Narcissa Lyons

Artless

I0677256

Artless

Narcissa Lyons

This book is a work of fiction. Names, characters, places and incidents are the product of the author's imagination or are used fictitiously. Any resemblance to actual events, locales or persons, living or dead, is coincidental.

Copyright © 2017 Narcissa Lyons

Published by if not for Passion

Cover image by Mark Spangler. Cover copyright © 2017 by Mark Spangler.

The scanning, uploading, and distribution of this book without permission is something we kindly ask you not to do. If you like the content and wish to share it, please encourage others to purchase from their favorite authorized retailer. Thank you for respecting the hard work of this author and this author's rights.

ISBN: 978-0-692-06570-9

To Panni and Paulette, my wonderful and goofy sisters, who have been very supportive of my writing endeavors and prodded this lazy writer into getting this written, and helped me finesse it to the story it has become.

Chapter 1

Garrett Darrs walked quickly and resolutely to the car waiting for him on Lexington Avenue. Although his usual gait was one of a casual confidence, his eyes fixed ahead of him, today was miserable and he just wanted to reach his car. He didn't believe in umbrellas, perhaps stupidly to his admission, so he bowed his head in the rain with the Wall Street Journal doing its best to shield him from at least the bad news of rain. He was grateful that Nick was on time, because let's face it, Nick was never on time. Nick, his driver, was a bad judge of traffic, a bit off with general direction, and prone to too many newsstand discussions that did not involve looking at his watch. Garrett had occasionally thought to oust him from his employment, and often wondered how Nick had made it long enough for Garrett to come to like him, but couldn't really bring himself to do it. He didn't know if it was because he liked Nick (and Nick always made sure he had a cigar for Garrett whenever the moment required one), or whether he was convinced Nick would not likely be hired by anyone else. But it didn't matter today. Nick was right there, his head hidden by paper news. Garrett opened the back door and stepped in (Nick also did not open doors because since he was usually late and Garrett opened the doors, he had forgotten that small but essential service).

Nick dropped his paper immediately, and turned to acknowledge Garrett.

"Hello Mr. Darrs". At least we've got that formality thought Garrett. "What a mess out here. The rain's made everyone ruder than usual, although at least it didn't slow them down much today. Where are we going?"

"Luigi's. No detours if possible." He paused. And then grudgingly "Glad to see you at the same time I came onto the street".

Nick was not ignorant of his failings. "I did what I could, but I think luck was also on my side. I'll get better Mr. Darrs. I've only been working for you for a few years". A shocking enough statement that Garrett left it alone.

He turned quietly to the streets outside his limousine haven, and watched the passers-by, which wasn't easy. There are many that do believe in umbrellas, and on days like this they were in abundance. Only here and there could he catch glimpses, and no one looked happy. In the face of New York City rain, no one ever looked happy he thought. As his interest waned, his eyes lost focus, staring outside his car but with no real sight at all.

Garrett Darrs was nothing short of gorgeous. Tall and lean, with deep gray eyes set in a head that bragged tousled dark hair, he was in fact beautiful. It would be strange to think a man with such looks was not at least arrogant, but Garrett's arrogance stemmed instead from his own intellect, and his intolerance of those that could not match it. He did not seem to care about this face enough to be boastful, although he cared enough about it to know that it had and would assist in his endeavors with women. As if money weren't enough. He was conscious of his health enough to run regularly, but not so obsessed with his physique to spend hours a day with a personal trainer as many of his colleagues did. His look was contemplative, if not sometimes dark. Although his smile would take the breath away of even a stony woman, he did not share it often, or even often enough. He was almost, but importantly not, somber.

Although Garrett had a short temper for inexcusable failings, he was patient and kind in moments that required it, and endearingly even when moments did not. He was fair in his business dealings, and possessed a devastating duende that women found disturbing, and men found likable. Certainly this was part of the reason he was so successful at marketing and selling the artwork that bedecked his gallery. Certainly that was some of the reason he was granted wall space in select locations around the city where others would wait months, and even years to hang artwork from their establishment. Truly it helped explain his countless bargain finds about New England for antiques to adorn both his home and his gallery. And obviously why women from all walks of life approached him and lingered for as long as they felt would not endanger their moral fiber.

Garret's gallery was something he was extremely proud of. He had bought the building about five years ago with some of the millions he had made on Wall Street, and he had invested heavily in the remodeling of the architecture, furniture, décor and marketing. All that he had done with the assistance only of his secretary Fiona Silvin, a devout employee who had begun working for him at Ocean Investments seven years ago, and left with him in his endeavor to change from the world of finance to the calmer, more beautiful world of art. He thanked her often, and even more often silently. She was efficient, honest, and rarely wrong, and she new how to handle calls he sometimes did not. She never flirted with him, and that was critical. He could not have an affair with his secretary, and she had never let on she would wish to have one—an oddity to him initially (analytically, not arrogantly), but over time he came to understand that although she was devoted to him when she was around him, she was devoted to William the rest of the time. Thank God for William.

So although it's quite true that Garrett was not born with a silver spoon, and that he in fact worked very hard for about ten years before he was able to purchase his gallery, he was a very lucky man. At thirty-nine he was wealthy enough to retire, and handsome enough to have a very good selection of women to choose from. And choose he did often.

Nick was winding his way in and out of traffic, occasionally swearing at the odd driver, and now and then nodding at passers-by. He was tired of the rain.

"Here we are, sir". He said to Garrett. He looked back at his employer to see that Garrett was drifting, as usual. "Sir." Garrett's gaze broke.

"Yes." He said. "Oh, right. Thanks. I'll let myself out" Garrett now made a point to say that as often as he could in the vain attempt to remind Nick of what he really was not getting away with.

"When would you like me back?"

"Well if that means you're not going to wait, then I'd say be back in an hour and a half". This he said knowing full well that he meant at least two hours.

"OK boss. See you soon." Nick nodded his head and smiled. He was an affable fellow.

"Yes. Thanks." Garrett closed the car door, and turned to walk into Luigi's.

Luigi's was an old restaurant, and an old favorite of Garrett's. He had been coming here for many years, and had come to know Luigi himself, the original owner, very well. The exterior was unassuming, with elegant, wrought iron letters, over deep cream walls, healthy ivy scaling the trellis and much of the walls. He opened the massive, thick wooden door and entered, a smile forming on his face, ready for the warm greeting that was his. The warmth and delectable scents greeted him first, increasing his appetite immediately.

"Hello Mr. Darrs." It was Daphne. She smiled.

"Hello Daphne" he said. "You are looking exceptional".

"Your table is ready. Come on" She said with a wave. He and Daphne had a sweet history. He followed her, his smile not fading, but gathering meaning. Reflecting on women always deepened his smile.

Garrett eased into his usual seat comfortably, and ordered himself a glass of wine. Daphne left him alone and he watched her depart. Life is beautiful he thought. He looked casually about the room, noticing that it was, as usual, well populated, even early afternoon as it was. The walls were peppered with mostly exceptional pieces of art, each lit strategically and tastefully. A good deal of it was from his gallery. A few were Marcus Poland, who he had shown several times, and was one of his favorite contemporary artists. His style was romantic and somber, sometimes desperate, rarely hopeful, but always stunning, even if it was not to everyone's taste. He noticed with a touch of curiosity that they had a new painting in a far corner by an artist he did not recognize. He thought it was of two women holding hands. He'd get a better look after his lunch.

Daphne delivered his wine, and after he thanked her he took a large sip, swallowing slowly enough to appreciate it. Today was

4

an important day. He was waiting at his favorite table in his favorite restaurant for a journalist to appear and interview him about his gallery and his accomplishments. True enough it was a bachelor column, and that didn't sit too well with him, but it was in one of New York's finest rags, New York Life. It would serve as excellent publicity for his already well-hyped Gallery, Gallery Darrs. He had planned everything he was going to say and everything he was surely not going to say. He was not a man of many words and did not want to give in to the pettiness of selling himself to any pining females reading the column, but instead to focus on the brilliance of his life's work, and where he intended to go from here. Not of course that he was quite sure of that answer. He had all the money he needed, the respect he deserved, the looks he could handle, and appropriate enough companionship on all levels. He was not a lonely man. The only things he was sure he still required in life was the acquisition of a larger sailing boat, a summer home in Italy, and perhaps at some point starting a restaurant. Other than that he was very satisfied and didn't see that anyone else should find that wanting. He was worrying too much, he decided, and instead looked down at his hands, his wine, the impeccable table linen. He had another taste of his chardonnay and looked at his watch. At any moment.

Luigi Paganelli strutted over to Garrett's table, a smile on his face. "Mr. Darrs". He nodded. "How are you today? You were looking a little nervous not too long ago" Luigi said with his heavy accent. "So I brought this over because you are drinking a very fast". He held up the bottle from which Garrett's glass had been poured.

"Luigi, you are kind and you know me so well" said Garrett. He held up his glass, and Luigi filled it. "I noticed you have a new painting in the far corner". He did not say anything else just yet.

"Yes. Do you like it?" He seemed proud. "I bought it last week from a young artist. She is very good." This last statement piqued Garrett's interest, because even though Luigi had purchased much of what he got from Garrett's gallery because he knew Garrett knew his art, Luigi himself had a good eye. His restaurant was evidence of that.

5

"Really? Who is she? I don't recognize the work."

"Carmen Carmine." Luigi's nose wrinkled. "I know. I don't like it neither. It's her real name, believe it or not...."

"Mr. Darrs?" It was Daphne. "Your guest has arrived. Shall I show her to your table?"

"Of course, thank you." He smiled at Luigi. "I'll have to take a look at it later. Meantime you'll have to make sure the chefs please this reporter".

"Anything you wish Mr. Darrs."

Daphne approached with the reporter. He tried to casually get a look around her, but would have to wait. He realized morosely that he was nervous. Nervous indeed. Not that being so would budge it.

Presently a young woman sat down in front of him. She could not have been more than twenty-four.

"May I get you something to drink?" asked Daphne.

"Yes, thanks". The woman (what was her name?) said. "I'll have what Mr. Darrs is having". Daphne nodded and walked towards the task. The woman believed her order required an explanation. "I know you like this place Mr. Darrs, and I trust your taste more than my own".

"You can call me Garrett" he said automatically, although he was not sure he meant it. "Or Mr. Darrs. It's up to you."

"Thanks, Garrett." Her eyes twinkled. "So what's good?"

She was one of those button cute people he thought. Petite, short cropped, modern purplish hair, wearing a very smart black suit that exposed just enough, and she wore plain silver jewelry. He imagined she wore quite different clothing during her off hours. She had a beautiful mouth and he made sure to only notice that this once. He did not like to give away any weakness of his during an interview—any interview. But he had a feeling she may have noticed him looking even for that moment. She looked very astute.

"Everything. But today the veal chop is the special. That would be my recommendation." He said this almost woodenly. He needed to know her name without telling her as much.

"By the way, I should tell you that Sharon couldn't make it because of another interview. She was ticked off about it, but had no choice. You'll have to manage with me, if that's OK" She smiled. "It's alright, though. I'm a better writer". She smiled again.

Garrett smiled broadly in return. He was both amused at her words, and relieved at his amazing luck. It did not seem to end. "And your name is?"

"Tabatha George. At your service." She went on to describe how the interview would go…

They chatted more or less casually during the meal, Garrett rigidly keeping as guarded as he knew how, and Tabatha seeming too much of a friend. It was enough to make the meal far less delicious by lacing it with edges of dread and false candor. Garrett did get one other chance to look at her mouth, and marveled at the contour, imagined there had to be talent, and wished he could invite her over for a drink. For starters, anyway. Tabatha, though level-headed, was nervous if only because she found his presence rattling. She was fairly certain she'd never been in the company of anyone, male or female, this good looking. Because he was a man who often looked away while discussing things (or, admittedly, that could have been his technique with her), she was able to devour his features in true appreciation. She imagined being in his arms, and knew it would have been too good. And she knew it wouldn't happen.

After dinner, Tabatha got serious immediately, ordering an espresso to jar her into clarity. Garrett ordered one as well, but decided to temper it with a glass of port.

"There have been articles here and there about you, Garrett, but it's true you keep to yourself. What about your family? Are you close to them?"

This brought Garrett's first genuine smile, even if not ear-to-ear. "Physically we're not close at all—most of them live in Colorado—but we talk often enough, and I see them at every holiday, whether I fly out there or I fly them here."

"You have three sisters and a brother, right?" Tabatha asked.

Something clouded Garrett's vision, but he said "Yes, that's correct. But it's a boring aspect of my life if you're trying to get a good angle. We're a fairly sane family, so no gossip." And Tabatha understood that was the end of that.

7

"Garrett, you're one of the most sought after bachelors in the city. What do you have to say to that?"

He thought it a stupid question. "I don't know how anyone gauges something like that. I don't think it makes sense. I'm lucky enough to be in the spotlight or good enough to be in the spotlight because of what I've achieved. There are plenty of exceptional bachelors out there. I'm just happy to be one of them".

"What do you mean good enough?"

"Through years of long hours and second guessing the market I was able to gain a more than sizable treasure to put me in the gallery I love."

"Do you like art as much as you like women?"

She was pretty good. "They are nearly the same, but no". He did not elaborate.

Tabatha did not like the answer. "Nearly the same?"

Garrett thought to say what he could in order to move the conversation along. "I cannot properly disclose my feelings on things about which I am passionate. And that passion is private. I can tell you that certain Monets invoke serious reflection, and certain Dali's a degree of amusement. Da Vinci more often than not will inspire profound peace, and Goya, solitude. Do you see any connection?"

Tabatha looked at Garrett with a quiet sadness. There was something to him, she thought.

The remainder of the interview went without too much excitement. Garret had set the tone, and Tabatha obeyed, only occasionally asking questions that prompted Garrett to first eye her admonishingly, and then find a condescending response. She learned to step accurately, but he did not so much put her off that she would write him a roué. She walked away that day pleased to have met Garrett Darrs, although part of her half wished she would not have been an inconsequential reporter in his life, but the woman that could entangle him, if only briefly.

After Tabatha left, Garrett sat a bit and contemplated his existence, something he was doing more and more often. He did not want to be locked with a woman. It's true, art and women were very similar. And he could never adore one painting alone.

Of course he knew it was not a fair analogy, but in his many years, he had not ever met a woman that was worth all his attention. This could have been written off as bad luck, but the odds did not point that way. Or it could be that he was attracted to the type of woman that would never satisfy him fully. He didn't know, but he didn't think it mattered. Why was the perpetual hope of apparently everyone to wed him off, to match him with the person they all knew to be ideal? The port was good and heady, he decided.

Once he realized that Tabatha and Co. had paid the bill, he decided to push off. Luigi came over to bid him good-bye. "Was the veal OK, Mr. Darrs? Neither of you ate very much."

"Luigi, please. It was exceptional as always, but I'm afraid today's meeting was not very appetizing".

Luigi nodded. "Yes, Mr. Darrs. I think I understand. Have a wonderful afternoon". Garret loved the accent, he decided for the one hundredth time. "Do you wish to see the painting?"

Garrett blinked. His thoughts had been too cluttered with the superfluous to properly understand Luigi. And then he remembered—the new painting on the far wall.

"Of course, Luigi. Please show me". He was indeed eager to see a new artist Luigi deemed worthy of his walls, although he didn't quite understand why he would not have been aware of the artist first.

Luigi led the way through the tables, most of which were unoccupied at this point. He caught snippets of conversation, and had his usual hesitations. He sometimes hoped to stop at a particularly interesting comment and sit with those engaged, but it was just that. A little desire. Presently they arrived at the far corner and Luigi moved out of the way for Garrett to see the piece.

It took a moment for Garrett's eyes to get accustomed to the light in this section, and to adjust to the colors and shadows immediately in front of him on the canvas. It was as he had thought—two young girls were holding hands. Tightly. It was a rather close up shot, and there was a long hallway behind them. There was nothing very remarkable about coloring, or texture, or even substance, he thought. It was the girls themselves. They

9

were probably in their early teens, and obviously sisters. The younger blonde was turned to look at her older, brunette sister. Her profile was mischievous, and happy. The brunette was staring at Garrett. She looked at him softly, with knowing, and understanding, and he felt that she liked him. He looked back at her, and at her sister. He then noticed they were dressed in shoddy clothing, and that they were a bit dirty. He realized they were urchins placed in the middle of someone else's grandeur, and it did not matter a whit to them. Maybe the port had something to do with it, but he fell in love with the painting. He fell in love with the girls, and most certainly the brunette. He wasn't sure how long he'd been standing there, and fully understood he had to find Luigi to buy it off him. But Luigi had been right next to him the entire time, because as Garrett was turning to seek him out, there he was, admiring the girls right along with him.

This would be trouble. Garrett immediately understood the negotiations for acquiring this piece would not be easy. Luigi was in love as well.

As if to read his thoughts, Luigi spoke. "It is beautiful, is it not?"

"Yes, Luigi". He was not helping his cause. "Really, it's more than that. What do you think of selling it?" He was fairly sure he knew the answer.

"I cannot, Mr. Darrs." He was sincere, Garrett knew, and was not seeking money with these words. "These girls have become my friends, even in the short week I have known them". Luigi then paused before he went on. As Garrett watched him, he noticed sheepishness taint Luigi's next sentences, and his own smile remained unexpressed. Luigi was loyal to him to the end, even with something this simple. "Actually", he began, still not comfortable with a truth he seemed bent on revealing, "your brother introduced her to me". He had been looking at the painting as he spoke, but now looked at Garrett.

This surprised Garrett. His brother was not a man who typically dabbled in the arts, even at all. "Finn gave this to you?"

"No, no, Mr. Darrs" He said, almost as if to assuage any possible sin on his part, if one actually existed. "He was in town a

10

few weeks ago, and told me about her." Luigi's comfort did not grow, and he continued. "Well, I think our love for art is obvious, no? Even your brother understands those that appreciate the beautiful". He stopped, and looked back at the painting.

Garrett was dubious, but was now also curious. "Well, obviously Finn did not come down from Boston just to tell you about an artist he could have phoned about, assuming, of course, he would be that considerate to begin with."

Luigi had turned back to Garrett, and was now more slightly rattled. "I don't know why he visited, though I got the impression it was just a pleasure trip, Mr. Darrs. He brought a pretty girl with him (here looking at Garrett with a look that simply stated, "what else would he do?") and they had lunch. He was about to leave when he looked around the room, only then seeming to notice some of the artwork. An after-thought." Luigi paused, trying to recapture what had been an apparently insignificant moment, but that he was now being questioned about. He nodded absently. "I don't really know what it was that stopped him, but on his way out he asked to see me. That was when he gave me Ms. Carmine's card, and told me I should stop by her home and see her work."

So now Garrett had gone from curious to puzzled, but no harm done. A little intrigue always bettered his day. "So you visited her shop just on the recommendation of my brother?" He asked.

Luigi shook his head perhaps too vehemently. "No, no, that would have been silly of me, truly, but the fact your brother even bothered to make such a suggestion made me interested, and just the fact he is related to you…" Luigi nodded deferentially before he continued. "…made me call her." Here he smiled.

"What a delightful creature" The volume of his story increased slightly. "So charming and modest! I love women, you know, all of them I think". He looked at Garrett apologetically, but Garrett waved him off. "We talked for a while, and it was enough to convince me a short ride to Connecticut would not be too bad. I must tell you I am so happy I did."

This Garrett did not doubt. "I understand." But he was not happy. He looked once again at the painting. He liked the idea

11

that someone could so kindly understand him, even if it was just a painted teenager. "Thank you for another wonderful meal, Luigi. I have to go make sure Nick is still waiting for me, or I'll have to cab it, and you know the difficulty that always presents." He started to walk off.

"Mr. Darrs." Garrett stopped and turned to Luigi. "I think she may be the next one." Who the hell is he talking about? Thought Garrett. "This is not her only beauty. Here!" Luigi shuffled around a bit for a moment and then handed Garrett a distraught business card. "She has no gallery yet, I do not think, but perhaps now she should have some space?!"

Garrett took the card. "Thank you, Luigi. I appreciate it." He smiled, nodded, and walked away.

Nick pulled up just as Garret stepped out of Luigi's after his 3 hour lunch. He couldn't say anything since he was there, but had he really just been circling the block waiting for him? He shrugged and then got in the car.

"Hello Mr. Darrs. Did you have a good lunch?" He seemed cheerful.

"Yes, thanks, Nick." He paused for a moment for effect. "It was a very long lunch."

Nick did not acknowledge any underlying meaning. "I like long lunches the best. The longer the better." Garrett saw Nick nod and smile in his rearview mirror. Garrett smiled, though tightly. "The Gallery, sir?"

"I think so. Take your time." Garrett eased back into the comfortable leather seats and then pulled out the business card Luigi had given him.

Carmen Carmine. He laughed a little then to himself, and then thought of the painting. Even though he had just seen it moments ago, it felt as though it had been hours or days. He remembered the kind girl's face eying him, and wished he had taken a few more moments to see what else she was revealing.

So Finn, his care-free brother, had happened to waltz into Luigi's and then mention an upcoming artist? Wonders really did not cease. He was a little annoyed his brother hadn't phoned him he was in town, but then realized it must have been a romantic jaunt of some sort. Garrett shook his head a bit with a small smile when he thought of his brother Finn's appetite for short but fierce relationships with beautiful women. Obviously, Garrett had plenty of his own trysts that he shouldn't pass judgment, but he would be biased if he presented his younger brother as anything other than a serious hound, a man almost suicidally bent on dating as many women as he could, and very often getting in a lot of trouble because of it.

So Carmen Carmine must be a past (or present?) fling of his, and maybe he felt indebted to her for some cad-like act he'd committed, and therefore had mentioned it to Luigi. That was probably too simple an explanation, but he knew very well it couldn't be far off. His pragmatic side joined his thoughts and told him it didn't matter. Soon enough he'd find this Carmen, and soon enough, even if she didn't have another copy of the one he'd seen, he'd get her to paint another. Chances were in fact that he'd like something else she had painted even more. He relaxed anew and turned to his favorite show outside the window.

Chapter 2

Like everything these days, Garrett was determined to get what he wanted immediately. He was no longer accustomed to waiting for anything. In Soho the following day at his gallery, he buried himself in his office while his gallery hummed with visitors. Normally he would stroll the gallery at least once in the morning after breakfast to look at his guests. Although he rarely spoke to anyone unless addressed, he watched closely the various characters that graced his gallery. Most of his visitors, though extremely varied, and strange in ways he found delightful, had a quality that the city's crowd as a whole did not always have. An admirer of art is one who usually does not lack passion. True enough, there were some that merely adorned the arm of an aficionado, and did not always share the adoration of the work that Garrett found breath-taking, but a vast majority would somewhere along the tour fall in love, if only briefly. After his casual walk, he'd roam upstairs and look over the balcony of the second floor, continuing to eye his fans. Or the fans of the art he had chosen, that is. Always he would find his favorite guest of the day. It did not have to be the one he deemed most appreciative, or the wackiest looking, or even anything outstanding—there was really no typical reason. He would find his favorite and then define the reason why he or she was just that, and then he would surmise at their existence. All about it; their age, wealth, marital status, happiness (or not), career, etc. Once, he had come very close to asking. It had been later in the day, after a particularly long alcohol-ridden lunch, and he had been leaning over his balcony as usual, if a little precariously. He had seen a striking woman, perhaps in her late forties, looking at a Gregory Thomaston piece. He was a modern painter, who most often used striking colors and slashing strokes to evoke a dramatic response. Garrett, not a modernist, still thought the work was an excellent representation, and found him stirring. The woman was looking at "The Black Sunset". She had, in fact, been looking at it for 10 minutes. She wore black pants, and a black sweater, and a wide red silk scarf in her short, blonde hair. She was tall and very thin and extremely serious. Garrett watched her closely, and did not see any muscle move. She did not shift her weight, or change any part of her body to get the blood flowing. The angle of her head remained the same, and her eyes seemed to absorb the entire painting (impossible, he thought, she was standing too close). He agonized over just this, and failed to notice the one betrayal that proved she was indeed feeling. She had been standing there now for fifteen minutes, and he had been looking at her figure, still too puzzled to even begin his guessing game. His glance had moved back to her face and he saw the tears. He was transfixed at the time. A woman crying is hardly an oddity, and tears at the sight of what a woman considered beautiful was nothing to take real note of, but she had never registered an emotion, or even the evidence of life, for that matter. At last she moved her black-gloved hands to wipe her eyes. She looked for about another 10 seconds and then walked on. He had absolutely no idea what her story was, and found the reaction to "the Black Sunset" a bit dubious, but in the end dubbed her a ballet teacher of the highest caliber, never married, well-off on the Upper East Side, and mostly sane.

Today he did not have time for his guests, although his work was still in line with providing the most stimulating art he could get his hands on in order to enthrall just those guests.

He dialed the number on the card Luigi had given him. He was not nervous, but he was not calm either. It rang a few times and then a woman's voice. "Hello?"

"Hello. This is Garrett Darrs. I was hoping to talk to Carmen Carmine" he said.

"This is she" said the other voice. "How can I help you?" She did not know his name.

"Yes, well I saw a painting of yours. Actually, I saw it at my favorite place, Luigi's--yesterday". He paused for a moment.

"Yes?" She asked, and nothing more. He thought he detected an accent, but wasn't sure.

"It struck me, well, rather deeply. I own a gallery in town, and I would love a chance to see more of your work, if that would be alright" he said.

"Ahh. Gallery Darrs, of course. Forgive my slowness. I'm flattered. And I'd love to let you look at my work." Friendliness had crept into her tone. A wry smile crossed his face.

"If it's OK, how about I stop by tomorrow?"

"That's fine, but I live in Connecticut, you know. Ridgefield."

He went on to tell her that was no problem, and they made the appropriate arrangements for him to stop by about lunch time.

"Thank you for your time, Carmen". Garrett said, relieved the conversation was drawing to a close. He did not like the phone.

"Thank you, Mr. Darrs" she said, pausing momentarily. Frustrated, he thought, because she had referred to him as Mr. Darrs, when he had not done her the same favor. "I look forward to your visit."

"As do I. And please call me Garrett."

They bid adieu and Garrett hung up the phone thoughtfully. She sounded fairly young, and she sounded enticing in other ways, he decided. So he began to play his game with a face he had not yet met. He could very easily find out all about her in advance of their meeting, and this was in fact a sage practice, but he never had as much fun with the obvious. A surmise is better than wise, he was certain.

Garrett lived on the upper east side of Manhattan, in a modest, but expensively decorated loft. His taste ran in the colonial style, and his taste was exquisite. He had decorated his flat as well as his gallery on his own, with perhaps only the required nod or two of approval from Fiona. He did most of the shopping himself, and she took care of the rest. A fair amount of his furnishings were in fact antiques. Many of his spring and summer weekends involved a trip through New England, with several stops at antique shops. He had run out of room by this point, and paid for storage of new buys. It was his full intention to buy a house in the suburbs at a time he found convenient, or at a time when life decided it was the next course of action.

He sat down in one of his large leather divans, a beautiful, old beaten piece with brilliant copper and wooden rivets holding the material fast. It was only mid-afternoon, but he was thirsty for a cocktail. What did it matter? He'd call Fiona and tell her he was taking the afternoon off. Up he rose, resigned to the fact that if he wanted a drink he'd have to get up and make it. He had not yet buckled to getting a maid or a butler, a luxury he could easily afford, and certainly wouldn't mind having. But would he then have true privacy? He did have a cleaning service come in twice a week, but other than that, he fended for himself. He was not a chef; so much of his food was either delivered, or preferably and more often, eaten out. Garrett Darrs worked hard, but did not deprive himself of that which he had worked for.

He fixed himself a fairly large martini and returned to his chair. He looked out his front windows, but not really to view the scene to which he was privy. He was looking through it. He eyed his living room appreciatively and smiled a little smugly. He was happy. His mind nudged him. Mostly happy. It's just that he really had it all. To a degree he felt there were no challenges left. He was successful to the extent that even though there were things he knew he had not yet done that he wished to, he knew he would succeed once he had the time. That thought alone was deflating to action.

He could travel, certainly. But a vacation is short if one isn't the type to travel alone (and, really, he wasn't). At any rate, so much of his everyday life was similar to vacation that he didn't think a different background would make all the difference. He frowned to no one, but at himself. He should rightly be flogged for some of these thoughts, since he was about one in ten million with a lifestyle as his. Besides, he thought with a smile returning, I not only love what I do, I'm good at it. He took a long draw from his martini and willed the gin to act the eraser of impudent ideas.

He spent the rest of the afternoon with a few other martinis, and television—a very rare companion. In the evening a little of his time was spent mulling over the adventure of the next day, and the companion that would be his for a few hours. He thought about her voice, and the slight lilt he thought he had detected. He

17

retraced the steps he had taken in his game, and realized he had concluded she was slight (of course), blonde, a little coy, a little sexy, and very cute. But he was off his game. Artists never turned out to be as one expected. He'd never been right before. Thinking about Carmen was driving him a little crazy, and he was driven by gin as well. With a hunger for skin that was getting the better of him, he picked up the phone and called his friend Annabelle. She would keep him company. She always did.

***

Nick arrived in front of his building at ten, a half hour after their scheduled departure time. Garrett decided not to mention it. He was in particularly good spirits, and though he did not sleep many hours, he had slept deeply.

"Good morning, sir" Nick said.

"Good morning, Nick." Garrett nodded with a smile.

"I'm a few minutes late" Nick kindly pointed out. Did he really think that a half hour was a few minutes? Did he truly think Garrett needed to be told of his lateness? "But I'll make it up en route. Checked the traffic reports, and we'll fly right in". He nodded his head with a radiant beam and waited for Garrett to settle himself into the seat.

Garrett smiled, bemused as usual. "Did I ever tell you Nick, that I think you've got the most interesting perception of time?" He waited a moment. "That I think you must have an adventurous watch?"

"Maybe, sir." Nick's brow was furrowed. Maybe he was thinking about it. "But really, I don't know." He paused again, and Garrett noted to his dismay that Nick was putting real thought into what he had said. "If there's....."

"I was just rambling, Nick. Don't pay me any mind." And then "I had a hell of a night." He waited for Nick to look at him in the rear view mirror, which he did immediately, and Garrett then raised his eyebrows in the suggestive manner that would tell Nick the story he'd appreciate.

"Excellent, sir." Nick nodded a few times to himself.

Garrett began reading the New York Times Nick had prepared for him, and sipped the lukewarm coffee at his side. He read a few articles, but found it hard to concentrate. There was too much to think about. He was slightly anxious about his meeting with Carmen, although he was fairly sure it would go in his favor. She sounded on the naïve side, even if she did live in Ridgefield. But he had to be careful. Although rare, an artist or two had gotten the better of him by his presuming naiveté. Garrett sometimes believed that stardust in an artist's eyes led them to hasty decisions, but through time had come to realize that the ethics of an artist are such that they usually value their work and what it means far more than promised fame. Fame was good, money better, but art was art and better left unblemished. Anyway, she sounded young. Just because her piece had made it to Luigi's place did not mean she was far ahead on the road to stardom. He thought about his strategy, but knew that honesty was generally the better bet.

If Garrett Darrs' charm would not sway Carmen Carmine, then it was likely his appearance would. He was clad in a dark royal blue linen suit, a crisp white cotton shirt, and an elegant red silk tie, held in place with his lucky tie-tack, a small gold lizard with a ruby eye. The sophistication was softened by his tousled hair, while the body beneath his clothing warned of something else. He looked only slightly tame. He was every bit prepared to seduce the artist in every way. Although Wall Street never elicited poor ethics on his part, his sense of doing business in the art world was another matter.

Garrett's thoughts went to Carmen again, re-picturing her presence. In truth he was very excited to see the rest of her work. Luigi's piece could not be a single stroke, he was sure. Finding an artist that painted with the rhythm of one's own soul was a miraculous feat in any lifetime, and having that artist's talent please most was nothing but treasure. His sense of money around the corner was at a peak. He imagined her studio as dark, and just shy of being gloomy. He pictured many easels—that she worked on several paintings at once—that she never abandoned something once begun even if she hated it. And he was absolutely certain candles abounded, even in the light of day. She drank a lot of coffee, but at night only red wine. She was not a drunk, but she drank too much. His reverie was taking him everywhere. He did not hear Nick.

"Mr. Darrs." Nick said rather loudly. He was looking in the rear-view. Once he noted Garrett's snap to attention he continued. "Would you like me to stop and get anything to bring for the lady?"

Garrett paused only for a moment. "Yes, of course. Thanks Nick." Nick was referring to flowers, a customary lure for female prospects, both practically and romantically. Flowers were what Garrett referred to as "scale tippers"—not that Garrett Darrs required something other than himself to tip the scale.

Soon Nick pulled over to a flower stand and purchased a beautiful but simple combination of daisies and lilacs, wrapped simply with yellow ribbon round the paper enclosure. Garret smiled a little smugly. He felt sure he was very ready for this meeting.

"What do you think, Nick?" He asked, fishing.

"I think she's half way to Mars before you ring the doorbell." Nick said.

Garrett laughed appreciatively. "I don't think I'll be too long. Try to stay close, but I have your number."

"Of course. Take your time." Nick was smiling.

Nick loved to hear stories or insinuations of stories about Garrett and his women. Although Nick himself was a charmer, he adored women, and knew that Garrett had a bigger selection, not to mention the fact that most of the time Nick witnessed at least part of the seduction while driving Garrett's dates around, at night, or in the morning. It made for interesting revelations, and sometimes, conversation.

Nick pulled into a driveway. "I think this is it, sir." He checked the number on the house. "Yup. Good luck." And he winked.

Garrett lost a shade of his smugness, and looked at the house, which was about 100 yards away.

Carmen Carmine was fairly certain the curtain behind which she stood was sufficiently closed to mask her inspection of her visitor. All she saw for the moment was a long, well buffed limousine, the windows at least as good a mask as her curtains. Her house was located on a modest but beautiful lot in one of the most elite towns in Connecticut, but still she thought the car too ostentatious. But it was beautiful, and she smiled just a little. Wealth did not captivate her or make her feel lacking, but it did raise the usual brow of admiration.

It bothered her that she was nervous, even though she knew why. But she was supposed to be a laid back artist, a character that suited her well. She was supposed to perhaps demonstrate a bit of humble gratitude (and that would be genuine), but that would be underlying a knowledge that her work was good. Carmen was proud of what she painted. Often so much she found it hard to part with a lot of her paintings, but she would then chide herself for such hubris. She knew this man, Garrett Darrs, was eager for her work. He had called her the day he had seen her painting at Luigi's place. The same day! It was obvious he wanted something for himself, but even better he would indeed want to show it at his very posh, very well known gallery.

So why was she so nervous? She gazed at the limo, trying to see behind the opaque windows, trying to see if what she had seen and read of him so far was true. That was it of course. It wasn't her talent, or his appreciation of her talent that had her twitching miserably like a schoolgirl behind a curtain. He was a well educated, wealthy, confident, devastatingly handsome man. This was unnerving. She had heard of him prior to his call, but then did a little research, and what she discovered was disturbing, even if in a delicious sort of way. Why didn't he open the door? Probably had only been a minute since she began her spying. She checked her forehead, and she wasn't sweating. Yet. This was silly, not her style, but of course she didn't move.

Carmen stood transfixed, standing as though ready to run a race as soon as Garrett's door opened. Handsome though Garrett was, and that she knew him to be, Carmen should not have been so nervous on that account. She had allured many a man with her large brown eyes housed in a delicately angled face. The only flaw to what might have been absolute beauty was a half inch scar over her right eyebrow, but it could be argued that this feature created a more profound, striking beauty, and at times it served as an eerie accentuator of her emotions. She had long, deep brown, almost black hair. She was of slight build, and not very tall, but her body was heavenly in all senses. She had inherited her father's Italian olive skin, though of course youth provided hers with the suppleness that those who are not young will envy. The suppleness of the skin would not be outdone by her generous, but firm breasts, which she was not afraid of coyly displaying. Despite the size of her breasts, the rest of her body was quite petite. In the end, any onlooker would conclude she had an excellent figure eight.

Carmen knew that to make her eagerness obvious by over dressing would be a mistake, but neither did she want to hide herself. She had opted for snuggish blue jeans and a pale V-neck silk sweater. She had added a bit of height to her 5'3" frame with tan leather boots. She wore her dark hair down, with a single antique pin on one side. She had been given the hairpin by her sister Sophia, an antiques collector and shop owner, back before she had begun to sell her work. Carmen considered it a good luck piece.

Carmen glanced at herself in the mirror for what she hoped was the last time, and ran back to the window side just in time to see Garrett get out of the long car. Despite herself, she sharply inhaled. He was quite tall. He was stunning. Confident. And carrying flowers. She stepped back from the window, almost tripping over herself, and cursed herself for not having poured herself a glass of wine. She looked in the mirror again and gave herself a dirty look. The doorbell rang and she screamed just a little, praying that it had been inaudible.

She said "Just a minute" and calmed herself resolutely as she walked slowly to the door.

She opened the door and saw his chest, so looked up, slanting her head and squinting a little. "Hello Garrett" she said. "Come on in". She moved out of his way so as he could enter, and it seemed to her as if he stooped to do so.

"Hello Carmen" he said, at the same time proffering her the flowers. "A pleasure to meet you. What a beautiful little Eden you've got going here". He seemed to mean it.

"Thanks so much. The bouquet is lovely--please make yourself comfortable while I put them in some water". She left to go to the kitchen, and very much felt his gaze on her retreating figure. She smiled.

When she returned he was looking at a small music stand on her baby grand piano. "This is beautiful" he said. "In fact, you've got quite a few beautiful antiques here".

"Are you a collector of antiques as well?" she asked.

"Only for pleasure" he said.

"Then I'd be happy to give you my sister's business card. She has a brilliant little shop a town over".

"Sure" Garrett said casually. "That would be nice. I'm surprised I haven't been there yet as I thought I'd been to all those in the Northeast". He paused, and both of them seemed a little uncomfortable.

"Can I get you something to drink?" she asked, hoping to break the tension and desperately join him in some kind of toast that would bring wine to her throat.

Garrett looked at her, into her eyes, seemingly willing her to be disconcerted by his deep gaze. It was brief, but ridden with intent, he hoped. "Yes, thanks" he said. "I'll take a scotch and soda if you've got it".

"Of course. I'll be right back".

When she left, Garrett watched her go, his smile fading. He didn't know what he was doing here. Or he knew what he was supposed to be doing here, but wished it was over with. He'd been present only a few minutes, and he felt the oppression of sexual tension. This is a dick of a dance, he thought.

But she was beautiful, no doubt. It was certainly obvious what his brother would have seen in her, though it inexplicably dismayed him now to bring Finn to mind. Something was

23

bothering him about the whole Finn involvement, even though he'd forgotten until just now meeting the artist. He found her movements graceful and alluring. He thought she walked as though certain she was being watched, a quality he enjoyed as it was a reflection of his own demeanor. He liked her in blue, and he liked what her blue sweater promised. In a few short minutes he had been rendered smitten, and he truly hoped it would not affect his business acumen, or any rationale, for that matter. He was blindly looking out the front window of the living room when he heard her returning.

She reached over to him with a glass of excellent amber hue. "There you go. Let me know if it needs anything" she said.

His hand brushed hers as he took it from her. He said nothing, but put the drink to his lips. He let the liquid quietly ignite his throat and stomach, and smiled. "Thanks. It's very good" he said finally. He looked at her. He noticed she had a glass of red wine. He wondered if he should mention anything at all about Finn, but quickly acknowledged it was none of his business and hardly relevant to his business endeavors.

"Well, Garrett" Carmen said. "Would you like to see my studio"?

"Mmm. Why not? Lead the way".

Carmen felt a little dizzy, and took a sip of her drink. The exchange between them was getting painful. She smiled at him, and began the tour. He followed her down a narrow corridor that opened to reveal a set of small staircases.

"It's not a very big house" she said. "But it's perfect for me, and it's got all the necessary quirks for an artist". It was just idle chatter, she knew, but it made her feel better. She went up the staircase to the right, and at the top it opened up into a very large, happily sun-lit room. Most walls were white, with the exception of the slanted ceiling, which was a melon color. There were many easels. There was also a large drafting table that was apparently being used as a desk. And there were many, many canvases, some blank, some work in progress, and the completed paintings were all in one area, cordoned off by a heavy rope.

Garrett stood in the entryway soaking in the environment while Carmen put on a few soft lights. He never tired of the feel of a studio, could easily feel the creative process in the air.

"My completed works are in the corner, as you can see. I think there are perhaps 30 or so, and I have some in storage" Carmen said and turned to look at him.

God, she thought. He really is devastating. The things I can imagine. She smiled, and of course he caught it.

"What's so funny?" he asked, returning the smile.

She blushed visibly, she knew. "Oh nothing" she lied. "It's just you look a little dazed". She walked towards the corner, and he followed closely behind her.

Garrett could smell her perfume, and breathed it in appreciatively. Something was happening, he was quite sure, and he had to keep his head clear before he led this elsewhere.

"Take your time" she said, motioning to the array of paintings, and then retreated, as if relieved, to the other side of the studio.

He was mesmerized. Although a few seemed slightly on the amateurish side, the rest were breathtaking, at least at first glance. He did a quick inventory, and then looked genuinely deeply at all of them, from time to time taking a sip of his drink. Each of the paintings evoked an immediate response, and the color contrasts were sometimes jarring, but strangely appropriate. He found some winsome, some dismal, some haunting, but all beautiful. They certainly rivaled the painting at Luigi's, although perhaps since he had seen that one first he still favored it. Quite honestly, he was astonished. Such a rich collection from an artist this green was nothing he had as yet come across.

"Carmen" he said, startling himself a little.

"Yes". Her voice was far off. She sounded engrossed in something.

He turned around and saw her sitting at her makeshift desk across the room. She had her head turned up, an inquisitive expression on her face; waiting.

"Please come here if you don't mind" he said, and watched as she rose and walked toward him.

"So what do you think?" she asked. "Do any of them attach themselves to you?"

He liked her wording. "Many" he said as she reached his side. "They are, in fact, beautiful. I would be very happy if you would consider letting me display them at my gallery". He chose to pause, but kept looking into her eyes. "I think you are very talented" he said. He did not stop looking at her.

Carmen looked at Garrett, praying he did not sense the mad beating of her heart. She felt that to look away would be a weakness, so she smiled, and of course, she was indeed grateful. "Thank you, Garrett. I must say I put everything, and all of me into my work. Hearing that what I create is noteworthy to others is always very gratifying." She chose then to glance at her work, still smiling, and then turned back to Garrett.

Garrett almost always did the same thing when a beautiful, smiling face turned up to him at this close a range, so why should he now resist? She was staring up at him, waiting for him to say something to continue their business, but the deal had just been completed as far as he required.

At just the point when Garret would have lowered his head to kiss Carmen, she looked as if she were about to step back, or worse, feint, so he grabbed her waist with his right arm. "You looked as if you were about to fall" he said, staring at her with some concern, but not letting go.

"I may...."Carmen began, looking and feeling more light-headed than ever. "I mean it's these stupid boots." She steadied herself by putting her hands up against his chest while he let her go slowly. Ever so slowly she thought. Did he do it deliberately or was it complete misconception on her part because he was so devastating?

Once separated, she felt better. Or did she? For the brief moment during which she had felt his body so close to hers, she had felt so safe. The sad part was she had not felt unsafe prior to that touch. Not at all, and now somehow she was bereft. Garrett wasn't adding anything to the conversation, and part of her was embarrassed at her clumsiness, so she decided to go with her only piece of rehearsed dialogue she had chosen in case of just such a moment. "Did you know I know your brother?" He was looking

26

at her strangely. Not amused, thank God. But also not exactly
happy. "Well, I guess you must by this point, silly of me." But
now she was starting to feel on the edgy side of talkative. "Well I
don't think he knew you'd see my painting at Luigi's quite so
soon. Not that I know, of course. I mean all he did was give
Luigi a card, and I know I certainly haven't spoken with Finn in
quite some time." She forcibly stopped herself. "Sorry, Garrett,
I'm going on and on for no apparent reason".

"Garrett?" She asked. He seemed to adjust his stare. "Did I
say something wrong?" Stupid question she thought. Of course
she had said nothing wrong. She had merely looked foolish,
undoubtedly, to this urbane gentleman, to this well heeled man of
the world. She felt suddenly perturbed at herself. What had she
been thinking? That this incredible specimen of a man might be
attracted to her? She knew she was pleasant to behold, but this
man must be able to bed anyone. Anyone.

"Not at all" Garret said almost too quickly. She had done
nothing wrong, other than avoid his impending kiss and bring up
his younger brother, who, as far as he could tell, had done nothing
wrong, had in fact assisted a young woman on her quest to paint
for a living. He couldn't decide if she had realized what he was
doing and averted it, or if she really didn't know what he'd had in
the works. He was fairly sure she was innocent of his intentions,
because she looked confused, and even flustered, although those
were also characteristics of one who avoided a kiss. And really,
wasn't it interesting that she'd brought up his brother the moment
after he'd made the attempt? This was silly. He shouldn't be
thinking like this. He was now irrationally annoyed with himself,
and also with Carmen. He acknowledged that he would only
further anger himself if he chose to dwell too long on the fact that
this woman alone should not be so annoying. She wasn't that
heavenly. But there was something, he knew. He looked at her
now while she was still standing so close to him, and a shadow of
vulnerability came over him. There was almost too much
sincerity in those eyes, and he found himself wondering what Finn
did when he saw those eyes. And really, maybe she was looking
at him like that because he was Finn's brother. It was a thought
that became vile the longer he dwelled on it, and he was thankful

he liked her now slightly less. No possibility such a woman, such an obvious bohemian, would be his type. "Not at all" He said again.

He was struck with distaste for his current situation, not his typical at-ease self, and not as in control as he liked to be. "Yes, Luigi mentioned the order of events. I have not spoken with Finn in a bit myself." He closed that subject. "I'd better get out of here" he continued. "I'd forgotten I've got to be back at the office in less than an hour".

"Garrett, really, is ...."

"No matters, really. It's just that I'd like to get back to my office and think about how I would approach a show for your work if we got to that point" He lied well, and he was now gaining composure and confidence, shrugging off the almost-kiss. She could not have known.

Carmen said "Oh, yes, of course", but was losing composure as Garrett was gaining his. She felt nervous and silly all over again. "Let me show you the door". She lowered her eyes, turned, and began to lead him through the various rooms and hallways.

The walk to the exit, though not a long one, seemed interminable to them both. Carmen was tense and feeling clumsy, sure that Garrett was watching her walk and noticing her timidity. She couldn't wait for him to leave. And Garrett was no happier. He was angry, furious at himself for not having had the strength to keep his distance, if it had not been perceived by Carmen. And that was the real issue at hand, after all. He didn't know whether or not she had purposely rejected his overture. Not knowing was prompting his slightly rude behavior (OK, maybe not knowing and Finn), but it's wasn't something he could do much about at this point. In all likelihood their relationship was now tainted, and would be fraught with hesitations, misunderstandings and innuendos. His unprofessionalism had cost them both. But on the bright side, he would be seeing her again, so he did have another chance of some kind to establish a better partnership. He smiled slightly at the thought. The front entrance was in front of them.

Carmen stepped aside for him to pass. "Well, thank you for the visit" she said, and she knew she came off as the humble novice, instead of confident as she had hoped, even if she didn't feel it. She felt stupid in front of this moody man.

Garrett turned to face her in the doorstep. "No, Carmen. Thank you for letting me visit. I look forward to working with someone so talented". He extended his hand to her, and she put her hand in his, grasping his hand as firmly as she could. They shook firmly, but not without the feeling that it was forced. "I'll give you a call" he said tersely, and walked away.

As he left her doorstep, Garrett grew less happy, now able to think and make expressions of his thoughts without having to worry she'd spot his emotions. He strode determinedly, silently demanding Nick be waiting for him, or today would be the end for him. His mind slipped for a moment, and he thought of her smiling face, and then her big, red taunting lips. Taunting sweater. He quickly returned to his mental tirade, and realized it was not just him, but in fact she had been mostly the cause. What kind of business relationship can start out with drinks, suggestive walks, and whatnot? But he supposed that fit in rather perfectly with Finn Darrs' type, and despite himself he smirked.

As soon as Garrett had departed, Carmen closed the door softly. And then she fell against it, sliding to the floor, a well-established pout on her face. She knew she was not far from naive, but what had she done to deserve his strange behavior? Why had he seemed so cross, so rude? He had prevented her from falling, an act she was actually grateful to him for, had said as much, and he then became a man of hardened stone. She thought back to those precious few moments, thinking of his arm around her waist, the clean scent of his closeness, the undeniable strength under his business suit. She felt lower stomach quivers at the memory. She played back the moment again, and could not identify any wrong-doing or rudeness on her part. But obviously something had gone wrong, because Garrett had changed personalities in an instant. It was just so aggravating, and completely unfair. How would this relationship progress if it had started off on such a precarious foot? She rose somewhat unsteadily, and walked to the cabinet that she knew would provide her solace. She hadn't heard an engine outside, and assumed

Garret must have started walking. Hopefully in the wrong direction.

Nick was there. When he saw Garrett approaching he fairly shrieked, and did something he never did. He hopped out of the car, stumbling in his rush, and opened Garrett's door for him. Garrett didn't notice, did not even acknowledge him, and entered the car like a storm cloud. Nick closed the door and got in his own seat, and began what he knew would be long ride back to the city. In the back of the limo he heard thunder rumbling.

***

Garrett and Nick got back to the city mostly silently, Garrett slowly recovering from his disgruntlement, and Nick steadily regaining his ability to be affable. It was only upon reaching the outskirts of New York, however, that any words were exchanged.

"Nick?" Garrett asked.

"Yes, sir" Nick replied, the tiniest bit of prayer in his voice.

"Take me back to my apartment, please, and be prepared tomorrow to once again visit Connecticut."

"Really?" Nick was not at all happy with the prospect.

"Don't worry. We won't be visiting the same woman's house." Garret said, and Nick noticed his employer smiling in his rear-view mirror. "Apparently she has a sister who sells antiques in the next town over". Garrett was beginning to feel smart again. "I think it's time I updated my flat, so to speak."

Nick could hear the smugness in Garrett's voice, and felt a mixture of pride and nausea. Whereas he would do anything for Garrett, he did not like the conclusion of today's meeting, and the thought of visiting a relative of Carmen's tomorrow, particularly one who might easily be forewarned of Mr. Darrs' behavior, did not sit well with him. Nick was an easy-going type of guy, and any disruptions to his equilibrium were not quite welcome.

"Yes, Mr. Darrs" was all Nick said at first, but then could not refrain from adding "Do you think that trip might result better if we take it next week? Less expensive furniture?" Nick was not pleading, but did not come off as jovial and nonchalant as he was hoping either. That would cost him.

"What do you mean?" Garrett looked at the rearview mirror to get Nick's expression. "Just because today was no smashing success, doesn't mean tomorrow can't be the opposite." He paused, knowing Nick would say nothing. "I've got plans, you see, and in case you've forgotten, I'm pretty good once the plans are in place. It's only when I've got plans in place, and people distract me repeatedly that things can go awry." Garrett felt agitation again, but forced it away. "I've got a plan, a simple plan, and it's hard for a simple plan to go wrong." He stated with conviction and a slightly rigid smile.

"Yes, Sir." Nick said, though he felt dismally anxious. He was experienced enough to know that "simple" and "women" rarely meshed.

Presently they arrived outside Garrett's building. "I'll see you in the morning Mr. Darrs?" Nick asked.

"Yes, thanks." Garrett said, but hesitated before getting out of the car. " I'll call you if it's otherwise, because to tell you the truth I never got her card from Carmen, which of course means I'll have to call her and ask for the information later today." This fact had obviously just dawned on him. He had left in such a stupid rush, he hadn't gotten the card, not that Carmen's sister's business card was on his mind at all while he had been visiting. He in fact could care less about her sister's business as there were more than enough shops that could satisfy his antique collection, but now he cared a bit more. "I don't think it should be a problem, though." Garrett opened the door, and got out. He leaned back in and smiled at Nick. "Anyway, see you at ten, unless you hear from me."

"OK, then." Nick knew better than to add "good luck". He pulled away.

***

Garrett opened the door to his flat, closed it, and then sank down into his couch, closing his eyes. What was he doing, he thought, dancing around with plans and ideas for this new woman? Why had she gotten to him? Her beauty alone was no answer, for as beautiful as she was, she was not exceptional. Was it his guilt for the days' events? Impossible. Though generally a gentleman, he had done many things in the past that might have been considered questionable for which he rarely felt more than a pang of guilt, and all he had done today was leave hastily. All he had done today was almost kiss a woman, wishing far more. What was wrong with that? That was natural, male, human-- required for procreation in fact. Why should he feel guilty about that, about fulfilling his role in nature? Especially since she didn't know. Of that he was now sure.

But he knew the answer. Natural were his instincts, and nothing wrong in them, but she had stopped him, albeit unintentionally. She had stopped him and he had turned almost mean, even as she was kindly asking him what was wrong, and looked at him with sincerity, with a sincerity that actually moved him a little. He had let the mere possibility of a kiss refused ruin his behavior. He had reacted as if he were a much younger, much more naïve man.

And of course there was the Finn factor, which he really was pissed about factoring at all. He and his brother had always gotten along well, cared very much in the usual older brother/younger brother fashion, and really only once had Garret had to step in on Finn's affairs to get Finn out of trouble. Problem is, he'd heard enough side stories from his sisters and poor mother that sometimes it just got tiring. Finn and he were the only ones in the family to have moved east when his family had chosen to remain in Colorado. Garrett had been drawn for obvious reasons—first the finance world that New York owns, and then the art world—ditto. Finn had left Colorado to go to school in the east where he'd bounced from New Hampshire to Providence (insert side story here as to why he really left New Hampshire, because it would not be his story), and then he'd gone to Boston upon graduation, and fell very much in love with the area. His original intention, bizarre to all that knew him, was law school at Harvard, and he'd easily been accepted, but after a few semesters he learned what everyone who knew him already thought--it was just too much toil without entertainment. Too much edification,

too much book time, all to be inevitably spent proving one thing or another whether he believed he should or not. He believed in justice, but he was too much of a cynic. Right about the time he was dropping out of love with law school, he became enamored with food, but more particularly, the preparation and presentation of it. So with the help of his parents, he'd bought a place in Boston's Southie district and began his culinary life.
Occasionally he popped down to meet Garrett and visa versa, and Finn would always have an entertaining tale or two, and they enjoyed each others' company. Nor was it always without substance. They didn't only go out to drink too much and find badly behaving women, which certainly had its merits, but they shared better intimacy, meaningful reflection. Garrett liked Finn, no doubt, but his involvement with Carmen was still nettling.

Finn hadn't mentioned an artist in his life, or her name, and Luigi had said Finn was with a pretty woman when he'd visited, so either his affair with Carmen was not exclusive, or it'd ended already. He begrudgingly admitted he might have mislabeled her unfairly at her house, and that he'd done so only at the prompt of her hypnotizing eyes, but Finn was involved.

And of course he knew what would happen now. He had wounded her pride, and crushed her spirit just a bit, so when they next would meet she would be cold or aloof, didn't really matter which. All manner of communication would be stilted and uncomfortable for them both. How he hated it. But he also could do nothing except have those communications, because he loved her work, and he would have to show it, and he'd have to buy some for his own pleasure, and he'd desperately like to get a copy of Luigi's piece for himself. All these requirements of his would mean at least a few chats with Carmen, but maybe it was not so bad? With each chat, things might go smoother, and with the acquisition of a few expensive pieces from her sister's antiques shop, as well as demonstrating as many excellent traits as he could to her sister, he could get in her good graces. Well, that's all he had for the moment. Screw it if it didn't go as planned.

It had now been three hours since his rendezvous with Carmen, which he thought ample time, so he took out her business card and dialed her number. Before it connected he put the phone down. Silly to call her without a cold drink with rattling ice cubes next to him he realized, so he made himself a lovely scotch and re-dialed. Why was he fidgety? And why was he what must be nervous? This was a WOMAN, a species he was very used to, loved dearly but very used to, and knew oh so well....

"Hello" said Carmen. She sounded normal enough—no trace of angst anywhere. It had of course been three hours.

Garrett hesitated only a moment. "Hello, Carmen". Sure enough, his ice was rattling as he held it. He took a quick sip and put the drink down. "Sorry about that" apologizing about nothing in particular. "This is Garrett—I hope I'm not disturbing you". He waited and also steeled himself another sip of his scotch.

"Oh, hello". She said. And right away he heard the temperature drop. She cleared her throat a little. "How can I help you?" She did not say his name, which somehow seemed worse.

"Again, I'm sorry to trouble you, but you had mentioned that your sister has an antiques shop. I'd very much like it if you could give me her name and location since I've got some immediate requirements, as does my office at the gallery" he lied.

"Oh. Yes. Of course." She stammered a bit, and sounded a little disappointed he thought.

"And I know our parting was a bit hasty this afternoon, but we should get together soon to discuss showing your work here at Gallery Darrs."

Mmm, yes, well...." She hesitated. "I'm not sure when I can come in just at the moment..."

"What's that?" Garrett felt an uneasiness creeping up his spine.

"You see, it's just that given a change in my circumstances, it might be better if we held off our joint venture for now" Carmen said. She was making it up as she went along, not entirely sure what she was doing. She knew Garrett was eager for her work, and part of her wished to punish him for his less than stellar attitude earlier in the day. How could he call her back on the very same day and act as though they were hunky dory now? She heard him take a sip of something with ice in it. Scotch. Hah. "Actually, I had another offer from a prestigious gallery that I found rather flattering, and...."

Garrett was not expecting that, at least not so soon. How the hell could that have happened in the space of half a day? "Which gallery would that be?" He said this coolly, but thought his voice might have been a shade too high.

Carmen was smiling. There was no such offer, but it didn't matter. "I'm afraid I'm not really at liberty to say at the moment. I haven't made any decisions, and think it'd be best for all parties if I didn't go into any details with anyone just yet." She nearly laughed out loud after that came out of her mouth. She heard the clinking ice again.

Garret knew he should get off the phone in case the vein in his head that was about to pop would be audible. He said only "I see. I think maybe we should discuss this before you go ahead and make any decisions, but why don't you sleep on it? I'll call you in the next few days. Thank you, as always, for your time Carmen." And he hung up.

Carmen smiled again as she put the phone down. How things can change in just a short time, and really, it was his fault....the phone rang again, and made her jump. She picked it up, and greeted her caller.

"Carmen, how foolish of me to now twice forget to get your sister's information" Garrett said coolly, but with just the right amount of self deprecation. "Would you mind giving it to me now?"

Why so eager for a few antiques, she wondered. Weren't his sources endless? "Of course. Her name is Sophia Carmine, and she lives in Ridgefield, on 73 Constance Lane. You can reach her at 203-764-1193. I'll let her know you'll be calling."

I'm sure you will, he thought. "Thanks again, and have yourself a good evening Carmen" and he hung up before she could wish him the same.

"You too, you annoying cretin of a man" Carmen said to no one in particular. She felt like a ping pong ball, up and down, low and high, silly game.

***

It was now early evening, so she poured herself a modest martini and went to her studio, quite sure she'd have the ability to paint something good, or at least begin the makings of something good. If for nothing else, Garrett Darrs was stimulation for emotion-ridden artwork, though nothing approaching anything happy. Despite her earlier smugness after possibly fooling him into believing another gallery was after her, that feeling had quickly vanished—had in fact vanished as soon as he had hung up. She was back to the familiar uncertainty.

She found a blank canvas, and put it on her easel. As she set about finding her paints and brushes, she thought about the day. She thought about Garrett Darrs, and she thought about other men that had been in her life. Strictly speaking, she was not a woman that normally required the company of a man. She often found that men were more trouble than the bit of pleasure they provided. Her past relationships had been fraught with passion, but aptly short-lived. She had never complained, had usually been ready for the ending, and sometimes thought she subconsciously or not-so-subconsciously had assisted in the demise. It was not that she didn't love men, for in fact she adored them, but she found most of them selfish, and then needy. She was not a doting female, as a lot of men were accustomed to. Generally men tired easily of doting females, so when they came across Carmen, who demonstrated qualities anything but doting, the change was too much. The men would become a little too doting themselves, and then resentful if such feelings were not at least slightly reciprocated. It was an interesting fiasco.

She could not logically imagine that Garrett would be any different, but things had not started well. She knew very well she did not have the upper hand, but she also knew he didn't quite have it either. Did he even care? A man like Garrett Darrs probably kissed a beautiful woman every other day and thought nothing of it, so why should she, pretty-ish Carmen Carmine, be special? After all, he had fairly run out of her house after he had caught her fall, and then he had been nothing if not curt. Is that why she was intrigued? Was it the trite reason that she was interested in something she might not actually be able to get? Was she as predictable as most?

Carmen sat down and prepared to paint, but she was feeling uncreative. She knew there was more to her attraction to Garrett than the fact she thought he might not want her. As they say, the eyes have it. He was a tall, strong, confident man, and yes, he was stunning. In his eyes, though, there was little arrogance. There was patience, kindness, and humor, and there was an appreciation for beauty—of the many beautiful things life offers always, but that too many don't even notice, let alone cherish. She recognized in him, even during the short time they had been together, qualities that mirrored her own. At this point, however, it didn't really matter. She would have to wait until they next met, and make sure she made a better impression, or better yet, make sure he wanted to make a better impression on her (assuming, of course, that he had no idea of the fabulous impression he had already made).

She thought then about Sophia, her sister, and that she would shortly be meeting Garrett. Rather tripping over herself, she went to her phone to call her. She would not let Garrett visit her sister without at least letting her know about this man, and without making sure that Sophia gleaned as much information from the meeting as possible. Sophia might even prove herself instrumental if she didn't louse things up. It was one or the other, Carmen knew.

"Sophia's Corner, may I help you?" Sophia said softly, seductively.

"Hello there Sophie. Just who were you expecting? You sound like you've just gotten some, or you really need some" said Carmen, admittedly rather crudely. She'd always been just a little jealous of her sister's timbre.

"Carmen! What a thing to say", but she laughed. "What's going on?"

"Do you have a minute or two, because I need to keep you abreast of a situation, and ask a favor."

"Ooh. Sounds good. The store is almost empty right now, so shoot." Sophia sounded intrigued.

"It's nothing that big, just this man, Garrett Darrs. Well, OK, so he's not just this man. He's a very rich art gallery owner who is interested in showing my work."

"Well that sounds excellent. What can I do about it?"

"He's going to be coming to your shop. I'm not sure when , but pretty soon, probably within the next day or so. I guess he's big into fine antiques, and he needs a few pieces for his home and office, so make sure you take advantage of it." Carmen was hesitating. All of a sudden she felt embarrassed mentioning the real reason she was calling.

"Excellent! I could use a large sale. Thanks for the heads-up."

"Mmm. No problem...." She was losing her nerve. Why?

"Yes? What is it?" Sophia paused, her mental calculations almost audible. "Is he an old boyfriend? An intended boyfriend? Has the contract been signed? What do you need me to do?"

"No, no no. Nothing like that, it's just that...." And Carmen went on to explain the events of the day, more or less, to her sister. She tried to impress upon her sister that she wished only for Sophia to get as many sales as she could, while at the same time taking note of everything he said. She was in high school again, for heaven's sake.

"Wow" Sophia said. "This guy must be something, alright. You've got me curious. Or he's got me curious."

This was not exactly what Carmen wanted, but she could live with it. Sometimes her sister meddled if she thought she could do any good. "Well, don't get the wrong idea, Soph. I am really interested in getting my artwork into his gallery, and things did kind of get screwy today, but please don't let him know that we spoke, other than my giving you a heads up, OK?"

"Oh, of course, of course." Sophia promised. "I'll just give him the hard sell on my junk, and practically leave you out of it."

"Thanks. Let me know what, if anything happens. Talk to you later." And after exchanging good-byes they hung up.

Carmen felt a bit better after the call, and relaxed. She went back to her studio and began to paint.

Chapter 3

Carmen and Sophia had grown up in beautiful Westchester County, New York, along with their brother Dominic. As children, they had been blessed with an exceptional environment, since their parents, Bella and Giorgio Carmine, did very well. Giorgio was the owner of a well established jewelry shop in Pleasantville, New York, the sister shop to their original shop in Milan. He had decided to move to the states to start another shop after the last of their children had been born. This was a move he regretted only in that the language was not second nature to his children, and surely would have been had they stayed another ten years. He and his wife had always spoken Italian with them, and had made sure to hire an Italian nanny, but things fade. Anyway, there were worse things to regret.

Though their surroundings would not have been considered opulent, their house stood on top of a gentle hill which was nearly the center of a pristinely maintained nine acre plot. Bella Carmine was born in Italy, and was therefore old school, so she did all her own cooking, but she did allow herself the luxury of a maid and grounds-keeper. Though she occasionally assisted her husband in accounting matters at the store, she mostly stayed happily at home raising her children. She herself had been raised by strict parents, and knew that while her children needed to experience certain things on their own, she didn't let them roam too far while it was under her control.

Dominic was the oldest, then Carmine, and Sophia the youngest. They had grown up, at least initially, as closely knit siblings, since there was no more than a total of four years between the three of them. Naturally, Dominic shied away as he grew older, but never strayed far enough away so that he could not keep an eye on his younger sisters. Like most brothers, he was very protective, a quality especially necessary with Carmen and Sophia since they were both exceptionally pretty, and everyone wanted to be around them—girls, boys, nice and not-so-nice.

Carmen and Sophia were usually best of friends, and for that matter, shared a few friends, particularly as they grew older. Though Carmen was older, she was shyer than her sister. Sophia's having been the youngest had prompted her to be a bit of a showgirl. Sophia cared deeply for Carmen, but an impartial onlooker would not find it hard to see that even Sophia's love for Carmen was perhaps slightly overshadowed by her love of attention. Sophia would not rob Carmen of attention in any direct fashion, but only subtlety, and only if she thought her stature within a setting was threatened. Carmen was well aware of her sister's needs, and didn't mind. She was older and could easily tolerate her younger sister's spotlight requirements; besides, Carmen didn't want the spotlight. She had always been an observer, and learned ever so much that way.

She started drawing at age two, but did not start drawing anything noticeably good until she was almost nine, and did not get truly interested in drawing and painting until she was halfway through high school, but then she was firmly entrenched. She took as many art electives as her schedule would allow without foregoing her academic requirements. Carmen regularly entered and won artistic contests in and out of school. Not that her other schoolwork did not suffer sometimes, because it did. Whereas she was very intelligent, her concentration was art, and she became immediately lazy when it was time to study for anything else. She failed nothing, but excelled really only in her art classes.

Sophia, on the other hand, was a natural at most subjects, and attained good grades without trying very hard, which was a good thing since she did not like studying either. As her personality demanded, she aggressively sought entertainment of all kinds. She shopped until her parents balked, hung out with her girlfriends until she grew tired of them, and flirted with the boys until her brother threatened someone. Her appetite for life, while heartening, at times teetered on the dangerous. She didn't like to be bored, not that anyone does mind you, but Sophia would not sit still at any given age.

Dominic watched fondly as his sisters grew, and once in a while found himself the mediator, even if a silent one, because he knew very well the differences between the two, and understood when to interfere, and when to cross his fingers from afar. It was so easy to have a soft spot for Sophia, just because she was who she was, but his true soft spot was for Carmen. He did not entirely fathom her quiet acceptance of Sophia, and everything else for that matter, but he also knew that she was, perhaps more so than any of them, very happy. Comfortable in her skin. And that's not easy for anybody.

How Carmen had come to her career is obvious, but some might not quite see how Sophia came to be an antiques dealer. It wasn't so much her means of making a living that enthralled her, though she did like antiques, and did make a stinking lot of money doing it (she had a stupendous talent for buying cheap and then nearly robbing buyers blind), but the world in which it put her. She lived and worked in a town that few others in the country could surpass as far as real estate, location, culture, hob-nobbery, snobbery, etc., and as always, she had the knack for making rich friends, and as a matter of course, then being regularly invited to posh parties in her town, as well as further reaching money-resplendent areas such as Long Island, and the Upper East Side of Manhattan. She made her hours such that she could maintain the life of a virtual socialite, and if she had to she completely trusted her one employee to stand in for her if need be. Sophia was exactly where she wanted to be—in the middle of it all. Like Carmen, she was not used to being tied down to one man for too long a period of time since she liked variety too much, but she did imagine she'd probably have to settle down in her mid to late thirties (she was now twenty-eight) just so she wouldn't die alone. She relied far too heavily on others to entertain her to believe she could entertain herself later on.

Bella and Giorgio Carmine continued to live in Westchester County in the same beautiful house. Too large for them alone, it was still a regular meeting point for the family, and they wouldn't sell it until it was too much. At any rate, they had the money to hire more help if they had to. They were happy and they were proud—proud of what they themselves had achieved, and even

41

more proud of whom their children had become and what they had made of themselves so far. They had little to worry about....

Chapter 4

It was early evening, and Garrett Darrs was uneasy, restless. The thought of the day ahead, while entertaining, was not enough to distract him from thoughts of Carmen. He knew he had fumbled a bit of their conversation over the phone, but thought it ended well. How vexatious a woman. How down-right nerve-wracking frustrating and petty. He wasn't sure whether or not she had another offer on the table, and in fact logically thought it unlikely, but that wasn't really the point, now was it? True or not, she had spoken of it. If, on the one hand it was true, then she would not have mentioned it out of courtesy to him and his offer, except of course for the events of the afternoon. If, on the other hand, it was not true (definitely the more likely), then she was saying so to possibly avoid signing on with his gallery for now. Silly woman. He'd maybe call her after he got home tomorrow, but therein was the problem. Calling her tomorrow was too eager, but he could not afford to wait if there was another offer. Silly, silly woman.

But her body was not so silly. And her full, sweet lips were not so silly. The way she walked, and the manner in which she held herself, the way her eyes almost could not hold his when she spoke—well, that was far from silly. He closed his eyes firmly, willing her image to disappear, but it was there for the moment. He could feel the weight of his desire in his clothes, and this did not make him happy. The wretched woman was going to ruin his night's sleep if this kept going. He thought then again of Annabelle, and wondered if ringing her two nights in a row would be too risky. He was pretty sure she did not expect much from their relationship, other than the exquisite sex they gave each other once in a while. But two nights in a row is hardly once in a while, and he didn't want her jumping to any typical conclusions. No, it couldn't happen that way. Nor could he think of anyone else he could conceivably call out of the blue, at least not without causing other problems he didn't need.

It didn't matter enough. Not getting a good night's sleep because of his troubled thoughts might work in his favor. When he was slightly edgy, he tended to intimidate people more, so perhaps he'd make a few great purchases. He got up from his sofa, resigned. After changing into his night clothes, he got in bed, opting to read for a while, a cozy sherry also his companion. Something had to help him sleep. Garrett read for a time, not always able to move on to the next sentence, as his thoughts were finding it difficult not to obsess. A line from a The Who's song teased him…"she's just a girl, just a girl….". But he guessed he really didn't think so.

***

When he awoke, Garrett was feeling better than he expected would be the case, and he was even rested, a pleasant feeling he attributed somewhat to the sherry, but also having eventually willed himself to have a good night's sleep, deprived of sensation. He was ready for his day, and he dressed with a replenished confidence he was happy to recognize. He shaved, had a bit of coffee while he read his required daily reading—The New York Times, and the Wall Street Journal. At 9:45 he dared to glance down at the street to see if Nick was waiting, but didn't see the car. He called him on his cell.

"Yup" said Nick.

"Good Morning, Nick. Are you near at all, or should I get breakfast somewhere?"

"Good Morning, Mr. Darrs. Actually, I should be there right about 10 as we discussed, but if you feel like grabbing a bite, I can read the paper."

"No, you know what, thanks anyway, but I'll see you at 10. I want to have an efficient morning so I can get back to the gallery, especially since I wasn't there all day yesterday. OK? See you shortly."

"Yes, sir."

They rang off, and Garrett did a last minute check in the mirror. Crisp, smooth and polished—the look of success. He smiled and went to meet Nick.

The ride out to Ridgefield was uneventful. Nick spent the time humming and driving, while Garret continued to read more of his paper. He did not dwell on the events before him, because he thought it would be far more straightforward than yesterday's. After all, he really only wanted to scout the place, and impress Sophia Carmen with his taste and ability to spend money. Getting to know the sister of a conquest, business or otherwise, was just sound logic. Get an in where you can. And if you could impress them in any way at all, it could only serve as additional positive fodder. He wanted Carmen to put her work in his gallery, and in fact he wanted her to fairly trip over herself to get her stuff through his doors.

When they pulled up to "Sophia's Corner", Garret put his paper aside. It was just past 11:30 in the morning. Other than a black BMW, there were no other cars in the parking lot, a good indication Garrett would have the place to himself. The grounds were small, but meticulously maintained, almost austere. The shop itself was a ranch, but seemed quite long. It was painted in cream, peach and light blue, not what he'd expect but friendly and inviting. There was a small, separate sign with the shop's name planted next to a cobblestone path which led to a large front door. Lights from inside seemed cheery enough, mostly chandeliers from what he could tell.

"OK, Nick" he said. "I don't think I'll be that long. I'll do my usual browse, but the place obviously isn't immense. I don't think it'll be more than an hour. Sit tight."

"OK, Mr. Darrs. Let me know if you need anything."

Garrett got out of the car. "Will do" and he closed the door. He stood and brushed himself off, vaguely wondering if he was being watched. He walked down the cobblestone path and entered the shop. A slightly noisy bell announced his presence as it jangled against the door he had opened. He let his eyes get accustomed to the light and looked around. Seeing no one, he began his mission. It was immediately apparent Sophia's boutique was full of excellent stuff. Here and there he spotted

45

questionable this-and-that's, but most of what he saw seemed authentic, and his eyes were well trained. The room into which the front entrance had opened was mostly a trinket area he realized, so he went about looking for the furniture area. As he walked he smiled at the sound of his steps on the creaking wide-planked, wooden floors. It was a sound he associated with antique shops, certainly, but also of his childhood. Creaky floors were one of many prompts for nightmares, and then later in the teenage years, a dead give-away for nights spent out too late. He found the room he was looking for only a few paces away from the front room, and was impressed with what he saw.

The room was spacious, and provided just the right amount of lighting, and of course the scents he associated with old, fine things. There seemed to be such a variety to look at, he decided to be methodical rather than random roving. His feet led him to the far left corner, still creaking as he went along. He felt almost self-conscious at the sound, and at this point was surprised someone had not met up with him. Maybe Carmen's sister knew it was him, and was deliberately keeping her distance, if only just for now. Or maybe she was right behind him, hoping to catch him unawares. He stopped fretting about that when he noticed a magnificent credenza, a piece entirely of mahogany, with exquisite detailing on the top and sides of the shelving. The wood was smooth, and there were only minor scratches here and there from what he could tell. There were a total of four shelves, all of which except the top one having the built-in bookends. Presumably Sophia had placed the books on the shelving, and the top shelf had several large volumes, but there was a matching jade bookend set holding them upright. They were two jade elephants, massive and also perfectly detailed, from the trunk and tusks to the heavily wrinkled base of the legs.

"Lovely, aren't they?" came a voice. Garrett was certain he made a startled noise, as well as a movement, and was very glad she had spoken before he had picked up one of the elephants, as he had been just about to do so.

"Ah, yes they really are" Garrett said as he turned to face the voice.

"Other than a slight crack on one side of one elephant, they are in perfect condition". Garrett had at this point turned around. "I'm Sophia Carmine" the woman continued as she extended her hand to Garrett. "You must be Garrett Darrs. My sister mentioned you'd be stopping by".

Garrett was good at maintaining his composure, and he quite needed to do so then. She had startled him, and now that she was in his sights, he thought her breath-taking, unsettlingly so. He had not even thought to consider that possibility, so he was all the more disturbed. But he was a professional after all, and addressed her accordingly. As he took her hand he said "Yes, of course. I had asked that she do so. Carmen had said she had a sister in the antiques business, and it just so happens I'm looking for a few pieces." He was looking her in the eyes, and she returned the gaze, a hint of amusement in them he thought. "A happy coincidence, really".

"I guess so." She said. "I'm always glad to part with my wares, especially the more expensive ones." She smiled at him. "I have a feeling you are a fan of buying just such expensive wares?" She was still smiling, and painfully flirting. Garrett now realized he was also dealing with a professional. His purchases would not be as easy as he thought, but he would neither let her win without his own form of bartering.

"Oh, I'm really a fan of many things—even new articles— things that have not had time to collect dust. Right now, as you noticed I was looking at this credenza, though in truth I really haven't had a chance to look around." Garrett paused for a moment. "If there are certain items or areas you recommend, please tell me, as my time is limited. My driver has to get me back to the gallery, you see." He hoped that slight exaggeration would help his cause.

Sophia's expression didn't change much. I'd be happy to assist you Mr. Darrs."

"Call me Garrett, please."

"OK, Garrett. And please call me Sophia. Let me point out a few rooms that might be of particular interest to you. Just follow me. Tell me to slow down if I go too fast, but remember I'm just giving you a quick walk-through. I'll let you off on your own

47

once I've shown you the basics." With that she was off on her tour. She began pointing out a few pieces in the room where they already stood, and he half listened. He was probably as knowledgeable about the stuff as she was, if not more, so he really didn't need to listen that closely. He was spending more time on watching her movements. She really was incredible looking, and of course she moved in the manner that told him she knew it. She looked very little like Carmen, actually. She was a few inches taller, and she was of a more slender build, though she was not too slender. Like her sister she had grace as she moved, but there was an extra slinkiness that Garrett found quite enticing. Every once in a while as she was leading him around her shop, she'd turn around and smile at him. She was beautiful, her white skin flawless, her blue eyes set deeply and always smiling. She had a very perfect nose, almost, he thought, one that had had work done on it, but it didn't really matter. She was just stunning. Strangely enough, he felt as if he was betraying Carmen by thinking it, but Sophia was the more beautiful of the two.

And Sophia was definitely sending some interesting signals. He had caught her more than once looking him over, and then looking him in the eyes. But she did not stop her tutelage as they wound their way around the house, and he noticed she was extremely good at pointing out lovingly items that had jaw-dropping price tags. Maybe her flirtations were part of the sale—that was far from an uncommon practice, but he still found it a little strange. Had Carmen explained their meeting, and the awkwardness he was sure she had felt by the end of it? Had it fazed her much less than he thought it had, so much so that all she had mentioned to Sophia was that he'd be stopping by and possibly buying some furniture? He decided to abandon that thought in favor of an easier one to swallow—Sophia was just one of those women—the type that was interested in a good-looking man despite what might be going on with her sister. Usually that sort of activity was abandoned after childhood, but sometimes the lesson was never learned. Maybe Sophia knew everything but had decided her own desires were more important Yes, that had to be it. Ahh, the life he led, the absurdity but excellentness of it.

48

"Now, Garret" Sophia was saying as he paid more attention to her words. "I'll let you stray, but come on over or call me if there's something you want to talk about. I won't be too far". She smiled, and walked away, swaying her sweet derriere as she departed, fully attuned to his watching her.

I just bet you won't, he thought. "OK, and thanks. I'm sure I can find something". Garrett didn't much feel like shopping anymore, and she had taken up a good twenty minutes going through the store with him, so he also knew he didn't have as much browsing time as he usually needed, but he got to the task at hand. He knew he could not leave without buying at least a couple of things, and without chatting it up a little more with the beautiful Sophia, a task he wasn't shy of performing.

After walking around for another half hour, and taking serious looks at seriously expensive pieces (very aware of Sophia in the back-ground), he decided he'd buy the credenza and elephants he'd first seen, as well as a ridiculously priced side table he'd spotted. He walked up to Sophia, who feigned interest in some inventory book. "Well, Sophia" he said. "I think I've found a couple of things, though frankly they seem to be priced rather high".

She looked up at him and smiled in her alluring way. "Garrett, I'm glad you found something, though I can assure you that while some of the prices seem high, in reality they reflect the true value of what are truly exceptional pieces, something I'm sure a man of your expertise in the field can recognize." She was teasing him he realized. "What, other than the credenza and the elephants have you found?"

"A side table, the one in the far room—I can show you" and he began to walk in that direction.

"Is that all you found today?" She asked, and she had a slight pout in her voice, an affected quality he did not like, and was surprised to think she found it successful.

"Honestly, if I had more time, I know there would be more, but as I said, I have to get back to my gallery." Garrett said. "I can assure you, however, I will be returning, especially if you'd have the kindness to inform me as new pieces come into your shop". The promise of continued business was always a wise

49

ploy, and this time it was also authentic. Despite the prices, Sophia's Corner was one of the better shops he'd seen, and the selection was nothing short of superb. Thief that she was, she had a very good eye for the stuff.

"Why Garrett, you do tease a girl" and she had dropped the pout to his relief. "I think I know the table you mean", and in fact she did.

When all was said and done he had paid nearly full asking price for everything, with only a few hundred knocked off for the promise of his continued support and the fact that he "was a friend of Carmen's". What a talented vixen was she.

"I'll have my movers come get my purchases" Garret told Sophia. "They'll be here tomorrow."

"Very well, Garrett. It was a pleasure meeting you and doing business with you." Sophia was looking at him meaningfully. "I'll have to come by and see that gallery of yours—hopefully while its walls are well populated with my sister's paintings."

He was not sure of what she knew, so he only said "Yes, I'd be happy to show you around. Thanks for a great morning, Sophia" and he headed out. She said nothing as he departed, but he knew she was watching him, and that she was smiling. Vixen with an antique shop.

***

Sophia watched Garrett's car depart, a forefinger on her chin—a look of study she was unaware she'd put on. A trace of a smile played about her face, and her eyes were on the way to far off. She'd made a tidy profit today, an easy task when dealing with the fabulously wealthy, as she knew Garrett Darrs was. She adored making money, was always thinking of ways to get a pinch more, though she hesitated not at all when spending. She didn't have to. While she made a good salary at her shop, she was a heavy spender and would be in the poor house if it weren't for her generous parents. They didn't care that she was still given an allowance at her wizened age, that if she wished a new car they'd grant it and ask what model. She knew the value of money, and she knew she was lucky to have what she did. They had taught her the appreciation and never to take any of it for granted. To them that was all that mattered. That and that she employed herself usefully, which she had done with the shop since just after she graduated.

The Carmines owned just two jewelry shops, but they had become famous throughout Europe for the design and quality. Giorgio's work was sought by the most affluent and influential people, and that only became more true as he practiced the art less and less. As he aged, his eyes got worse, dexterity dwindled, and patience all but disappeared when dealing with his own limitations. The one thing that hadn't waned was his imagination. So he would draw what he envisioned, and convey it to the men he had hired to translate it into fine jewelry, and now both his New York and Milan shop were bigger than ever. There was talk of (from his wife) opening a shop in LA, but Giorgio had had enough. Maybe Madrid. Maybe not.

Sophia was more like her mother, Bella, a woman of small stature but large personality. In her youth she had been virtually unattainable physically and philosophically, but she had met Giorgio Carmine and at twenty-one had fallen quite hard. Giorgio had not wanted to tame her, or even adore her too closely. He was an artist and understood the need to let beauty flourish and sometimes run wild. Bella had given herself, a virgin, to Giorgio on their first outing together, and from that moment on the pair did not separate. When they were not being physical, they were engaged in conversation or shared silence they believed resonated with each other's thoughts. The passion they shared for and with each other was not something that abated, just shifted in nature. Even now and even often, their children would catch a swift spark exchanged across a room, and it made them tranquil and it made them glad.

Sophia had received the lion's share of her mother's neon blood, did not care to taper it or hone to something reasonable. The shop, and the degree of responsibility it took to run it, was what she allowed of the even-keeled world. She smiled with a bit of mischief as she turned back to ring up the sale and go about

51

orchestrating its departure. Something to this man, Garrett Darrs, and her sister felt the vibe, she could tell.

She was mostly happy with the purchases Garrett had made. She had, after all, bought those pieces at a fraction of what she had sold them to him for, but she knew well he could have bought more, and thought that he seemed in a rush to depart, despite the fact he was a man that really did not have to rush at all. But there was something else. He was extremely handsome, sexy— extremely her type. Carmen had said he was good-looking, but had not elaborated, and she had also said things had gotten a bit uncomfortable between them, but again did not elaborate, even when Sophia had pressed the matter. Which could only mean that Garrett had made a pass at her, and it had gone awry. Doubtless, Carmen had screwed something up in her own somewhat innocent way, and probably she fancied the man despite the voided passion. This was all speculation on her part, but Sophia knew her sister well. Why else would she have been so evasive, yet made sure to call her prior to Garret's visit?

Yes, her parents now gave her what she wanted and needed, but she'd also been accustomed to getting any attention she wanted. She wanted Garrett, or she certainly wanted his attention. Every part of her body understood what it would be like to share a bed (or whatever) with him, and the fact he had a huge bank account did not detract from the man, of course. She did care for Carmen, however had Carmen actually said she was interested in Garrett as more than a business partner? No. Sophia could surely not be held accountable for any future relations she might have with Garrett if Carmen had not said what she meant.

Maybe, in fact, Sophia had met her inevitable mate earlier than expected? She did love partying and dancing with as many handsome men as seemed fit, and being escorted here and there by the beautiful, and she had imagined it would go on for a few more years, but what if she shouldn't wait? After all, Garrett Darrs was perfect in all ways since he had everything she required in a partner, and she could tell he had an admiring eye for her as well. She remembered the glint in his eyes when first he saw her, and she could sense something else as well. But she would not chase him—she never chased the boys—she'd just make him chase her.   She was getting tipsy at the thought of her future, an impossibly strange occurrence, as Sophia Carmine had never been the sort to dream of her wedding day, or dream of even anything lasting beyond Christmas, but there she was.   Bedazzled.

Chapter 5

It had been nearly a week since Garret Darrs had bought the furniture, which now sat, still wrapped, in his gallery's warehouse. He had not phoned Carmen, and she had not phoned him. He had determined Carmen had been making up the bit about another gallery making her an offer, and now, having made that decision, was equally determined to beat her at her game and make her nervous. The whole thing had initially been addling him, but now he just found it amusing. His confidence in this game was perhaps derived from his lack of proximity to the woman. The further the events of the past became, the less the effect Carmen had on him, and the more power he wielded, but time was getting to be an issue. His walk through the gallery the other day had proved he needed to populate his walls with at least Carmen's work, or get someone else to fill the gap.

He made his way down to the warehouse because he wanted to inspect what he had bought. He remembered the grain of the mahogany credenza, and he wanted to make sure it was as beautiful in the lighting of his warehouse as it had been in the more dimly lit, romantic atmosphere of Sophia's shop. As he walked, he used his cell phone to contact Fiona.

She answered on the first ring.

"Yes, Garrett?" She queried.

"Fiona, I need you to do something for me." He said.

"Yes?" She waited for him. "I'll try to accommodate you once you actually tell me what it is you want me to do" she added after the longish pause.

"Funny girl, I've always said. Easy enough. I need you to get hold of Carmen Carmine for me and arrange a lunch meeting at Luigi's." He said. He knew that would be the perfect environment for their meeting.

"When?"

"Today."

"Today's lunch time is past, Garrett. I will call her today, but for what date should I arrange the lunch?"

"Of course. I'll give her a few days. Make it for day after tomorrow, and don't let her make excuses to miss it. If she attempts to do so, it's OK to imply that others are in the wings."

"My Oh my, Mr. Darrs. What are you up to?" Fiona said, not really curious since she was used to his games, but enjoying the occasional banter they shared.

"Nothing" he said, and then "Never mind. And you know what that means." Which meant to both of them that she was not to discuss his plans, as usual, with anyone.

"Call you back" she said only.

"Mmm." And they rang off.

No one was in the warehouse, but he easily found his way over to the antiques. He found a utility knife, and after careful slices, began to unwrap everything. The elephants were well polished, and just as stunning as he recalled, and the side table was also unharmed. That purchase he cared little about but at the time felt he had to make as he was quite certain Sophia was expecting him to buy a lot. He finally unwrapped the credenza, and it too had been well polished. Sophia cared about her product at least. Charge a fortune and a polishing was a good idea he thought, a bit perturbed. But it was an excellent piece, even here in the harsher light of his warehouse, and he now had the time to appreciate all the detailing. Satisfied, he started to walk off, but noticed a paper right next to the credenza on the floor. Assuming it was some sort of packing list, he picked it up and unfolded it. It was a note from Sophia.

***

"Hello?" Carmen said.

"Miss Carmine?" Fiona asked.

"Yes. Can I help you?" Carmen did not recognize the voice.

"Hello, this is Fiona Silvin, Garrett Darrs' Secretary. I hope everything is well?" She politely waited for a response.

Carmen's heart, having nearly stopped, made her hesitate a little. "Um, yes. Everything is fine, thank you."

"Glad to hear it" Fiona said kindly. She had learned over the years to make sure her voice sounded sincere, even if she hardly knew these people well enough to mean what she said. "I'm calling on behalf of Mr. Darrs, as he's in meetings all day, but stressed the importance of getting hold of you" she lied. This would hopefully allay any concerns Carmen might have for not being called personally.

"Oh. I see." Though she really didn't. "What can I help Mr. Darrs with?"

"I am told the both of you had a possible arrangement for you to display your work at his gallery, but that you needed an opportunity to consider his proposal, among others I guess?" Fiona knew the real story, as much as Garret had explained, and hoped her own skepticism was not conveyed in her words.

Carmen did not like being caught off her guard, and chided herself, because she should have been preparing for just such a call. "Yes, that's right...."

"I know you may not have come to any conclusions as yet, but Mr. Darrs would like to discuss this, and perhaps finalize the matter over lunch on Thursday at Luigi's. He would of course have a car pick you up."

"Well, I wouldn't want to waste his time, Miss Silvin...."she stalled. "I'm not sure we could arrange something over lunch, and...." Her pause cost her.

"Call me Fiona, please. And don't worry about a thing. I don't think you'd be wasting Mr. Darrs' time at all, especially as he so admires your work. His gallery is at a critical point, if you must know. As is par for the course, most of the paintings on display have sold, and will be flying off the walls shortly." Fiona hesitated briefly, but meaningfully. "So he needs an artist to fill the space."

Carmen noticed the anonymity of "an artist". No need for a hammer. "Of course..."

"Carmen" she said in a conspiratorial manner. "You are his preference right now—really, and you should take advantage of it. I don't think I have to tell you how competitive the art world is, especially when it comes to vying for walls in a gallery that has as much prestige as Mr. Darrs"."

56

"No, I guess you don't." Carmen tried to think of any other way to get out of it, even though she didn't know why she was trying to dodge the chance of her life-time. Nothing, however, came to mind. "I think Thursday should work out fine. Let me just double-check my appointment book" She said, trying to make a last attempt at showing a modicum of power. After the right amount of time and paper noises she said "Yes, that's OK."

Fiona smiled, though she did feel a little sorry for her. "Great. Expect the car to arrive at noon on the dot."

"Thank you, Fiona". Carmen said, unhappily.

"You're very welcome." She said sincerely. "And don't let him give you any guff", which she also meant.

It's too late for that, Carmen thought. She felt bullied even before having seen him. She was two days away from seeing that grouchy man and she didn't feel ready, even though it was only a matter of saying yes or no. Her hesitation was only because she felt in some small way that she was prostituting herself if she agreed to let his gallery have her work. Logically, she knew this was sheer stupidity, and nothing more. This was a business transaction, and she stood to gain a lot. She would get excellent compensation for her paintings, but more important, her name would take off. It was difficult not to succeed if your work was displayed at Gallery Darrs. But he had not treated her well, and then had, of all things, gotten his worker bee to call her for their meeting, as if such dealings were below him. He couldn't be that busy.

At least he had given her a few days to think about it, because think about it she would. She would go to that meeting, and even though she knew she'd sign her soul away, she'd make sure she got the better deal and that she would exit the meeting head held high.

Chapter 6

Fiona Silvin was an exceptional woman. She had been with
Garrett Darrs for a long time, and they had learned to trust each
other implicitly, and they liked each other very much as well.
Quickly had their professional bond grown, for Garret saw Fiona
immediately for what she was—an extremely intelligent, intuitive,
devoted hard worker. During the first years of their relationship,
when things did not run quite as smoothly as they did today, she
toiled many hours as necessary, not once mentioning the extra
time she was putting in—just making sure that things got done.
Such behavior never went un-noticed. Garrett paid Fiona highly,
and gave her generous raises and bonuses, but sometimes more
valuable than that, he gave her respect to the degree he let her
make many important decisions without him, gradually doing so
more often as he realized she rarely made a mistake. She had, in
fact, done the lion's share of presenting the gallery as Garrett had
wanted it to be—the crème-de-la-crème, one of the most sought
after galleries in the city—on the east coast.

Fiona was married to William Silvin, a man she had been in
love with from maybe date three. He was a piano player, and a
good one at that. He played in many lounges all around the city
as often as he liked, or as rarely as he wished, depending on his
writing schedule, because he also wrote music for pleasure
sometimes, but for hire more often. William was blonde, tall and
lanky, had a funny sort of jovial swagger, and twinkling,
understanding eyes. You couldn't say he was gorgeous really, but
after looking at him and listening to him and letting him listen to
you, you could be convinced that maybe he was. He had an easy
manner, and an affable style, bringing with him into a room an
aura of happy calmness. Fiona knew his serenity was merely a
reflection of his self confidence, and a real satisfaction of who he
was—where he was. She found him brilliantly dazzling, and
couldn't believe her luck when he chose her for his future. Not

that she didn't think she was worthy, but they had dated for only five months before he had asked her, and she was very aware of the many pairs of female eyes that watched him, a few following him in fact, from act to act.

But William Silvin was smitten right away by the reserved beauty that was Fiona. She had wandered into Bishop's during a Tuesday night act, and she had been on her own. He saw her enter peripherally as he played, since it was not a busy night. He never actually saw her fully until the break after his first set, which was when he approached the bar. She was sitting at the far end, and was just looking around, a small smile on her face, an almost dreamy expression he thought at the time. She had very dark hair, and it was pulled back loosely into a casual chignon, a few wisps dangling on either side of her face. She wore smart glasses that accentuated her expressive eyes, and high cheekbones. She seemed perfectly comfortable being there, yet did not seem to be the sort to go out on her own on a regular basis, not that William was really sure what type that was. This was New York City, after all. She took a sip of her drink (he didn't know what it was and shortly after their eyes met he ordered the bartender to promptly get her another), and as she put the drink down their eyes met. He had felt his heart lurch, and he gave her an acknowledging nod and smiled, a move that must have appeared a little goofy he had thought, and cursed himself. She had smiled easily back at him, and the smile had lit up that exceptional face. She had held his eyes for a moment and then looked away. What devastation he had felt when she had looked away! He watched as the bartender delivered the drink to her while saying a few words and nodding in his direction. She thanked the bartender and then looked at him, raised the glass and smiled again. He had taken that as his cue and ambled over to her, a growing smile on his face that he could not get rid of. As he approached he grew a little dumb-struck, because she held his gaze, and she was even more glorious than he had thought.

"Hi" he said to her.

"Hello" she replied. Her voice was steady. And silky.

"I'm William Silvin." He held out his hand.

"Fiona Hastings" she said and extended her hand to shake his, but instead he brought her hand to his lips and kissed it, and she didn't seem to mind.

"Fiona. That's beautiful."

"Thank you."

"Are you planning on staying for the rest of my show?" He asked hopefully.

"I hadn't actually planned on it.....but you play so wonderfully that I'll certainly stay longer than I had intended." Fiona smiled at him warmly.

She had never talked to such a charm. True his eyes twinkled, but really it was as if every movement he made had a twinkle about it. She was fairly sure he was the sexiest thing she had ever seen, and she was nervous--of all things. Men did not usually make her nervous. For the most part they tended to bore her, probably the main reason she had not dated that much. William was talking about how he had gotten into piano playing, and she listened as best she could, hoping he didn't ask her any pertinent questions, because she was really mesmerized by his voice, his expressions, his abundant humor, his occasional chuckle (she adored chucklers—they seemed rather rare).

William, for his part, hoped he was making sense. He thought he was because Fiona didn't question anything he said, but he was close enough to her to smell her perfume, heady and delicious. He wanted to sink his mouth into her neck right there. She was dressed fairly business like, but her pale cream silk blouse was unbuttoned dangerously low, and he subtly (hopefully) found a way to look at her sweet cleavage, her breasts, he noticed, held by a pink lacy brassiere. He was starting to feel a little dizzy, so he paused and smiled at her. "Well, I suppose I don't want to bore you anymore" he said. "And I think I better get myself one more Chivas before I have to go back on stage."

"Let me get it for you, please? You weren't boring me at all." She said. The bartender handed them both a replenishment without charging them. She thanked him and turned to William, but found she didn't know what to say to him, so she only smiled.

William didn't notice. He was entranced. "What brings you to Bishop's tonight?" he asked. "I play here a fair amount, and I know I haven't ever seen you."

"I've never been here before. It was on my way home from a successful job interview, so I thought I'd pop in and congratulate myself with a drink." She said.

"Really?" He said in a rather daffy way, but he was delighted for her—truly—that's what she invoked in him. "How excellent for you. Cheers."

"Thanks." She was simply radiant after that reaction. They clinked glasses, took a good swig of their respective drinks, and continued to smile inanely at each other.

After a long pause that was not awkward, William said. "Well, I guess I'll get back up there. Will you be here at my next break?"

"Count on it" she said confidently, happily.

He was walking away from her, but he turned his head, his blonde mop half covering an eye, "You're beautiful, you know?" He smiled, and then turned back to his walk.

It went from there. She had stayed for that set, and the last, and he had walked her home, which had been a good twenty-five blocks. They had conversed openly, warmly, walking closely, but nothing more. When at last they had reached her apartment, he had again kissed her hand, his mouth lingering a bit longer this time. "I'd like to see you again, Fiona Hastings" he said, wishing he could grab her hard and kiss her for an hour or more.

"And I, you." She said, wishing he'd just kiss her. Her hand was still tingling from his kiss, and such tingling had spread to other parts of her body. She was sure she'd faint if this didn't end soon.

He handed her a business card. "I'm trusting you to call me." William said. "Tomorrow morning if you could…" And then he did kiss her. He couldn't have waited any longer anyway. He grabbed her as he had wanted to, and pulled her painfully close to him. He put his hands behind her neck and pulled her face towards him as he bent his own head down to meet her. She made a small cry of surprise, but was other wise pleasantly silenced by his mouth. He was aggressively kissing her, his tongue claiming her mouth as his. Fiona did not resist, but let him do what he was doing, her knees growing weak in the process. She responded in kind, driven wild by the feel of his desire beating against her stomach. It was a full minute of desperate kissing, before William forced himself to abandon the endeavor. He had been about to rip her clothes off, and they were in the middle of the sidewalk, already showing off a bit more than he was used to. He gently slowed his kiss, and pulled her head away from him, looking down at her with a strained smile. He was breathing hard, and he would kill to take her in the closest alley.

"I.." was all he managed to say.

Fiona was dazed, and her eyes were even a little glassy, but his severing of the kiss had assisted her in getting some logic back. "I'll call you in the morning." She smiled at him. "Good-night William. Thanks for all the music." She went up her building stairs, opened the door, and turned around to wave to him, for he was watching. William Silvin waited for her to get in her elevator, and he stood there a little longer, reveling in the previous hours, the many exciting moments, the perfection of her features—of her soul, he knew, and of course the perilous kissing. After about 10 minutes of standing there (all of which were happily witnessed by Fiona from her apartment), he slowly made his way home, his head in the best kind of fog. William Silvin was in love.

***

Fiona had delivered on the promise of calling him the following morning, and for the next five months they saw each other virtually every day. She went to almost all his acts, and during their off time, they'd do everything else together. William had had a few girlfriends right up to the evening on which he had met Fiona, but met with each of them over the immediate following days and broke it off. He did not like to make girls weep, but he would not be unfaithful to the likes of Fiona. He just didn't need anyone else, a fact that might have normally amazed him, but served only to amaze his friends. For her part, Fiona had no one to break it off with, but she was intensely happy, and all aspects of her life reflected that. She was an immediate success at her new position as a Secretary for one of the top financial advisors of Ocean Investments, Garrett Darrs, the position she had obtained the day she met William. Things were going swimmingly.

Their sex life was stupendous. From moment one there was no hesitation or inhibition. Fiona had early on abandoned the notion of abstaining past their third encounter (third day after meeting, that is). She didn't know how she stopped herself at their second meeting when he picked her up at her apartment for breakfast, but she did. After spending that entire day together, they did not go out until after lunch on their third date. They had met at the park to go for a walk, and it did begin that way, but perhaps innocent intentions quickly unraveled. It was fall but still warm, cloudy and misty. They were walking in a quiet area of the park, and there were not too many people about. Fiona had stupidly worn higher heels than she would have liked, and tripped slightly on the pavement. They had been holding hands, so William easily stopped Fiona from falling, with his strength righting her position, and pulling her in. He overcompensated a bit—easy to do, she was so light, and she fell a little into him.

"Oops." Fiona said. "Sorry. Stupid shoes. Well, stupid me" she added as she attempted to part herself from him and continue the walk.

But William's heart had started to beat erratically, and he felt suddenly possessive of his clumsy Fiona, and decided not to let her go. Fiona felt his resistance, and looked up at him. Neither of them said anything for what seemed a few seconds, and then very tenderly William took Fiona's face in his hands, and bent down to kiss her. It began slowly and ever so lovingly, Fiona's arms going around his neck, through his hair, Williams' arms wrapping around her waist, but William's patience faded, and he found his hands digging into her back a little, sliding down to her buttocks, and pulling her in even closer. Fiona had moaned slightly, and felt authentic weakness, but his arms would not let her teeter. He stopped then almost abruptly, and looked around.

"Come here" he said, leading her into a more secluded glen. Fiona followed, barely able to keep up with his pace. He

63

apparently found what he was looking for, because he stopped and then gently steered her to a large Oak. "How're you doing?" He asked her as he pushed her against the tree.

Fiona was weak and a little perplexed by the question, but said only "Fine". She was looking at him and breathing hard. William nodded ever so briefly and ever so slightly, almost as though he was getting rid of a question he hadn't had time to ask in the first place. Then he kissed her ferociously, almost too quickly, then deserting her mouth in favor of her neck, and all she could do was whimper. Expertly he whipped off her jacket and then unbuttoned her blouse, his hands going beneath her bra and squeezing her breasts hard. Fiona cried out, but was not objecting, her hands in his hair, on his back. She desperately wanted to feel the skin beneath his clothes, but he was too distracted. Fiona vaguely wondered about on-lookers, though the spot seemed safe, but she knew they were not silent, so promised herself not to make anymore noise.

William could no longer tease himself, and abandoned her breasts, choosing then to lift her skirt up, and very quickly slide her panties down her long legs, which he proudly noted were trembling. Fiona raised one of her legs so he could take off her under-things, and held tightly to him as he raised her up against the tree. He kissed her hard again, while he unzipped his own pants, and then slid himself into her. She nearly screamed with satisfaction and pain when he entered her, for it had seemed like she had waited a long time. William groaned as well, holding Fiona up gently, penetrating her slowly, but hard and deeply, her back scraping against the tree. Fiona seemed not to notice the pain, and reveled in the depth he found, the smooth cadence of his penetration.

Not many minutes later William cried out forcefully, as if he were claiming Fiona, as if he now had that right. They were breathing heavily. William seemed to come out of a fog, and suddenly noticed where he really was. He looked into Fiona's eyes and smiled, and then gently, so gently, William let Fiona down, and made her lie down on the cool, wet grass while he pulled his own pants up. He lay down next to her and spread her legs.

"What are you…." Fiona started to say.

"Sshh…" He said, and he put a finger to her mouth. His other hand found its way between her legs and went to work. He watched her face as he excited her, but she was almost oblivious. Expertly, rhythmically he brought her to her climax, so that she was actually shaking, and she had to bite her own arm to stifle her cries. He kissed her quietly and dressed her as she recovered. For long minutes they lay next to each other on the grass, William on his side looking into Fiona's eyes.

"Let me take you back to my place now" William said. "Let's do this again, but slower, my Fiona".

And so it went.

***

William asked her to marry him at Bishop's after the place had closed. It had been a particularly busy night, and they were relaxing after the show together, sitting side by side on the piano bench, each drinking a glass of champagne. He was wearing a tousled black suit, tousled even before the night had begun, but still looked dashing, especially against his tousled blonde hair Fiona thought. Fiona was dressed in a revealing, sparkling black dress, long, with a very high slit up the left side. William was looking at her exposed leg, while they were exchanging light banter about the night's guests and performance, and was suddenly shy about asking her the most important question he'd ever ask anyone. Sure, she seemed happy enough, but look at her he thought as she continued to talk, her hair lazily caressing the side of her face, her head tilted slightly to the side. He had purchased a ring for her about a month prior, but over that time couldn't find the best moment to ask her the huge question, and he also thought (incorrectly he later found out) that she'd think he was rushing it. But that night he could wait no longer, and the dwindling of the crowd had given him the moment.

"Fiona" he had said.

"Mmm?" She said lazily, and looked up at him, slightly tipsy from a few drinks, but also from an evening of a great

65

performance by her handsome entertainer, an excellent audience, and a general buzz in the air that night.

"I'd like to ask you something."

"Go right ahead. I'm listening." She was still looking at him, and smiling a bit, but she was also humming a little, not adequately focused on him, he thought. William then got off the piano bench, went around to her side, and got down on one knee.

Well, that did the trick. Fiona turned around, and an immediate alertness came into her eyes. She looked down at him. "William?" She queried.

"Yes, Fiona" He said smiling. "Listen to me for a few moments, OK? Then you can ask me whatever you want." Fiona was looking at William, fascinated, though more seriously than she had been. Logic had set in and she knew very well what was happening, but she couldn't quite believe her early fortune. William took Fiona's hand in his own. "You are without a doubt the most beautiful woman I have ever encountered. You dazzle me." William's eyes were intense and sincere as he began. "Over the past months, I have with each day been struck by just how much you have added to my life, and just how happy it makes me to try and do the same for you. I can no longer imagine a life without you, and I would be honored, simply elated, and forever indebted to you if you promised to be my wife." Fiona was still gazing at William, but there were tears coming down her face, and she was smiling. "Fiona, my beautiful and wonderful muse, will you marry me?" In his hand he held a box with a brilliantly sparkling diamond ring, which he now proffered her.

"Oh, William." She said quietly, her voice shaking, "Yes, of course, yes." And her tears fell more freely as she got off the bench to kneel down with him. William had taken the ring out and slid it gently, sensually onto her finger. As they embraced they heard a "Bravo" somewhere, and a "Congratulations" elsewhere, along with scattered but enthusiastic clapping. The near silence of their exchange had drawn the attention of those cleaning up, and a few late staying customers. The two acknowledged the crowd briefly by turning to them and smiling, but then they rose, a little shakily, and embraced each other more closely, ignoring anyone else, and they were respectfully left alone.

That night they didn't stay long, and they shared just a sip more of champagne upon returning to his apartment, because they had better things to do.

* * *

They married very soon after that evening. It was a small wedding, family from both sides, a few friends, and Fiona had invited Garrett as well. She respected him, and had a feeling he'd be hurt if he wasn't invited even though she'd been with him only a short time. The ceremony had been carried out in a small Catholic church in upstate New York with the reception in a large room of an up-scale restaurant not far from the church. It had been a beautiful fall day, the proceedings romantic, the partying intimate and fun, and it had crossed the minds of many that day that the proceedings in general boded well for the couple.

Chapter 7

Dear Garrett,

Thanks for coming by yesterday and making the purchase you did. It was lovely to meet you, and I hope the future holds for us many mutual benefits. As I said, I'd love to get a personal tour of your gallery upon a day that affords you time. You have my number.

Yours,
Sophia

Garrett read the note and smiled. He had read it originally when he had first found it, but then forgot about it. Now he read it, and it gave him a fresh perspective. What a flirt was this Sophia, he thought, a friendly, beautiful......devious flirt. He'd give her a tour alright. And then he would take her to dinner, and whatever else she wanted him to do. The hell with Carmen. If Carmen was so uptight, and so hesitant even to do business with him, or at least so coy as to try and impress that upon him, then he'd woo her sister. Besides, he didn't want to involve himself with Finn's left-overs—better to entertain the company of her un-Finned sister. Sophia was an enticing woman, and who knows, maybe she was just what he needed—a fun beauty to wile away the time that needed wiling away. His gut told him she was greedy for pleasure in all senses, and that maybe even he would find her too energy-depleting, but at least he'd have some fun out of it. At least he'd have reigns on a Carmine, even if it wasn't the Carmine he knew he was truly after.

"Got your note." Garrett had said to Sophia without first saying hello.

She smiled. "I meant you to", not hiding her pleasure. "You liked your shipment, I hope".

"You don't disappoint". He chided himself at the unintended double entendre. "Nor do I wish to—at least when it comes to an invitation." He paused, and Sophia waited. "Would you like to go out to dinner? Forget the gallery—it's not filled with the good stuff yet anyway". This was plainly amateurish, but he knew she wouldn't be picky about it.

She had agreed and named a time, and they said their good-byes, both of them hanging up, Sophia smiling knowingly, and Garrett twisting his mouth, vaguely glad but also as if he wasn't sure exactly what he'd done.

In the mean time he'd have to deal with Carmen, which he meant both literally and figuratively. Today was the day of their lunch appointment, and it was fast approaching show time, so he had to get his act in order. He dressed quickly, but confidently. He felt like a little boy, and whistled a little. The match was almost too easy, almost mundane, humdrum, but of course Garrett Darrs did not really expect to be bored. He had now met both Carmine sisters and though logic told him his tasks ahead seemed cake-easy, the personalities of his women (his?) would probably hamper the course of things. Still, he carried about preparing himself and comporting himself in the manner of one slightly deluded, happily deranged. At least today would be entertaining. Furthermore, he would be able to gaze at Carmen for a few hours without it being questioned.

He met Nick at the street right at the appointed time. What was going on? Garret wondered. "Hey, Nick. Good to see you?" He got in and closed the door.

"Mr. Darrs." Nick nodded and smiled.

"You know where we're going?"

"Yes, sir. If memory serves, same old, same old." Nick said casually.

"Yes." Garrett paused for a moment and then asked "Nick, by the way, who did you send to pick up Miss Carmine?"

"Unfortunately, the only one available for the job was Jean". Nick shrugged his eyebrows.

"Oh." And then, "Excellent". Garrett was happy to realize Carmen, if things went as they normally did when Jean was driving, would be slightly frazzled upon arrival. Jean was notorious, among Garrett's skeleton driver's crew, for his talking. The man would not shut up, even though he didn't have much to say. Usually it was easy to tune this out merely by raising the partition glass, but Jean always began the trip with it down, as did most drivers, and if you didn't know Jean, or were even slightly shy, you'd be intimidated to raise it. Which meant you'd have to listen, and maybe even answer sometimes. To make matters worse, his talking tended to distract him so that his driving was adversely affected. Bottom line, it was not a relaxing ride.

It was a beautiful October day, leaves cascading gently from the occasional tree, the sun bouncing off the many windowed streets. Though it was not quite warm, the crueler cold of late fall had not yet set in. It was the kind of weather that brought to mind long, breezy walks, sharing a warm drink in a cozy bar overlooking the streets, or sharing the morning in bed with a favorite woman, sometimes talking, sometimes reading, and sometimes just enjoying each others' bodies. Garrett's expression faltered as he continued this mode of thinking. Sure, there was a respectable list of women with whom he could spend the day in bed, some of whom he could likely even have a tolerable conversation with, but when was the last time he had shared that cozy drink? Had taken a pleasurable walk with a female? Again he was struck with the idea that perhaps he was getting lonely, that perhaps his solitude was getting dull, that maybe, just maybe, he was not as interesting as he thought he was, and so therefore time spent with himself was not as entertaining as it had been. It was during this contemplative mood that they pulled up to the restaurant, and Garrett quietly thanked Nick and got out. Luigi met him at the door, and seated him personally.

"Mr. Darrs, good to see you again. As you see, your guest has not yet arrived." He said. "As usual, you have the advantage".

"Thank you, Luigi. Good to be here, my friend. In fact, you know my guest today." Luigi raised his eyebrows inquisitively.

70

"Carmen Carmine is coming here to discuss displaying her work at my gallery."

Luigi's eyes lit up and he grinned happily. "Wonderful, wonderful, Mr. Darrs. I knew it was only a matter of a short time. She is a lucky artist indeed to be able to show her work at your fine gallery."

Garrett smiled with gratitude. "Thank you, Luigi. Kind words, and let's hope you're right. Though I'm fairly sure she's up for it, she's playing me a little. Put a little magic in her meal".

"Oh, Mr. Darrs, you are a funny man. The meal will be exquisite, I promise, but she won't need any magic from me. Who would dare refuse such an offer? Ms. Carmine does not seem foolish to me".

"Thanks. Well, anyway, could you have Daphne bring me a Dewars on the rocks?"

Luigi nodded kindly, and walked away. Garrett noted the place was buzzing with people, and felt the usual good vibe from the place. He looked over at Carmen's painting, the one he had fallen in love with, and something stirred inside him again. Even at this distance he was affected, and deeply so. There was so much passion and kindness in the eyes of those girls—so much sincerity. The depth of the goodness the sisters conveyed was beautiful, certainly, but Garrett realized it was also disturbing if only because it was humbling. He felt somehow inferior to those girls even while he felt a gratefulness to them. He considered getting up and having another look, but then thought better of it. He was not feeling himself, and the painting was not helping him at all. Besides which, it would not do him much good if Carmen caught him gazing adoringly at her painting, not to mention he wanted to watch her walk in. It was one of his favorite things, really—watching his guests walk in. So much was revealed, regardless if it was a man or woman, though of course it was a lot more fun to watch a woman walk in. More unpredictable.

He slowly began to cheer himself up by imagining Carmen's entrance, and she would be predictable—dressed smartly casual, not too sexy, walking with her easy, graceful sway, her expression pleasant, but guarded. She would not look comfortable. No, maybe she'd even be tentative, and slightly irked after her ride with Jean.

Luigi brought the drink over himself. "Here you are, Mr. Darrs. Ms. Carmine has just now arrived, and Daphne is about to bring her in".

"Thank you, Luigi." He nodded, and Luigi made his exit, all too aware of Garrett's habits.

A tickle of apprehension hit him just then, and annoyed him. He willed it into submission and sipped his drink. And then he leaned back, and crossed his ankles casually, intentionally. He turned his head in the direction from which he knew she'd be arriving. Daphne came around the corner, and sensing Garrett's desire to watch his guest, stepped to the right and gestured to Carmen so she knew where to go.

When the lovely Daphne stepped aside, Garrett had his drink in his hand and his eyes on the runway. Carmen Carmine walked towards him, a shy (amused?) smile spreading across her face as she approached, and predictable she was not. She wore a soft grey turtleneck sweater over a long, almost to the ankles, wool black skirt, but any semblance of demureness ended there because the skirt had a slit that ran all the way up her left leg, ending not so promptly at her upper left thigh. As she walked, which Garrett now perceived as slow motion, he saw that she wore tall black boots with three inch heels. He had absorbed this much of her quickly so as to meet her glance, but knew he was at least partially unsuccessful. Her dark hair, black in this light, hung loosely about her face, moving provocatively with each of her steps. He looked her directly in the eyes.

Carmen saw Garrett as soon as the hostess stepped aside. She immediately noticed the way he was sitting—handsomely, but decidedly posed. She felt sure his posturing was well practiced, which amused her, and boosted her confidence, something she desperately needed after that horrendous ride; another experience she thought might have been contrived by Garrett. To what end she was not sure, but she had done everything to smooth her features, comb her hair relentlessly in the car upon their arrival, and she now knew that she had done the job well because he wouldn't stop staring. Whereas she understood his staring must be part of his domineering business routine, she also knew he couldn't have looked away. The black skirt and grey shirt combo had never steered her awry, and boots seemed to get to any man. She felt the desire to swagger. He took longer than was wise to look her over, but when he finally met her eyes and held them, she longed for a railing. Just a few more steps.

Garrett stood. He offered his hand for Carmen to shake and said "Hello, Carmen. You're looking well."

Carmen took his offered hand, and they shook firmly, but quickly. "Hello, Garrett. Thank you." She sat down as he waited, and did not return his tepid compliment. Looking well, my ass.

Garrett sat down calmly, resolutely. He was uncertain of his words, didn't know if he should be more flattering, at this point addled about what should be done for the sake of the "deal", managing their relationship, and his honesty. Complexities invariably ruined his appetite so he would not let them in. After Carmen seemed to make herself comfortable, Garrett said "It's good to see you. I hope you traveled well". An atonement of sorts, even though he knew quite positively she had not traveled well at all. "It's a gorgeous day for it, particularly from your neck of the woods."

Carmen was leery, not wanting to seem suspicious of him in case she was being paranoid. She made every effort not to let her skeptical eyes show when he mentioned her trip to the city. She only smiled slightly and agreed with him. "Thanks. You're right. It's beautiful out there, and the driver was….informative."

Garrett smiled, starting to feel ashamed of his earlier glee upon hearing from Nick that it was Jean who had fetched her. Carmen returned the smile, and Garrett thought he saw a barely perceptible hint of challenge in her eyes. Obviously, she was in top form now, knowing damn well her allure. He didn't yet want to discuss business because he wanted to focus more on improving their friendship which had been a touch marred by his performance not more than a week ago. He felt it had been months since he had seen her last. He hadn't remembered her being this beautiful. Why had he been so brusque again? He decided he liked her scar a lot, could probably get attached to it if

73

he saw her face enough. She was talking about her year in France, spent painting the countryside and city scapes, as well as learning about food, and invariably wine. How had that gotten started? He had not been paying attention to anything other than the way her lips moved—so softly. She had a generous mouth, and he was certain a generous nature with that mouth. He consciously broke the spell she was trying to cast and took a large sip of his scotch, enjoying the way it lit up his throat, reminded him of what he was doing here.

Carmen had paused and was looking at him. "Well" he said. "It seems as though it was extremely good for you, artistically and spiritually". A fairly good commentary he decided. "I enjoyed my trips to France, though I'm sure I didn't glean as much from them as you did, since my visits were never longer than a few weeks. Italy is where I seem to spend most of my time when I go abroad."

"Yes" she said. "Italy is lovely. Though I've visited our home town a few times, I should have spent more time there, and I mean to in the future."

Daphne came over and delivered the wine that Carmen had ordered, and Garrett ordered lunch for the two of them. Daphne retrieved the menus that had never been opened. Carmen was tempted to question Garrett, because how would he know she liked beef? That maybe she was a vegetarian? But then she opted to accept it because she thought perhaps that's just what he was waiting for—her to tangle with him. She only said "I hope you know what you're doing, Garrett."

"As do I" he replied, enjoying the double entendre.

"This is your eatery of choice." She stated.

"I guess it's fairly obvious? I can't seem to stay away, and Luigi not only treats his guests superbly, but his chef is uncanny. I eat here at least twice a week."

They then turned to the topic of favorite restaurants and foods, and they both seemed to enjoy the conversation, because it was something they were both passionate about. They were both adventurous, and each listened to the other, seeming to forget the discomfort they had felt at the beginning of their meeting. Carmen felt at ease, and Garrett saw her beauty enhance as she became more comfortable with herself, her surroundings, and him. She radiated a warmth he found enchanting, and he thought she might have been a nice pick for taking that autumn walk.

For her part, Carmen watched Garrett as they conversed, and welcomed the fact she could talk to him so freely. How differently today was going! The man in front of her was kind, humorous, attentive. She saw no signs of the Garrett from their last meeting. She understood intellectually that he would have to be nicer to her regardless of what he truly felt if he wanted their partnership to work, but still, it seemed as if his interest in her was genuine. He looked into her eyes and she saw reaction to her words not just in his expressions, but in those amazing eyes, and quite often he was smiling—warmly. So, yes, she did get comfortable, and she did not think she was in danger of losing any ground. Maybe they really could forget about their odd shared moment not long ago, and forge a sincere friendship in addition to their partnership.

Their meals came, and Carmen stopped thinking about it. She would leave reflection for later in the day, when she was kicking back at home. As for now, she relaxed and ate one of the best sautéed steaks she had ever had, savoring each taste as it hit her palate, and washing it down with an exquisite Bordeaux Garrett had ordered.

There came a pause between the main course and their next indulgence, so Garrett chose the moment. They were both, after all, relaxed. "So, Carmen." And he smiled at her, letting just those words sink in so that she understood he was going to switch to business. She smiled in return, acknowledging and accepting. "As you know, I'd like to have your paintings grace my walls, and all I'm waiting for you is to agree right now, and then obviously in writing. Before I continue with all my ideas, why don't you tell me if you're interested, and if so, what sort of terms you were hoping for."

Carmen was pleased to see he wanted her input, and was not ordering her about, though she understood the logic. Regardless of any fronts he put forth, or any subtle warnings she had gotten from Garrett's associate, she was mostly in the driver's seat.

"Well, Garrett, I won't lie to you" she said. "Your gallery is about as prestigious as they come, so not displaying my work there might be silly, despite any other offers that might have come along during the last week." She tried to see if there was any amused doubt in his eyes, but saw nothing except the eyes of an interested business partner. "I think we could work together, and since you are so very knowledgeable in the field, and I am a relative novice—as you are aware—you could also help me to understand the world into which I am formally entering. I guess I would refer to it as the commercial end--and I hate to use that term but have to be realistic—and you could assist me in the transfer, if you will." She realized then that she had inadvertently (maybe) invited him to be by her side rather regularly, and that she would likely be closer than a phone call from his gallery if she were to actually learn anything.

"Of course. I'd be delighted". Garrett at the same time conjured up the possibilities. Proximity to her perfume, her walk. Control over her environment. The meeting was going better than planned.

An uncomfortable yet not altogether unpleasant feeling was welling up inside Carmen. She was putting herself in a precarious position, and one in which Garrett Darrs would have almost complete control. While daunting, the prospect was exciting. She was entirely unsure of what their future held, but she knew that the meal they shared today was an important one, that it signified a strange beginning of things. She was pretty sure she wasn't ready for most of it, but she had to put the success of her art first. If all else failed, she had that, and that was something indeed.

Garrett and Carmen spent the next half hour discussing the nitty gritty over port. Coffee had been offered, but coffee had quickly been declined. They came amicably to an agreed profitability margin for them both, and then Garrett pulled, seemingly out of nowhere, two copies of their discussed agreement, with only the final numbers and signatures to be filled in. Carmen watched as Garrett filled in everything except her signature. She felt a little shaken, a little betrayed, though she couldn't really justify it. He was an experienced businessman, and must always be prepared.

Before she could say anything, as he sensed Carmen's surprise, he said "Forgive the ready paperwork, Carmen. I have to go to every meeting with the expectation that things will go my way, because if they do, I cannot leave my prospective partner with the time to regret—to change his or her mind. You understand?" His look was apologetic.

And she was convinced, even if a little sobered and de-romanced. "Yes, of course. Give it over, then." And with only a slight hesitation, she signed both papers. His reputation was such that she didn't think she needed to read the fine print. She gave them back to him, and he put them absently in his inside jacket pocket.

He was looking at her, not smiling, but serious. "Let's shake on it."

Carmen was a little taken back by the tone, but almost too quickly proffered her hand. They had to reach across the table, so the leverage was not ideal, but he grasped her hand firmly, strongly. She knew she was not allowed to look away from his eyes, so she stared back at him, even if nerves had her smiling a little. Garrett was still serious, and would not let her gaze go. So this was how he pronounced his power, she thought, and she was trembling inside. He was suddenly so tall, so virile, so handsome, and the handshake seemed to last forever. Weakness would overtake her soon, she was sure, and she'd have to pull her hand away. But it never came to that. Her hand was freed, and she was sure that simultaneously her body was ensnared.

As bravely as she could, she said "Let's drink on it then". Even to her, her voice sounded feeble.Garrett nodded and lifted his glass to greet hers. Again their eyes met. He waited, but was now smiling. Triumphantly she thought. "To our mutual success" she managed. And to attempt some sort of separation, "To our partnership". She hoped she had underscored "partnership". She thought she did, but was no longer thinking clearly. It could be the alcohol, or it could be Garrett, or both those toxins combined.

"Here, here" Garrett replied, and they clinked.

They shared a few quiet moments before the bill came, and Carmen found herself wondering why Garrett had not mentioned her painting, had not even glanced over at it that she had noticed.

77

Undoubtedly some sort of power play, but a silly one. She knew that he loved that one, so it would hardly be odd for him to comment on. Just something else to mull over later.

While Garrett attended to the bill, he brought up her debut party. "As I'm sure you know, Carmen, we'll present you to my gallery's clients, and a larger part of the art world, by throwing a debut party at Gallery Darrs, as is customary. It's my expectation that we should do so as early as a few weeks from today, since I need to start filling up my space. Is that time enough for you?"

Carmen's expression did not change. "I'll have to do some quick work on some of my paintings, but truthfully I have done quite a lot over the past week." She paused, and maybe the wine made her add "Brooding makes me paint more—and better."

Garrett looked into her eyes, and though she knew that he knew exactly what she was saying, he merely nodded and said "I can agree with that, at least as far as my own work is concerned."

His statement was as elusive as she expected, so, fed up, she changed the subject. "Please let me know all things necessary to be prepared to the utmost, and please let me know all such relevant facts almost before you know them. I do not want to disappoint anyone."

"Of course. My success relies on just that sort of communication. You will usually be hearing from Fiona, but I will be involved when it comes to the more delicate piece of the business." He looked almost bored at this point, she thought. She was also starting to dislike Fiona.

"OK then, Garrett. I suppose I should get back to my studio. I've got work to do, as you can guess. Would you mind calling Jean for me?" The prospect of riding home with Jean was making her weary already, but she had no other practical means by which to travel.

Garrett didn't answer right away, and a small smile crossed his lips. "I hope you don't mind, but I'm going to have my driver, Nick, take you back. I've got some things to do in the area, so I won't need him anyway. He'll take care of you." He had no things to attend to, but could not bring himself to set her out with Jean again.

Carmen was certain anyone would be better than Jean. "Thanks Garrett, if you're sure about it."

They walked together towards the door, and both of them simultaneously turned to glance at the painting in the far corner, though for different reasons. And they each quickly turned their attention back to the walk in front of them when they realized what had happened. The remaining distance to the door seemed interminable, but Garrett did not let the moment go unacknowledged. "It really is beautiful" was all he said.

She was more grateful for this simple statement than for anything he had said to her or would be doing for her, not that she said so. Once they were out in the street she did stop, turn to him, and quite sincerely say "thank you". Garrett tipped his head gallantly and was then shooing her off with Nick.

Chapter 8

Mack Fordham stomped through the stable somewhat distressed, though for anyone watching, his demeanor would seem nothing other than one of calm resolution, if maybe a little too intense. He was tired of people coming in, using the horses, telling him and the horses how much they cared about them, etcetera, and then not actually tending to the basics. Obviously the stable had hands for doing the cleaning and grooming, but to rely on the owners and lesson takers to put the gear where it belonged and to do so neatly was not a lot to ask. Problem is, these people had money, and, Mack knew, people with money bent toward the spoiled side, and didn't always think of the obvious. They just weren't synced properly. They did not seem to understand the very simple relationship in place—the relationship that people had with the horses, the stable, the hands. This was a community, not a playground for one owner, or one well dressed child hoping to win the equestrian of the year award. And so it goes. Mack was not by nature a complainer, but witnessing regular arrogance on the part of the monied patrons of Twilight Stables had certainly added a bit of a cynical nature to him.

Mack Fordham was rough around the edges, and more often than not people would shy away from him if they had not met him, and even then it could be intimidating to approach him. This was not his intent, just who he was and how he comported himself. He stood about six feet, and his structure reflected all the physical work he had done during the course of his 37 years. Though Mack had gone to school through college, he had not pursued any career that took advantage of his degree in engineering. Since he had grown up on a farm in Ohio he had always been around animals, and found them good companions— certainly dependable, if perhaps moody sometimes. But he had learned how to handle them ages ago, and he liked the tranquility that farm life offered. He loved the pungent, fresh scents that greeted him every morning when he woke in the country—the cut wheat, stinky but lovable pigs, weathered barn wood, the occasional waft of wild flowers. He would never be able to handle forgoing that kind of environment by getting up, wearing something uncomfortable, getting in some metal contraption, be it car, train, bus or whatever, and then looking at walls and a computer all day. Not to mention the far more daunting task of talking to all sorts of people all day that actually preferred the steel contraptions to the joy of country life. No thank you. He wouldn't have any of it, so for the moment he managed Twilight Stables for the Carmine family, and that was just fine. He had started the job just a few months ago, having moved from upstate New York because he wanted to be closer to the ocean. He wanted to be able to see that part of nature occasionally as well. He was certain he now had the best of everything. He knew it was a modest life, but this didn't trouble him. He lived comfortably in a one bedroom cottage on the estate, managed ten men, and was trusted to do what needed to be done. He had very quickly demonstrated his appreciation for stable life and work, and his lack of tolerance for anything less than a job done perfectly.

On his time off Mack would often go riding, usually on his own, but sometimes with one of the hands. And he had started to visit the coast as he had promised himself. He'd pack a bare-bones lunch and a book and find a decent place to park himself. He had not actually started reading at the beach yet since he'd only just moved close by. Sometimes he would walk, hands deep in his pockets, and watch the surf as it rolled in, how it rolled in, how immense yet comforting it sounded. The ocean was something. Having lived in the heartland most of his life, he had never had the opportunity to visit the shore more than for a few brief visits, and those visits had been during his youth when he really couldn't have given a rat's ass about the sea. It was different now. The ocean instilled in him a solemn sort of peace, and he reveled in it.

What a picture Mack Fordham made, walking down the beach. Not as fearsome, maybe, as the man who made Twilight Stables run so smoothly, but just as unapproachable. His shortly cropped dark blonde hair was not military, but it wasn't soft, and his angular face added to the sense of sternness one got. He boasted a 3 inch scar on his upper right cheek from a nasty farming accident when he was 15. The only thing that softened his face just a little were his hazel green eyes. Though often frosty, usually concentrated, and mostly unreadable, there was somewhere a warmth. Mack just made that warmth difficult to see, and it's not that he'd had an overly tough existence, for that couldn't be further from the truth, but he had just gotten jaded by meeting too many people he thought did not appreciate what they had, what was around them, what real beauty was. He was just too used to seeing lack-luster.

This sort of stoniness that Mack exuded left him mostly to himself when it came to men he didn't know, but quite the opposite was true of women, at least at first. The force of his presence, and his apparent aloofness was a tough combination to ignore. He was immediately thought of as a challenge, someone worth getting to know. But here there was a sad sort of irony. Mack did not dislike women, but he was not entirely trusting of them, and for that reason did not begin, maintain or end conversations very well. He was in fact just as difficult to get to know as his appearance led one to believe. The women he might have liked to get to know better invariably gave up. It was the ones he had no patience for that stuck around because they had nothing but patience, lacking as they did something inside the skull.

He had had some casual affairs, but not many. He found it difficult to go too long without sex, and alleviated such requirements on occasion, but the resulting consequences generally left him dismayed, so these kinds of encounters slowly abated. He sometimes hated to admit it, perhaps because of the intellect he possessed which argued his logic, but he found women mostly intolerable. Flouncy. Frivolous. Often ridiculous. So it was with these thoughts he began to avoid further trysts in his cottage, passionate rendezvous' in his car, in the field, barn or anywhere. He tended these days not to go out very often, and if in a public place made sure to avert his admiring gaze on a woman before it was even noticed. It cannot be said that Mack was lonely, because by nature he was a man of solitude, a man at peace with simplicity, and in fact the beauty of simplicity. And it should not be said that he missed the better looking gender by any great degree, or that he may have actually resented them a bit because of his own self inflicted celibacy. It cannot and shouldn't be said, but it might be why he genuinely flinched when Sophia walked into his barn.

Chapter 9

Sophia Carmine, a few days after having sent her shipment to Garrett, had received a call from him asking her to dinner. When she heard his voice, she immediately felt a slight quiver in her stomach, recalling as she did the man behind that voice. Being sure enough of herself as a world class flirt, she did not betray her eagerness one iota while they spoke. Although she wasn't a big fan of accepting a date the same date of a call for it, she managed to do so without tripping over herself, and thought she pulled off a bit of casual "oh, what the hell" upon acceptance.

When she hung up, she began to think about it. She also began to wonder, not quite idly, if she should contact her sister. Would Carmen find this odd, or maybe even inappropriate? Carmen had a different set of rules than she did, Sophia knew, but Carmen was also not without romance. Just because Carmen had business dealings with Garret, did not mean she couldn't go out with him, right? At least there could be no objection to one harmless date. She had made the right decision, but also decided that she ought to tell Carmen about it, just so as not to let her get caught unawares.

Carmen answered on the second ring. "Hello?" she said.

"Hey Carmen, me. How's it going?"

"OK, I guess, how about you?" She sounded a little faded, Sophia thought.

"Good." She paused and searched for a word. "Interesting."

"Really?" Sisterly curiosity had edged into her voice.

"At least I think so." Another pause. "I thought I'd run it by you, not really sure why, but anyway, Garrett Darrs asked me out to dinner tonight." She realized she had spoken a little nervously, even though she was not at all. She calmed herself and continued. "I didn't think it would be any big deal to you, but also didn't

want it to interfere with any business you might have going on.
Would it?"

There was just a moment of hesitation, and then "No, no."
Was her voice a little stiff? "I agree. I don't see why it would."
Then she quickly added "I don't even think you had to check with
me, but thanks for the consideration." A little formal, Sophia
thought, but she was in no mood to go back and forth. She had
gotten the seal of approval she sought. She was about to end the
call when suddenly Carmen added "So where are you going
anyway?"

The nature of a seemingly innocent question such as this was
enough to set Sophia on a bit of a tangent, and off she went about
the possibilities, and soon enough about what to wear. They
shared some feminine banter going over the details, and
exchanged some genuine laughter.

Sophia felt quite good when she got off the phone. She was
not, after all, privy to the expression on her sister's face.

***

Carmen hung up the phone after talking to Sophia, and sat
down in her favorite settee. She marveled a bit at the news and
the timing of it, mostly certain that it was a good thing her sister
had told her after her lunch date with Garrett earlier that day. Had
she known prior to that, the event could have gone differently,
even though she would have tried not to let it. What she now
wondered, and could not call her sister back for, was when exactly
he had asked her. Had he phoned her in the morning, before their
pleasant business meal? Or had he rung her up afterwards? It
was a monumental difference, of course. Making such a date
before she and Garrett had met up for lunch was passably OK,
though still suspect. Making the date afterwards was cryptically
bad. A celebratory date? A "see Carmen, how easily I can play
the both of you" date? Or, worst of all, a date made simply
because he wanted one, but with Sophia, not her.

Her house seemed suddenly dismal, and her stomach was
unsettled. She was supposed to do what, now? Sit around, watch
TV, read a book, while her sister and Garrett were out on what

would obviously be a wonderful, heady night. Was she really even expected to paint, of all things? She thought of how they would look together, to each other. She knew it was only a first date, but she also knew the power of attraction her sister had over men. She was a stunning woman, no doubt about that. And how she could dress and adorn herself. She oozed enough sex appeal that her clothes did not have to. Not understated, but only barely suggestive. She dressed, in fact, more conservatively than Carmen. Where Sophia's boldness required less outer flair, Carmen's stiller waters demanded she dress herself more brazenly, and so she did.

She imagined Garrett arriving at Sophia's (just down the street!) in his polished limousine, stepping out gracefully, no effort required. She saw him walk to her doorstep and ring the bell, a bouquet of exotics in his hand, hair just a little tousled. Is that sort of man ever resisted?

She rose in a trance from her seat, a somber little look haunting her face, and went to pour herself a glass of wine. It was still early afternoon, but her work for the day was done. There would be no more productivity, no more progress, so she decided to begin her lethargy with a glass of red. She took a sip and vaguely appreciated the depth of its flavor as she walked back to her settee.

She resumed her ill at ease ponderings and tried to picture Sophia. What had she said she was going to wear? The cobalt blue silk thing, was it? Yes, that was it, and what a color against her sister's red hair. Sophia would open the door and instantly disarm Garrett with her stupendous smile, and her flashing eyes. Carmen had never been outright jealous of her sister, but just then a pang of it jolted her out of her reverie.

"I'm torturing myself with something that hasn't even happened." She said out loud. "Yet". She added, got morbidly to her feet, and walked into her studio to look for a blank canvas.

***

Garrett knew why had called and asked Sophia out, but after his lunch with Carmen that day, he thought about the significance of the call. And why he had made it. Why had he made it? Yes, she was beautiful, and yes the evening would undoubtedly be entertaining, and quite possibly satisfying in the most basic of ways, but why had he made it? He reminded himself he was a little put-out with Carmen's past with Finn, and that had assuredly justified his asking Sophia out. But again, he almost said aloud, he had had a wonderful lunch with Carmen. So wonderful he had written about it in his oft-ignored journal. There had been a depth to that meeting, to that woman, to the way he had been at ease that he had been left a little struck, a little starry-headed. He was not accustomed to it. And never once did that ease of presence negatively influence his attraction to her. He'd come to understand, through various friends of his, that it wasn't unusual to lose some attraction to one's partner as friendship grew thick, as comfort came so naturally. He had not experienced it, but instinctually knew it must be accurate. He had not experienced it today with Carmen. What he had experienced was a new level of communication, of mutual understanding, even if it was expressed silently.

He thought about her proud stride, her exquisite, close-fitting outfit, the sweep of her dark hair over the sweater that could not have gotten closer to her skin. He thought about her deep, smoky brown eyes, and the promise behind them, even if, admittedly, the promise wasn't being made to him. At this his expression balked, because he didn't want to think about who it was she made such a promise to, who it was that could captivate her if he couldn't.

Thus the date with Sophia. He would love her company, he knew, but he had made the date because he felt sorry for himself, sorry that he could not have asked Carmen. He could not risk it, because if she refused it would not only anger him unduly, it would jeopardize their future together at Gallery Darrs. He would not let her devastate him in that way.

***

Sophia thought the conversation with both Garrett and her sister had gone pleasingly well enough, so she put on her riding gear. She had not been to the stables in several months, and it was time to start riding regularly again. She was a very good rider, and until recently had gone two or three times a week. Her thriving antiques store and social calendar had made her lazy, and she thought her pants might be tighter because of it. That was one consequence she was unwilling to allow, so feeling heartened by the prospects of a date later that evening, she went to Twilight to say hello to her horse and hoped in earnest that she would not be too obnoxious because of Sophia's long absence.

She drove up the long, winding vehicle pathway and parked her car in the shade. As she got out she was warmly reminded of the beauty of these stables. The main barn itself stood majestically about 50 feet from the drive, painted freshly in white and green. Although from here she couldn't see them, she knew that behind the barn sat several quaintly presented cottages, each with its own garden, and, depending on the tenants, neatly trimmed gardens or something a little bit more wild attended each one. She would make a point later to say hello to some of the people she knew lived there. There was also a smaller barn set further back that housed some ponies and all the tools needed to maintain the property. As she drew nearer the barn she noticed how well the place looked. The grass outside the grazing fields was cut low, bushes trimmed, and she thought she spotted additional sunflowers to the right of the main barn. The sight pleased her and made her smile. It was with this half smile that she entered the barn of Twilight Stables, ready to go on an all out ride with Envy, her favorite, her only horse.

As she rounded the corner she noticed a tall man on the far side of the barn grooming a large stallion, a new horse to her eyes. She could not see very well because the sun was behind them, so she assumed they saw her just fine.

She waved a high hand and said "Hello".

She did not hear anything right away, but continued on to her horse. Envy was the fourth one on the left, and she could hear the horse whinnying since she had recognized Sophia's voice, and may have actually seen her walking across the driveway. She sounded a little frenzied, so Sophia walked a little faster.

She got to the fourth stall and peeked in, just about to greet her when she realized that in fact it was not Envy. "Uh?..."

"How can I help you ma'am?" boomed a voice immediately behind her.   She screamed louder than she wished and whirled around.

"You scared the shit out of me" she said, angry she'd sworn (though in truth liked to swear and did so often at her store when no one was listening).

"Sorry, but I don't believe we've met, so I don't know how I can help".   He said this evenly, but she sensed something a little more ominous.

She did not like to be questioned on her own family's estate, at the hands of some brute.   "My name is Sophia Carmine.   My parents own the joint."   Since when was it OK to be sassy so soon she thought, a little dismayed.

Mack was not happy.   She had the mouth of a vamp, and the attitude of his least favorite type of people—the spoiled rich ones, a fact that surprised him since he knew the Carmines fairly well, and didn't think they would be parents unable to discipline. Worse than rude, she was also intensely good-looking.   This could not have helped in her upbringing, and it certainly wasn't doing him any good now.   Actually, she was unbelievable looking, and he could feel his staunchness begin to lose its veneer.

"I mean…." She continued.   "I mean, I have not been here for a few months, sorry to say, because I've been extremely busy (why was she telling him this?), which is why my face is new to you." She said.   She was not thrilled with herself for acting guilty, so she decided to turn the table if she could.   "What, may I ask, is your name and position?" She added a pert smile to convey her slight annoyance at the situation.

He looked away for a moment, a little resigned.   "I'm Mack Fordham, Miss Carmine." He then looked at her directly in the eyes.   "I manage the place for your folks." He waited a moment. "My job to make sure everything is running as it should be, you understand".   He kept looking at her.

She had not been quite ready for his eyes.   She was not ready for such honest dislike brilliantly conveyed by a shade of hazel she had as yet never seen.   "I see." She said, too softly.   When she briefly averted her eyes from the coldness of his, she was faced with the rest of him.   She noticed the harsh scar on his cheek, the ruggedness of his features, the sheer physicality of him. He stood almost stoically, and she realized that he was close to handsome, but he was also rather frightening. She mentally added iron to her backbone and said "Nice to meet you Mack. Please call me Sophia." She knew he would hate her even more for having assumed it appropriate to call him by his first name without his permission, but she couldn't help herself. Just who did he think he was, anyway? He'd been here for a few months, and he was allowed to treat her as an intruder? Not ever.

His eyes, stony before, were now positively ice. "Sophia then." He started to walk away, and she was sure she saw a slight shake of his head.

"Mack?" She questioned, though it was really the last thing she wanted to do.

He stopped and turned his head. "Yeah?"

"Could you just point me in the direction of Envy's stall?" She regretted the question immediately. He would be thinking she was too lazy to walk up and down to figure it out. His expression said as much.

"You passed her on the way in. First stall on your right." That had been said smugly. As though he found it pathetic she had walked by her own horse.

She was seething. Worse, she no longer felt like riding. Maybe throwing rocks. She was unaccustomed to this kind of behavior from any man, let alone a stable hand, or manager, whatever the hell he was. She knew, however, that it would not be safe to stay in the barn and stew, because he'd had the audacity not to leave, so she walked as calmly as she could to Envy's stall.

As she did, she could hear Envy's neighing increase, and it soothed her a little. Maybe that good, hard ride would be what she needed after all. Gallop at full speed to stomp out her embarrassment at the whim of this Mack, the new guy, the new pain in her butt.

"Hello you gorgeous animal, you" she said to Envy as she came upon her. Envy was there waiting, and didn't seem too upset, surprisingly. Her horse nuzzled her, and with each touch she found herself calming down, letting the anger subside. She would approach her new found situation with logic and poise.

One unfortunate meeting did not have to mean more to follow. She let her shoulders relax as she saddled Envy and groomed her fine dark mane. She let the simplicity of the task recreate the happiness she had been experiencing before entering the barn.

She knew that Mack was still on the other side of the barn, and that she would have to pass him in order to go riding. Going out the door she entered would seem an obvious maneuver of avoidance. But she was no longer fazed. She pulled on Envy's reins and led her out of her stall, gently coaxing the animal along. As she walked towards Mack she studied him. He was grooming a different horse at this point, seemingly absorbed with the task. She was impressed again with the sheer size of the man, and the strength he easily emanated. His profile was a hard one, but not unpleasant, and she decided she was a fan of the scar. Though she still thought him frightening, she was sure she detected tenderness somewhere, perhaps only visible because of his obvious admiration of the animal he was grooming. So he was one of those. Someone who was sure all creatures were inherently good, except for those on two legs. She felt some twinge of annoyance, but made sure to ignore it. Now was not the time to bare her teeth.

As she approached him, Sophia could see him visibly tense, which made her react in kind. She deliberately stopped her horse. He looked up at her, a bored question on his brows.

"I don't think things went very well before, and I wanted to re-introduce myself" she said. "I am Sophia Carmine, and I'm sorry if you thought me rude". She just didn't quite have it in her to apologize for in fact being rude.

He had been crouched down in a squat attending to the legs of the horse, but now stood to face her, and his face seemed to grow less tight, less bored.

"It happens. I'm sorry I didn't know who you were." He extended his left hand to her. "Mack Fordham".

She met his hand and they shook, her hand dwarfed by his. As she smiled she looked into his eyes, which was difficult, but she hoped he saw a little bit of the defiance she had earlier felt. Their hands dropped, and there was a bit of awkwardness as she started to move Envy on again.

"Have a good ride" He said, but when she turned to thank him he was already tending to the horse again. She looked away and continued on, shouting a "Thanks" as she did so.

Sophia thought their second meeting mostly a success, even if a little forced. She didn't need headaches when she wanted to go riding, and since she intended to go more often now, Mack Fordham had to at least accept her, if not actually like her. She had a feeling he was a puzzle, but right this moment, before her adventure into the woods, she did not want to dwell on him, but on the beauty before her, and the welcome feel of Envy's strength beneath her.

Chapter 10

Nick pulled the car up to the antique shop, and turned to face Garrett.

"Here's your rose Mr. Garrett" he said.

Garrett had been off in some other world and shook his head a little. "Hmm?"

"You asked me to pick you up a rose for Ms. Carmine. Sophia Carmine". Nick had not actually met Sophia yet, and was looking forward to it since he had rather liked Carmen.

"Oh yeah, Nick. Thanks". And he took the rose from Nick's outstretched hand. "Anything else I need to know?"

"I don't think so. You look good."

"Thanks, Nick." Garret replied. "I should only be a minute or two. Find a good station, or put in one of my appropriate CDs". Garrett opened the door, got out and headed for Sophia's house. He was not sure where the entrance to the living area of the shop was, but decided to head towards the side of the house, since he noticed another pathway.

He was wearing a tailored dark blue suit under which he had donned a maroon shirt, the ensemble finished off by an exquisite blue and yellow tie from Milan. The suit enhanced his eyes as well as added a degree of mystery to the man; a very appealing touch of danger. Garrett did not think of his reflection in that manner, but soon Sophia would. He found a large door as expected and knocked.

Only a few moments passed, and he heard footfalls approach. He was calm, but not without apprehension, due in part because he was still not sure what he was doing. Sophia opened the door and Garrett was rendered breathless for a fraction of a second. She was without a doubt one of the most beautiful women he had ever seen, and she knew it of course. Her radiant smile said as much, but it was not the smile of a braggart, just a woman proud of her luck.

"Hello Garrett" She said. "Don't you look dashing! Please, come on in." This she said as she backed up to let him in. He noticed soft music in the background.

He didn't yet step in, but proffered her the rose instead. "A single rose for a singly beautiful woman" he said, and nodded his deference to her. He then walked by her and paused in order for her to let him in.

"Would you like something to drink before we go?" She asked.

Garrett had not intended to, but now was suddenly thirsty. "If you have any scotch, that would be great". He could not very well stop looking at her, and was hoping it was not awkwardly noticeable.

She was still smiling, but said only "I'll be right back."

He watched her walk away, mesmerized by her walk, the slinky confidence with which she held herself, and wondered just how much havoc she'd left in her wake over the years. She was wearing an almost floor length spaghetti-strap blue dress, and the nature of the material was very flattering to the nature of her body, sent him thinking wildly nasty thoughts too early in the evening. He would have to get a better grasp of everything. It was all about control, and having it.

She was coming back from wherever it was she had been, holding a drink in front of her. The task of carrying the liquid did not affect at all her impossibly wavy walk, a walk, he noted, that did not at all seem practiced, but hellishly natural and relaxed.

As she approached she said "Here you are, though it's the last of it I'm afraid."

"Thanks. Don't need another though. Where's yours?" He asked, daunted by the fact she didn't want one.

"Oh I had one before you came. I don't want to ruin my enjoyment of the evening, do I?"

Sophia now had her opportunity to drink in the man if not the liquid. She gazed up at him and engaged him in conversation about antiques since it was a shared interest, and as he spoke she watched the shape of his mouth, the amazing intensity of the blue in his eyes. When he occasionally glanced away from her to look about himself as he spoke, she was able to get a look at the rest of him, and she was excited anew about their evening together. He was dressed far more elegantly than he had been the first time in her shop, and the look seemed comfortable to him. He was a man used to looking polished. Every movement resonated masculinity, even to the way he shook his glass a little to let the ice clink. He had a smile that was beautiful, but he seemed selfish with it, not ready to really let loose. She'd do something about that.

"You really do know a lot about this stuff" she said somewhat idiotically because she had not been paying very close attention to the content of talk, but she wanted him to think she had been.

"A bit, but I've been collecting a while. I'm sure I'm no match for you."

"Maybe not with antiques" She said and smiled up at him daringly.

He had no idea what to say to such boldness, so simply smiled at her and shook his head just a little. Was this what the night would be, he wondered? Sexual innuendo he had to somehow respond to? It wasn't his forte, and he wasn't any good at it. He far preferred directness.

"I'm just playing with you, Garrett". She said, still smiling. She could tell she had surprised him. "Don't worry about little ol' me. I'm pretty harmless".

"No problem, I'll just have to catch up." Harmless my ass.

"Shall we head out?" She asked since she noticed his scotch had vanished.

"Why don't we. We've got some time, but it'll give us a chance to enjoy the scenery. I love this area."

As they walked together towards the limousine, Garrett's left hand lightly touching Sophia's back, Garrett noticed Nick get out of the car to open the passenger door for the second time in a week. Nick's etiquette was certainly self serving.

"Thanks, Nick" He said and gave a meaningful look to him that Sophia couldn't see.

"Yes sir" was all Nick managed to say in return.

"Hi, Nick" Sophia said and smiled.

"Ma'am" he responded, hypnotized.

"Watch your step" he added as she bent her head to get in the car.

Garrett closed the door behind her and said "Smooth, Nick, smooth."

"Yes sir" was still all he could say.

Garrett went round the other side and got in. The bemused ensemble was off.

***

Carmen stared at her canvas bleakly. It was evening, and she had been toying with many ideas, and as she grew more and more aware of the time, that witching time when she knew Garrett and Sophia were out together experiencing all things excellent that two beautiful people will experience on a first night out, she became less sure of what she felt. Why was she acting like a foolish woman for a man she had only met in the last week? Why was she so deeply smitten when Garrett had only had the opportunity to demonstrate to her his public personality, albeit a mostly good one? Other than his odd bout of terseness on their first meeting, he had been nothing other than gentlemanly, honest and kind. She knew he had business on his mind, but she knew that that interest was not what prompted his politeness. She knew by her own instinct and by the reactions of others, that he was a basically good man. But she did not know more. It was unusual, she thought, to be this woozy over a man one knew very little about, but when someone looked the way he did, carried himself the way he did, implied passion of all kinds in the way he did, rationale was perhaps out the window. And that was really it. She wanted to get to know him. She was very sure that something cool, something extraordinary was lying in the heart of Garrett Darrs. She sensed it keenly, and she knew she sensed it accurately.

As she thought about it, as she slowly completed the analysis of her feelings towards the man, she began to paint. She wasn't at all certain of where she was going or what would transpire before her, but she began to paint furiously and with vivid colors. The movement of her hands did not cease for quite some time.

Carmen became somewhat hypnotized by the quiet of the studio and the gentle sounds of her paintbrush as it conveyed the hues she commanded to the canvas. She had forgotten about the exciting date that had obsessed her not long before, and that was unfolding still as she painted on. When evening had turned to night, when her arms were no longer able to support her instruments, she stopped and looked at what she had done. It was not nearly finished, but it was the very beginning of something divine—this even she could recognize from a subjective standpoint. She marveled at the sheer audacity of it. She was suddenly not sure if she could continue, and if she did she was convinced she could not allow it to be displayed for anyone other than herself. She stared at it a bit more, and before retiring to bed she knew where the painting was going, and she felt a welcome peace. The art to which she was so profoundly tied was also a great healer, offering her solace in times when maybe no other could. She cleaned up her brushes and palettes, and quietly went to bed, a small and content smile playing upon her lips.

***

Nick could not help looking back in his rearview mirror more often than was appropriate, or for that matter, what was safe enough to get them to the restaurant, but Garrett did not have the heart to raise the partition glass just yet. He and Nick had a tacit agreement that, at least at the beginning of the evening, Garrett would let Nick appraise the gem.

The vehicle hummed along quietly, matching the comfortable silence within. Sophia was content to look outside, occasionally commenting on landmarks of which Garrett might not know anything but about which she found some significance. She pointed out Twilight Stables, what little they could see from the road, and Garrett listened at her brief description of the place, but then how it launched her into a more descriptive narrative on her love of riding. That was something he could share, though he'd ridden only a handful of times in his life. He imagined the peace experienced in the sport would not be unlike that of his appreciation for art, and said as much.

"Well you're right about that" she said. "I hadn't been in quite some time, at least a few months, and I went today. It made me realize I've got to put more time into it". She seemed then to go off in her thoughts, on odd look on her face, a bit of a cloud before her eyes. "Anyway" she added, "you've got to go out with me some time."

"Absolutely".

Presently they came upon a drive with two lamp posts at its base, giving a hint of a grander path beyond. Nick turned onto it and said "Here we are." He then glanced back and smiled at Sophia, an almost adoring gleam in his eyes.

"Thank you, Nick" said Garrett. "I suggest you wait for us, even though we'll be a few hours".

"I expected as much, Mr. Darrs. Brought a book and a deck of cards." He pulled up in front of the restaurant, "Frank's Bistro", and stopped the car. Again, Garrett noticed he got out to open the door for Sophia. His eyes were still puppy-struck as he bid Sophia a good evening.

They walked in together and, a bit early, decided to have a drink at the bar.

"You've got a nice driver in Nick" Sophia said as she sat down.

"I do" He agreed. He looked at her appreciatively. "He's of course exceptionally nice to gorgeous women".

"Thank you, but I'm sure he sees quite a few of those".

"Less than you think" he lied. "Anyway, I'd like to concentrate on the beauty in front of me if that's alright" he smiled.

"Perfectly."

He asked her about her family, for in fact he was intrigued. He was curious about a couple that had done so well, and had brought such beauties into the world. He watched her as she happily spoke of them, the love she felt obvious in her speech and motions. He found this woman alarmingly sexy, almost decadent. She gestured a lot and looked at him very directly. She was suggestive in almost anything she did, but he was sure it was not always intentional. She'd been so used to the attention of men, toying with men for so long it was part of who she was.

She did not remind him of Carmen. This fact served, however, to remind him of her. He wondered what she was doing this evening, if she knew of his and Sophia's date. He suspected she did, and the knowledge satisfied him to the point he was almost ashamed. He was very unsure of himself around Carmen, not just because he didn't know quite how he felt about her, but because he couldn't quite read her. He knew she was at least a bit attracteded to him, because judging by her reactions, she cared what he thought, and she listened intently to what he had to say. This was not just good manners he was sure, but genuine. He reflected fondly on their lunch only just that day, and a gladness touched him, but also sent a bolt of guilt since he was supposed to be paying better attention to Sophia. She was now talking about her brother, Dominic. Garrett was glad he had snapped out of his reverie in time to hear of this individual about whose existence he had been unaware until this point. Well why would he know? These two women were fairly new to his life, and that acknowledgement hit him strangely, for it seemed that now his life was well populated with the Carmines. All in the space of a week or so.

They were ushered to their table, which was located in the center of the dining room, among other well spaced tables. It was not a quiet spot, but Garrett had thought it was not a night for a quiet table. He would rather they enjoy the ambiance of the place together, especially since he had known Sophia would be lively, attractive company. She seemed to appreciate it because she was smiling radiantly.

"This place is lovely, Garrett." She said. "How do you know of it?"

"Actually, I don't" he replied. "A friend of mine recommended it. It is nice, isn't it?"

After Garrett ordered a bottle of wine, they looked over the menu together, exchanging idle bits about various entrees, and they each enjoyed the topic. The waiter arrived with their wine, and opened it without too much fuss, making them feel relaxed. It was a place to feel at home, and in some ways reminded Garrett of Luigi's. For a second time that evening he thought back to earlier in the day, but this time his mind traveled to the painting of

Carmen's he so loved. He wondered how Carmen was coming along with her work, if she would have enough completed over the next few weeks to be able to present a good body of work. When he had been to her studio he had seen many complete, but quite a few that had to be finished. He did recollect now that she had vaguely mentioned a storage area where she housed more. He would have to take a look....

"So Garrett" Sophia was saying. "What's going on with the gallery? My sister has been quite busy and has not been as chatty as usual on the subject."

He hoped he hadn't been obviously absent. "We're on." He said. "We'll be putting on a show in a few weeks. I wish it could be sooner, but I don't think Carmen will be ready, and I don't want her to feel that much stress for her first show."

"Two weeks? That's excellent. I wonder why she hasn't mentioned it." Sophia frowned slightly.

"Well we only just closed the deal today." Garrett replied.

"Today?" She seemed surprised.

It now dawned on Garrett he probably should have kept his mouth shut. "Yes, we had a closing lunch in the city" he said, hoping it sounded official enough, not sure why he cared. Instinct, he guessed.

A curious, but not altogether kind smile formed itself on her mouth. "So you had lunch with my sister, and this prompted you to call me for a celebratory date?" She asked, tilting her head in a fashion that looked an awful lot like she thought she had him caught, and could not quite wait to see how he answered.

"Actually, I called you before we had lunch" he said. He did not smile because he knew a smile would make it seem like he was asking for her forgiveness, thereby admitting guilt. He just looked at her, and then continued. "It's going to be a beautiful event. Your sister, as you know, is very talented."

Her smile turned from ironic to appreciative, if not for the explanation itself than for the well delivered nature of it. "Yes she is" Sophia acknowledged. "We are a talented family", and she just stared into his eyes for a few moments, audaciously not looking away.

He knew those talents could not be disappointing, and he couldn't help but at that moment imagining her without her beautiful blue dress, with it carelessly thrown perhaps by his bed and her laying back against the pillows looking at him, waiting. The thought dazed him some, distracted him to a place he was not ready to go, but he said "I believe that, Sophia", and he would have added more, would have played her obvious sexy game to please her, but their waiter arrived with their dinner.

They dined peacefully, and without any other dangerous conversation. He told her a bit about his history in finance, and she told him of her days at Cornell. Slowly creeping into the mood, of course, was the apprehension of later moments, at least for Sophia. Garret knew how the evening would end, since he had planned it. Not that he was never spontaneous, and not that a date couldn't sway him, but he liked a first date to proceed in a particular manner.

Sophia was beginning to tingle at the thought of kissing this man. She would love to be able to seduce him completely, but knew it would not be prudent. Garrett did not seem to be the type of man to wish for such a thing immediately, at least in the logical sense. She was quite sure that he didn't want to hold himself back, but just did because that's who he was. Such information she was able to have gleaned, even after only a few hours, because he had demonstrated his reserved nature. She was openly flirting with him, and only occasionally did he take the hint, even though he was aware of what was transpiring. She was tantalized all the more, because most men would have reacted differently, all too eager to accommodate her double entendres.

They shared a lovely piece of apple pie for dessert with a few cordials to wash it down. The alcohol had started to take effect on them both, and Sophia was sure she should not have any more for several reasons, most important of which she didn't want to forget her decorum or ravage Garrett before she should. As for Garrett, he felt the nice vibe of the liquor, but he was a tall man and accustomed to drinking a bit more. He sat back and enjoyed watching Sophia as she chatted on, a bit more talkative now, maybe even a little conspiratorial in some of her musings. She was very amusing, very playful. He liked this one, but he had a nagging suspicion she was not tamable. This was not always a bad thing, and any woman he admired had to have an independent soul, but he was not a huge fan of the fanatically wild. He could be wrong, and he thought it might be interesting to find out, even if just to assuage his curiosity. Again Carmen's face flashed before him, smiling gently as she listened to what he had been saying about the use of color and how it enthralled him. He shook his head absently.

"Why don't you escort me to Carmen's Show?" He asked, feeling very in the moment, and immediately regretted it. What the hell was he thinking? What would Carmen think? It was one thing for her to know about the date he was on tonight with her sister, but entirely another to bring her to Carmen's show. It could easily place too much importance on Sophia in Carmen's eyes. He was angry at himself for caring.

Sophia was surprised by this, but pleasantly. "Well that's a great idea" she said. "I mean I'm sure I would have been there anyway, but it would be even more exciting to attend as your date. Thanks, I'd love it." She felt a warm flush creep throughout her body as she thought of the prospect.

"I'm going to get the check" Garrett said.

The bill was taken care of, and they walked lazily out to the limousine. Nick was talking to some other drivers at the side of the building, smoking a cigarette and speaking animatedly. When he saw them, a little smile and shrug of his shoulders was his reaction. He dropped the cigarette, and walked quickly towards them.

"Hello, again Sophia, Mr. Darrs" Nick said. "I hope you had a nice evening". He led them to their car since there were several others parked along the curb.

Once they were inside Nick said "Where to now, Mr. Darrs?"

"What do you think, Sophia?"

"I think it's been a wonderful night, Garrett, but I have to get up somewhat early in the morning for the shop" she said, which was true. She didn't want the night to end, but knew that was the perfect reason to end it.

"Please take us back to Sophia's, Nick".

102

"Yes, sir" Nick replied, a little disappointed. He'd had a nice enough evening chatting with the guys, but he'd been hoping to drive around a bit more with Garrett and Sophia. Romance vicariously. Then Nick noticed the partition rise and his face turned dismal, though not without his regular sense of happy pride for his boss and his amazing accomplishments.

When Sophia saw Garrett hit the privacy button she felt a tremor. She knew it probably meant nothing, but she felt nervous, very odd for her. And she was not comfortable, also pretty strange. Even the effects of the wine seemed to dissipate.

Garrett looked at her. "It's been fun this evening, but I've got to say I'm glad you wanted to go home" he said, waiting almost, for a response.

Sophia did not know what that meant, because it could obviously mean a few things. "Why's that?" she asked. "Bored with me?" She added coyly; glad to see at least her speech was not affected by her misgivings.

"I'm not sure how anyone could be bored with you, Sophia. I find you extremely interesting." He said quite honestly. "But you're right. It's a school night, and I don't want to keep you, or get Fiona angry at me for being late." He was joking about that, but no matter to Sophia.

"Fiona?" She asked.

"My devoted secretary. I'd be dead without her." That was probably the truth. "But anyway, I'd like to see you again, and I know we've got the show coming up, but that's a few weeks away. What do you think about going out this weekend?" Just what was he doing? He had not really had time to think whether or not he should be or wanted to be seeing her again, was in fact flying by the seat of his pants.

Sophia felt that warmth again, thinking he must genuinely like her if he was willing to ask her out for two future dates on the same night. Her frazzled nerves were easing, and her recognizable calm was replacing it. She had it, she'd always had it, and she always would have it, damn it.

"What did you have in mind?" She asked.

"Dunno, really. What about a surprise?" He asked. "I'll call you tomorrow to let you know how to dress."

103

She couldn't imagine it would be a bad surprise from Garrett, but men were funny creatures. "Sounds fine. No bungee jumping, though." They both laughed and then let Nick drive them the rest of the short distance back to her house in relative quiet.

When they arrived Nick let Garrett handle the opening of the door, so that he would not be interrupting anything. Garrett held out his hand for Sophia and she accepted. Once she was out of the car he shut the door and guided her to the side entrance with his hand on her back, a back that felt very smooth beneath the silk.

As they got door-side and stopped walking, Garrett said "Thank you for a very pleasant evening, Sophia".

"You're welcome, and I had a very nice time as well. Excellent little restaurant I'll have to frequent". She paused. "And my company was absolutely handsome and debonair".

"Really?" He said, teasing. They had already been standing in close proximity, and now he pulled her closer.

"Really." She replied, a little out of breath.

Garrett decided to end any hesitation and kissed her. He had thought he'd not do so tonight, but the air was clean and warm, Sophia beautiful, and the wine still zinged in his veins and affected his judgment some. The ambience of their date and the mood of the night had turned him vibrantly on, and he would have liked to twist tongues with Sophia, but something was awry. He felt passion, and knew that Sophia was just as caught up, but the moment he had leaned down to kiss her, Carmen had popped into his mind. He lived through the moment when he was hoping to kiss her, could not erase her face, and it was distracting him—not to the point of ruining this simple kiss with Sophia, but by making him believe he was kissing Carmen instead. He was about to erase Carmen, teach her a lesson for butting in by turning the kiss into a Frencher version, but Sophia then chose to stop the moment by gently pushing her hands against his chest.

"Garrett, I think I'd enjoy a longer kiss" she said, "but I won't put myself in that kind of danger" and she smiled.

Garrett's head was spinning, partly because of the pleasure of the kiss, partly because he knew he would remain physically unsatisfied, but mostly because Carmen was intruding on them. He was at a loss for words. "And I could kiss you all night, but I will say good-bye as you wish. Wouldn't want to show my wild side too soon." Wild side? He needed to leave.

She opened her door, and turned to look at him.

"Thanks again Garrett. I'll talk to you soon."

"You will. Good night Sophia." And he gave her his winning smile, quietly hoping it came across properly.

She returned the smile and closed the door.

Garrett walked to the car and got in. Nick seemed surprised to see him.

"Nice night with a good ending?" He asked.

"Yes Nick, thanks." He said distractedly. He saw a glass of scotch sitting on the side ledge, waiting for him, a few ice cubes easing its sting. He reached for it and took a good sip. "Thanks Nick." He said again.

Nick looked back at Garrett. "No sweat Mr. Darrs" was all he said, but Nick didn't like what he saw. Garrett was usually much cheerier upon ending a date with a beautiful woman. Maybe not as cheery as a morning departure, but still happier. He decided not to disturb his boss further by talking.

Garrett pondered the recent kiss, and it's near demise by the presence of Carmen. He was getting annoyed. Three times this evening, at least, he had thought about time spent with her. He couldn't help it, and though he had loved kissing Sophia, a part of him truly did wish it had been Carmen, which might be why he had asked Sophia out in the first place—not as a punishment to Carmen, but as some sort of 2nd prize to himself. Was he that pathetic? Maybe he should just ask Carmen out and be done with it, regardless of what her involvement was or may have been with his brother. At least then he would know. Even if he didn't do that, he should rethink his decision to take Sophia on another date. But she was so beautiful, he reminded himself. Why should he deprive himself? He knew, of course, that was not a good enough reason, especially if Sophia was too interested, something about which he knew nothing. He wouldn't cancel anything just yet, but wait until tomorrow when his head was clearer. The light of day would surely promote a wiser decision.

***

After Sophia closed the door, a smile still on her face, she went into her kitchen and poured herself a glass of wine. She probably didn't need it, but she was not quite ready to go to bed, wanting instead to think about her evening, because it was definitely an evening she had to think about. She relaxed on her favorite couch and absently turned on the television, switching the channel to local news. She'd had a very good night with Garrett, of that she was certain. Of much else she was decidedly not. It had gone mostly smoothly, and she knew Garrett hadn't sensed any of her reservations, and a delightful sexual tension had been present from beginning to end. So what was nagging her? Why was she not totally satisfied? She thought back to her doorstep, when they had shared a teasing kiss, and she felt the familiar tremors in her abdomen. She closed her eyes and tried to relive the moment, one of her hands seeking herself between her legs, starting to rub where best she liked. She thought about their tongues interlacing, and what a good kisser he would be. She thought about his incredible physique and what he would look like naked. Thinking of him in that fashion, and doing things to her that she willed led her higher still, and her hand quickened its movements. There was sweat on her brow as she rose to her climax, and she moaned audibly, her eyes still closed, picturing now very clearly Garrett on top of her, entering her again and again in a not very gentle manner. These last images were what she saw when she let out a final cry of relief, breathing very heavily.

After a few moments, Sophia sat up, feeling physically much better, though still somehow not quite satisfied.

The next morning she woke with a completely different outlook on things. She had slept soundly, and felt better, a renewed sense of confidence within her. The date had been fine, Garrett had been fine, and she was just searching for things. It didn't really matter anyway, since they'd be going out in just a couple of days and she would pay closer attention to gestures and nuances. With that knowledge, she put thoughts of Garrett behind her since she was a busy woman. She was also looking forward to going riding that afternoon, and at times thought she was a little impatient with customers, as if hurrying them out of her shop would let 4 O'Clock arrive any sooner.

When she pulled up to the driveway, she recalled the Stable Manager, Mack, and a frown crossed her face. She hoped he was in a better mood, or not around, so that she could enjoy herself. She had the funny feeling, however, that he had not been in a bad mood at all, that in fact he was just some generally aggravated sort of man. This replaced her frown with a slightly amused smirk. Nothing was going to get to her today. She hadn't the patience. Envy and she were going to tear through the hills and woods, letting nothing get in the way of their joy.

Chapter 11

Garrett arrived at the office on time, right at the stroke of ten. Fiona looked up at him as he entered and smiled.

"Good Morning, Garrett" she said cheerily. "You look pretty tired….late night?"

"Thanks, Fiona." He said sarcastically, but smiled. "Your honesty is so refreshing, but coffee would be more so. Did you make any?"

"Funny you. Can't you smell it? You really are tired".

"I wasn't out that late, but then I didn't go to bed soon enough—you know me".

"Yes." She said with perhaps a tinge of admonishment.

"I had a date." Not really sure why he was telling her.

She looked up. "Oh?" She was not used to him telling her such things.

"Well sort of…..you know, with that Sophia woman." Would this forthcoming spasm not stop?

"Sophia woman?" She was now looking directly at him, a puzzled look on her face. He felt himself shade a bit red, and hoped he was not about to stammer.

"For heaven's sake, Fiona, Sophia Carmine" he said in a perturbed fashion so as to hopefully draw some attention away from himself.

Her face was deadpan. She would not be bullied in her own office, not thinking it strange for one second that she thought it her office. "Sophia Carmine." She stated.

"The antiques dealer" he said plainly, but he was getting uncomfortable. Why didn't he just walk into his office and close the door? Why did Fiona's stare hold him fast like this?

"The antiques dealer." She stated, further aggravating him, because the statement was weighted. She continued. "Carmen's sister, you mean."

"Yes." And then "So what of that?"

"Be careful Garrett. That's all I'm saying" Fiona said, still staring at him as if he were a misbehaving little boy.

"I'm a big boy, Fiona" He said stupidly.

"I know who you are—in fact too well. Just be careful is all I'm saying. Don't jeopardize something important for something that is far less so."

She began working on her computer, indicating to him she was done with the conversation. He tried desperately to think of some quick retort, but he had nothing. She was right even if she was unaware of the exact dynamics. She looked up at him, a question in her eyes. "Yes?" she said, waiting.

"Nothing, Fiona. Nothing." And then he finally moved and walked into his office, closing the door behind him. Behind him Fiona smiled.

"Fuck" he said as the door closed. He went to his desk and sat down heavily. It had started out a pretty good morning, he recalled. How did he let himself louse it up so early? Why had he even mentioned it to Fiona?It didn't matter. He had decided he'd go out again with Sophia, if only just as friends and on that evening would decide if he should somehow try to get out of taking her as his date to the show.

In the meantime he had work to do with Carmen. He had to get a better idea of how much work she had, and how he should place the work. This is something he rarely did personally, but sent Fiona to do since he trusted her taste sometimes better than his own. Carmen's project he would handle, and he promptly decided he would do so unannounced. That would surely give him an advantage, not that he knew what he needed the advantage for at this time.

He went to his office door and opened it. "Fiona?"

She seemed a little startled at seeing him so soon. "Yes, Garret?" She said calmly.

"I need you to do whatever you need to do to get an amazing lunch basket ready & delivered to the car within a half an hour. And I need you to call Nick and tell him to be in front of the building at the same time or sooner. "

"That's a tall order, but I'll do what I can." She had the amazing decorum, Garrett noted, not to ask him what it was all about.

"Thanks. Let me know if there are any hang-ups." And with that he closed his door and went back to his desk.

***

Carmen was in her studio drinking a cup of tea, lazily. She had begun to paint at 9 that morning, early for her, and now at almost lunch she was nearly complete with the work she had started the previous night. She would need another few hours perhaps of touch-up, but the brunt of it was done. And it had been exhausting. She looked at the canvas, and she was sure it was the best she had ever painted. Though most of her paintings were personal, this was deeply so. The kaleidoscope of emotions expressed was at least thought provoking, but she thought staggering. She was very proud of it, had in fact been admiring it for a solid ten minutes while she had her tea, when she thought she heard the door-bell. She wasn't expecting anyone, so dismissed it. She put down her cup of tea and picked up her paintbrush, ready to begin the last touches when she heard the definite ring of her bell. Fed Ex? She put her things down and walked softly to the front door.

"Who is it?' She asked.

"It's Garrett, Carmen". She heard him say.

She heard herself scream internally very loudly. What was he doing here? What was he doing here without having called her first? The internal scream would not shut up, so she decided the best way to turn it off would be to answer him.

"Garrett?" She said, her voice riddled with shock. "Hold on." She unlocked it and opened the door to see him standing there, beautiful and frustrating as ever. He should have called. She was wearing painted jeans, and a tight painted top, and her hair was messily held back by a kerchief headband, and she knew her face could not be free of her work.

"Hello Carmen" he said. "I'm sorry to arrive unexpectedly, but I was in the area and was hoping you'd be in".

110

In the area? Why would he have been in the area, but then it dawned on her exactly why he would be in the area since her sister was not far away, and she hoped her face was not turning red, because she felt a heat. "Nonsense. Excuse my appearance. I've been working all morning." She paused and realized they were still standing at the door. "I'm sorry, Garrett. Come on in." She got out of his way and closed the door behind him. As he passed she was pleasantly reminded of his masculine height, and it also immediately brought to mind their first meeting here only just a week prior. She felt herself blush again. He was looking at her, a strange expression playing about his eyes. She smiled. "To what do I owe this pleasure?" She asked.

He wanted to drink in her appearance, because she looked even more beautiful than she had yesterday when she'd had on the tight-fitting skirt and sweater. She was free of make-up, her hair was mussed, and her clothes were obviously work clothes, but they fit her well. She looked natural, at home. He imagined she might even have looked peaceful had he not barged in on her as he had. In today's light her eyes seemed very dark, almost brooding, but she'd had no time to build any walls around herself, and he felt happy to be with her. He realized he'd better answer the question.

"Well, a bit of business if it's alright. And a bit of pleasure to hopefully forgive my rude arrival" he said.

"No apology necessary, Garrett. Would you like some tea?" She asked.

"Actually, I brought us some lunch if you'd like to join me— it's perfect outside for a picnic and I've got all the things we need." He knew there would be no way she would say no.

She didn't know how much she wanted to sit through a lunch with Garrett because she was not sure she had the strength to look at him, listen to him, dine with him yet again, and not stop herself from wanting him. "Well, Garrett, I don't know…."she said.

Garrett found himself on the brink of being perturbed. This house was just no good for him, but she had hesitated. "I promise I won't keep you from your studio too long, and a refreshing lunch outside will do wonders for the creative process." He wasn't sure about that, but thought it sounded logical enough.

"We could also go over some ideas on the show". That was a direct lie. He had no intention of talking business unless forced.

She decided it would be rude not to take him up on his offer, especially since he'd brought it all with him. "You're right." She said. "I could use a break."

"And I'm also here to take a look at your paintings again, if that's OK. I'd like to get a better idea of sizes, moods, etcetera for the lay-out of the gallery space."

"Of course that's OK." She said. "Would you like to do that...." Her voice trailed off as she thought about the painting she was working on. It was not covered, and it was not something she wanted him to see. Not now. She was mostly sure he would not see it for what it meant, but she couldn't afford to be incorrect.

"Carmen?" Garrett asked. He was looking at her, waiting.

"Yes, Garrett."

"You were saying...?"

"I'm sorry. Why don't we have lunch first—I'm actually famished." She recovered. "Then we can go to the studio and you can do what you need to do." That would give her plenty of opportunity to move the painting.

"Sounds good. Unless you have any recommendations, I'll go out and find a spot and get Nick to help me unload. Sound OK?"

She was grateful for the opportunity to wash up. "That sounds perfect. I'll see you out there" she said and smiled. She turned and walked towards her room, and she heard him head towards the door. She did not hear him turn around to look at the last of her figure as she turned a corner, and she did not see the half smile that crossed his mouth.

Garrett felt comfortable and genuinely happy as he and Nick laid out a blanket, a beautiful silver bucket with ice and champagne, and everything else Fiona had brilliantly put together. He felt no apprehension like he had on his date with Sophia, though he reminded himself this was not really a date. Carmen had no thought that it was anything other than lunch with an associate, but he didn't care. It was a beautiful day, her property was nice, and he had chosen what he thought an ideal area to relax. When they were done setting up, Garrett told Nick to go for a drive.

"Don't come back until I call you. And try not to drive farther than an hour from here" he ordered, assuming something would go wrong, but fearing it might be Nick coming back too soon. Too soon for what?

Nick smiled affably. "OK, Mr. Darrs." He said meaningfully. "I get you."

"Nick, you don't get me, it's just….he paused. "Never mind. Just go."

He was still smiling. "OK, Mr. Darrs", and he walked off to depart.

Garrett wasn't really irritated, but he raised his eyes to the sky never-the-less. He wondered exactly what Nick thought about the last week and his various get-togethers with Carmen and Sophia, but he supposed that ironic smile had said enough. He sighed and sat down, and moved to open the champagne. How could she say no if it was open already? He didn't know what he had in mind for their afternoon, other than getting to know Carmen Carmine some more—to see if the magic of yesterday's lunch was an illusion. After that, he didn't know what he was doing.

He heard the door to Carmen's house open, and he waited, looking in the direction from which he knew she would walk. She came into view, and he noted her fresh attire. She had exchanged her painting clothes for a different pair of tight jeans, but had opted for a loose, cream-colored turtleneck to replace her T-shirt. It was casual, but flattering, and she had brushed her hair down. He did not take his eyes off her, and she couldn't hold his gaze, occasionally looking instead askance at the garden as she approached.

"Hope you weren't waiting too long" she said and sat down. She felt like a school girl with Garrett, and the way he looked at her unnerved her.

"Not at all. I just finished opening the champagne" he stated. "Would you like a glass?"

She did not hesitate. "Yes, please." She said, and then added "I'm thirsty, and probably deserve a glass after all my hard work this morning."

He thought she looked beautiful, and said as much.

The statement addled Carmen, but she thanked him, and reached for the much desired champagne. She studied him as he went about preparing their lunch which looked so good she realized she really was hungry. He was dressed in blue-jeans, a black T-shirt and a magnificent thin, dark brown leather jacket. It was a casual look, but a well groomed casual she thought. His blue eyes were a deeper hue with the black T-shirt back-ground, and they were penetrating as ever. She watched him go about the business of fixing their lunch, and she relaxed. He seemed preoccupied, which was good. When he was paying attention to her she felt a lack of control, and she was certain it was a visible lack of control.

"I have some pretty excellent cheeses here, along with good bread and the requisite fried chicken, but I wasn't sure what you liked so don't feel you have to have any of it. I also think I have some butter and ham in here somewhere" he said, searching.

"Don't worry about me. I like almost everything I see" she said, too late realizing it could be taken incorrectly.

He sat back and smiled. "Well then help yourself."

She blushed, still not sure if he was teasing her, but she let it pass. It was an innocent comment, and she, at least, would treat it as such.

"How is the planning for the show going?" She asked, in between bites of chicken.

"Well enough" He answered, "But it's too early for me to tell you any of the interesting details". He changed angles. "How are you doing preparing for the show? Are you excited?"

He was smiling casually, a look of earnest curiosity in his eyes, and she was a little mesmerized by his dimples. "I think so, but it still seems far enough away that it's unreal." She paused. "I suspect I'll start to freak out in a week or so, because I know I won't be calm. You might be used to it, but this is absolutely huge for me. I'm a rube, as you know."

He sat up a bit, and his look got more serious. "You're not a rube. You've been in art since you can probably remember—you just haven't shown your work." He touched her knee, and she felt something electric shoot to her stomach. "This is not a moment to feel anxious of ridicule, but pride in being the belle of the ball since it's your debut." His hand was still there, lingering, and it almost felt as though it had gone up her thigh just a little. Her heart was beating wildly, and the heat emanating from his hand to her leg was beginning to take its toll. It felt like a small sun, each finger radiating strongly enough to send odd tremors between her legs. She tried to distract herself and looked at Garrett nervously, desperate for something to say. He was looking at her strangely, not smiling, but it was a look she could not read.

"You're right, I guess" She finally said. "I'll just need you to guide me through it." Was that also a double entendre, she wondered? This must all be in her twisted head. There was no way Garrett would be having such thoughts, and almost to prove it he removed his hand gently, and sat back on the blanket once more.

"That's what I'm here for" He said, an odd waver in his voice, and then he looked away, apparently interested in an overhead object. And he repeated himself. "That's what I'm here for".

Garrett was trying to collect his wits. He had only touched Carmen's knee to reach out, to create a bond that let her know he was there to help. He hadn't even been thinking about it, until he actually touched her leg. He was surprised he spoke so evenly while his hand was there, because the moment he felt her jeans, the heat of her leg through them, he was hit with a rush of desire. She didn't remove his hand or say anything, so he did not let go immediately. In fact, because his mind was transfixed with the idea of moving it higher, he may have done so. He could not once again jeopardize their relationship, so he reluctantly let go.

"May I have some more champagne?" Carmen asked, startling Garrett.

He looked into her eyes then. "Of course" he said, slightly cheered.

"Maybe we could walk some of the lunch off after this before we go in to the studio." She wanted to prolong the afternoon.

"That sounds good, actually. I need to be sharp when I go about my measurements."

The mention of the studio brought Carmen upright. "Garrett, I'll be right back. I just want to run in before we do go." She said. She handed him her champagne. "Could you keep this upright?" She asked.

"Sure" he said, thinking crudely that he could keep a few things upright. He watched her quickly walk back towards the house, and thought that even in haste she was graceful and sexy, her long hair wafting as she went.

She was not Sophia, and today made him realize it would be unfair for him not to tell her he had gone out with her, would be going out again, and would probably be bringing her to Carmen's opening show. Whereas she might already know about last night, it had not come from him, and that would have to change. They had spent enough time together, and established some kind of relationship, still uncomfortable though it might be, that he should not treat it frivolously. He was certain Carmen would not forgive that sort of behavior. He would tell her today, not quite sure of how to time it.

Carmen returned and took her glass from Garrett. "Thank you". She said. "Why don't we put all this back together so it's out of the way?" She asked, referring to the picnic.

"Forget about it. Nick will take care of it when he gets back. That's what I pay him for."

"I had a very pleasant ride with him yesterday" She said. "Very easy to talk to".

"Yup. Just not so easy to find all the time."

They began walking in the direction Carmen led. The comment by Garret regarding Nick began a discussion on the trials and tribulations of having him as a driver, and the conversation amused Carmen. She had an easy-going laugh, and let it sound often, which only fed Garret's desire to make her laugh more. He told several anecdotes just to keep the joviality going. Such a beginning of their walk prompted other idle banter, and they walked for a few miles in this fashion, each not wanting

116

the walk to end, the easy glee to stop, but neither would divulge that to the other.

Just once did Garrett's mind happen upon the thought of his brother, and only because he was listening fondly to Carmen about a prank she'd pulled on someone at school involving toilet paper (what didn't?) and feathers. He was paying just half attention because really he couldn't get enough of her expressions. He decided that she and Finn were on good terms since Finn was trying, if only casually, to promote her, and he decided to believe their past was just that. Perhaps he should stop behaving as though Carmen had some wicked side just because she knew or had known his brother intimately. And he hoped she hadn't been hurt. He hoped Finn had behaved.

At last Carmen realized they had walked farther than she'd ever gone, and she didn't think it was a circular path. "Garrett, we'd better get back" she said. "I'm not really sure where, when or if this path ends." She said.

Personally, he didn't care, but said "OK. Why don't we turn around".

They did so, and the walk back was a little quieter, possibly made only so because they both, separately, did not like the thought of returning to the house.

Eventually they arrived back, and were surprised to see their al fresco dining area cleaned up. Nick was sitting against a tree apparently napping, a newspaper in his hand, and did not stir when they approached. They tacitly agreed to go to the studio without waking him. Garrett had an urge to put his hand on Carmen's back, but withheld. He could then only think of his hand on Sophia's thinly covered back the night before, and he felt a dash of shame, but there was no time to dwell on it as they had arrived at her studio.

" I'll just let you go about your business while I prepare a canvas for my next painting." She said.

"Thanks. It's good that you can stick around, because I may have a few questions."

As they both began working on their individual projects, Carmen said "Do you have a finite number of paintings you can

117

put up Garrett? Or if I have a few more pieces than you count and measure for today—will that be alright?"

He answered right away. "I will make room for whatever you have Carmen. And I'd like to get to your storage area too, if we can. The more I have the space prepared, the better I can imagine the final presentation."

"That's right. I can just give you the key, if you like."

That more or less concluded their conversation for a while. Carmen had started painting again, another idea having popped into her mind. It seemed this was the case recently, material just flowing to her and then through her. Garrett was busy, or made it seem so, measuring her work, and also imagining how he would go about doing the show. He'd still rely on Fiona in the end. Unbeknownst to Carmen, he also spent a fair amount of measuring the nature of who she was, watching her expressions, the movement of her body. He was entranced by the allure of art to the artist of course, but he was able to see it today so vividly. Only once did she catch him, and she quickly smiled and looked away, but he thought he saw appreciation on her face, and maybe just a shade of red.

Chapter 12

Mack stared frustratedly at his truck's engine. It was not the time to break down, if there ever was one, but he needed to pick up a lot of things from the hardware store, not to mention some treats for the horses. The truck had been with him a while, had been steadfast and true, but he thought now repairs might be beyond his basic skills. He'd been tweaking things for half an hour or so, and was quite greasy. He wiped the back of his hand across his brow, a final demonstration of his bothersome predicament.

He heard the familiar sound of wheels churning gravel at the bottom of the drive, and he was thankful, for a change, at the arrival of a rider. He was fed up and needed the variety of some farm-related activity. His welcome attitude changed rather abruptly when he saw the maroon Mercedes pulling up, knowing it was no other than Sophia Carmine, the well-to-do heiress of Twilight Stables. How could she be so different than Carmen? Carmen, who was quiet, nice when talking, and generally out of his way? He thought back to only the day before when he and Sophia had met, and realized he was clenching a fist. It's true she had apologized, and he was fairly sure it had been genuine, but she had still rubbed him the wrong way. She had seemed almost condescending, almost presumptuous in her demeanor and actions, both qualities he could not and would not abide. He didn't care who she was.

But then she was beautiful, achingly beautiful. He had watched her leave the barn the day before, her close-fitting riding pants on hips that reminded him of sculpture. He didn't know if it was real or not, but her hair reminded him of fire in the full of its rage. Despite himself, he was eager to see how she looked today. He got back to busying himself inside the hood of his truck so he would appear occupied.

Sophia noted, with dismay and a strange anticipation, that Mack Fordham was not to be avoided today. He was looking at his truck, it appeared, and she would not very well be able to ignore him. She got out of her car and walked in his direction. She thought he was probably pretending to tinker since he did not look up until she said something.

"Hello Mack" she said, and stopped by the truck.

He turned to look at her and then stood up. His gaze was fixed and unreadable as he said "Hello Sophia. How are you today?"

Yesterday she had not been this close to him. Yesterday he had been a little farther, and easier to respond to, easier to sass at. He had dark grease marks on his forehead and a few on his cheeks, and somehow they accentuated his angular, almost cruel face. He was bigger than she recalled, more solid. More virile, she thought. She had not quite noticed yesterday his hazel eyes and the intensity with which they presented themselves, and the audacious manner in which they looked at her. He thought he knew her, is what she saw.

She had a feeling he didn't truly care how she was, but still, he was being polite. "I'm OK, I guess. I've been looking forward to this ride all day" she said truthfully.

"Really?" He stated more than asked. "But you only just rode yesterday".

She was amazed at the boldness of this. "And I'm going to ride every day" she said just as boldly, though now committing herself to something she was not sure she could. "It's part of my spiritual resolution". She had added that so it did not seem as though her first statement had been retaliation to his comment.

"That's quite a resolution" he said, still looking directly in her eyes. "But I'm sure it'd be good for you."

She was not sure how he meant that, but decided to take it at face value. "Yes, I think so." She had been returning his steady gaze, but now, at a loss for words, she found she had to look away.

"Enjoy your ride". He said, and when she looked back at him he was returning to what he'd been doing. She didn't yet want to end the faltering conversation and said "What's the matter with your truck?"

He did not stop what he was doing, but said "I'm not sure, and I don't think I'll find out."

120

"You can borrow my car if you like—if you need something" she offered, surprising herself.

Mack stood again, and looked at her with the same unreadable expression. It was a stare that was not cold, but miles from warm, and still it was doing strange things to her. "That's kind of you to offer." He said, truthfully. "But I need to pick up quite a few things and your car probably doesn't have the trunk space."

She shrugged. "Up to you" she said. "But here are my keys in case you change your mind." And she handed them to him.

"OK, thanks" he said, and she thought she caught the hint of a smile.

"See you later", and she was off.

Mack was watching her walk away again, just like he had the day before, and he found the pleasure of beholding her departure just as good. Sophia turned around as she was walking, quite unexpectedly, and she smiled at him brilliantly—as if to say "Ha ha, I knew you'd be watching me". He nodded tersely and turned back to his car, thoroughly agitated by the haughtiness of her.

Sophia was laughing, but quietly. She did not want Mack to hear her because she knew he'd already be angry at himself and probably at her, if she was a good judge of character. She greeted Envy, and groomed her lovingly, feeling confident and happy.

Mack waited until he knew Sophia had gone off with Envy, and walked over to her car. He chided himself for being this stupidly eager about driving her car, but he was admittedly curious. He convinced himself that it was actually a good idea to borrow it, if only to pick up a few of the necessities, and why not take the opportunity to drive a good-looking car. No, he was not a materialist, but he did appreciate a nice car with a good motor, plus he might find out a little about Sophia Carmine in the process.

He opened the door and got in, adjusting the seat so he was not getting crushed, and the first thing that hit him was the very female scent within. It was not overpowering, but pleasant, reminding him of what he'd recently been giving up, reminding him of a female neckline, and here he pictured Sophia's long neckline, beautiful and inviting. He shook his head physically to

121

dodge the thoughts out of his head, and looked around her car. It was a mess. There was at least a load's worth of clothes strewn all over the back seat and floor sharing space with papers, quite a few books, an inordinate amount of matchbooks, and an empty champagne bottle. The front passenger floor had a handful of empty (he hoped) coffee cups & just as many soda cans. He looked at the clothing again, casually wondering whether or not there was anything racy, but was disappointed in that search. He decided not to do any more looking around until he left, since with his luck she'd come back for something. He turned the engine and felt the motor turn on and purr. He maneuvered the car out of the driveway and drove out onto the roadway, appreciating the get-up-and-go it offered. Ridgefield itself offered no long stretches of fast driving, but it had some good windy back roads he knew about, so he opted for that direction before heading to the hardware store. The Mercedes was not an automatic transmission, which could only mean Sophia liked to drive—fast he suspected. He shook his head a little, disapproving.

Mack switched on the radio, pre-flinching at music he was sure he'd hate. After listening for a few seconds he realized he was listening to Pink Floyd, a band one did not hear frequently any longer. He checked the screen for which station, but noted it was a CD. He was impressed. She did not look like a Pink Floyd appreciator, a group he also happened to be a fan of. He noticed the music system actually had a six CD changer, so he forwarded to find out what other music she had plugged in. He recognized all remaining five selections of which he liked four. The last was Billy Ray Cyrus and he crinkled his nose and made the gesture for vomiting with one of his hands. But overall, she had gone up a notch in his mind. Hers was not a collection of only the popular, mindless crap he heard so much of when he turned on the radio. He went back to Pink Floyd, and relaxed, understanding it was time to get to the store so he'd be back in time for Sophia.

While Mack enjoyed her music and her car, Sophia was enjoying the beauty of riding quickly and on landscape that was handsome terrain. Twilight Stables sat on over one hundred acres, so there was plenty of space on which to roam. She knew the many paths well as she'd been riding since she was quite

122

young, but simply riding hard in some of the fields was even more fun. As she rode she found her mind going back occasionally to Mack. There was something about him that drew her to him, made her curious about what he was really like. It was not just that he was such a physical presence, and he was certainly that. She thought it was all in his eyes, eyes that spoke of something abandoned, of something quiet but passionate, but maybe most of all eyes that showed a lack of tolerance. She was immediately impatient with those that lacked tolerance because she thought it egotistical and falsely stoic, but at the same time it was magnetic since he obviously applied this attitude to her. So quickly he had judged her, and maybe she had provoked that, but he had not forgiven her as she had him. He was guarded, suspicious, and, worst of all, apparently aloof.

Envy seemed to be tiring. They had been galloping for too long a stretch as Sophia had been steadily getting more annoyed with Mack Fordham. But she knew today had proved useful in that he could not help but think her decent to have offered her car, a Mercedes no less, and then she chided herself for thinking like that. The offer had been self-serving, though she would have offered it regardless of the situation. Even if he was reluctant, he had to credit her with a modicum of something OK. She smiled at this, and then vaguely wondered if he had taken her up on her offer. Probably not. She thought of the way he held himself, the attention his proud stance commanded and she knew he would not have taken it even if he wanted to. It was just a stupid borrowing of her car, but she knew he would not have done so. Not Mack Fordham. Boob.

Mack was humming as he came out of the hardware store, and once he realized it he promptly stopped. A frown crossed his face as he walked over to Sophia's car, trying to figure out why he was happier now than he'd been just a half an hour ago. He popped her trunk and dropped his packages in, slammed it and then got in the driver's seat. He sat there for a few moments, briefly going over a list in his mind, wondering if he shouldn't go to the feed store as well. As he did so he noticed the glove compartment, and realized his earlier detective work had been incomplete. Was it OK to open her glove compartment? Was that considered snooping?--a quality he would immediately condemn others for, but he dismissed the idea, reached over and opened it.

Except for too many lipsticks, there was nothing to confirm any suspicions, something he was unaware he was looking for. The usual vehicle paperwork, a bottle opener, a broken pendant, and a very beautiful crystal angel, which he picked up to look at more closely. He didn't know why that struck him, probably just a trinket from some craft fair or jewelry store, but it did make him pause a little, and it did bring the onset of just a pang of guilt. He put the angel back and closed the compartment, saying out loud to no one "Shit", and then he started the car.

The ride back to Twilight afforded the time to hear the beginning of a stormy Mozart CD, which matched his mood. He had been humming when he left the store, he remembered, but now his mood was contemplative, subdued, and generally only just so. He could not acknowledge it yet, but Mack was a shade miserable because he had misjudged Sophia and was angry that she seemed, at this point, to be a better representation of the Carmine family than he had given her credit for. The original manner in which she had presented herself had been apparently deceitful, and she might not in fact be that shallow. Most would consider that a welcome discovery, but the grievous pride with which Mack had been born would not allow that, and he was, bottom line, not convinced. Even some criminals had good taste in music, she might have been condescending when she offered her car to him, and maybe the angel was a gift from an old boyfriend she had not yet discarded. But now he was being utterly absurd, and he knew it. He hit the gas pedal harder than was wise, and made his way the last few miles of the trip.

When Sophia got back her car was as she had left it, and she smiled. She unsaddled Envy, groomed her a bit, and locked her in her stall. She walked over to the car with the idea that Mack might have put the keys on the front seat or in the ignition, but saw nothing. He had not been in the barn so she went looking for him at the cottages, assuming he would have the largest one. She found that right before she rapped on the door her body began to betray her. There were butterflies (for freak's sake, butterflies?!)

in her stomach, and she was hesitant. Ridiculous, she thought. She banged loudly on the door to punish herself and waited. Just before she was about to bang again she heard footsteps approach.

When Mack opened the door he was wearing only a pair of loose-fitting jeans that stopped just below his abdomen. Sophia could not help but look at his flat stomach, in fact could not help but let her gaze linger there too long and then travel achingly slowly up his well defined chest. Finally to his face. She was feeling odd and put her hand against the doorframe. He had obviously been in the shower, because his hair looked wet, and he smelled freshly clean (and manly).

"Sorry, Mack" She managed. "I was just looking for my keys." She shook off her shyness and decided it would be better to act casual. She smiled.

Maybe there was amusement in his eyes, she couldn't tell, but he said "Sure. I'll go get them" but did not offer her into his home. Not a surprise. She watched him as he turned and walked back in. His back was broad and strong, and his rear looked promising in the low-hung jeans. Her thoughts became steamy and devious as she waited, and almost randomly she thought of Garrett. She would be going out with him in a few nights, and the thought pleased her. She did not have to dwell on this particular beast, dewy-skinned as he was, because she had a social life. She had a devastating man available who she knew could please her in all the facets she cared about.

Mack returned with her keys, still unclad from the waist up. She idly wondered if he thought this gave him more power over her, if he had seen quite how slowly she had appraised his uncovered body. "Here you go" he said. "And thanks".

Sophia asked "Did you have the need to use it?"

"I did end up taking it to the hardware store for the barest essentials."

Her prediction had been incorrect, and suddenly she thought of her car's interior, the squalor in which she kept it. She found it somehow funny, but still commented. "I suppose you think I'm horribly sloppy now". She could see he was about to say something, but continued. "I suppose it just confirms the horrible things you already think about me. You don't strike me as the

125

messy type." She beamed at him largely. It was an odd variety of flirting, she realized, and likely not one he'd recognize.

"I don't think it would be very fair of me to think horrible things of you" he said.

"Which hardly means you don't".

At this he actually did smile, the first one she'd seen. "Riding has agreed with you today" he said, and she wasn't sure what he meant, but maybe he just meant what he said. And his smile faded as quickly as it had appeared, though he did not become unfriendly. "Thanks for the use of your car—I mean it". He handed her the keys and began to make movements toward closing the door.

She stopped the process by saying "You like being in control, don't you?"

He stared at her, an iciness steeling into his eyes. It almost seemed to her the edges of his hazel eyes clarified to become a hardened emerald hue, which prompted a chill up her spine. "Why would you say that?" He asked.

She was not really sure why she had asked, other than to prolong another moment, but she guessed it to be true. Mack liked things just a certain way, work completed in just the appropriate manner, people acting as Mack Fordham thought they should. "Am I wrong?" She questioned the question while smiling.

He seemed to ease up a little, but sighed with exasperation, which she also thought amusing. He was an easy target. "Sophia, I don't really know you and you really don't know me." He stated quite factually, and seemed as if he thought that would be enough of an answer, but then continued. "So I don't know why you think it's OK to ask that kind of thing, but to answer you, since I know you won't leave until I tell you, who doesn't like control? Who doesn't like to know that what they're doing contributes importantly to the way the day goes, a job gets done, etcetera? Yes, I like control, but so do you." He had been looking in her eyes the entire time, and still did look, but said more quietly. "You just get it differently".

He was right of course, but it had been good to hear him say a little more than two words, even if he had said them in a tutorial fashion. "Touché Mr. Fordham, Touché." She looked at him with her hopefully daring eyes and added "And sometimes I say things not to provoke, but to elicit. A subtle difference between the two, but still a difference." She shrugged her eyebrows at him, turned and walked towards her car. "I'll see you tomorrow!" she called, her hand waving in the air.

This time she did not turn around, somehow sensing it would be a bad idea, but Mack was staring after her, not, this time, appreciating the enchanting recession of her steps, but contemplating the woman behind those steps. He did not know if she was really trying to be nice, if she was playing some silly female game, or just feeding an already sizable ego. He shook his head and closed his door, heading for his fridge. It was very much time for a beer. And maybe a whiskey partner.

***

It had taken almost an hour, but Garrett had finished his measuring and assessing. Carmen looked up when she noticed Garrett was approaching her.

"All done?" She asked.

"I think so." He looked at her canvas, which for the moment had nothing other than the beginnings of a field and sky scene. "What are you painting today?"

"I'm not sure yet" she said truthfully, even though she did have a partial idea.

It was beginning to get dark, and the light in the studio was soft, reminding Garrett of candlelight, romance. He wondered what Carmen was doing for dinner that evening, what she might be cooking, because she struck him as a cook, not one to order out. He found himself picturing her in an apron, preparing various foods, a glass of wine somewhere and some casual music playing in the background, and the thought made him wistful. He had been looking at her almost absently, perhaps too long, and now focused, and stared into her eyes. He could have kissed her just then; she was still sitting as he stood beside her, and he could have lightly touched her hair, bent and kissed her. It was such a strong desire, he was nearly pained.

127

Garrett was staring at her strangely, Carmen thought, but she returned his gaze dutifully. She had to look up at him, and he was standing very close to her—if she stood they would be body to body, an unnerving realization. He was looking at her, and something about him made her think he was going to kiss her, which started her stomach going, and she realized she wished it to be. She found that she was no longer uncertain of how she felt. She very much wanted him to kiss her, do whatever he wanted, really. But she suddenly understood her own foolishness. Why would he want to kiss her? He had just spent the night with her sister. The beauty and flow of the day had made that fact all but forgotten. She felt ridiculous, silly, little girl-ish. She knew where he had been, even if he didn't know it. She also understood that if Garrett wanted Sophia, it was hardly likely he'd want her. They were entirely too different. That aside, she had to stem such feelings, because maybe Sophia was interested more deeply than her usual light-hearted adventures. It was almost certain they had spent the night together since Garrett had all but admitted it, and that was something Sophia did not do so easily.

He said "Thanks for everything, Carmen. It's been an exceptional day—really". He was smiling at her kindly. Kindly? And his face seemed almost stiff, almost as if he had to force the smile. She was reminded of that first day in her studio, and she desperately hoped he wouldn't turn cold again.

She moved to get up and Garrett backed up to allow her the space. "It was a good afternoon, Garrett—a welcome surprise to my day." She hoped he understood her complete sincerity in this, despite her current state of dejection. "I'll show you out".

Her fears on any possible change in his personality turned out to be strictly paranoia, since his demeanor was affable enough, though maybe reserved. "I'll give you a call about the storage facility tomorrow" He said.

Garrett should have said something at some point in the studio about Sophia, and now his chance had passed. Something had changed this afternoon. Whether because of the beautiful weather, pretty countryside, relaxing meal and walk, something between them had altered. He felt that he now knew Carmen well enough that he should be honest with her. And it was obvious

128

something else was happening. A moment had taken place at the end, a certain magic or electricity. It had not just been the lighting. Why he had not kissed her he couldn't figure, because he was sure she would have been receptive. Perhaps his unconscious had stopped him, fearing a similar rejection or perceived rejection as had occurred last week, but no matter, the moment was over, the opportunity missed. And now he had the additional guilt of having had such a pleasant day without having owned up to his having begun to date Sophia, something about which she might already know.

They had reached her door, and Carmen said "Oh—let me go get you the keys" and she walked towards another part of the house. He found himself wanting to see the parts of her home he had not yet seen, which was most of it. He really wanted to see the kitchen, make more solid his earlier vision of her cooking. He began to walk in the direction she had gone, hoping he'd have his wish granted. He meandered through what must have been the living room, and briefly glanced around at the décor. From what he saw she had beautiful taste, but he supposed that made sense. She was an artist whose work he liked. It was logical their eye for beauty might be similar. He thought he heard keys being jingled, and continued in that direction, turning a corner and going through the dining room. And then there she was, and there it was, her kitchen. When he stepped onto the tile-work it announced his presence. Carmen let out a tiny shriek and turned around.

"I'm sorry, Carmen" he said. "I didn't want to scare you—I was just being a little nosy" He made a sheepish face, and she immediately smiled.

"That's OK"

"I realized I hadn't yet seen the full interior, and being somewhat of a décor fanatic myself, I figured you would be too—as an artist, I mean. You can just shoo me back to the door if I'm treading where I shouldn't."

She waved him off. "Don't be ridiculous, Garrett. I should have offered you a tour". She paused. "Well, this is my kitchen, quite obviously" she said, bowing a little.

Upon entering the room he had not looked around, concentrating solely on not alarming Carmen further, but now he did take a view. It was a large, warm and inviting room, a pumpkin-colored background with many accents of red. The oven was old, but attractive, and the rest of the appliances were modern looking, clean. From the red ceiling hung two black, wrought iron chandeliers, pieces that looked imported. The room was a large rectangle, and closer to the oven's side was a large, chunky butcher block island, the bottom of which was mostly open, and he saw many copper pots dangling from the underside of the block. The floor itself was the most attractive part of the kitchen. It was a sporadic but handsome array of Mexican tiles, a pattern he hadn't seen, and he wondered if somehow Carmen had fashioned them.

"I actually made the Mexican tiles" she said, noticing his interest.

"They're beautiful. Maybe I'll have to commission you for a project, if you do that sort of thing." He said earnestly.

"Never thought about it. C'mon, I'll show you the rest of the place."

She brought him everywhere, including the basement, and every room was not only neat, but inviting and enchanting to the eye, but they were also vastly different from one another, each a different story.

At one point, going down the bedroom hallway, she stopped short because she had forgotten to point out the library. Garrett must have been right behind her, because his hands went up against the back of her shoulders to let her know his proximity. Something seismic ran through her body, and she closed her eyes for a moment. It took all of her effort to calmly, lightly say "Sorry. Forgot about the library". She had been turning while she said this, and his hands were still on her back, but lower, seemingly sliding off. The trail of those hands, even through her sweater, must have marked a red path on her back for the heat that she felt. As she got to the doorway, she felt his hands leave her body, and felt disappointment.

"Here it is" She said a little too brightly. Her heart was beating very quickly, and she felt a little faint. Being too close to this man would surely be her undoing. She'd have to make sure to keep such meetings at a minimum, not that she could really prevent surprise visits. And then she realized, sadly, there'd be no more need for surprise visits—he'd gotten his measurements.

"It's lovely" he said from right behind her in his deep voice, somehow deeper, somehow sensual. It almost felt as if he had spoken his words closer to her left ear, had lowered his head to say it intimately. Would that be possible? She was not thinking clearly, and did not feel much strength of any kind, physical or mental. If she turned around and he was right behind her, she would reach up, grab his face and pull it towards her. "Your desk is magnificent" he added, but that voice was farther, not so intimate, and this woke her swoon-state.

"Thank you." She said with a sigh in her voice.

As for Garrett, he'd had to stop her with his hands on her back in the hallway, which he did gently, but his hands did linger longer than he intended, retrieving them only when he knew it would seem something other than a gentle stop. As they approached the library he had been looking at her neck, the curve, the skin he knew that would be supple. He had become transfixed, in a way, and when he had commented on the loveliness of the library he had been referring to her neck. Or he could have been referring to her perfume, because it wafted up to him only just barely, and it reminded him of flowers and the sea.

They completed the tour, Carmen deciding to use the term "master bedroom" when showing her own bedroom, not sure what it accomplished, but needing to say it none-the-less. By the time Carmen showed Garrett back to the door, they were both a bit distracted and reticent.

"Thanks again, Garrett" Carmen said as she looked up at him in the door frame. "I suppose I'll talk to you tomorrow."

"Thank you" he replied. "You were a very kind host. I'll see you later". He turned and walked towards his car, and Carmen closed the door. They both sighed deeply.

***

131

When Sophia got into her car after waving good-bye, she immediately noticed she'd been wrong about Mack borrowing her car. "Huh" she said aloud, and then looked around carefully. In back, all things seemed pretty much the same, not, she supposed, that she would notice the difference. Everything in front seemed in order as well. Wasn't he even the least bit curious about her? Anything? She puzzled a little more, and then opened her glove compartment, but that too seemed as she usually kept it. What an odd, miserable man, she thought, a thought prompted because she was a little disappointed. It's true he was cold-eyed, and said very little, but how could he be so disinterested?

She started the engine and began her short ride home, a little annoyed, but then she purposely put her mind on her social calendar for the weekend. Friday night she was going out with handsome Garrett again, and Saturday was a party in town being thrown by a good friend of hers. She turned her stereo on, and noticed it had been taken off random, and was currently playing Mozart. A classical man? But, yes, a classical man she decided. Mack was a brooding type of man, and brooding was best done under the influence of violins. That made her snicker a bit, and she felt better. Who needed him?

Chapter 13

That night Carmen decided to call Sophia. They were close enough sisters, but did not see each other as often as either of them would like, and they rarely talked on the phone more than once a week, and usually that once a week was prompted by a necessary item to discuss, an event they wanted to share. Carmen would talk about the show, but she really needed to know about the date with Garrett. It had been gnawing at her from the very moment she knew of it, but now that she had spent more time with Garrett, she needed more information. She needed to know, even if it had only been one date, how they had gotten on, what had happened, particularly once they had gotten back to Sophia's house. She also wanted a true gage of her sister's feelings for Garrett, whether it was a real interest or another dalliance, desperately hoping it was the latter.

She had fixed herself a simple pasta dinner, and now was washing dishes while she enjoyed a glass of wine. How many times she had gone over the afternoon in her mind, she didn't know. Enchanting was the only word that best described it, and yet she was haunted by a tiny fear that would not let go, and a fear she could not name. He had been devastating, debonair, masculine, and yet maintained a modicum of humility. There was no arrogance in a man otherwise destined for such. She could not shake the thought that he was attracted to her, despite her earlier misgivings. Too much evidence pointed to it, but then why would he have gone out with her sister the night before, sharing who knows how much passion? Such were the sort of questions that now left her with no choice but to call Sophia. She put down the last of the washed dishes and went to her phone.

Sophia answered the phone and Carmen heard a slightly drowsy "Hello?"

"Hi Sophia, it's me…..you sound like you were asleep." She said, starting to feel sorry about the call, but glancing at her clock noticed it was only 8:30.

"Me? Asleep at this hour….don't be ridiculous, you silly". Carmen then realized she was not drowsy, but tipsy. "So, sis, what'sss up?" She asked.

"You sound awfully happy, Sophia" she said, a little amused, a little concerned.

"Happy? Now why wouldn't I be happy, Carmen? I'm always happy." Carmen heard a slight hick-up.

"What did you do today?" Carmen said, right now forgetting about the more pressing question of what she had done the night before.

"Me? Well, I worked, like I usually do." She sounded perplexed at the question. "Well, and then I went riding."

"Wow. You haven't done that in a bit".

Sophia scoffed. "It's only been a month or so, and anyway, I'm going to go every day. So there".

"OK" Carmen said, placating. Something was irking Sophia. "I didn't mean to imply that you were slacking off or anything…."

"No, no, no….of course you didn't….not like you." I think I've made myself a bit of an nenemy at the stables, that'sss all."

"Maybe you should go to bed, Sophia." Carmen thought she might not get anywhere asking questions tonight.

"Oh, I intend to, don't you worry…..so what do you think of Mack Fordham, that stableman?"

"Stable Manager, actually, Sophia. Mack? I don't know him very well, but he seems OK. Why?" She was all of a sudden on the alert. "What happened?"

"Manager, shmanager." She said, sulkily. "Nothing happened, that's what. Man's got no sense of interessst, apparently no curiosity of life in general."

Carmen did not understand where she was going, but she calmed down when she realized Sophia was just complaining. "Like I said, I don't really know him—he's rather quiet—"

Sophia was laughing a little wickedly. "Quiet? Ya think?" She laughed some more, and then let it fade. "Anyway, here we are…what's up with you?" She asked.

Carmen decided Sophia was not on a mission of depression, and answered her sister. "Oh, nothing really, just called to say hello, see how last night went and tell you a little about my show."

"Oh, the show—Jou know what?" She didn't wait for an answer. "Garrett's taking me to the show, isn't that funny?" She was still talking, Carmen knew, but Carmen was not listening. Her eyes had glazed a bit, and her hand around the phone began to tremble. She could feel silly tears well up in her eyes, and she was mortified at her own stupidity, ashamed at her own foolish feelings too soon putting her in ruin. He had gone out with Sophia for one date and had asked her to her debut? How could that not be monumental? How was that not significant? She slapped her own face to elicit a sting, thankful that Sophia would not notice. This horrible news could not have come at a better point from that standpoint—over the phone and with Sophia drunk—nothing to recall of her sister's apparent undoing…"so what are you going to wear?' Was now what Carmen heard.

"Wear?" She asked weakly. She walked over to the nearest chair and sat down heavily.

"Oh, Carmen. Tell me you haven't thought about it…" But Carmen was getting tired.

"You know what, Sophia, I'm sorry, but I'm not feeling quite right. I think I need to lie down—had this questionable fish dish earlier."

"Oh." She sounded a little hurt, though only in the inebriated fashion. "Thought ya wanted to hear about ma date."

Carmen was tempted, but was actually beginning to feel ill. "Maybe you can call me tomorrow when the shop's empty." She said encouragingly, though at this point she didn't think she needed to know anymore.

"OK." She said lightly. "But you'd be proud of me. He's awfully cute, but I stuck to my guns." And then she added "And not his", laughing hysterically after she said it.

That last statement made Carmen pause. She said "What do you mean?" adding a laugh to go along with her sister's crude humor.

"Sent him packing. OK, not true—he didn't really try anything other than a kiss, but I wouldn't have let him either, not this kid…"

She would have kept mumbling, but Carmen had heard enough. "So he went back to the city last night?"

"Are you not listening at all? Sheesh, Carmen, sometimes it's very difficult talking to you."

"Sorry, love, like I said, I'm feeling crappy. Please call me tomorrow." Then she quickly added "And go to bed, Carmen. You need some sleep."

OK Doke, sis. Right you are….night night." And she hung up.

Myriad thoughts were bombarding Carmen at that moment as she continued to sit. She should have felt relief that last night's evening had not gone on to the bedroom, and maybe there was that, but the show. He had asked Sophia to the show. It then very clearly dawned on her that she could not enter her debut solo. She could not, not with Garrett bringing along her sister.

And now anger reached her. How dare he? Even if he did not have any interest in her romantically, deciding to date her sister at precisely this time seemed unbelievably inconsiderate. And they had enjoyed such a pleasant day together, and never once, never once had he been an honest enough associate to tell her what was going on. And he had not been man enough. It was then that she cried silently, tears streaming for a lack of understanding, tears at what she deemed betrayal, even if unfairly so labeled, tears for misjudging perceived magic moments. She cried for that, but she cried mostly because she was humiliated, and she was not used to that. No man had ever made her feel that way, and the unaccustomed feeling was plain and simply no good.

***

Garrett called Carmen the next day just to let her know he was going to her storage facility to check out the balance of her work. Of course she had given him the keys, so perhaps the call was not necessary, but it was a courtesy, and it might have been another way to talk with her again, to somehow make more real the day before and what it had meant to him. When she had answered she had sounded somehow jaded, though he had not called her that early, and when she had realized it was him she had turned strange, or at least that was only how he could interpret the short answers, the nothing answers, the almost frantic desire to get off the phone. He had not called to chat idly about anything, but found it strange how many times in a short interval he heard the words "OK, well I should go now", even when they did not apply. She almost sounded robotic.

At last he couldn't take the about face in personality. "Carmen, is everything OK?" He asked. "You sound extremely odd."

"Odd?" She asked. "Really?" She sounded as though she was reaching for words, but then she said nothing else.

Exasperated, Garrett said "Yes, Carmen. Odd. Are you OK?"

Something jolted her, because she then said "I'm sorry, Garrett. After you left I stayed up painting endlessly. I'm more tired than I should be. I should really go now". And then she hung up without saying anything else.

Something had happened. He didn't know what, could not even begin to guess, but that was not Carmen. At least not the Carmen to whom he had bid adieu only yesterday.

He had started the day well enough, but now felt the tasks ahead of him to be heavy, even that time when he'd been looking forward to--looking at paintings of Carmen's he had as yet not seen. The show was only just over a week away, and there was too much to be done, too much he had been putting aside whilst wooing Carmen in his own fashion. And Sophia in another fashion.

He beeped Fiona. "Yes, Garrett?" She asked, expectantly.

"I need your help, Fiona. I know, I know, just get in here, please."

"Right there." She responded, and three seconds later the door opened, Fiona entering, elegant, finely suited, and ever smiling. What a delight that quite immediately calmed his stomach.

"Fiona, my love." He said, meaning it more than usual. "You know the shows not far off?" He asked stupidly. Fiona knew everything before he did. "Could you help me? I was going to go to Carmen's storage to check out the rest of her stuff, but I've got neither the time nor the energy. I need you to do it, if..."

"I'd rather do it. It'll give me a better overall scope of the show. I don't know why you've involved yourself so deeply in this one anyway." She said, looking at him fixedly. She looked down, and quietly said "Or at least I hope I don't know."

Garrett was tired, and did not want a lecture from the one person who was most qualified to give one. "Fiona, here are the keys." And he threw them across his desk. "If you could find a way to get them back to Carmen when you're through I'd appreciate it."

***

Sophia woke that day in a fine enough mood, though she had a bit of a head-ache. She had had to open the shop two minutes late, but was quite pleased to see two couples waiting for to her unlatch the door when she did get there. She passed the rest of the day happily enough, now and again traveling to her previous day, her yesterday's ride, and all that accompanied the adventure. She did not like to think about Mack, and until today had not been, but yesterday had etched itself on her, so much so she had gone home and ordered a pizza, eaten half of it, and consumed an entire bottle of Chianti. She was not sure why she was more bothered— because when he had finally spoken he seemed condescending, or because he had borrowed her car when she had thought he would not, or because he had answered his door half naked and did not blink an eye. It was all so frustrating she wished she could scream at the next person who came in the door "Yes, that's more than twice what it should be, but just pay the fucking price you cheapwad!". And then she laughed. She'd go riding again today and give Mack a piece of her mind, even if right now she could think of nothing to say. She supposed he really had done nothing wrong in the true sense, but that just made it worse.

Once again, she walked, discussed through the day with those that entered her reputable shop, and today not one left without purchasing. She smiled, walked lively, and pointed to the pieces she thought her buyers were looking for, and she made it to closing time. She hated herself for the desire for four O'clock, hated herself, but that did not stop the smile when the hour arrived.

She drove quickly to get there, but made sure to drive slowly up the gravel. What would she say today? What would she say, could she say to prompt something from this silly stableman who thought he had her number. She parked her car but did not get out, not caring whether or not it was noticed. In the end she concluded she was an idiot, and that thoughts she was trying to put into regular conversation were counter to actual meaning. What ever happened, happened—such a wise sentiment. She smiled, and got out of her car.

As it turned out, she did not see Mack that day. She went in to Envy, and began grooming her, almost certain Mack had some kind of radar for when she arrived, and that he would come sauntering out and ignore her when she was there. It didn't happen. She fed treats, groomed and saddled Envy, and it took a better part of an hour, but there was no sign of Mack, or anyone for that matter. All the while, she spoke to Envy, related her past evening, how she finagled some customers, anything that Envy would listen to.

"Time for a ride, my friend" she said as she put her foot in the stirrup and got on. She made a few comforting clicking sounds as they rode through the barn, and then out beyond. "Let's do better than usual" she said.

When they were safely off, and hardly in sight, Mack stepped out from the shadows of one of the stalls. He did not know why he had stood in hiding, though he suspected he was not in the mood for any more confrontational banter as yesterday had provided, but he had indeed stood still while Sophia had groomed her horse. In recollection he smiled. She was quite a talker when it came to animals, and in fact she hadn't shut up. If horses could

139

talk, Envy would not have gotten a word in edgewise. This made him smile a bit more. And part of him smiled just because he was having fun at Sophia's expense, but the larger, more generous and grateful side of him smiled because for once he had witnessed someone, Sophia, doing something natural—no pretenses, no thoughts of being watched and acting just so. Maybe Sophia Carmine was OK. But he double checked himself. It was probably too early to tell. Though the smile slowly disappeared, a frown did not replace it.

***

called Carmen as a courtesy to let her know she'd be going over her storage material, and asked her whether or not she wanted or needed to come along.

"Oh" was all Carmen said for a few long moments. Fiona was about to break the awkward silence when Carmen added "Sorry, just thinking about something. I don't think I need to go with you—it's fairly straight-forward."

"OK…"Fiona began.

"You know what" Carmen interrupted. "Maybe I will meet you there. I haven't seen some of those in a while, and it'd give me a better idea of the show if I get to talk to you about it while I work." She said, and she meant it. She wouldn't mind reviewing the stuff, something she hadn't thought of as yet. She also wanted to get to know Fiona because she knew Garrett relied on her heavily, and having her as an ally or friend could only be a good thing.

Carmen gave her the address, and they made arrangements to meet later that day.

Until Fiona had called, Carmen had been sitting on her couch staring into space. Her Garrett/Sophia predicament had so thwarted her emotionally that she was still dazed. And now it appeared Garrett wanted to distance himself from her further by having Fiona go assess her storage work, or at least that's what it seemed to her. She puzzled and puzzled over what she'd do about the show, and how she'd present herself. There was nothing wrong with going solo, she knew, but her ego was damaged now, and going alone while having to watch Garrett escort Sophia on one arm would ruin her confidence. Maybe not outwardly, but she would not be bearing it well at all.

The significant problem was of course that she knew no one who she could take that was a reasonable companion considering her circumstances, and she couldn't ask Sophia for her inventory of men because Sophia would want to know why. She needed to find someone handsome, intelligent and fun to be around. And who didn't? She had only a week or so to capture such a gentleman and could think of no recourse other than possibly placing an ad on the internet locals, and then what? She would have to interview the prospects, and then hope that nothing catastrophic would happen during the debut. She was certain that was asking for disaster, and doubly certain that somehow it would come out she'd had to advertise to get a date, and then it would just get worse.

She spent the better part of an hour thinking it over, and finally came to the conclusion Sophia may have inadvertently solved her dilemma. It was a desperate move, and she was not sure how she would go about asking him, but Mack Fordham seemed a good choice. OK, her only choice. It's true she barely knew him, for the life of her could not remember even the color of his eyes, but he had always been polite, and she knew his men respected him. All she would have to do was present the idea in an attractive manner, making sure to let him know that his answer had nothing to do with his position at Twilight, and that he would only be doing her the grandest of favors, and might enjoy it. Though that she doubted. She could not really picture him hobnobbing with the type of people she assumed would be attending, and that thought brought on a new onslaught of ponderings, because until now she had thought nothing of who would be coming. How would she fare? For a second time she thanked the fact she'd soon be meeting Fiona, because Fiona would give her the scoop on attendees—it was in the best interest of the gallery for her to be prepared as much as possible. She walked over to an antique mirror she had always cherished, and stared at her reflection. Was this it? The faith she had always had in herself, in her artistic abilities, in the very essence of her family, her existence, had it come to this? To asking a virtual stranger to accompany her to a life-altering event just to present an illusion to a man she had known for a week? She kept looking at herself, a somber expression never changing, but then, and beautifully slowly like the melting of ice, she let a smile cross her face. This was the ridiculous, and how apt for an artist. She would warmly embrace absurdity, and in so doing would make it un-so. She had a debut, and a polite cowboy would see her through it.

* * *

When Carmen got to her storage Facility she pulled up and waited for Fiona to arrive, but then noticed a black limousine further down the lot. Didn't anyone ever drive themselves, she wondered? But she did not really begrudge them. If Garrett was able to supply cars for his employees and customers, all the better for him. As she got out of her car, she noticed that Fiona had also spotted her, and was walking in her direction. As they approached each other, Carmen suddenly felt under-dressed, though she should have expected Garrett's right hand assistant to be dressed smartly. She was his top executive. Naïve, Naïve, Naïve. She was not dressed slovenly, but she had chosen dark jeans and a leather jacket over a white spattered T-shirt. Hell with it, she was an artist. She watched Fiona for the brief moments remaining in their approach, and admired the elegant, dark blue suit, noted that it was tailored to a very sweetly slender figure. She wore her dark hair in a tight chignon, and sported slick black sun-glasses, and above all carried herself with assured confidence, yet still with a sexy gait. Carmen felt she dwindled with each step, but quite quickly Fiona put her at ease.

Fiona was holding out her hand to Carmen. "Hello Carmen. I'm so happy to meet you—Garrett is thrilled to have you on board." She said genuinely, and a sincerely kind smile prettied her face.

Carmen took Fiona's hand and shook it. "Hello Fiona, I too have heard so much about you and how much you run the show. I'm very much looking forward to working with you, and hope

142

you can put up with my naïveté. I'm sure you know everything, but I truly am nervous, and suspect that will just get worse as the show approaches. Frankly, I am counting on you to guide me through this.."

"That's exactly what I'm here for, and if I weren't any good at it, Garret would have fired me ages ago". An exaggeration, but a comment she found soothing to those that needed it.

Carmen laughed, and Fiona liked the tone of it. "I doubt that. From the little I've heard, your powers know few bounds." They smiled a bit longer at each other, only slightly awkwardly and Carmen said "Let me now show you the space, and of course you've got the keys."

They then walked together, walked through the lobby after showing the front guardsman their IDs and keys, and Carmen led the way.

When Fiona opened the door, the smell of dust and paint and canvas hit them in a pleasant caress. They both smiled separately at the task in front of them.

"I don't know what you need me to do Fiona—I can just hang out and answer any questions you have while you uncover some of these or all of these—up to you, and do your measuring, etcetera."

"I will have a question from time to time" she agreed, "but why don't you find a chair and relax—maybe the guy in front has some magazines to browse while I go about my business. If I need any help maneuvering large pieces, I'll also let you know."

Carmen returned with a few issues in hand, and sat down to read, though in truth she was more in the mood to watch Fiona, and found it to be an impressive sight. The woman was efficient. She wasted no time in taking covers off canvases and doing what needed to be done, and she was ever so delicate with the work, and Carmen could see that Fiona had at least as much of a passion for art as Garrett did. She could see in her eyes a degree of envy for a talent she did not have, but the envy in no way overshadowed the obvious respect she had for the artist. It was quaint, really, because most of the while Fiona worked there was a smile on her face, sometimes of surprise, sometimes quizzical, and sometimes bittersweet. Carmen liked this woman.

143

***

Sophia had had an exceptional ride, for two hours riding on, thinking of her exceptional sales day, a strange couple she had met in the process, and funnily enough, the time that had so far passed her that was her life. She was not accustomed to extensive contemplation, did not spend an inordinate amount of time delving into that which did not get her immediate satisfaction, but today proved itself different. She did not know if maybe all the riding she'd done in the last few days was the cause, or the closeness she felt to Envy, and perhaps animals by default, but she felt like thinking more, not so much living day-to-day, not so much wondering about the next party. Not that the next party was not attractive, because how could it not be? But just these last few days had made her ever so slightly more spiritual. She briefly let herself think about Mack, but despite her own desire for honesty, could not allow for the fact that he may have had a small influence. How could he have?

When she arrived back at the barn, she saw no one about, and unsaddled Envy quickly, groomed her a touch and left. She did not spend the right amount of time cleaning the stall, brushing Envy's mane, or leaving adequate water and grain. She knew others would do it, and since no one was there to see that she had had a good ride, that same no one did not see her haphazard exit. When she drove away, she immediately felt guilty, and almost turned around, but she could not overcome the largest fear that if she did return to do a proper job, Mack would be right there doing what she should have done, and would look up at her scornfully. She stepped more forcefully on the gas pedal, but to little avail. She only just lived a few miles from the stables.

As she walked in to her house, the phone was ringing.

"Hello?" She asked, a little impatient, a little out of breath. An unfair reaction, since she'd been the one to rush to answer.

"Sophia." A statement.

Sophia calmed her breathing. "Hello Garrett" She said and smiled, and let the smile ooze into her response. "How are you?" She was truly interested. She'd spent enough of her day thinking of things far away.

144

"I'm well, Sophia. I was wondering if we were still on for tomorrow night." He sounded nonchalant, distracted.

The smile in her voice slipped a little. Sophia did not appreciate either nonchalance or distraction when she was being spoken to. "Up to you entirely, Garrett." She said somewhat coolly. "I could always go out for a dinner in the hopes of being spoiled somehow, but it's also Friday night. If you're tired, I can always go out with my neighborhood party gals. They're tiresome, but once a week they're fun enough." She was willing to abide only a degree of hesitation.

He seemed to wake up because his voice changed, and focus held his words. "Sophia, let's go out. I could use it, really, and I've been looking forward to it for the last two days." He said. "How about we pick you up at 8?"

"See you then, Garrett", the smile back in her voice.

She hung up, and wondered at her Sybility. Hours and hours trotting, cantering in bliss thinking of all things away from social, and the second she answered the phone, her vanity wakes her to the less attractive reality.

Chapter 14

It was later in the day, almost five, but Carmen knew Mack would still be working, so she drove out to the stables, and sought him out. He was not in the barn, however, and after looking around for a bit, and stopping to say hello to the horses, including her own beloved Thomas, she knocked on Mack's door. She supposed he could have gone to the beach, since she knew he liked to do that occasionally, but she stopped that line of thought when she heard foot-steps.

When Mack opened the door, a look of concern came over his face. "Miss Carmine." He said. "Is everything alright?" He was looking around behind her as if he might find something amiss.

Green, his eyes were green. Well, maybe more hazel--and he was tall. It seemed she had forgotten. He was also rather broad, intimidating in his stance, unapproachable in carriage, but here she was. Her stomach was uneasy, and she was regretting this hair-brained idea already. What if she just asked about getting a different color saddle for Thomas instead? Probably stupid.

"Carmen. Call me Carmen, please, and nothing is wrong, really. I was hoping you have a minute to talk to me."

The look of concern seemed to deepen his features. "Of course. Come in." And he stepped aside, and let her pass. "Please sit down, Carmen". He added. "Can I get you something to drink?"

"Well tea would be good for me, but I'd love a beer if you've got one."

"Silly to have a fridge without one" he said and got her a beer and a glass.

"You keep a very tidy place, Mack" She said appreciatively.

"Force of habit, I guess." This he said as he sat in a chair opposite her. He seemed to sense that she was having a difficult time trying to phrase her request, because he said "So, what would you like to talk about?"

She looked at him and smiled meekly. "I'm not really sure how I'm going to ask you what I'm going to ask you, but I do have a favor I need to ask of you—you should know that right out. I don't want to insult you by saying this, but you must know that whether or not you decide to help me has absolutely no bearing on your post here. The favor has nothing to do with this place, just a personal favor for me..."

"I will gladly help you if I can". He said this without hesitation, and was looking at her intently.

"Oh Mack, you're so nice, but I haven't told you what it is yet, and I'm not sure you're going to like it, but instead of me blabbing on and on about the fact I've got a favor to ask, let me just ask it." She took a deep sip of beer, and then smiled at him. "I have my debut into the art world in a bit over a week at a very prestigious gallery in New York." Here Mack just nodded. "I need to bring a date, for reasons about which I'd rather not get into today, but I was hoping you could be that date." She rushed on before he could say anything. "I am well aware we don't know each other very well at all, though I can tell from the few meetings we've had that you seem to be a good man, and I know my parents think the world of you—as do your men. Honestly, I'm not seeing anyone now who I could ask, and the prospect of placing an ad for this event seems like too much work and not enough time."

"OK, I'll do it." He said, stopping her from explaining herself further. "I don't know how much good I'll do you since my knowledge of art is limited, though my appreciation for it is great, but if you need an escort, I'd be happy to do it." He looked and sounded sincere.

"Really?" She almost squeaked, she was so happy. "And, well, this may seem stupid, but I would appreciate it if you didn't say anything to anyone about this, particularly my sister, because then she'll start asking all kinds of questions that I have no idea how to answer."

"I won't say anything to anyone."

She took another sip of beer. "I've got to say, Mack, I feel a lot better. I was in a bit of a quandary, but it was actually Sophia that gave me the idea, inadvertently.

"Oh?" He looked at her quizzically.

"Well in so much that she had mentioned you in conversation." To that he only nodded. "I think you've made quite an impression on her."

"That I don't doubt" he said, and smiled just a little.

"Thank you, Mack. Really. This will help me out a lot" she said, rising to her feet. "I'll call you a few days before the event itself, but it's a week from Sunday at 3 in the afternoon. You don't need a tux, but I think suit and jacket are advisable. You know, I don't really even know. I'll find out and let you know— I'm sorry for not thinking about that ahead of time."

"Don't be sorry Miss Car...I mean Carmen." He reassured her. "I've got a few suits from which to choose, so it won't be an issue unless I do have to where a penguin get-up." He then did finally show a full smile.

She opened the door to leave, and laughed a little. "I'll call you next week, then. Bye, Mack."

"I'll talk to you later" he said, and closed his door.

Carmen felt a huge weight lift. She had a date, and he had agreed. Everything from here on should be fairly simple. And he had a few suits, something she thought she might have had to purchase for him, an embarrassing offer she was glad to avoid. She got in her car, humming.

And while Carmen drove off, Mack walked to his refrigerator and grabbed another beer. He was deep in thought about the Carmine family. He did not know if there were secrets—they seemed straightforward enough—but he was admittedly puzzled. Why should Sophia not know about Carmen bringing him to the event? Surely it would be an event that Sophia would also attend, and would therefore see him. So why couldn't she know in advance, although Carmen was obviously the more sedate, level-headed of the two. Perhaps she really was just concerned her wilder sister would not be able to keep her mouth shut, would somehow botch up the show. He shook his head at the prospect, totally sympathizing with Carmen. He thought about how he'd go about the evening, and frankly thought he'd enjoy it on some level. True, there might be plenty of the sorts of people he didn't appreciate, but he guessed he wouldn't have to talk to them, and if he did he could make a game of it, an acting bit of fun, as long as he remained true to Carmen's request. He respected Carmen, and even a little more so after her difficult task of asking him, and he was also impressed she'd had a beer. He took a long draw on his own and switched on the television.

* * *

Sophia was not in her element, did not appreciate the passage of time as it had been so doing this week. Yes, it was Thursday, and yes the weekend approached, but she felt unfulfilled. There was not a bit of her shop and duties involved that she didn't like, and most of it she adored. It was just so easy. She met with people, people inevitably with more money than they could spend, and most of them were even interesting. And they had time on their hands. Which meant they would shop for quite some time once they entered—she had a lot to offer, and they would talk because they needed that extra bit of service, camaraderie. And many of them, particularly men, would linger, reaching for conversation, advise, if only falsely. Sophia understood the allure of her shop, but she even more sagely understood the allure of her face and her body. She was at least half the selling point. Mostly, agreeing with people was all that was necessary, even if they were totally off on dates, material, names—she just needed them to purchase. Other times, she could glean from them their wish to be taught, or at least taled to, and they bought, and they bought, and they bought.

This Thursday was different. She had ridden yesterday, would ride again today, but she felt it was of little consequence. The fact she had not seen Mack hit her ego, a fact she did not like to admit. How vividly she remembered their last conversation, and she had taken it to heart, was convinced he had done the same. But not so, evidently. She was not one to feel this much about anything, and she was determined that today, Thursday, might be a little bit different. She had been unable to close her

149

shop until late, but she still had time to ride. It was not yet late October when time would be less in her favor, so she drove quickly. She passed her sister en route, and wished she had known of her plans, because a ride together would have been nice today. She could have used a chat. The last chat she remembered had been just the day before, and really, she remembered very little—just that she had been rather drunk, and may have said things she should not have, but what else were sisters for?

She parked and got out of her car, understanding the requisite to hasten, and in that moment vowed she would not do as she had done last time—leave too hastily and not do a proper job. She was too old and too polite for that. And now she knew the staff well enough, or at least Mack, to know she should not be remiss to that degree.

It was getting cooler, and she regretted not having brought a sweater. She had not even bothered to don her riding clothes and wore only blue jeans, tall brown leather boots, and a simple white long-sleeve oxford shirt. Her hair was down, and blowing about mildly in the autumn breeze as she walked into the barn. Mack was standing towards the center of the barn, hosing down one of the stalls. He seemed intent on getting the job done, because he did not turn upon her entry. She walked over to Envy's stall and opened it, not looking in his direction though she knew he would have heard the creak of the stall door and turned at the sound. She went about unhooking Envy's gear from the wall, and saddled her. When that was done, she grabbed the brush to do a brief grooming job. Her back was to the door when she began the soothing task, and she tried to think only of Envy and the chore at hand.

"It's a little late for a ride". She heard Mack say, and nearly jumped through the roof. His approach had been silent, almost stealthy, but she supposed the wind may have hidden footsteps.

She turned to face him, and noticed he'd opened the stall door and was drawing nearer to her and Envy. This was unnerving, and possibly not fair play she decided. "You scared me to death, Mack" She said. "Creeping up on people is not nice, or hadn't your mother taught you that?" She asked, not quite coyly.

150

She was looking at him, and his expression didn't change, but he merely said "I don't creep, Sophia." And then he looked her up and down—not in a sexual fashion, but it was a slow scan, and she somehow did feel naked.

"Why are you looking at me that way?" She asked. She tried to smile a brave smile, but he made it difficult.

"You're not in riding clothes, and you're not properly dressed."

"So there's a dress code under your rule?" She challenged, and turned back to brushing Envy's mane.

"Sophia, obviously I need to be concerned about the safety of all my riders." When Mack said this, he realized he might be exaggerating, and added "It's also beginning to get dark, so I hope you are not planning a long ride." He prepared himself mentally for a lashing comment from her.

"Why, Mack Fordham" She said, turning and smiling tauntingly at him. "I do believe you're beginning to like me, much to your distaste." She felt a bit clever, a bit cavalier.

Mack's expression took on a shade of disdain, and he said "I don't think it would be distasteful, necessarily, if I liked you." He did not go so far as to stress the "if", but she got the meaning just the same, and laughed playfully.

"How serious and handsome you are, even when you're awful." And she meant it, even if he did not take it as such. His height and quartz-hazel eyes matched so well the mood of the day that he was eerily breathtaking.

She thought he looked angry at her comment, because his face was more red, and his stare at her more severe. She felt a touch of satisfaction that she was able to get a reaction from the rock that was Mack, even if it was misplaced anger. "I'll be back" he said almost softly, and walked out. Sophia stood there, marveling at such a man, and such a man she could not read. To this point she had felt mostly frustration in his presence, and then even upon later musings of the man such frustration did not evaporate, but now she found herself saddened. He was a difficult man to read, even to her rather skillful talent, and he would make himself more difficult to read because he apparently condemned her so. Just for being who she was. Which she supposed was what she found so sobering. She would not be able, ever it seemed, to convince Mack that she was very worth getting to know.

She looked outside the barn, saw the trees bending in the increasing wind, and glanced at the rapidly setting sun. It would have been a very cold ride, almost an unkind ride, possibly a bit dangerous—just the kind of ride she appreciated, but her heart was no longer in it. It was just another challenge, as if, almost, Mack had set his personality into the weather, the mood, the beginning pall of the evening, and this time her strength had waned. She had finished grooming Envy, and began to unsaddle her, feeling tired and listless, barely able to do the perfect job she had promised herself she'd do.

"What are you doing?" Mack asked, still in a soft-spoken fashion.

Sophia turned around, and looked at Mack. "You said I shouldn't ride." She said with resignation. "Maybe you're right. Maybe...."

"I didn't say you shouldn't ride, just that you weren't dressed for it."

She ignored his statement. "You're the boss, here, Mack. So I'm calling it a night. You win."

"I win?" She heard steel creep into his voice, and felt too late regret. "Just what did I win, Sophia?"

She turned back to cleaning up, becoming a coward in the face of his weary-soaked mood. "Control" she said, and heard that her voice was a little too high. "It's all you seem to want" she added, wishing she'd shut up. No wonder he didn't like her. She heard him drawing nearer to where she was, sounding as though he were almost directly behind her so that she stood up quickly and turned around.

And indeed, he was only a foot away from her, towering over her, and looking down at her, still, always, in a way she could not fathom, and she was agonized right then with the strongest desire to weep or to rip at his chest, but she did neither. She suddenly feared he was going to hit her, and shied away, backed against the back wall of the stall. She saw Mack wince when she did that, and regret slapped her viciously once more. Mack stood there for

152

a moment, looking at her, and strangely she thought she saw a lack of understanding in his eyes.

"You astound me" Mack said only, with an expression Sophia could at last read. He turned around and walked out without making much of a sound, and it was only then she noticed he was carrying a large sweater in one of his hands. Her back still against the wall, she slid down to the hay covered floor and let frustrated tears fall.

Chapter 15

Friday finally arrived, and all those who rose breathed various kinds of sighs, for it'd been a long week for everyone. Garrett was exhausted between arranging the debut for Carmen and pretending to be arranging it, while he was possibly wooing Sophia, though he was not even sure of that, and though Friday was thankfully here, it also meant he was going out with Sophia that evening, and he was not looking as forward to it as he had been earlier in the week. He would not deny that he liked to look at a beautiful woman, particularly over a fine evening meal, and in general he was a man made for being in the company of women, but he was not sure he had the energy tonight to meet Sophia's expectations, or even to live up to his own requirements of dating. He was also still not sure if he should take her to the show, especially since he had not so far gotten the guts to tell Carmen, but he could not very well cancel something like that with Sophia without a reasonable explanation, since no matter what, Sophia would be in attendance with or without him. He thought it might be best if Fiona arranged a meeting between he and Carmen, maybe another Luigi meeting, where he could tell her what was really going on. The more he thought about it as he got ready for work that morning, the more he began to look forward to the evening with Sophia. The prospect of lifting guilt from his shoulders suddenly upped his energy level, and even though he didn't realize it, Garrett Darrs was whistling.

When Sophia woke that morning, the first thought that hit her was the incident in the barn, and her cry in Envy's stall in the fading of the evening, the absolute feeling of desolation she had felt, no comfort coming from the tears that fell down her cheeks. The wind had continued to blow, becoming more relentless, and made her feel less welcome than she already did. Mack had not returned, and why would he? She had insulted him with both her words and her actions when all the while he had actually been intending to make her ride more comfortable. This was not an easy way to wake up, but she had the evening to think about, at least. She relished the thought of being in the company of a man who at least appeared to appreciate her company, to look into her eyes, and to look at her admiringly for the woman she was. That was what she was used to, and that was what she deserved. She was a woman who cried rarely, and she had even been occasionally accused of being hard-hearted, so the week had done a number on her emotionally, and after having ridden every day, she was also rather physically spent. She rose from the comfort of her bed, got in the shower and soaped herself with an extra degree of care and gentleness. She was determined to begin and end the day with the old Sophia at the helm, a brilliant smile at the ready. And knowing that she had to run her shop the full day since Fridays tended to be busy, and she then would be preparing herself for the evening, she knew she would not be able to ride, despite her promise of a daily ride. The absence of a ride today, however, was better than alright. She could not imagine having to face Mack and the eyes that she knew would hold nothing but coldness and a well-deserved resignation. In fact, she would not go riding at all this weekend she now decided. She'd call Carmen and they'd go to the beach together, go for a long walk, maybe even go to a spa at some point later in the day. Her heart lifted a little just thinking about having a little sister hang-out time, something they never really got to do anymore.

Carmen was making her coffee, humming quietly and thinking of her weekend ahead, a tiny but harmless frown crossing her mouth. She didn't have any plans, but that was good time to spend working, not to mention going out and finding just the right gown or get-up for the show, a prospect she out-right feared. She was not a shopper, and then thought she'd call Fiona for some tips. Normally Sophia would handle these types of questions, but Fiona had more experience in this arena, and now Carmen felt perfectly comfortable calling her. That settled, she felt better and sat down to breakfast, still in her pajamas. She had learned so much in the past few weeks, and most of it had been good, but that which that had been bad, had been quite bad. She was ever so grateful to Mack for agreeing to be her date at her debut, and she would not tell Garrett. Let him be surprised for a change, unprepared for an occurrence. Let him be the one to have to hide an expression, whatever the expression might be. But then she chided herself—if he was taking someone to her debut, regardless of who it was, he was not there for her, so why would he bat an eye, or have to hide batting an eye? She once again thought back to the way his hands had seemed to linger on her back, the seemingly genuine depth in his eyes when they talked with each other. She shivered a little, but she felt no drop in temperature. She realized, as she bit her toast distractedly, she was lonely, and she knew who could end that loneliness, but it was not to be. She sighed, and thought that at least it would be another good day to paint. She painted misery well.

Mack woke up very early every day, but not this morning. It was 8 O'clock and he'd usually have been up for several hours, making sure the horses were getting tended to for their morning feed. His men had gotten concerned and visited his cottage, but Mack just yelled that he was not feeling well, which would not have been a lie. He'd stormed back to his cottage last night and went straight to drinking the hard stuff, something he never did. In fact, Mack couldn't remember the last time he'd gotten drunk before then, it had been so long. Leave it to a woman. He had left Sophia feeling angry, but more than angry, disappointed. He didn't know if he was disappointed in her or in how she reacted to him. She was always taunting, always with some façade, and it was not something he could very well endure—and then she had backed away from him. That had struck him severely, that she actually thought he could hit her, that he was the type of man that would hit any woman. Granted, they'd only met a handful of times, but there are some things a person should know, should pick up right away. He had left the barn with his sweater, angry at himself for even having thought to lend it to her, when he decided he'd go back and give her the sweater, and plant it in her face, make her eat her silly words, and maybe next time she wouldn't be so quick to send jabs. So he had turned back and began walking in Envy's stall's direction, when he heard the distinct sound of crying. This stopped him dead in his tracks, and froze him for countless moments as he literally did not know what to do. The obvious choice was to turn back and go home. This was not territory he liked, and he also knew he was not a delicate man. He thought of her then, her red hair covering her face as she bent her head and cried, and she could only be crying because he had upset her. What had he said? But he knew the answer to that, and had even remembered purposely putting a look in his eyes so that it would be unmistakable what he thought of her, even though it had only been self-defense, and he was learning more and more every day that Sophia was a woman around whom he could not predict or understand his actions. But it was unmistakable—she was crying, not loudly, but in such a manner she knew she was alone, so he went farther and walked to just the edge of the stall. It was odd, really, because all the horses were quiet, some shuffling, some eating their hay, but it was a silence akin to reverence. Having been around animals all his life, Mack knew they had a type of innate perception, and he guessed they were just respecting the moment as they knew how. Very carefully, he looked around the corner of the stall, and there he saw what he had already pictured in his mind, only the truth was more unforgiving. He almost made a sound that would have meant remorse, but he bit his finger instead to silence himself. It was obvious he didn't know this woman, certainly couldn't predict what she'd say or do, but he did not want to see her cry. There was, of course, nothing he could do. She would not have wanted him to see her like this at all, and by standing there any longer he was infringing on her privacy, so he quietly turned and walked out of the barn, but he did not return to his cottage until he knew she was safely off in her car. When he did get in, he found his whiskey and poured three measures' worth in a tall glass and drank half of it at once, and it just went from there. He did vow to himself that he would try not to lose patience with her in the future. He might not be her friend, but he would not make her cry again.

***

"Fiona?" Garrett asked as soon as he walked into the office.

157

"Hello, Garrett." She said as she came walking out of his office. "How are you today?"

"Fine, fine, you?" He asked quickly, really just getting greetings out of the way.

She looked at him, a mock annoyed expression on her face. "OK, what do you need this early in the morning?" She asked, now with her arms crossed in front of her chest.

"Can you arrange a lunch date with Carmen for tomorrow at Luigi's?" He asked as nonchalantly as possible.

"Tomorrow is Saturday, Garrett." And she walked over to her desk, dismissing him, apparently.

"I know what day it is, but I still need a lunch meeting."

"Why? Everything is taken care of." She said, looking at him not understanding. "I just sewed things up with her yesterday. Measurements, check. Placement plans, check. Background music, check...."Before she could continue Garrett interrupted her.

"I know the basics are all taken care of, and for that I thank you as always, Fiona, but I am not quite done ironing out some last minute details." He said, looking at her in as boss-like a fashion as he could.

Fiona, of course, would have none of it. "What kind of details, I wonder, Garrett, would need taking care of before Monday?" She really was nosy, he decided, and made a mental note to mention that at her performance review.

"You're going to have to leave this one to me, and I don't want to hear anymore about it. Trust me that it's something that needs taking care of promptly" he said, and would not look at her, but strode into his office. He closed his door, but not before he heard Fiona shout.

"You better be nice, whatever you're doing, Garrett."

Fiona was not happy, never was when she was kept in the dark about important things, and getting hold of Carmen on a flipping Saturday was important, as far as she could tell. Not only that, but how would Carmen even agree to it if she couldn't tell her what it was about? Silly man. Obviously, she had to give it a try anyway.

"Hello" Fiona heard Carmen say.

"Hi, Carmen, it's Fiona."

"Oh, Hi." And Fiona heard a smile in her voice, which she returned. "I hope I wasn't disturbing you, but I was hoping I could arrange a meeting at Luigi's with you for tomorrow." She half lied.

"A meeting?" She paused. "I suppose so—is everything going as planned? Did something horrible happen?" And now Fiona heard concern, and fairly so.

"No, everything is absolutely fine—sorry to alarm you, it's just that Garrett has some last minute ironing out to do with you."

There was a long pause. Fiona uncharacteristically tapped her fingers on her desk. "Oh, a meeting with Garrett" Carmen finally stated. "I'm sorry, I thought you meant with you."

There was another pause, which drove Fiona enough to say "But you know what? I'll just tell him you're not free, after all it's Saturday. I'm sorry for even asking you." And she was cursing Garrett all the while.

Carmen had not known what she wanted to do about this turn of events, and couldn't imagine what Garrett wanted to meet for, but now she realized not going might jeopardize Fiona's position, so she quickly said "Saturday is fine, and especially if it's at Luigi's. I loved that place—it might not seem like a meeting at all." Which she sincerely hoped was true, but remained skeptical.

Fiona sighed happily but inaudibly. "I'll arrange a car to get you at eleven, if that's OK" She said.

"Perfect, but there's actually something you could do for me, Fiona."

"Anything." Which she meant.

I know I'm coming off as some kind of bumpkin, but I would really appreciate your help in finding a dress. I don't mean for you to shop with me or anything, but if you could give me a general idea…."

"I'll take you. No problem. I'd be happy to, and don't argue."

Carmen adored the way Fiona had responded, and laughed a little shyly. "Really? That would be so helpful. I'm really at a loss and…"

"We'll go Tuesday, and think nothing of it. Let's make a day of it. We'll go to lunch as soon as we've found the dress that'll knock 'em all dead."

And then they brought the conversation to a close, Fiona delighted she had made Saturday palatable to Carmen, and looking forward to helping her dress for her event, and Carmen happy at least to have the dress shopping out of the way. And then she thought about the next day's appointment, and twitched her mouth. What could he want? Everything was done. But she wouldn't let it weigh on her, because there was no bad news as far as she was concerned that would have outdone his bringing her sister to the show. No more damage could be done to her ego, and it would also give her an opportunity to tell him that she would not be walking into the show with her arm unadorned either.

***

Sophia had dressed in an elegant shin-length, black dress, a turtle neck, but closely fitted all the way, and she wore sleek sandals, and accented her red hair by wearing a blue, green and black scarf as a headband, which she then pulled back with her hair. It was a beautiful effect, and when Garrett opened the door, he bestowed upon her the only reaction she liked best—a few moments of stunned silence followed by a very sincere complement. She felt good, had gotten over her morning blues, and was ready to be more social than she had been the past few days. What was she thinking, going about pretending she wasn't a party girl? She most certainly was, and here was this incredible man to pick her up and help her prove it. Horses, country, fresh air be damned. She'd remind the town who ruled it and why.

When she had opened the door to Garrett, she almost hugged him; it was such a delight to be met with those eyes and those words. "I guess I'm ready if you are" she said.

"Ready?" He said. "I just hope everyone is ready for you." He could not help but notice her lithe figure, made more so by the black dress. She and Carmen were a similar height, but Sophia was maybe the more athletic build of the two, and Carmen the more voluptuous. Either way, he was having a hell of a time taking turns looking at them both, and he was surprised just then that such a thought did not make him rueful. Maybe the days of his guilt, undeserved though they were, were over. Maybe he could at last enjoy his situation for the moment, since he knew it was coming to an end, and would come to an end honestly.

Nick was off for the evening, and on a date, Garrett believed. So tonight, since Victor was also unavailable, they were stuck with Jean. Not so much a problem for Garrett since he had no qualms whatsoever about raising the privacy glass. After introducing Jean to Sophia, he raised it almost immediately, cutting Jean off in mid-sentence.

Sophia said "He was in the middle of saying something, you know" she said, somewhat reproachfully.

"I can lower it if you like, but he's in the middle of saying something all the time." He answered evenly.

Sophia smiled, and said nothing more for a time. She was off in her thoughts, and had to remind herself she was in a lovely stretch car with a handsome man, though Garrett too seemed a little far away. "What's a girl got to do to get a drink around here?" She asked.

"She shouldn't have to do anything. She should have been offered immediately. Sorry, Sophia" he replied, and poured her a glass of champagne.

"Where are we going tonight?"

"Actually, since it's Friday, I was thinking of going into the city for a little more oomph to the night, if you're up for it."

"Let's go. No curfew, no hesitations. I'm yours." She said, but stopped herself short from adding "for the night". She did not know how she wanted the night to end, and she did not want him to believe that he knew.

They spent the evening together in a happy harmony, but more distant than their first date, yet neither of them was uncomfortable. In fact, there was an ease of banter present this time that hadn't been before, and they neither forced conversation nor endured long stretches of silence. Sophia was relaxed, in her element, soaking up the enchantment that New York offered in the daytime, but a thousand-fold at night. She grinned with

161

hidden glee at the attention she got, attention she was used to, but she was far more secluded in Connecticut than in the city lights. As for Garrett, he was proud to have Sophia at his side, but he was accustomed to beautiful women, and he was accustomed at being stared at by everyone. Together they were a stunning couple. Surely they were famous, some would often wonder as they passed them in the streets.

Garrett could have taken her to Luigi's, but he was going there tomorrow with Carmen, and somehow, he did not feel it the best choice for this evening. Luigi's took on a whole other, deeper personality at night, and somehow, he felt this date did not quite deserve a visit there, though he realized he would not have hesitated had he been with Carmen. He felt a bit guilty, as if he were depriving Sophia in a way, but she'd be no one the wiser, and besides, he knew he was making too much about not enough. Instead he ended up taking her to another favorite haunt of his in Little Italy, Bella Notte. It was loud, friendly and spontaneous with song, the sort of place where an entire room might get involved in a conversation, or a play of words with the owner, who went about from room to room, making sure everyone was enjoying themselves to the fullest extent. It was not exceptional cuisine, and the wine was home-made, but the ambiance was hard to beat. Garret felt, and it turned out Sophia agreed, it was the perfect way to spend the night together. They ate happily, talked here and there about nothing in particular, and they even danced to a few haphazard numbers performed by the restaurant's schmaltzy band. Garrett held Sophia closely, but not intimately. The music didn't beg for proximity, but he knew that wasn't really why he maintained a gap between them. As for Sophia, she didn't seem to notice or care how far or near she was to Garrett, but glided on the floor as Garrett led her, smiling at him, but also smiling at the band, and even a few audience members. He came to realize she was a bit of a ham, even if only in the sexiest way. From there on he relaxed, and they both enjoyed the light-hearted steps they took before they finally rested, both of them laughing, sweat at their brows.

Sophia felt in her element, and Garrett was an exceptional lead. She was more used to dancing separately from men, rhythmically to the cool, throbbing sounds of nightclub music, but this was enchanting her, made her laugh. It was easy, maybe not quite as sexy, but a hoot none-the-less. For one fleeting moment in the middle of an Italian-polka like number (was that possible?) Mack's face had appeared in her head. No warnings, no obvious prompts, but there he was, his look stern but not unkind. It skewed her rhythm for an unnoticeable second, but then it skewed her thoughts a bit longer. She couldn't help but quickly wonder if he danced at all—if maybe he was loathe to dance, which was what she concluded at the end of the brief thought she forced out of her mind. She'd not let Mack intrude on her date, and she ignored the sign in her brain saying "too late".

When they were seated they each took a long drink of water, and looked at each other and smiled. "That was fun". Sophia said. "I haven't danced to this kind of music in a while. You're quite a dancer, Garrett."

He nodded a thank you. "You held your own, and then some." He said. "And I think you captured the hearts of most of the men in the room—intentionally I might add". He pretended admonishment. He'd reached a comfortable enough moment in the night, and a self-acknowledgement of what it was all about, that he thought he could tell her he noticed the flirting with other men—and imply that he didn't mind.

Sophia tilted her head to the side, and smiled oddly. "Maybe I did." She softly added "And it doesn't seem to bother you".

"I guess I don't know" He answered nearly honestly.

Sophia could not deny the attraction of this man, but she had somehow come to know tonight that they were not destined for a great romance. She wasn't sure how she had come to that conclusion, but it was obvious, and now it seemed that Garrett's sentiments mirrored her own. Part of her wished right now to go back to her house and spend hours simply enjoying each others' bodies recklessly, passionately, even cruelly, but she didn't think she could do it—unlike her, and she knew it would have been wasteful. Perhaps it was because she really did like him as a man, or because she wanted him to continue to like her even if they were not Romeo and Juliet. She wanted to continue to see him occasionally and have fun. Surely that was acceptable?

But all she said was "Maybe we should end this wonderful night at its peak".

Garrett thought the idea a good one. Maybe New York had been too grand an idea--they were not so young they wanted to go clubbing all night, though he was sure Sophia might have without him. Taking her home, and all that it could mean—should mean so much to him in the face of Sophia, but did not. He should have, would have, been on the verge of ecstatic thought had this date occurred a few weeks ago. Something he did not altogether approve of was barring him from an otherwise exquisite sexual adventure, and even elicited guilt when he pictured her without her black dress. He looked at her across the table, and she was never more beautiful, but he noticed somewhere, deep within her incredible eyes, a sadness, or perhaps a resignation. He knew she, along with him, had enjoyed the night immensely, had reveled at the rare opportunity to frolic, because that's what it really had been, hadn't it? They had frolicked. He could easily envision much more than a frolic in her bed, and it was a tantalizing thought, but only in the scientific sense. At this moment, he knew it would never happen, not only because he wanted to maintain a modicum of decency, but because despite the obvious delight of the act itself, he was not excited by it, a realization that frankly scared him. What was the artist doing to him? What sort of long distance powers did she apparently have?

"I would be honored to take you home, Sophia". He said to her, smiling a scant smile. "Thank you in advance for a really great night. You're something."

Garrett paid the bill and summoned Jean, who had been there waiting, sure they'd be going elsewhere. He guided Sophia gently with his arm around her, and she was led willingly into the car. They sat back and relaxed, and Garrett gave Jean instruction. He also added a polite dismissal to him, remembering Sophia's earlier scolding.

Once they began the drive, Sophia said "Garrett, I hope you don't mind, but I'd like to get a little tipsy on the ride home". She smiled at him mischievously. "Just a little".

He looked at her, a crooked look of concern on his face. "Why would you want to do that, Sophia?" He could not imagine the answer.

"I feel like it, I guess." She looked down at her hands, a little feigned sadness on her face. "You know as well as I do the things we could do at my house, Garrett. I've thought of it a few times, and it always turns out excellently." She finished her statement by then looking up into his eyes, a rueful smile on her lips.

"But?" He was thankful on one level that Sophia was making this an easy night on him, but of course now that she told him the prospect of fucking was a virtual impossibility, he found himself feeling a shade hasty about his own virtuous conclusions.

"Something ain't there, sugar" She drawled in a southern twang. "I really would like a drink before I continue, though." As she watched him accommodate her request she said "You are, without a doubt, the handsomest man I have ever met, a man I would do everything with, to, and for, but I don't know that we've got it. Don't get me wrong. If we got into my bedroom I know there would be no problem with chemistry, and that we'd not regret the event on any physical level." She took a long sip of the wine he had given her. "But, I don't know. I don't know if I'm going through something, or you're sending odd signals, or what, because trust me, maybe only a month ago I would not have hesitated regardless of what I thought the outcome would be." She looked at him, but didn't seem to be waiting for anything from him.

"Lucky me." He said jokingly, and she laughed.

"Maybe I'm growing up, though I really hope not. But maybe my needs are changing in the natural order of things, if that makes any sense. Like I said, I don't know what I'm thinking from one day to the next these days, but I think I know it'd be smarter and happier for both of us if we just didn't go any further tonight. Possibly ever."

"You are an astounding woman, Sophia." Garrett said with sincerity. She could be so frivolous, and yet she obviously was not. "But why does all this require your getting a little tipsy?" He asked.

When Garrett had said she was astounding it sent Sophia swiftly to another occasion altogether, and a hollowness so treacherous hit her stomach that her hand reached and touched it, soothingly. For a second time that night she thought of Mack's face, though this time it was a colder expression. She felt darkness would overtake her thoughts if she wasn't careful. She forced herself to concentrate, and looked Garrett in the eyes, focusing. She remembered she had a glass of wine, and finished it off right then.

She tried to maintain her casual attitude, and answered him. "Because, Garrett, I am an anomaly. Unlike probably every other woman you know, alcohol does not make me hornier. Just makes me want to drink, so I'd rather do that and stave off my true desire to rip your clothes off." Then she winked at him, and slowly her dark moment passed. "If you would be so kind, I'd like one more glass of wine before we reach my lovely home." She made the request serenely, the first glass starting to do its magic.

"Of course" He said, still looking at her a little oddly, a little amused, but also a bit admiringly.

They spent the rest of the ride chatting, listening to music, and playing cards. Jean pulled up Sophia's driveway, and got out of the car to open their door. Both Garrett and she got out, and as usual, he led her to her door.

"Thank you for a lovely night, Sophia. You are enchanting"

"Mmmm, I know. But so are you." She leaned up to kiss him on his mouth, and he leaned down to meet her. After their lips had gently touched and lingered for a mere second, she pulled away from him and smiled up at him. "You are a gentleman, thankfully, because sometimes I'm no lady."

He smiled back. "That I doubt. But before we say good-bye, may I still assume you'll be my date for your sister's opening?" Originally it had been his intent to perhaps undo the invite if the opportunity presented itself without his being rude, but he had changed his mind. This was a woman he liked and had come to respect, and she happened also to be a lot of fun. He might just need something of that nature on a day he fully expected to be on edge.

"Oh, that's not affected by my ramblings tonight, unless it is to you. I'd love to be your escort. How could I not?"

Garrett reached down, took Sophia's hand and kissed it. "Thank you, and enjoy your sleep."

"I'm regretting my sudden bout of morals already. You better leave." She said ominously, a wicked smile on her lips and irony on her brow. And she backed into her house, waved a bit and closed the door.

Garrett said through the door "It's a bit more than a week away, so I'll call you with the details a week from today if that's OK."

Garrett walked towards the car, filled with a slew of emotions. Happy (though with some trepidation) he was still able to take Sophia to the show, glad that she was wise for them both this evening, and rueful he would not be touching skin—any skin. So what if it would have been for one night? So what? Really, who would have to know? He should feel no guilt if it was consensual, and for God's sake he had no commitment to anyone. He had half a mind to turn around and make her let him in. Despite her claim on the effect of wine on her, he could sweep her up in one moment and let her know what she really wanted. Surely what they both deserved. But he knew he was just lying to himself, and that his need for intimacy was not superficial this time. The thought rendered him surprised, dubious, and ultimately wary of himself. What did it mean when the only reason he wanted to touch a woman was so that the act served as an erasure of what he really wanted? As he got in the car to go home his mind provided the logical, simple answer, but he wasn't really ready to believe it.

***

The following morning Sophia called Carmen up to plan their day of fun she'd been hoping for. Beach time, sun time, walking, and maybe a spa date, and she'd be a new woman. Though truthfully, the night before with Garrett had done wonders for her. It had brought back the self esteem that had been dangerously seeping from her soul of late. Of Mack late. She furrowed her

167

eyebrows crossly, but not today, she thought and forced serenity into her expression.

Carmen answered her phone with a yawn. "Hi Sophia. Little early for you, isn't it?"

"Maybe. But I've got a day planned for us, what do you think?"

"What did you have in mind?"

Sophia excitedly began the description of the ideal sister day together, starting with the seaside, and mentioning all her ideas, but promising nothing was etched anywhere and they could gallivant as they wished.

"That sounds perfect. We haven't done something like that in a while, and....Oh, well I just realized I can't meet you 'til mid afternoon or so. Is that OK?"

"What?" Sophia sounded mildly distressed. "Why not?"

"Well, I have to meet up with Garrett to finalize some details for the show, I guess."

Sophia paused. "Oh." And then "On a Saturday?" Briefly she wondered how he managed his time, and understood he'd never intended to stay at her place if he'd planned a lunch with Carmen the very next day. Would be a little rushed. Unless he would have driven straight to Carmen's from her place? The thought amused her, more so because none of it mattered anymore.

"I know. I asked the same thing, but I only spoke with Fiona."

"Did I tell you I'm going to escort him to your debut?" Sophia asked.

"You did happen to mention it the other night. Not quite soberly, I suppose." Carmen was beginning to feel uncomfortable, and did not want the conversation to continue along these lines. "I'm sure you'll have a great time. Just make sure you're walking around talking me up like you do your antiques."

"Bet on it. So when can you meet up with me?"

"I'll call you when I'm heading out of town, but I can never predict the duration of these things."

Sophia laughed just a little. "OK. I'll have my cell on me." She said, hanging up, and then added "And tell Garrett my dancing muscles are aching from last night, the brute."

"Um, OK...." But the receiver had gone dead.

Carmen was left looking at the receiver, trying to diminish any significance of what Sophia had said, but the scene in her mind, brought to you by Sophia thank you, made her a little dizzy. Dancing. Last night. Obviously, the two of them had gone out the previous night. So it was official. Her sister and Garrett Darrs were dating. She put the receiver down, and walked to her bedroom. It was probably time to start getting ready for her day. True, she had a few hours before 11 a.m., but a long shower was in order. What kind of dancing? It was a private joke, of course, the brute. Where had they gone dancing? Probably something chic, snazzy and over-the-top sexy—made the most sense.

And then Carmen's mind went where only it could—thinking of her sister dancing for Garrett, with Garrett, closely. She was quite a dancer, Carmen knew, not that she even had to be. She was feeling a little queasy, and sat down, but she realized her stomach was empty. Everything was empty.

Chapter 16

Mack was thrilled to have reached Saturday. As far as weeks went, it had not been a very good one, and he was quite ready to kick it in the ass good-bye. He had packed himself one of his favorite sandwiches—tuna-fish on rye with pickles—and put it in his cooler along with some other snacks and a bottle of wine. He really was not a wine drinker, not the biggest fan, but somehow he thought it matched the ocean. He had wasted Friday morning hung-over, and generally miserable, and then he had spent the better part of the day riding. He had worked his men harder than usual, and probably too hard for a Friday. He usually had a few beers waiting for them at the end of the day, but none of them had stuck around to find out if this Friday would be like the others, sensing as they did that this was not a Mack Fordham they felt like socializing with.

He was diligent in his work at the main barn where the Carmine horses resided, arriving at those chores late afternoon. He went from stall to stall, carefully grooming, washing, checking feed, and even treating the saddles to a good shine. The whole thing took him over two hours, and when he was done it was almost dark, and he had seen no one come to ride. He imagined that most were starting their various weekend ventures, and though he didn't want to, he caught himself looking at Envy. Sophia had today broken her vow to ride every day, a vow he knew she had made in the moment because she was being impetuous and ridiculously girlish. But the vow had been broken, and he could not help but wonder if it was because he had broken her. Not more than a week ago such a thought might have made him feel a bit of triumph, taming the likes of a sassy better-than-thou person, but on Saturday it did not make him feel that way. On Saturday he looked at Envy, and very vividly remembered the evening before, the soft but distinct whimpers of a woman undone.

Mack got out of his truck after having parked, and grabbed his cooler from in back. He decided today to park and walk north of his usual spot on the beach, and set out with all his gear. It was a cool day, but not unkindly so, the sun shining brightly, a good breeze jostling the passers-by. He nodded at those he saw, and noted everyone was in good spirits. The country-side could do that to people, he knew from experience, but the ocean was the most effective seductress. People were just at peace. Normally Mack prided himself at being able to pick out personalities when he went out on errands, seeing many different people. He could spot a fuss-pot, a ding-bat, a rude SOB, a truly good human, but not here. Here everyone looked like a truly good human being. The power of sun and water immense was humbling, and ever so divine. Eventually, after having walked a half a mile or so to an area he knew he had not visited, Mack walked towards the sea. Being fall it was not overly crowded, but still populated well enough. It was high tide, so the walk to the water was not long and there was really no wet sand. Finding a suitable spot, he laid down his blanket and then the rest of his belongings.

Mack knew he was still a newcomer, but he was sure his appreciation for just this arena would not change. How could anyone get jaded by this? And then he thought about the incredible cost of beachfront housing and realized maybe he was not alone. There were others with the hearts of poets, those that understood what it was to grasp life passionately, face the spell of it, the brazen untouchability of it, and sometimes, the terror of it. It was moments such as these that changed him, gave him the faith he knew he lacked. True enough, some of that faith would fly out the window when he drove away from here, but when he was oceanside, a positive feeling would almost overwhelm him— a positive feeling towards his fellow men, of all things. Mack smiled to himself in a self deprecating manner. Maybe he needed some lunch.

***

Carmen had taken her long shower, letting the steam warm her, coax her into the day ahead of her. When she had started the

171

water she was fairly sure she would not go to meet Garrett, would tell whichever nimrod was driving her that she would not be getting in the car, that she would call Garrett and tell him she was not up for it, but that she'd see him at the show. As far as she was concerned, there was nothing to go over. Then she had stepped in the shower, let the hot water pelt her body, and stood there for many minutes without moving much, just relishing the searing heat, slowly and excellently erasing all brooding from her body, her mind. She tried to imagine what a real Zen feeling would be like, but then realized it would not include thinking about what the actual moment would feel like. It would just be. She mentally turned the shower into a cleansing, somewhere far off understanding the corniness, and maybe futility of it, but she needed to go through the motions. From calamity she wanted to find correctness, correctness in decision. Was it wiser to call Garret as she had originally decided, or better to meet him in person, feigning a rosy veneer? What would make her stronger, happier, triumphant? What was right?

Was it right for him to be sleeping with her sister? Was it right for him to befriend her so fervently without ever once mentioning that he was sleeping with her sister? And why did he befriend her so adamantly, a surprise visit no less, even after she had signed his blessed papers? What was he doing, what was he doing, what was he doing? But over-thinking was a forte of hers. She was an artist, after all. Maybe he really liked her, liked to hang around and picnic and chit chat and take walks. But he could do that with whomever he was dating. Garrett Darrs was not a man who would have time enough to get close to everyone he thought was good company. It ended up being too much for her to think about, and she had been in the shower for at least a half hour, the skin on her hands looking very wrinkled. She eased the temperature a bit lower to waken her, and spur her to exit and to action.

After having dried off, and treating her body to creams and scents she knew it deserved, Carmen walked to her closet and dug deep. She knew she'd be meeting Sophia at the beach later, and would therefore bring a change of clothes, but for her lunch date it was time to change it up a bit. With not too much detective work

172

she found what she had been looking for—a deep brown satin dress that had a neckline that literally stopped at the waist of the dress. It was not a tight dress, but it did plunge most nicely, and met a large silver belt that wrapped around her small waist. It was a dress that ended just above the knee, and a dress that had always done her well. She was not dressing for Garrett, but for the date she would tell him she had following their "business" meeting. It was time for her to start sleeping around, time to stop being the wall-flower available at the drop of the hat for an impromptu lunch or a Saturday meeting. She smiled as she looked at it, because she knew what she looked like in it, and giggle she almost did.

She took her time getting ready, sometimes thinking about how she'd tell Garret about her date, or the fact she'd be bringing that date (or maybe a different date?) to her show. True enough, he'd be in his element at Luigi's, being fawned over by the entire staff if she remembered correctly, but it didn't matter. The dress would be her first devastating move, in that it would keep him distracted. Even if he was not after her in that sense, she happily knew that her cleavage still had its power. She would make sure she led the conversation, and not let him guide them into any pleasant discourse. She laughed at that—avoid pleasant discourse would she? This is what it had come to, and this is what it had had to come to. Pre-emptive Carmen was long over-due, and though she was not a woman that wished for guises or masks of any sort, and really Garrett had led her to believe she needed no such pretenses, she had now been forced. She and Sophia had as yet never had an intimate conversation about Sophia's relationship with Garrett, but enough had been revealed. And by Garrett, enough had been hidden.

So be it. She would wear her brown satin armor to help protect herself, and she would speak some words to imply a different story of herself, but none of it would be borne of malice. She marveled in advance at the meeting, at her hopefully well-timed, well-postured responses, and couldn't help but think some of it would have to be robotic. Carmen, the artist! Carmen, who just a week ago had been ecstatic at the prospect of having her work displayed to the public, now cared more about the gallery owner and what he thought of her, not so much her art. She thought this made her pathetic. She thought this made her the opposite of an artist. She thought and she thought until she could think no more. She had been sitting on her bed, contemplating still the day ahead of her, and when she looked at her clock she at the same time heard the arriving of a vehicle on her driveway. As always, the long, black car was on time. She stood, glanced again at her full-length mirror, and smiled at her reflection. But this time, it was a smile less gleefully haughty, less domineering. She heard the driver get out and close his door, obviously headed towards her door to summon her. She pulled breath into her lungs, doing her own sort of summoning for her confidence, with the full knowledge that it was she who should own this particular day, and such a call did not go unanswered. Carmen kept that smile on her face, and she walked towards her door knowing it was about to be knocked upon, and she claimed herself as ready, and swore that by the time she got to Luigi's she would be.

**

Mack had eaten his sandwich in relative peace, save the seagulls, but he didn't really even resent them. He'd slowly had his lunch and a glass of wine while reading a book he'd been working on just as slowly. The tide had begun to go out, and the breeze had subsided just a bit. He looked up from his book and gazed at the beachgoers. Some were doing what he was, though usually paired up; some were flying kites or throwing Frisbees, and a few were even boogie boarding. Couples were walking, most of them notably holding hands, either simply walking or involved in what must surely be a good conversation. What would he talk about if he were talking with a woman, or if he had a date on the beach right now? He found the thought an intrusion. He was not with a woman right now, was much happier because he was not, and having to converse with a woman right now did not seem an attractive picture. It would not be an easy endeavor, he knew, because he'd done it many times before.

He would not mind, however, lying his head on someone's stomach while being read to, or possibly holding a hand of someone who was paying attention to him even if he was being silent. What about a glance? What about all that could be exchanged in just a solemn look? OK, exchanged in one of sheer happiness? The only meaningful glances he'd had of late were those with his men at Twilight in reference to the greatness of the end of a day, or the riding of a beautiful horse—if you could call any of that meaningful. What had happened to him? What essential ingredient was he missing to help him enjoy life more— he appreciated life, that was not the question—but did he enjoy it enough? Was not at least half of the enjoyment of life sharing that feeling with one other or more? He was starting to get introspective, a common occurrence with him, but he tended usually to rid his mind of such thoughts when at the beach. He reached for the bottle of wine and poured himself a new glass.

What an exquisite wine he had purchased, he decided. True, he was no connoisseur, but he knew that, so wisely asked the advice of the shop's owner, a man very well versed in grapes all over the world. This was a 1986 Cabernet that had just the perfect weight, and a dramatic beginning, middle and finish. Take that unschooled opinion and shove it, he thought. A smile crossed his face, and he scanned the beach anew, determined to abstain from questioning the way he lived.

Which is when he saw Sophia. And how could he not have seen her before? He stopped mid-sip to stare at her, watch her movements she thought were unobserved, or at least unobserved by him. This brought him to fuller attention. She was flying a kite, or trying to, and he did not see anyone immediately around trying to help her. He quickly looked around at surrounding blankets, attempting to find any man that might be interested in her actions. But that was stupid. She was a stunning woman, again did not appear to be wearing enough for the weather, and there were quite a few men watching her, she oblivious to her beached audience. There was no man coming to her rescue, because rescue she needed if she wanted to fly the blue kite she was throwing at the sky, and this somehow made him satisfied, which then quite soon made him disgusted. He watched her some more, now quite relaxed at his advantage, feeling almost criminal at his current abilities to look at her. But he of course discovered nothing new. She had not become some hideous creature in the blazing sun, and was more relaxed herself, enjoying her time in the sun, despite the lack of success with her toy. She smiled most of the time, lighting up her pale face, pushing back her flaming hair as if she thought she could. And even when she did not smile, the expressions were never anything other than amused frowns, curious twists of her eyebrows, mock petulance. Her feet were bare, and she wore very short jean shorts with a loose fitting tee that was some kind of cover-up for a bikini top underneath. Her legs were long, specifically lined in an athletic, yet feminine fashion, and that part of her seemed tanned. Unnaturally? But he didn't think so. As she went about her task, which had started to grow tiresome to watch even to Mack, her body was graceful even if her skill was absent. He then saw her stop, a little out of breath, and begin walking in a particular direction, focused on something. He turned his head to follow her gaze, and saw a boy looking at her, waiting. So that was it. Must be his kite, and sure enough, she reached him and began talking, outlining their dilemma with words and gestures. She also, laughably, made a motion as if to say that the kite might be faulty, and the boy looked like he believed her.

Mack had enough. At the beginning of his discovery of Sophia, he had wanted to stay in the background observing, undiscovered, but now she'd brought a boy into the fecklessness. He took a sip of his wine, put the glass down, and stood. He was unsure how to approach, but his instinct held its own, choosing to get closer to her out of her view. He chose then not to dwell on such a maneuver, not deem it stealthy or unfair, or even survivalist, but just something that seemed better. The nearer he got, the more he began to regret his action. He had, after all, made her cry only just a few days ago. But she didn't know he knew, he chided himself. In fact, if logic were to work itself into the quotient at all, she would be feeling remorse for the way their meeting had gone, so in theory, she'd almost welcome him.

None of these thoughts let him stray from his course, and as he got closer to her and the boy, he heard her laughing, and realized the boy also was laughing with her.

"I'm sorry, Cory. I know I've done this before, and I know the damn thing has flown. Maybe you can go find someone who's already flying a kite and watch them, or ask them what the physics are or something." She said.

Cory had too late noticed Mack come up behind Sophia, though he had been only in the last few seconds watching him close in.

Marveling at his own movements, Mack reached around in front of Sophia to take the kite from her, his inside right arm reaching between her outstretched right arm and her side, the skin of his lower arm touching the skin of hers. It was such a short sensation, just his skin on her very soft skin, but the effect was intense. At the very same moment he physically touched her he said "You're doing this wrong, Sophia", but still his words could not stop her shrieking at his sudden presence. She whirled around to see who had interrupted in such a fashion, Mack's arm dropping in the process. .

When she saw him, he watched her closely. He saw a movie pass through those eyes, but it went so fast he couldn't determine what he had seen. She then said "Mack". She didn't smile, but kept looking at him, and then asked "What are you doing here?"

"The beach isn't yours too, is it?" He asked, and immediately regretted it, but she only looked down and said nothing.

"I'm sorry, Sophia. I didn't mean that how it came out." He said.

Then she did look up at him. "Oh, I think you did, Mack, but that's alright. I may have deserved it once." She was looking at him deeply, and seemed to want to add something, but Mack wanted to lighten the moment quickly. He could not bear to ruin either of their days.

"Why don't you let me show you?" He asked.

"Have you done this before the right way?" Asked the boy, Cory.

Mack looked over at him, not minding at all the presence of the youth. "Not on the beach, but all the time in wide open fields, and the principle's the same, Cory."

177

Sophia looked at Mack, and he could see in her eyes the recognition that he'd heard at least some of her exchange with the boy.

"OK, Mack. Why don't you show us how it's done." She reached towards him, as if to hand him the kite, but Mack shook his head.

"I'll show you, but it's still you that has to learn. Turn around" He ordered, and she did so. Mack got closer to her and brought his arms around her, then grasped a hold of her arms. He said softly down to her "It's just the wind you want to harness."

Sophia realized that was not true at all, and she had also lost her concentration. There was a large man with his arms encircling her, his hands holding her arms, and the man was Mack. Only two minutes ago she could not have imagined anything of the sort happening, and now that it was two minutes later she was not sure she still could. He was very close to her, and she could feel the warmth of his body through her thin T-shirt, and one of his thighs was brushing against the back of her right thigh. The beauty of his strength behind her was making it particularly hard to focus on the goal at hand. If Mack sensed her ineptness he said nothing, merely continued to hold her arms and speak in a gentle, guiding fashion. She was unaccustomed to this Mack Fordham, and found it fascinating, alluring.

What devastation! She was falling for this brute of a man, and, if she was honest with herself, had probably started falling for him at one of their first meetings. Maybe that was why her evenings with Garrett had been a bit muted, a bit dimmed. Maybe that explained how a man as smashingly good-looking as Garrett Darrs couldn't keep her concentration. Stupid, stupid, stupid to fall for a man that loathed her, but typical she supposed. She was astounded she could think so logically with Mack holding her, and now his hands had moved up her arms from behind her, and she was immediately distressed that perhaps he had determined she knew what she was doing enough to let go of her. She did not want to lose his touch just yet. She wanted to extend this moment for as long as possible, to extend the illusion just now that maybe he did not dislike her so much because he was being helpful, and he did sound kind.

Mack was not entirely himself either, and he was beginning to find it harder to justify his hold onto Sophia since things seemed to be going just a little smoother. Her skin was soft, and holding her arms made him recognize the frailty of a woman, at least physically, and at least next to him. He knew Sophia was the opposite of frail, but touching her taunted his thoughts, made him think of her in other ways, in his arms, but turned around.

His wits were keen on that beach day, because he moved his hands to her waist while at the same time saying "OK, you're getting better, but the wind is strong. I'll just guide you until I know you can stand up to it." He smiled a little at his ingenuity, but was too distracted by the feel of her skin beneath her T-shirt, the thinness of her waist, and the promise of the curvature of her hips. This was a "G" moment he reminded himself, and there were many people around, most notably Cory, but to revel in one's own thoughts was neither sinful nor visible.

"I think it actually might be a little too gusty out here for me" Sophia said, hoping still for her extension, but the fact was, the kite was soaring fairly high at this point, and her arms were starting to give in. She realized then that Cory might want to take over. She raised her voice a bit. "Cory, you want to try it now?"

Cory looked as though he thought it was about time he got his kite back and got close enough for Sophia to hand it to him. Mack let go of Sophia and helped Cory take hold. "You sure you got it?" Mack asked.

Cory looked at him with half an attempt at frustration and said "Of course I do. Thanks." He then looked at Sophia, an obvious soft spot for his red-headed rescuer, and said "Thanks Sophia".

She smiled at him. "Have fun, Cory". Then she turned to Mack, finally face to face, and she said "Thanks. I needed that help. Poor kid was a goner with the likes of me."

Mack smiled a little at that, and said "No problem. I've always liked flying kites".

The moment was approaching the uncomfortable for both of them because now there might be nothing, and neither knew how to continue without being the first one to make the request, something they were both averse to.

"I have a bit of wine over there," Mack said pointing to his blanket "if you'd like to join me." And then he quickly added "It's fine if you don't, though—up to you." He was looking at her, but not looking at her, willing this moment to pass regardless of her answer. He felt weak for asking, but couldn't quite fairly let her go without the question.

"Truthfully, it's hard for me to turn down a glass of wine, even though I should really be offering you since you helped me out, but sure I'll have a glass if you don't mind."

He started to put his arm out, as if to take her hand and guide her to where he had been sitting, but then drew it away and tried to turn it into a forward looking gesture, saying "Just over there. Follow me."

Sophia smiled inwardly, because she had seen what Mack had almost done. She smiled because she was glad he apparently thought she was OK enough to want to assist in that respect, and she smiled because he didn't quite have the guts to pull it off, for whatever reason. She obviously had some effect on the man, but deciphering just what it was wouldn't be easy.

They reached his camp, and he motioned for her to sit. "Sorry, it's not a little more plush, but I wasn't expecting anyone".

"It's fine. It's the beach. No matter how plush your stuff, you'll still find sand in your pants when you get home". She said, and then laughed a little at her own joke.

Mack laughed a little too as he poured her a glass, and Sophia realized it was the first time she'd heard it, and how pleasant, how rejuvenating it was to hear. She voiced her thoughts. "That's the first time I've ever heard you laugh." She looked at him, and she saw his features grow more serious, but wouldn't let that stop her. "What a great sound it is." His features didn't change, and he looked at her.

"You know, Sophia, I'm not without humor. Maybe until now circumstances haven't allowed it."

"I find it hard to believe that you're a laugh a minute type of person—not that that's a bad thing. I am merely telling a simple truth. From my perspective. I know you might be tempted, but please don't take it as an insult." She took a sip of her wine. "This is very good".

"Thanks. I'm trying to learn about the stuff. The owner of Casks has been teaching me some things, and selling me some wine—and not actually trying to rob me." Mack sat down next to Sophia, not having an option of sitting anywhere else because of his belongings.

Sophia refrained from telling him she thought he must have a bad impression of people until they proved innocent. The conversation was for once headed in a pleasant enough direction, and she was glad to be sitting here on the beach next to him. "Casks is a good place." She paused and then said "Do you mind if I lie back a little and get some sun?"

"Of course not. I can get back to my book. You must be tired from your battle with the kite."

She looked up at him, not knowing what his expression would be, but he just had a little well-meaning smirk.

"Night, night handsome" She said and closed her eyes.

Sophia wasn't all that comfortable physically, having nothing to really rest her head on, but she was simply ecstatic. She let a smile cross her lips since she didn't think Mack would be looking at her now. Something about him, more than just his physical strength, made her feel safe, and it was the safety she suspected many women wished for, wrote about, envied, and it was a safety she hadn't felt before. Not only that, but for the first time she had witnessed kindness that she knew was not forced, and sensed that maybe he had eased up on his dubious opinion of her. She let the smell of the ocean calm her further, and the breezes lull her, and it was not long before Sophia was truly asleep.

***

Carmen had spent the ride into the city mostly reading, enjoying a glass of wine from the car's bar. She was not using the alcohol as a crutch, but as it was intended—as a drink of enjoyment, as a celebratory concoction at her willful confidence. The distance between her home and the restaurant had diminished, but her self-regard had not. Even while she'd been reading she'd been smiling a gentle smile. It was her turn, and regardless of what Garrett had in store for today's meeting, she would walk out of there the victor. She refused to mull over just what she'd be the victor of right now, but there was electricity in the air. She felt the city welcome her as they drove in, and she felt every bit as glamorous as she looked.

Garrett as usual was first to arrive, having done so almost a half hour prior to Carmen's arrival. It had been a half hour well spent, slowly but appreciatively sipping at a scotch, going over a few times in his mind how he'd tell Carmen about Sophia, how he'd explain the situation without divulging his feelings for Carmen—that it was she who he'd rather be seeing, that in fact it was only Carmen's reserved actions that had made him over-think the whole thing. Carmen didn't have to know anything about that. All she had to learn was that he'd be bringing Sophia to the show as a friendly escort. With one simple sentence over a well ambianced glass of wine he would erase his guilt, and he could pursue her honestly. He sat at the table almost glibly, very well assured once again of who he was in the world, and thought his recent bouts of regret were almost perverse. At the same time he realized it was a powerfully attractive woman that could prompt such feelings, and it was time to do something about it. He might not tell her how he felt about her, but he'd ask her out, of that he was certain. It was captivating, really. The thought of taking out his artist, the realization that moments such as they had shared just a few days ago could return, and could then grow. He turned and looked at his favorite across the room, and with an audacious hit of ego thought about asking her to repeat that painting for his own collection once she had fallen under his spell. Just a day ago he would have thought "if she would fall under my spell", but such is the way of the human heart and the human mind. He could get used to the absurd if it felt this good.

Daphne approached him, and he knew what that meant, since his glass was far from empty.

"Garrett, your lunch date has arrived" She said with a large and meaningful smile on her face.

"Thank you, as usual Daphne, for the notice." He said, and she left quickly for him. He put a smile on his face without effort because all he felt like doing was smiling. He didn't have much time to think about what she'd be wearing, because quite out of nowhere another charming creature was walking his way. The mirage that it was not her lasted only for a moment, but it was a moment that stilled him disquietingly.

She looked stunning; without flaw. And as she walked towards him, he watched every movement he could catch, including the beautiful, confident smile on her face, the sway of her hips, and the obvious knowledge on her face that everyone who could was looking at her. He tried to devour her as much as possible, but she'd quite soon have reached the table, even if the moment now passing seemed somehow interminable. Here was Carmen, his artist. But who else was she? Because there was a dash of something additional at play here, and it wasn't just the astonishingly daring brown dress he'd immediately fallen in love with. In every gesture, glance and step was an additional Carmen. That's the only way he could think of to put it.

Carmen loved every long drawn moment she experienced walking towards Garrett, and she was nearly entranced by the fact he couldn't or wouldn't take his eyes off her. It only served to fuel her pride, and her gait felt almost like a female swagger, whatever that was. She tried to return the gaze, but he wasn't really looking into her eyes at all, so her approach was easier. She looked instead at him, this beautiful man, and she knew that this might be one of the best moments she'd yet experienced, that this exceptional male was rendered immobile by her.

"Hello Garrett" Carmen said to him when she got to the table.

He was already standing, and said "You are breath-taking, Carmen". He took her hand in his and brought it to his lips. "I'm sure you noticed I couldn't take my eyes off you."

"Thank you." Her hand was returned to her, and she sat down across from him. Garrett also sat down.

A somewhat long moment, not uncomfortable, but perhaps assessive, passed between them. "There's something different about you" Garret said, breaking the silence.

"Really? Like what?"

"Haven't figured it out yet." He said honestly, and added "But I will."

"I think maybe you seem a little different too." She said, meaning it. There was a measure of something else to the man across from her, and it was nothing she could name, but it made him seem somehow less close. It wasn't that they were close of course, but they had established a very good degree of camaraderie, and she felt it had diminished somehow. His smile was friendly, all his actions were admiring, but something was awry--a fly in the ointment.

"I'm just in an exceptionally good mood today, Carmen." A waiter came over and handed Garrett a new drink and a glass of wine to Carmen. "It's a red I thought you'd enjoy" He said.

Carmen had no issue with items being ordered for her and right now she could use a "celebratory" sip of wine, but she realized coming once again to Luigi's could have been a mistake. Why had she not thought of that? Perhaps the wicked vapors of her recent found ego had erased that knowledge, for here he was in all his glory. Even if he was the true gentleman, and so far as she knew he was, he couldn't help but be self-enhanced by his second home. Before she took a sip she held up her glass.

"To a lovely lunch". She said. "And a mystery lunch at that" She added.

"A what?" Garrett seemed perplexed by the statement.

"Well I've no idea what you'd like to talk about, Garrett, not that I don't of course enjoy your company, but Fiona indicated you wanted to go over some last minute details for the show, and I didn't think we had any. I thought it was all wrapped up. So, a mystery." She explained.

Garrett made a sheepish expression, and Carmen smiled. "Sorry." He said. "Didn't really know how to get you out here, and I didn't want to drop in on you unannounced again."

"Well that day was wonderful, though. You know that, I think." She said, briefly traveling back in time to their shared afternoon.

"It was" he said somewhat ruefully, casting his eyes away. He took a bold drink from his glass, but not so big as to reveal nervousness, because he wasn't at all. In fact, he wanted to draw the moments out, sit back and enjoy their meal, talk as they had done at her house in the garden. In the end, however, his boyish side would take over, he knew. She just looked too beautiful, and he wanted to talk and then enjoy their lunch, clink a few more glasses and basically just be smug looking at each other.

"Well here I am Garrett". She said. "And as I've said I like your company, but I'm not going to let you keep me all to yourself today". There. She'd started the ball rolling, and now her heart was aflutter with anxiety and daring, knowing what she'd be saying, but not how the moments succeeding would unfold.

This sobered Garrett a little, and his totally relaxed demeanor flickered. "Oh?" He mentally kicked himself in the head for stating a surprise. "Oh." He corrected, stupidly. "I'm sorry, Carmen, I've been inconsiderate. Why don't we order." He called the waiter over, and they both ordered and smiled at each other at the prospect of a good meal they'd be sharing, Garret momentarily forgetting Carmen's distracting words.

"So, Carmen" Garrett said after the waiter had gone. "How arrogant of me to assume you wore that amazing dress just to meet me for a business lunch."

Carmen felt her stomach turn. She recalled to herself her mantra for the day, "You are the Victor". The victor in her did not, however, have forthright conviction in her voice or sentiment. As she looked down at her hands picking up her wine, which thankfully didn't shake, she said "Oh, this old thing?" Once spoken, she almost choked on her wine. Really, she thought, that's all she could muster?

Garrett was amused, but decided to prod none-the-less. "Don't be modest, Carmen. You're an artist—you can't afford it." Here Carmen looked at him, a question mark in her eyes. He had sounded a bit flippant. "What I mean is, you do look stunning, heartbreakingly so. I was just curious what lucky bastard you'd be seducing." He smiled at her widely.

The sentence was an odd one, and it dismantled Carmen in several ways. In saying she looked so good as to be seducing someone, he was really saying he didn't think a date was in her plans. "Actually" she said with a little smile and a scheming raise of her eyebrows, "I do have a bit of a date in a few hours, which is why I had to wear this rather date-like dress."

"That's quite a date" Garrett said instinctually and too quickly. Something had been set in motion. He understood that he had strangely been the one to invite it, and wondered if somehow he could undo it, because this was not something he had planned for. At all. This was in fact the opposite of anything he could have planned for, and he knew he had to think quickly, because she had once again, amazingly, spurned his attention. But he would not turn unkind as he had that first day at her home in Connecticut. He suddenly realized it'd been too long since he spoke a short sentence, and thought it would be better to say something. "Well, I'm sure you'll have fun." Brilliant.

Carmen did not feel as satisfied as she thought she would, and she did not like the way their lunch seemed to be heading— unruly waters hard to swim in. "I guess so. I'm not one to date that often, so it's a little nerve-wracking." She searched his features but could see nothing other than a replication of Garrett. She could see he wasn't thrilled with the prospect of her going out with someone, but that's all she could tell. A pall had not so neatly settled.

Garrett made a snorting sound, and Carmen looked at him sharply, for it had not been a kind snort, if there was such a thing. "I know what you mean" He said, and there was little nice in his voice.

"Oh?"

"That dating isn't easy sometimes." He looked at her and smiled, but it was a robotic smile, and Carmen felt cold. What, exactly, was happening here?

A welcome addition to the moment was the waiter, who arrived with their food. Garrett raised his glass. "Cheers to you kid, and I hope you have the afternoon you've been hoping for." He was getting tired thinking about his requirement to carry on as if he was just as happy now as when she'd first arrived, because of course he was not. Some unknown male was ruining his lunch, but he did hope she had a good afternoon. Mostly. And then he wondered how long she'd been seeing the man in question, and surely, with a dress like that, it wasn't a first date. Would there be hands that would pull her dress apart from the front and devour her breasts? He took a large sip of his scotch, this time not caring how large it looked.

Carmen was hungry; a little confused with the mood of their conversation, and was beginning to feel self-conscious in her deep diving dress. But she stoically raised her glass to meet his and said "Thanks Garrett. I'm just hoping I enjoy the show".

"Oh?" He said. "What show is that?" He felt like he might be getting a little drunk, and was thankful of at least that.

"Miss Saigon". She replied. "I know quite a few people who've seen it, so I hope my expectations aren't too high".

Garrett did not answer immediately. He looked at the beauty across from him, took a few moments to absorb her, who she was, her kindness—the genuine article, he realized, and it soothed him. No use being jealous when it wasn't her fault. "I think you're going to love the show" he said with a hint of a smile.

"You alright, Garrett? Ever since I mentioned going out after this you seem like changed company. Is there something you're not telling me?" She was puzzled. He seemed a little up and down.

Garrett looked about them as if troubled. He then looked at her seriously. "I'm sorry, Carmen. Really I am, but it's my natural instinct I guess. When in the company of a beautiful woman, I deem her mine regardless if facts are otherwise, and your plans took the wind out of my sails a little. Forgive my idiotic jealousy."

"Jealousy?" Carmen felt somewhat allayed by his admission, but now dumbfounded at her next remark. She'd been successful in her endeavor to educate him about her date, just more than she expected. "Oh, well I'm yours right now". This could have been a silly comment, so she changed the topic. "How about we talk some more over the chocolate torte they mentioned after we finish this excellent stuff?" For truly her meal was heavenly. It was a veal scaloppini dressed with saffron cream and sliced artichokes perfectly seasoned.

He seemed not to hear. "And it's selfish and ridiculous of me to be jealous anyway. I'm sure you know I've been seeing your enticing sister. Maybe that's the problem—I extend my feelings for her to you a bit, and that's why I act so foolishly."

Garrett was indeed delivering the information to Carmen he'd promised himself he would, just not quite in the fashion he had hoped, plus he was blatantly tainting the truth to hopefully hurt her, but maybe hers were deaf ears. Maybe she did not mind that he and Sophia were an item, had that been the case. Even with his scotch-addled reasoning, he still knew that she would not have appreciated the glib way in which he spoke of her sister. He had a way with being ugly at times, a quality useful occasionally but today decidedly not. But it was not he to blame, after all. It was whoever it was that would later be holding his Carmen. He forced himself to look at her so that he could understand truly how she might feel about what he had said, if she showed anything at all.

And Carmen was in fact not well. Her arms were at her side, and her hands gripped the edge of her bench. Just who was she dining with today? She could be no more saddened about his seeing Sophia than she had been, but the manner in which he had admitted the courtship had been more than blunt. She would not, however, let him see her turmoil. She would not waste all the precious moments that had preceded today's lunch go wasted just because Garrett Darrs had several personalities. He had finally chosen to mention his involvement with Sophia, but it seemed to her he had tried to hurt her with it, something she would not have expected from him. These thoughts had taken place in less than a few seconds, and she braced herself for further conversation.

"Yes, I think Sophia mentioned something to me the other day". She tried to smile lightly, but her face felt taut.

"Did she?" Now he knew, but he also did not know what else to say without giving himself away. He took another drink of his nearly empty scotch and asked "Would you like an after dinner drink? To go along with the chocolate torte? Which, by the way, is a great idea." He knew the answer, but also needed things to say or ask. Nick had better be waiting at the curb to take Carmen home.

But Carmen was having second thoughts about the chocolate, and sharing it with the man across the table. She was pretty sure it would be a better bet to leave sooner than later. "Would you hate me if I changed my mind?" She knew he wouldn't, but she also knew he'd think something of it. "I'm actually a little more full now than I was a few minutes ago. I guess that's digestion for you." She almost laughed at that one, and just a tiny smirk did twist her mouth.

"I could never hate you, Carmen" he stated simply, quietly, and it sounded as if he were talking about something quite different than cake. Then he seemed to shake his head out of an unseen cloud, and said "I'll just get the check so you can start the rest of your day."

Garrett looked around, hoping to find one of the staff quickly, but they'd been watching, and while one person quietly took their plates, Daphne brought over the check, saying only "Thank you, Garrett, Miss Carmine. Have a good afternoon".

"How charming it must be to have everyone at your beck and call." She thought it might have come out a bit more derogatory than she intended, and hoped she wouldn't pay for it.

Garrett, distracted just a second earlier, looked at her and laughed a genuine laugh. "You're sassy for all your demureness. What do you think, Carmen? That I'd arrange a meeting without the advantage?"

Me and my big mouth, she thought, but she did not back down. "A meeting." She paused to add some weight to the words. "You still haven't told me what this was about".

"You're right, but it's nothing really." And for a second Garrett recalled not too long ago when he'd been looking forward to this moment, when he'd utter the same fact, but surrounded by truth instead of what would now be something masked.

It was Carmen's turn to snort. "Nothing, really?" She was now feeling insulted, especially in the face of his new haughtiness. "You scheduled a Saturday meeting with me that's nothing really? Honestly, Garrett." She was exasperated, and she was fairly sure her food was not digesting properly.

Garrett tossed some money on the table next to the check, while thinking to himself that he wished some moments in life were scripted. There was not much more he could say. "I don't mean that, and I'm sorry if I inconvenienced you, but the meeting was really a formality to let you know I'd be bringing Sophia to your opening." He needed to add something more since his guilt was getting the better of him. "I just thought I should tell you in person, and I thought at the same time we could share a bite to eat."

Carmen could not fight against the sincerity she heard in his voice, and softened. "I see. Well thank you for thinking of me in that respect, but you needn't have." She looked back at him, but her veneer was chipping away, and she needed to exit. "Not that it matters, but I'll be bringing along a date as well to carry me through what I'm sure will be a trying evening for a newcomer such as me." She had said none of this in retaliation, but almost in surrender. She'd had enough.

Garrett's heart ached. Despite the rough and tumble of their discourse, he wished to reach across and touch her face, because she was showing her humility, her weakness, and it was rarified beauty. He said sincerely "You'll have more than just one person to lean on, Carmen. Quite a few of us are there for you, and will help you dodge any rare bullet. But you'll see. It'll be magical."

They looked at each other and smiled, and Carmen knew that her eyes looked teary, but she didn't care. He had left his haughty behind and was back to the Garrett she so cared for. She felt better—tired, but better.

Garrett rose and extended his hand to her. "Let me walk you to the car. Nick will take you wherever you need to go."

Carmen took his hand and eased out of her seat, conscious again of her diving neckline. "Thanks."

When they stood, their hands parted, and Garrett automatically put his right hand on her back as she walked towards the door. It was a natural move, and on any other day might have gone unnoticed, but today had not been such a day, and he felt Carmen stiffen. Briefly his hand came off, but then despite his polite upbringing and regular instincts, he put it back, and as they reached the door which was being held open for them, his hand ever so gently pushed into her left side to guide her through. It wasn't much, but it was a modicum of the control he needed. He'd already lost so much.

They crossed the sidewalk to the waiting car, both of them noting Nick deeply buried in the newspaper, and also on a cell phone. They were done with lunch early, so Nick would not be looking for them yet. Before she got in the car, Carmen turned to

Garrett and said "Thank you for lunch, Garrett. I guess I'll see you at the show."

His hand took hold of her wrist and he said "Don't thank me, Carmen, though I do thank you for coming in. Honestly, I'd had a different idea about today." He looked into her eyes as if searching. "But nothing's that predictable, I guess. Anyway, no matter what a jack ass I might be sometimes, know that I hold you in the highest regard, and that has nothing to do with the high regard I already have for your work as an artist."

Carmen wondered then, why did sincerity always have to come at the end of things in a rushed moment, when it was too hard to think of a good answer? "OK, Garrett" was all she could think of to say. She noticed he was still holding her wrist, and she was about to knock on the window of the limousine, but Garrett pulled on her wrist so that she was forced to face him once again, and he had also pulled her closer in the process.

Garrett wasn't entirely sure what he was doing would end up shining a positive light on him, but he was not about to let one more minute go by without kissing the woman he'd been trying to kiss since the first time he saw her. They had each doused the tension, let a calmness set in, so a proper closing could surely be just such a kiss. She was looking at him after he had stopped her from rapping on the window, and he had no time. He leaned down and kissed her gently on her lips, just ever so gently. It was light, almost of no consequence, but slow enough so that the skin of their lips did not want to part right up until it did. In that singular moment, Carmen accepted that unexpected; they both closed their eyes, and a brief and tiny smile danced behind their closed eye-lids. Carmen opened her eyes to look at Garrett who had pulled his head back to look into hers, searching. She was about to gently push herself away from him when she felt Garrett move his other arm around her to pull her in further, press against her back. He knew now he was crossing a line, but he was not ready to let her go. Her lips were so soft, and she had not stepped back, and though it had been a small kiss, she had felt inviting. He believed now a kiss might be all that was required to make everything finally perfect. Hesitation might prove costly, so as he drew her to him he leaned in once again and kissed her harder this

191

time against her lips, and when it did not seem as if she would protest, he began to open her mouth with his tongue.

Carmen was swept up with the feel of Garrett holding her closely, and his strong mouth claiming hers. The kind of passion she felt and felt him feeling was not what she was used to, but it was making her weak, dazed, and utterly tuned to her body. When his tongue parted her lips she did nothing to stop it, welcomed it, kissed him back just as fervently as he was kissing her. She felt his heart beating against her, and just that sensation was ecstasy as lip touched lip, tongue glanced tongue, and as he still held her forcefully close. What had passion been before this? What had passed for a beautiful kiss before was nothing, and part of her wept while the rest of her remained spell-bound with the movements of their mouths together. Somewhere inside her head she knew this had to stop, even though it had been but a few ridiculously short seconds. What was she doing kissing him right now? What was he doing kissing her--when he was sharing similar moments with Sophia? The calamity of thought eroded her enjoyment just enough to bring her to sanity. The arms that had been so inactive against his chest suddenly came to life, and though she loathed the movement as she did it, hated the wrenching away of such sweetness, she pushed against his chest.

Garrett immediately sensed her wish and pulled away from her. He stammered for words "Carmen, I'm sorry, I...."

"Um, it wasn't just you. Sorry, I...."

"But I would do it again." He knew that now was the time to be honest, get it done with.

Carmen's expression changed, or froze. She looked at him startled and a little dismayed. "This was a mistake." She shook her head. "Must have been the wine and the scotch" making excuses for them, ignoring what he said, not wanting to have to confront it just now.

Garrett would not let it go, though he sensed that it might not be easy. He glanced at the driver's seat, but Nick was still deeply embedded in a lively conversation. "Carmen, I'd do it again, because...."

"What?" The unsatisfied passion flowing through her body needed an outlet, and now it seemed she had found it. "Why would you say that, Garrett? I'm not saying I'm any better than you because I was part of that kiss, but you're sleeping with my sister, taking her to the show, and…."

Now it was Garrett's turn to be taken aback. "Carmen, you don't know what you're talking about." He said calmly, trying to rid her of any concerns. "Where did you get that idea? Is that what Sophia told you?" He felt the onset of a headache.

"Oh, Please. She and I don't kiss and tell." She paused to collect her thoughts. "The other day, on your lovely surprise visit, you told me so yourself, well in so many words. Remember? And Sophia said…well never mind what she said. I wasn't really born yesterday, even if I might be a rube in the art world…." Her embarrassment and annoyance was getting the better of her, and now she desperately regretted having kissed him. Was he trying to addle her? What was the strategy? This was getting to be too much for her to think about, and she was ready to get into the confines of the limousine. She looked into his eyes, but saw only a serious expression that told her nothing. "I have to go. As you know, I've got a date."

"Are you going to kiss him like you did me?" Garrett said, turning suddenly cold. He had been amazed at the turn of events, at the fact she felt certain of the nature of his relationship with Sophia. He would have stopped her in the next moment had she not mentioned him. It was OK for her to go around kissing others while involved with someone, but not him. Wasn't really fair fighting as far as he was concerned—might even be considered hypocritical in some circles.

Carmen felt as though she'd been punched in the stomach, and for a second did not respond. She looked at him as though she did not understand, and in fact she did not. "I'm going". She said, whirled around and knocked loudly on the window. Behind her Garrett stood immobile, angry, but also sorry.

Nick was so startled by the knock he dropped his phone, but ignored it when he saw Carmen at the car and the expression on her face. And then the expression on Garrett's face. He unlocked the doors hastily, and Carmen got in. As she did so she heard Garrett say "Carmen, I'm…" before she slammed the door shut.

"Please take me home….I mean please take me to Central Park" She said, realizing she was supposed to be going on a date.

"Yes, Miss Carmine" he said, still ignoring his phone which he believed was mid-conversation on the floor somewhere. He glanced briefly over at Garrett, who just waved him off.

In the back, Carmen was holding onto herself, hugging herself mentally. She just had to wait until they were out of Garrett's sight. She just had to hold on that long. It seemed as if many minutes had elapsed before she could say anything, but when she thought it safe she said "Nick, I've changed my mind. I'm sorry, but I'm not feeling so well. Could you take me home?"

"Of course. And help yourself to the first aid back under the seat just next to you."

"Thanks, Nick." She smiled weakly. "Also, Nick, I'm going to raise the glass and take a nap 'til we get there." She smiled again, and waved good-bye, closing the glass as she did so.

As soon as it was up, Carmen began to cry. She was so tired. She was not used to arguing, to so much tension and then so much passion shared with someone. She couldn't stand how it seemed so easy for Garrett, and she really couldn't stand how mean he could be, even just seconds after having kissed her like she were the most precious woman on earth. How could she face him in a week's time? At least time would pass, which would certainly help, but she would also have to live the days in between wondering, and she had no strength for what her own mind would put her through. She did lie down on the seat then, letting the tears and the gentle roll of the car quell her into an uneasy doze.

On the other side of the glass Nick called his boss, feeling almost like a spy, but loyalty was loyalty.

"She didn't go to Central Park, sir." He said into the phone.

Garrett furrowed his eyebrows. "What?"

"I'm taking her home, sir. She's not feeling well." He paused. "You OK, Mr. Darrs?"

Garrett didn't answer the question. "Get her home safely" was all he said.

"Yes, sir." Said Nick, but Garrett had already hung up.

194

Chapter 17

Sophia heard a man gently saying her name, and she also felt a large hand on her shoulder, softly nudging her.

"Sophia" Mack said a little louder. "Sophia". He had not wanted to wake her, but she'd been asleep for over a half hour. He didn't care if she snoozed for hours, but he wanted to check with her to make sure she had no plans. Last thing he needed was the likes of her wrath if her nap would delay her calendar.

Sophia lazily opened her eyes and looked at Mack, who was hovering over her just a little. His proximity woke her up quickly. "Oh" She said. It now dawned on her she'd been sleeping. On Mack's blanket, no less. Wonders never ceased. As she began to sit herself up, Mack backed away.

"I didn't want to disturb you, but I didn't know if you had to be anywhere." He explained.

"I can't believe I fell asleep." She was still a little sleepy-headed.

"The sun'll do that to you, and so will running around in it". Like she needed to be taught that, he chided himself.

"I'm just meeting my sister here at some point, but nothing pressing. Thanks for thinking of that."

Mack only nodded. "How's your book coming?"

He looked at her as if trying to judge whether or not she really wanted to know, but he said "Boring, really. But I'm only 50 pages into it. I'm a slow reader."

"Me too. She said. "Actually, it's terrible. I don't read much at all anymore."

"What made you stop?" He asked. He didn't understand people that didn't read—so much to miss.

"I graduated college" she said and laughed.

Mack shook his head, as if he should have known but was also a bit amused. "I saved your glass of wine if you want it." He said.

This surprised her. He was extending his invitation to her willfully, and she felt a bit of a glow because of it.

"Yes, thanks, that'd be great." He handed it over to her, and she took a sip. He also handed her some water.

For almost the next hour they sat together, occasionally exchanging thoughts, but more often than not exchanging silence, and Mack was impressed. Not that Sophia could be silent, but that he was not uncomfortable, did not feel as though she were waiting for him to speak. He thought it might be silly, but he believed it was because she had fallen asleep in his presence. Something that simple, that trusting, even if accidental, changed things.

When Sophia was done with her wine, she got up and put it in his cooler, making sure she shook out any remaining droplets first. She wanted to stay, but it was much easier to be the one to leave. "Well, Mr. Fordham, I've got to say, it was an actual pleasure spending beach time with you today." She smiled, and Mack stood to meet her. "Thanks for inviting me over, and thanks for the kite lessons."

He nodded slightly as an answer, and said "I'll see you at Twilight". He couldn't help it then and added "You missed a day".

Sophia's movements froze just a little and she looked askance at the beach. "I did. Way too much business at the shop".

Mack felt a little bad and said "But you can always go riding a few times in one day".

She looked at him, looking relieved and amused. "Wouldn't that just drive you crazy".

"Probably". But he made a forgivable expression, and she walked away.

* * *

When Sophia got back to her space on the beach she checked her phone, but there was nothing. She called Carmen to check on their plans, but only got her voicemail and left her a message. It was unlike Carmen to blow off plans, but she knew she'd had a lunch in the city, and delays happened. Which was a perfect reason for Sophia to do the blowing off. Maybe she could get an hour ride in, and not make it two days in a row that she wasn't riding. It was only 4 O'clock, so she could be with Envy before 5, enough for a short ride. And suddenly it was all she could think of, and she set about packing up her things hurriedly, knowing she did not want to be too conspicuous about it in case Mack was still around.

And what would Mack think about it? If he were even going to be there today? Quite possibly he wouldn't, especially since he thought she'd be out with Carmen. Now she laughed to herself almost giddily. The conceit she had! To assume that Mack's plans would actually be affected by what she did. She was in danger of laughing out loud for no apparent reason to her surrounding beach-goers, the thought of which did nothing to allay the threatening fit. She took a moment to collect herself and realized she didn't care who was at the ranch. She wanted to go riding, and that was all.

Once packed and sorted, she strode towards her car. She looked over to where she knew Mack might be, but he had already left. This didn't surprise her, but she let out a small sigh. How could she feel as though she had missed something if she'd said her good-byes to him? She packed her car and got in, mulling the day over as she did. She really hadn't had that pleasant an afternoon in a long time, and so comfortable. As she drove home to grab a change of clothes she thought about what it might have been like if when Mack had leaned over to wake her he would have kissed her awake instead. What if he'd been looking at her for a little while before he woke her? That was certainly possible. She let her mind go all over the place, and take things where she inevitably took them, but logic did at last bring her home, both literally and figuratively. As she pulled into her driveway she thought she should not let one happy and peaceful afternoon persuade her that everything would be bliss from here on in. It had been a good experience, but she mustn't forget that it'd been preceded by several rather bad occasions, and that he was not a man to be taken for granted so easily. As she ran in to change quickly with clothes strewn over a chair, she countered herself by affirming that neither was she someone you could toss around.

Not Sophia Carmine. She finished dressing, slightly annoyed with the clothing option the mess in her room had provided. She could nowhere find her riding pants, and had donned a long, loose peasant skirt and a close-fitting button down white top. It wasn't the most fashionable, but she doubted anyone else would care. Besides, it'd been a long time since she'd ridden bareback, and tonight she would. She looked in the mirror, and despite her disheveled hair, she looked good, healthy. She smiled, picked up a jacket and ran back out to her car. She thought of his eyes, the very depth of them, the quiet and utter power of them. She shivered just then, not quite convinced the fading of the sun was the cause of it. As she drove the brief ride to Twilight Stables, she thought about the other night in the barn, the last time she'd seen him there, and those were the eyes she'd never forget. Those were the eyes that promised no forgiveness for sins committed, no redemption for failings, but somewhere she knew there was a promise of something else—something benevolent and loyal.

She shook herself to get rid of thoughts so distracting. That night was over, and even if today didn't mean a perfect future, it had done something good for the both of them. She felt confident they had both moved on. She parked her car and walked to the barn. She noticed that it was quiet, which was to be expected for the time and the day, and despite herself she looked in various directions to see if Mack was around, but he was not, and as far as she could tell, his truck was nowhere to be seen either. But she wanted to ride no matter what, right? She smirked a little at that, but still bid hello to Envy politely. No sense sharing her mood swings with an innocent horse.

She made fast work of brushing Envy's mane and putting on her bridle, wanting to get as much of a ride in before sunset as possible. She was not a fan of hurrying pleasure, but she knew she had once again cut it close sunset-wise, and she didn't want to get scolded by Mack or whoever was acting on his behalf upon her return. She smiled as she found a stool to help her mount Envy's bare back. The feel of the horse's close cropped hair against her bare legs was warm and sensual. She gently nudged the animal forward and out of the barn.

It was a beautiful late afternoon, the sun gently teasing the sky with exceptional shades of orange and yellow before it would finally decide to go farther around the earth, taking with it any vestige of color. Just this much more inland, and the breeze was not as strong as it had been on the beach, but still added a cool presence and brought with it the comforting scents of the ranch and other outdoors. She breathed in deeply as she rode, very content and glad she had opted to come out for a ride—no matter what. She thought even in the last week she'd gained some form of lucidity, and even if riding was not the sole contributor, it definitely played a role. It was not a bad resolution she'd made the other day in haste to a man she'd resented right away.

She wondered where Mack was right then, since he had not been at the ranch. He didn't seem that social, but what did she know? He was the hardest person to read she'd ever met, though part of that she knew he forced on those who were trying. The thought crossed her mind that he might have a girlfriend, but she crossed that off the list. Surely a girlfriend would have been with him at the beach. She continued to ride in leisure, sometimes a comfortable canter, and sometimes an all-out gallop, but eventually the waning light was telling her it was time to head in. The ranch was unusually quiet, and she did not want to be caught out too late. She slowed the horse down, wanting to take it easy on the way back, breath in the evening pine. Maybe when she got back to her car Carmen would have called her, and they could do something this evening, still make a sister-date of it—maybe even talk about men.

She had left only a ¼ mile or so of terrain before she'd reach the barn, and she mulled over the evening she was beginning to plan with her sister. It was just then that a noise somewhere behind her and to her left startled her. It was too large a sound to have been a small animal, and it was getting harder to see. She had turned her head sharply when she heard the sound, her immediate peace shattered.

"Hello?" She said as loudly and bravely as she could. She was used to running into riders, of course, but she knew the stable was full, and it was too dark. There was no response, and she immediately dug her heels into Envy's side to let her know it was time to speed up for the last stretch. As she did so she was sure she heard a distinct shaking of brush and a heavy footfall. She wasted no time at all and sped back the remaining distance, hoping she'd be able to scramble to her car and avoid the noise-maker, grooming be damned. Envy would forgive her. "Go, girl, go" she whispered hoarsely. She was not fear-stricken easily, but the more she thought back on what she had heard, the more she thought it odd and threatening.

Once she reached the barn she still cantered all the way to Envy's stall, pulling her up short just shy of the door. She tried to hear if anyone was coming, but her heart was beating so wildly she felt deafened. As she took off the little of Envy's gear, cursing all the while because it seemed she was working so slowly, she glanced behind her shoulders constantly, sure someone was about to abort her mission violently. She briefly wondered if Mack was back from wherever he'd been, but knew she'd no way go look.

It all happened at once, and Sophia's fragility did not help right then. She had left Envy's stall after hanging her gear, and turned to go to her car. And there he was, tall, broad and silent. Sophia screamed piercingly even while part of her knew it was OK. Mack was looking at her with a hint of pity and winced at the sound of her scream. She stalled the end of her scream, her brain kicking in to shut the awful sound, and she began to cry and shake in the process. She didn't care that Mack saw, she cared only that he was there, and that she would surely be safe.

Mack could do nothing but go over to her silently and hold her up, let her cry into his chest. It had been the second time in too few days that he'd made this woman cry, though right this moment he wasn't sure how he'd tell her. They were standing to the side of the entrance of the great barn, and Mack looked around to make sure her emotions were not being shared with others, but he knew everyone had either gone in or gone out carousing. Her heavy breathing and tears subsided, and Sophia pushed against him to let him know it was safe to let her go. She backed up a few feet and looked up at him.

"I think there's someone out there, Mack." She said. "I heard a very strange noise, almost like there was someone lurking in a bush very close by to me, but no one answered me when I called. I don't know if he's still out there. Or it." She was looking at him beseechingly, waiting for him to provide her with a reasonable explanation.

Mack thought he'd never seen a woman more beautiful. Sophia's hair was a windblown mess with an occasional piece of leaf or stick, her face was tanned from the afternoon at the beach, and her eyes were wild, feral. He wished he could keep looking at her without spoiling the moment, which he knew he had to do. "There's no one out there anymore". He said.

She raised her eyebrows in a question. "What?" She said, unsure but sounding a bit relieved. "How do you know? And who was it?"

"It was me out there" was all he said, and looked down before looking up at her again.

Something in her features had changed, but she looked no less wild. "What?" She said quietly, still not understanding.

"I'm sorry, Sophia." He said. "At the time, it seemed like a fun idea—to play a prank on you, so I didn't answer when you said something. It honestly surprised me when I realized I'd really scared you—you're out alone all the time, so I rushed down here as fast as I could when you took off like that."

Sophia looked like she was at a loss, and started to pace a little, but then she rushed him. She began pummeling her fists into his chest, and said "Who the hell do you think you are, Mack? You think it's OK to scare the shit out of someone, a woman, me, at the brink of darkness when there's no one around?" She had begun to cry again in her anger. "You think that's OK? What do you hate about me so much anyway? You make me so angry with your stupid smugness, and your idiotic judgments, and yet you can go around messing with people in any way you deem appropriate." Sophia knew she was talking wildly, maybe going overboard, but she had been scared, and he had been the reason.

Mack understood that it was the fact Sophia had been so scared that she was going on and on, and unfairly at that. He might have made the wrong decision, misjudging her reaction to his antics, but it was an innocent enough action, and he'd

201

apologized. He wouldn't let her continue to hit him so he grabbed hold of her wrists, holding them firmly, and looked down at her.

She looked almost like a teenager, all aspects of her disheveled and unruly, and she was staring at him still angrily, her eyes fierce as ever, but he had silenced her when he grabbed her wrists, which he had not done lightly. "Enough of this" He said sternly, not letting go of her, beginning to enjoy the fact that just a little effort on his part rendered her powerless. The moment allowed him a few extra moments to look at her, dare her to try and fight him, and then he acted on what had been starting in his groin for the last week. He took her wrists and locked them in only one of his hands, using his other hand to grab the back of her head, and pull her mouth to his roughly. Sophia gasped, unable to react as quickly as he'd made the movement. He felt her head push back against his hand in resistance, but he only held on stronger, and bit into her mouth, forced her to kiss him.

Sophia had been thusly caught, and though she made an attempt to free her hands, just his one hand was far too strong. She felt herself giving in to the kiss. It was, after all, what she had wanted. She had not intended it be so hard, and seemingly devoid of any feeling other than the will to conquer, but she had yearned for this moment. And she was not strong enough against even that wish of his, could not ignore his tongue and how much she felt like being devoured whole. When Mack felt Sophia respond, it was the last thing he needed from her, and his hand moved from the back of her head. He could not control himself with her, was uncannily turned into the beast that she had earlier feared. He pulled his face away from her and looked down at her, but still saw the anger in her eyes, though she said nothing. He did not let go of her hands, and instead pulled her aside and against the wall of the barn.

Sophia was entranced, if somewhat scared, because in front of her, ravaging her, was a man she thought she knew, but who seemed someone else. He had begun to kiss her again, no less savagely, and then his right hand went down to her breast and grabbed it, squeezing hard. Sophia let out a cry of pain, hating herself for showing any reaction. She did not want this to end, but didn't want Mack to know that. He did not lessen the assault on

202

her, and she felt dizzy, glad for the wall against which she was held. She was filled with a desire she had never known before, and heard herself cry out again, but knew it was a sound of pleasure.

Mack let her hands go, and pushed himself off her to look at her. She stared at him wantonly, some of the anger gone, all of her defiance intact. He was a man unbound, and used both his hands to force her shirt open. Sophia's eyes rolled back into her head as he again grabbed her breasts through her brazier, and then he captured a nipple through the material with his mouth and sucked on it to the point she again moaned. Mack reached into one of his back pockets, and Sophia vaguely noticed he had a knife. She stared at it, mesmerized, wondering if she should be afraid, and now one of his hands was holding her against the wall, and faster than she'd ever seen anything, he slid the blade under the middle front of her bra and cut clean through it. She took in a sharp breath, and was again glad for the hand that held her. He threw the knife to the ground and pushed the bra to the sides, and looked at what he'd uncovered. Mack fell to his knees and once again took a nipple in his mouth, and used his hands to roughly caress her other breast. With her arms now free, Sophia dared to touch him. Though he seemed almost apart from her, she reached down with one hand and touched his short hair. He did not notice her touch or did not acknowledge it, and moved his mouth to her other breast while the chill of the air tantalized the damp nipple he had just deserted. She moved her hand to slide it down behind his neck and down his back as far as she could reach, made newly aware of the muscle that was this man.

Mack had never felt this hungry, had never tasted skin so delicious, so feminine. He had not ever witnessed such a combination of smoothness and firmness, and doing so now did nothing to put him at bay. Despite the fact he felt Sophia's resistance no longer, he did not feel he had less to command. There was a basal part of him that wanted her to understand this moment was not up to her, that he could take her because he could make her want him to. And now she very much wanted him to, he knew. He explored her belly with his tongue, acutely aware of the skirt she wore, not sure how long he'd be able to stop from

203

ripping it away. His pants had long ago reached too tight, and a guttural sound escaped him, led him to move his mouth where it was naturally drawn. Through the material of her thin skirt he sucked where he knew he would taste her, and then exhaled hot breath against her. He did this several times, and Sophia was lost--began to slide down against the wall as she made sounds of a woman in exquisite pain. Mack moved both of his hands to her hips to steady her and stood as he did so, needing to get on with this, take care of what had begun. He swung Sophia up into his arms without effort and carried her around the side of the barn, as far from any sight as possible, horse or otherwise. He put her down on the ground, almost gently and then stood over her. He stooped and pulled her legs apart with his hands, feeling more resistance than he'd anticipated. He then knelt between them, and leaned down to kiss her mouth again, deeply, passionately, with greed and no remorse.

Sophia felt on the verge of tears once again, but tears caused by the awe of the intensity of feeling inside her, around and all over her. He made her feel as though no matter how much of her he had, he could not get enough. She didn't quite understand how she had gotten to this point, but was sure it had to be part magic that she was almost naked with her legs splayed and shaking. Mack moved from her mouth and bit against her neck with his teeth and tongue, making her cry out and mentally picture a wolf. It had been him in the brush, but it had been an animal. He moved his mouth and gently put his tongue in her ear, and then drew it out. He whispered then to her "I'm going to fuck you now, Sophia". A part of her feinted, but she didn't know if it was more from fear or desire.

The bold, confident words echoed in her mind, and then dared to disturb her growing passion. Her skin, and in fact she was sure all her organs, had been tuned for this moment alone, and despite herself she thought she could feel everything in her body reacting to Mack's body and all its seeking. But the echo of Mack's statement would not cease, and she shook her head visibly, though Mack would not have noticed. How she adored confidence in a man, and how well he was exhibiting the quality! And all the while, her body held captive by this talented madman,

Sophia's mind would not be quelled into quietude. Of course confidence, in the brain of a strong-willed woman, can so easily be twisted into brash assumption, and Sophia, against even her own wishes, was making that translation. She doubted, didn't want, to physically deny him, but she couldn't let him think it was solely up to him either.

Mack could not take anymore kissing, or touching or foreplay, and wanted to give Sophia a last warning in case she was not sure what his intentions were. After he spoke he drew himself up so that he was looking down at her, still on his knees, parting her legs. He pulled the vestiges of her shirt and bra to both sides, wanting to see the beauty of her when he penetrated her, and then he pushed up her skirt roughly, revealing cream-colored nothings. He looked into Sophia's eyes as he reached up to undo his own belt, wanting to lock with her, let her see he was not brutal, just hungry. He couldn't read her, but he thought in addition to desire he saw a hint of a smile. He unfastened it hastily, the metal of the buckle making a meaningful sound. He was unzipping his jeans, and heard Sophia quietly say something that was otherwise very loud.

"I guess you've won." That was all Sophia had been able to come up with, distracted as she was with an otherwise perfect moment, and as she said it she knew it would not be well received. Maybe the words alone could have been ignored, and taken as a sexual invitation, but she could feel her twisted little haughty smile present itself on her face, knew exactly how challenging her expression was, and it was too late.

Mack's hands froze. He stared at the woman lying in front of him, legs wide apart, breasts firm and inviting, and looked back at her. The defiant look was back in her eyes, perhaps it had never left, and she had a smile on her lips that reminded him of a hungry tiger. He felt anger rise up inside him at the thought she'd turn a moment such as this into a contest of wills, as if that was all it had been. He did not unzip or re-zip his jeans, but slung himself low, just above her face. He supported himself above her with one arm, while he deliberately slid his free hand over her bare stomach, and over her underwear, letting it come to rest gently between her legs, his thumb teasing the top of her panties by

205

sliding back and forth, as the rest of his hand applied enough pressure to elicit heavier breathing from her.

He looked directly into her eyes, just inches from her face, and said "I think we both know that's true." He paused, and as he did so one of his fingers began to rub her clitoris slowly through the material. He spoke much more slowly now, still rubbing . "And if I wanted to, I'd take everything and you wouldn't say another word." As soon as he finished talking, he took his hand away and got to his feet. He looked down at her while buckling his pants, difficult now that his erection was back. "I'm sorry I scared you". And when he looked into her eyes she knew he was not referring to outside earlier, and that in fact he was not sorry at all. He turned and walked out the door.

Chapter 18

Carmen woke to Nick's gentle calling from the front of the car. She was surprised she'd been able to sleep, and grew more so when she realized they were parked in her driveway. Nick got out of the car and went to open her door. He extended his hand for her to grab, which she did, still dazed from her nap.

"I can't believe I slept that long". She said as she climbed out of the car.

"You needed the rest, Miss Carmine. Now go inside and make yourself a nice cup of tea and relax."

She smiled at him, appreciating his genuine nature. "Thanks, Nick. And thanks for the lift."

He walked round the car saying "Pleasure's mine, always mine."

She waved, and turned to go inside, feeling no peace within. She had napped, and was perhaps better physically, but she still felt mentally exhausted from her experience with Garrett. She replayed the conversation and events, and tried to determine what had happened, how it had gone awry. She fixed herself the tea that was such a good idea and brought it into her living-room where she melted into her couch. She tried to get it out of her head, but could not. All she kept really going back to was the kiss they had shared. Despite the fact that it had been inappropriate, it had been so exceptional a moment that even now her body tingled at the thought of it. Perhaps the thought of Garrett brought on the guilt induced realization she owed Sophia a call, because her original plans had been to meet her sister at the beach and then out elsewhere. She knew she wasn't up for the beach, and she wasn't really up for much. She desperately could use a sisterly talk right now, but Sophia was the one person with whom she couldn't raise the topic. Even though they'd only been out on a few dates together, because they hadn't spoken much it was difficult for her to gage just where her sister and Garrett did stand. And she'd feel sneaky and unloyal if she snooped with innocent sounding questions that were in fact the opposite of innocent.

She had risen up lazily from her comfortable couch and phoned Sophia, but all she got was her voicemail. It was four in the afternoon and she was likely still at the beach, so she simply left a message telling her she wasn't up for much but to give her a ring when she got to her phone.

She tried to imagine the conversation they would have, because inevitably Sophia would want to talk about her relationship given that they hadn't yet and that today was supposed to be "their" day. What were the chances she'd say something like she wasn't really that into Garrett? That she found him not as attractive as most women did? Carmen laughed out loud in her quiet house as she thought of this. She continued her amusing line of thought, placing odds on what type of woman would look elsewhere if faced with Garrett as a prospect, and decided she'd take no such odds to the casino.

In the end, she knew she was too tired to go out, but would gladly have Sophia over if she felt like visiting, so she changed into her comfy stuff, and went back to her couch. She turned on the TV, and soon enough it distracted her enough so that she relaxed, and even enjoyed some of the inane programming offered.

She was startled when the phone rang and when she looked at the clock it was a bit after 6. "Hello?" She said.

"Hello Carmen, don't hang-up" Garrett said.

There was a silence while Carmen tried to figure out what to say. "Garrett, how can I help you?" Realizing she shouldn't be at home she quickly added "I'm not feeling well."

"Yes, Nick told me. I'm sorry to hear that, and I guess I thought perhaps I might have something to do with it—I—was unreasonable outside the restaurant." He paused, and continued because Carmen was still silent. "Maybe you were right about the scotch". Though he knew otherwise. How he hated apologizing, especially when he wasn't sure he should.

"It's not your fault my body went ill on me today" She lied, but did not want to give him credit. "But it was not the best afternoon in hindsight."

"No" He said, starting to regret the call, but he brought back to mind the fact that she'd never had an afternoon date, yet had felt the need to tell him she did. "Do you want me to pick you up something from the store?" He continued in the same futile vein because he was not good at shutting up once started. "Or maybe some dinner? I could pick up soup".

"That's nice of you Garrett, but Sophia and I are getting together tonight."

This stopped him cold in his intent to smooth things over because he thought it was likely Sophia's fault he was in this predicament. "Oh". And then "Maybe you should have her bring something to you. You don't sound yourself."

"Ah, OK, thanks."

Garrett did not want to have to draw a line in the sand when it came to seeing Carmen again, but it was time to do so. "I guess I won't see you until the show, Carmen".

"I guess not."

"I hope you get better, and please call me if you need anything or have any last minute questions."

"Thanks, Garrett. See you then. Bye." And she hung up, an odd look in her eyes, an odd feel in her stomach that had nothing to do with her earlier queasiness. She wished Sophia would call her, because she decided she might just have to be underhanded in the way she asked questions—if she had to be. Why had Garrett called her? There was no way it was business—the business had been an after-thought. She mulled it over, but in the end could come up with nothing other than a call of a real apology.

By the time 8 O'clock rolled around and Carmen had not heard from her sister, she tried her line again, but still got her voicemail. When she decided to call Sophia's home line she got better luck.

"Hello?" She heard Sophia say quietly.

"Soph? That you?" She knew it wasn't a smart question, but her sister sounded odd. "You OK—you sound funny."

Sophia cleared her throat. "Am I alright?" She said a little louder, and she laughed a strange, hollow laugh. "I'm OK, just tired, worn and beaten." She laughed again, a little more genuinely.

"I guess the beach can do that." Carmen said.

Here Sophia laughed heartily. "The beach". She laughed again. "That's true, Carmen. Oh, you're a riot."

Carmen started to get annoyed. "Well you don't have to make fun of me. What happened?"

"Well I could be like most women and say "men"". She said. "But I'm not most women."

"No, Sophia, you are not." Carmen agreed.

"But today I can in fact say "men"". She sighed heavily, but with an amused sound to it. "Sophia Carmine has finally been found."

"Found out." Carmen corrected, but mentally chided herself because the thought of her having had a row with Garrett was disturbing. And unfortunately elating at the same time. "What happened?"

"Something like a hurricane, I guess. Not really sure, but...."

"Please stop speaking in tongues, Sophia. I have no idea what you're saying."

"Speaking of tongues.." She began and snickered.

"Sophia!"

"Oh, Carmen, thanks for shaking me awake. I've been in a stupor for the past few hours, and only just now realizing it."

Carmen sighed. "Do you want to tell me about it or not?" She asked, not totally keeping the annoyance out of her voice.

"There isn't much to tell". As she lied to her sister, she thought back for what seemed the hundredth time to being trapped by Mack, pawed, man-handled, and yet again she went weak. She forced herself out of the reverie. "I think this fool could be in love." And she laughed again, though there was an uncomfortable sound to it.

Carmen heard herself groan, and put a hand over her mouth. "Wow. That was fast." She said, meaning it, but realized the spell that had been cast on her had taken only just a bit longer.

"Maybe." She agreed, still sounding dazed. "But I wouldn't know. Never been here before."

"Sophia...."

"I know you don't believe it, but you don't really know, now do you? Or at least I didn't know until now, but I don't want to debate it too much. It's already made me humble." And then Sophia said nothing.

Carmen let out a snort before she realized her sister was serious. "I'm sorry, Sophia. Does he know how you feel?"

"He didn't, and he probably doesn't" She said, feeling thankful for at least that success. "You know, Carmen, I'm at least good at reserve." She said.

Carmen could feel a quiver threatening her voice. "What made you realize it today?"

"I think I just admitted it today. I think I might have known it almost the first day I saw him. OK, second."

A tear fell out of Carmen's eye, but she said only "Well I'm sure he feels the same way about you."

Here Sophia laughed with derision. "Don't bet on it."

This startled Carmen. "What do you mean?"

"I think he might actually hate me even while he wants me."

Carmen found the idea disturbing and had the withering experience of picturing Garrett over her sister, doing to her what it was she wished he'd do with her, but she couldn't imagine Garrett hating anyone.

"Don't be ridiculous, Sophia. Or childish. If that's how you feel about him, maybe you should let him know.

"You're being quite defensive, and I can't imagine you know him much more than I do."

"Sorry. Just give it a try. It can't hurt to put yourself out there honestly. I mean, it can hurt, but then at least you know."

For a while they spoke of other things, and then made sure they'd get together for their "date" later in the week, since neither of them was up for an evening this day.

Carmen said "Well, I'll give you a call on Thursday before we go out."

"OK" Sophia agreed.

"And don't be so hard on Garrett. Tell him how you feel."

"Ah…"

"Talk to you later" Carmen said and rang off, eager to return to her couch, because she knew now she would not stop the tears.

Sophia laughed when she'd hung up the phone, and then voided their conversation, almost having thought she should heed her sister's advice. If only Carmen knew.

***

Mack had left Sophia lying beside the barn on the grass, had gone straight to his house, opened the door and then closed it loud enough to be heard, but not so loud as to be interpreted as a slam. He wanted to make sure she got safely to her car, and headed back to the barn breathing heavily, his pants still not fitting him right, his hands still alive with the fresh sensations of having had them all over Sophia, seeking, holding and grabbing as he had not done since high-school it seemed. He was still perplexed, possibly dumb-founded by what had unfolded, and how it had done so. He was not one to be timid around women sexually, but he couldn't recall that kind of urgency or greed. He tried, but his mind would not let him erase the picture of her body against the wall of the barn, her half closed eyes as he had continued the adventure of seeking her skin, more of her scent, more of anything his senses could get hold of. What it was that had driven him was so blatant it was shameful, pedantic, almost rude. He knew it had to do with the anger she often made him feel, the chaos that was within him when his desire to be the gentleman to the lady fought with his wish to shut the lady's mouth.

He reached the back far side of the barn and saw Sophia simply standing in the same spot she had been laying, and she was looking out towards the moon. He tried to hear if she was making any sound but could make nothing out. Her hair wafted slightly behind her in the breeze, and he realized her profile could possibly be more elegant than a straight on shot of her face. At long last she reached up and stretched. She let out a long, satisfied cat-like yawn, and let her arms fall once again to her side. She glanced around, seemed to shrug, and then walked toward her car. Now that she was walking away from him, Mack approached quietly to see if he could learn anything else. She walked lazily, almost haphazardly, and Mack then heard her actually humming.

212

He was somewhat awestruck, a little disturbed, but above all suddenly content. He shook his head, smiled to himself and marveled, not for the first or last time, at the woman that was Sophia. She had her fronts, her various devices, but she was as much an enigma and a beast of passion as he was.

He had gone back to his cottage after her car had departed, and quietly closed the door. He had poured himself a modest dash of whiskey and sat down in his living area, staring blankly at the TV, which was off. One day to another was the way life happened to everyone, and mostly, changes were minimal. The large events of most lives were planned for and expected--going to college, weddings, babies, and even funerals in many cases. But then there were the unexpected deaths—freak accidents, discovered adultery--that flew in the face of what was rote. That had been today, and Mack found it ironic his mind thought of only the morbid to equate his tryst with Sophia. He was a changed man, but he was not a changed man. He had been altered by her in some basic way, but at the same time knew they had been mutually scarred. They were the same. He was missing something in his life, even though he had wished it to be that way, almost wore his loner label as a banner. She just didn't know she was a loner, or at least she had not known it until she had met him. She was utterly, superficially satisfied with life, obviously because of her family, her wealth, and most of all her beauty. She had always gone where she wanted, done what she wanted, and been with whom she wanted, never challenged enough to believe there was anything not within her reach. That kind of innocent power could make the soul listless, eventually lonely. And once she had met him, maybe she recognized who he was—the representation of what she did not have, may not be able to conquer, may in fact be someone who would not let her have anything she deemed hers. And maybe it was that subconscious knowledge, along with his own innate resentment towards those of her background that had caused clashes between them from the onset. Mack was tired of thinking about it, and the whiskey he'd been sipping was making him sleepy. It was too early to go to bed, but he could make preparations just the same.

Chapter 19

The week between Carmen and Garret's street-side fait-mal and Mack and Sophia's entanglement and the day of Carmen's art debut went by slowly, and with a general background headache for all. Each of them had their own reasons for viewing the coming event with trepidation, baseless or not, and each went about the days in between in some sort of trance, likely for the sake of self-preservation.

Even Fiona found it difficult to address Garrett's day-to-day requirements, as he was oddly subdued, and simultaneously demanding. His usual adherence to his office calendar was met with disdain, and outright omission, and the means by which he asked her to fend off clients and suppliers was unprofessional to the extent she had to create her own strategy and write it all down for Garrett to later verify if prompted. She was used to managing, officiating, delegating as required, but having to recover after Garrett's too frequent flubs that week required drawing on an altogether different set of talents which were not quite as well honed.

Fiona did not like to delve into Garrett's personal life, mostly because it scared her, but something was going on. She knew he was going to the debut as Sophia's date, but he had not mentioned her name more than once. She knew for a fact that he'd had a woman over on more than one night, probably Annabelle, because he was so ridiculously awful at hiding it. She knew better than to think that Garrett needed any recognition for having had a romantic rendezvous, but it was hard not to think that way since he would absolutely never come in the next day before ten O'clock, and he was never shaven. His clothing would be almost impeccable, but his hair, though groomed, would always be at a different angle. Did he have them brush it? As some sort of sentimental/kinky ritual? When he came in to work, she'd always have a respectable choice for his breakfast, but he'd eat twice as much, and always say something stupid like "Hungry I guess", and then smile sheepishly. And that's what was doubly amusing—that he felt such that he smiled sheepishly. Most telling was his suddenly diligent work ethic and his almost pathological avoidance of her. What sort of church-like personality must she exude for him to act like she'd send him to the far corners of hell if she knew who he slept with and how often? Frankly, it was offensive and something she'd talk to him about, she resolved, as soon as the week was done with.

But for now she had to concentrate on Garrett, because apart from acting out of sorts, he was not looking well. Each day somehow the circles under his eyes seemed more pronounced, and she was certain he'd never even had any circles to begin with. When she managed to stop him, now and then, and look into his eyes as she spoke to him, she thought he looked strangely haunted. Of course he still laughed and joked some, and strove hard to appear as though this week was just like its 51 brothers, but something else played about at the back of his eyes that she couldn't identify. It was annoying, because he was not giving her all the information. She couldn't do her job properly if she was not given all the data, and he'd always been forthcoming before.

"Garrett, what are you hiding?" She'd asked him one day as he walked by her desk, again not looking her way.

He'd stopped and turned around, and said "Hiding?" A frown played with his eyebrows and mouth. He walked up to her desk, now looking at her. "Why are you asking me that?"

She had not expected him to sound and look so serious. "Don't be so sinister, Garrett. I mean only that you're not yourself this week." She gave him an inquisitive look so that he could not continue to turn the tables on her. "You don't even look like you."

That had seemed to irk him. "What does that mean?"

She got out of her desk and walked around to him. "Have you even looked in the mirror at all? And I don't mean just after your date evenings, I mean in general?"

He had interrupted with a hoarse, but genuine laugh. "Date evening?" He looked at her, daring her to go further. "What do you know about a date evening?" He said pointedly.

Surprisingly, she had heard a challenge in his voice, uncharacteristic for this subject. Sometimes he knew her not at all. "I know, Mr. Darrs" She said, teasing, "that I am being very polite when I call it that". She smiled broadly and wisely enough so that he didn't respond to it.

"OK, Fiona, why don't you tell me what's wrong with my face".

She'd then taken the cue and told him what was awry, and what could be done to mend such darkness in his features, and gave him direction for sleep, healthy eating, and honesty. The last was an attempt to get something out of him, but it fell on deaf ears. They parted, one wiser and one less perturbed, but it was still only a brief respite from the constant battle that Fiona later referred to, not quite fondly, as the "Pre Carmen" week.

Garrett may not have been himself, but it was not for lack of trying. The most recent days hadn't played out as advantageously as most things did for him, and naturally it was unsettling. He was a man who had gotten to where he was by a good deal of nose to the grindstone, but the days when he was truly toiling away were distant enough in the past so that he'd started to get a little lazy—an entitlement, absolutely, by this point—but also a likely cause for finding his moods of late unpleasant. And he was prone to mistakes, or at least actions he never would have taken even months ago. For instance, having asked Carmen into the city on that ugly Saturday for a "business" lunch—absurd. And then calling her later to see how she was doing. It had been enough to ruin the entire weekend, because if she was a thinking woman, and he knew she was, she'd very easily have gleaned too much information from him—that he was sorry for how he'd acted (a perceived weakness), that he was jealous of the man she talked about (pathetic), that he couldn't wait to talk to her only hours after their meeting (catastrophic). The entire situation was disaster, but worse, he could only acknowledge that if she'd made any such assumptions they'd have been correct.

It shouldn't be admitted or stated that Garrett Darrs was falling in love, and it oughtn't be proclaimed that his actions were solely focused on "getting the girl", or that when Annabelle came over to sweeten his nights he pretended she was another, but it must be noted that Garrett was each day less able to convince himself that any of it wasn't true. Fiona was directly right when she had alluded to his affairs, but for the first time he actually felt guilty, which may have partly explained some of the cruelty that accompanied many of his words that week. To Fiona. The Curator. Dave's Catering—didn't really matter, and he found there was nothing he could do, other than hole up in his office.

It was a matter of less than a week from when he would see Carmen walk into the gallery, but what a monstrous amount of time. He knew that Carmen couldn't be serious at all with whoever it was her beau would be, but it was aggravating just the same. He tried to imagine what kind of man had captivated her enough that she asked him to escort her. Generally speaking, artists liked to go solo on such an occasion, unless it was a well worn relationship. It was far more distracting if you had to worry about someone else having a good time, or whether or not you were ignoring them. And this was her first show—there'd be far too much attention on her for her to adequately attend to anyone she'd bring. He had enjoyed that revelation and mentally made a note to task Fiona with tasking Carmen.

There was the additional nerve-twitching fact he'd had to call Finn ,and invite him—not to be avoided considering Finn's involvement in the whole process, even if likely unintentional. He would not tell Carmen about that, because he didn't think it appropriate. Besides, it was more than possible she'd had a conversation with Finn about his contribution, because even if Finn hadn't told her (and he wouldn't have), Carmen would have connected the dots easily enough. She would have thanked him. What else they would have spoken about was not knowledge he could acquire, but it didn't matter. Finn's attendance would likely not skew the success he envisioned for the show.

He had been tempted, so tempted, to lightly ask Finn what his history was with Carmen, but by the end of the conversation he had been unable to do so. He wasn't sure what he feared most— that Finn would say, "Oh, it was just one of those fun romps. You know me, Garrett" a smile and a shrug in his voice—or that he would say it had been an unstoppable love, but one that just somehow didn't make it. He would process both differently, but neither would be comfortable or easy to forgive (unfair though that might be). There was, he knew, the possibility that there was nothing. He simply did not have the courage to find out, and that was that and he had hung up dissatisfied, shoving the nagging to the back of his head.

And then there was Sophia. No matter what, he couldn't help but smile when he thought of her, mostly because it seemed he just relaxed when he thought of how amusing she could be, and that he felt no tension when he was around her. For that reason he was at ease, knowing he wouldn't have to put up any false fronts for her, and he knew there were absolutely no expectations on either of their parts. At least not everything would be fraught with tension. Inconveniently, however, it seemed Sophia hadn't told Carmen what exactly was going on, and he'd spoiled his chances to do the same. The fact he'd kissed Carmen couldn't be easily forgiven if he were still seeing Sophia, obviously.

Such was the nature of Garrett's thoughts the days preceding the show, and so he did not get enough sleep regardless of Fiona's advice. He'd made love to Annabelle two occasions that week, and fervently, desperately, and with almost too much passion. On the Friday before the event he picked up his phone to call her yet again, but this time couldn't do it. Finally, the need to assuage unadmitted loneliness was not as great as the wish to be faithful to what he really wanted. And the need to just be still.

In that fairly short moment during which Garrett put down his phone, a tilt in his universe may have happened, because he relaxed for the rest of the weekend until minutes before the opening. A perhaps unrealized resolution had set in his mind to let things fall as they might, and recover as things went. Sure, he would set the stage properly as he always did, so that no one looked better, was more accommodating or cavalier, but he'd leave the fretting to others. When Sunday morning arrived he looked in the mirror and saw the man he had missed. The edges were gone, the darkness disappeared. He thought of Carmen then, of the extreme pleasure he'd have watching her walk in (and he'd make sure to be there before anyone else), looking at the features if her slightly off-kilter face, and serenity was his. He no longer cared about some escort bringing her in, and he was beginning to forget why he had ever cared. He made an expression of "gimme a break", snorted, and walked away from the mirror.

Carmen knew ahead of time what that precise week had in store for her, so she had made preparations. She had made sure she was fully stocked with art supplies, candles, tea, and she resolved to have soft, beautiful music playing all day long. She spent most of her time in her studio, painting light-hearted scapes, not wanting to tap into anything that would invoke introspection. The other night, after Sophia had told her she was in love with Garrett, she had cried for longer than she cared to admit. It was bizarre to love a man after having known him for only a few weeks, and particularly when that man was loved by her sister. It was also not comforting to think Garrett may well not be in love with Sophia if he had only just kissed her. And she had thought about it to exhaustion, the fact that his kissing her made no sense against who he was, or who he seemed to be. She knew it might be idiotic since she'd known him only just so long, but she was sure Garrett was not a man that would kiss so haphazardly. And even if she was being naïve, it didn't make business sense. He wouldn't put his gallery at stake by offending her or her sister.

Where did that leave her? If she had come to such logical conclusions, what was left? That Sophia was in love with Garrett, who might actually care for her instead? Such thoughts were just as damning to the future, and she tried hard to abandon them, and hated herself for hoping there was truth in any of it, and as the days passed by it became more apparent that "light-hearted" might not be the best description for her artwork.

It was almost the end of the week when, sitting blankly at her easel, she realized she hadn't spoken to Mack since her request to him that he be her companion to her debut. He had no way to get hold of her short of showing up at her door-step, really, so where had her head been? She breathed a sigh of pseudo-relief that he likely had not made other arrangements due to the nature of the life he led, and then she heaved a sigh of guilt for having thought that way. The very next day, first thing in the morning, she had gone to Twilight and sought him out, hoping he hadn't forgotten, or worse, changed his mind. He seemed very independent, and she could have caught him at a weak moment. She had had no success at his door, and strode off towards the main barn, with each step feeling more resigned to a solo entrance. A solo entrance, that if she timed just right, would have the room looking curiously at her, and then appreciatively when they looked at who she was, and realized that she was the one behind the blazing talent on the walls they'd all by then had the chance to glance at.

What a reverie! She was walking quite proudly, not noticing any longer it was on hardened mud she virtually paraded. And just as terrifically as her moment of splendor had begun, it abruptly ended, for she tripped on a haughty, protruding root and fell. The jolt of the fall did much more than remind her of her mission, and her knees were aching as she pushed herself away from the ground. "OWWW" she exclaimed, and began the achy process of getting up. From behind her she heard a voice.

"Carmen?" Mack said, hesitantly.

She was brushing herself off, and spun around. "Oh, hi Mack."

"You OK?" He asked, smiling just slightly.

"Probably. Walking too fast, I guess." She said, hoping her thoughts had not translated into a strange promenade he'd witnessed. She continued. "I was hoping to find you".

He only looked at her, and she had a moment, in the sunlight, to see more of his rugged features. She felt comforted, safe, and fervently wishing he remembered and still agreed to what she'd asked of him.

"I just realized I hadn't spoken to you since last week." She looked at him with a question in her eyes, and went on. "Are you still up for going with me to my debut?"

"Why wouldn't I be?" He asked.

A fair enough question, but still unexpected. "Well, it's not that...I mean...I just wanted to confirm it with you. That's all." She felt a little silly.

"Well I haven't changed my mind." He said, and was looking at her curiously. "Is there something else you want to tell me?"

"Ah, no. Well, I think Garrett is sending a car. Would you mind meeting me at my house?" She asked, feeling younger by the moment.

"I'll be there when you tell me to." He paused, looking around at the fields, and then added "I don't think you want to worry about anything". She thought it a lovely way to put things, and smiled at him.

"I think you're right, Mack." She dusted off a bit more dust from her jeans. "If you could be at my house at one, I'd appreciate it."

"A promise." He said, and they parted.

Mack stood and watched her go, feeling satisfied, but not totally understanding why. He was looking forward to the occasion, but acknowledged it would be foreign to him. He didn't mind mingling with people who were totally different than he was, and was even looking forward to doing a lot of watching, but he sensed his duty that evening would be to help Carmen feel at ease. He felt protective of her, an odd sensation given their almost non-existent past, but he also had a foreboding of the unknown.

It was a fact Sophia would be there, and it was also a fact she didn't know he'd be present, a thought that while not entirely comfortable, held promise for an evening worth wanting. He didn't know much about art, although he knew much about real beauty, and he was positive he'd see much of both. He felt an unaccustomed spasm of glee at the thought of surprising Sophia, and watching her react to the unexpected. Truthfully, he was slightly ashamed at what he deemed a school-kiddish eagerness, but he wouldn't let that stop him from whistling for the rest of the morning.

It was such a hearty whistle that when Sophia arrived that morning to ride, having decided to close her shop for an hour or so, she'd heard it and smiled, thinking somebody was happy to be here. Not that she wasn't happy—far from it. She was not such a fool as to have put herself in the vulnerable and unenviable position of the wishful thinking lass, pining away for a man that wanted nothing to do with her. She knew very well that Mack definitely wanted her around for something. That he wanted her around for more than the evident was another question, but this was not something she planned on worrying about. She would not go away, in case that was what he was hoping for. He'd been

221

angry when they'd parted company, true enough, but his anger would fade far more quickly than her allure, and though she wouldn't change who she was for anyone, there couldn't be anything wrong with backing down on the offense a little, letting him maintain his sense of control. Not that she'd apologize, since technically she hadn't done one thing wrong, had in fact conceded a victory to him, really. At any rate, those were her thoughts of the week. She would keep to her promise of riding every day, and she wouldn't seek him out or arrive when she knew he'd be in the barn, but she'd be visible and happy, just like the unseen whistler.

Other than riding every day, however, she had no plan, and for the first time, she found she wanted one. Once she had something in her sights, patience was soon worn thin, and even though her nights and parts of her days were spent reliving their passionate tryst, it was not enough to sustain her, and too much to endure without the completion she needed, the completion, alas, she had stupidly forfeited. She was able to keep to her plan of not seeking Mack out for the better part of the week, but Sophia was not as lucky as she tended to be, and she didn't see Mack at all, no matter when she showed up. On Friday morning while showering, she at last came up with a simple ruse to have some kind of contact with him, and she made sure she believed it wasn't a feeble one. She grabbed one of her favorite books she'd read on one summer break from school, and brought it with her to the ranch.

She had worn tight, tight cigarette jeans with a crisp white shirt, and had been feeling superbly spiffy until she got to his doorstep. Her body betrayed her, and her stomach twisted into nervous knots, and she was aghast that her mouth was starting to feel dry. Angrily, she knocked on the door. She would not be party to any schoolgirl butterflies because she was not someone who should have to be nervous about talking to anyone, no matter how weak her knees were made by them. Such a thought of passion made Sophia more forgiving as she knocked for a second time, calling on logic to explain the fact it was perfectly acceptable to have a few jitters before seeing a man for the first time after a row, or whatever it had been. But there was no answer, and Sophia frowned. She had been wise enough to bring pen and paper and wrote Mack a note:

Hello Mack:

I found this book while looking for another.
It's one of my favorites--thought you might like it.

Sophia

She stared at it blankly, wondering if it might be pathetic at all. It did at least cast a positive light on her reading habits, which he'd approve of, even if it wasn't true. She took the note and placed it on top of the book she'd brought and put them at the foot of the door. She found a good sized rock and placed it on top, and then she walked off to go riding.

She only once let her mind happen on the weekend's event and going with Garrett. Just a month ago the prospect of going to one of New York's most exclusive art galleries on the arm of possibly the best looking man in the city would have had her hooting. She was looking forward to it, but now mostly because of Carmen, and being able to proudly watch her sister's well-deserved entrance into the art world. Not only that, but she hadn't been privy to all of Carmen's work, and she'd have the opportunity to gaze at it just as everyone else would, and the thought excited her. She was proud and excited for Carmen, but also petrified for her, because she knew her sister. The outward appearance of exotic poise might well have been created by her, but it was not always a good mask for the turmoil within, and the anxiety she thought Carmen might go through that night. Plus she'd been strange of late. She seemed not to talk as much, to grow impatient with her more readily. But maybe it all had something to do with the show. As she rode along on Envy in a thoughtful sort of harmony with nature, she resolved to help ensure the success of Carmen's debut. Maybe that meant fanning her ego constantly before Sunday, or maybe it meant just hanging back. She didn't know, but today they were finally supposed to go out together and have fun, or at least talk more than they'd been able to recently.

Such a conversation would have to yet again be delayed, and this time Carmen was the one stalling behind the scenes. Much as she loved to be with her sister, even though it could be exhausting, this was not the week. She was quite simply not up to the task. The other day when she'd begged off the line crying silently, she'd actually found herself getting angry at Sophia, which was the wrong reaction. It wasn't Sophia's fault she was so light-hearted about falling in love, if in fact she really was. How was she supposed to sit across a table from her and listen to her go on about Garrett? About their future? About, full dread setting in, their sex life or what little of it Sophia would reveal? She knew herself well enough, understood her differences from Sophia enough, to know the likelihood of their luncheon turning into an awful event. She didn't want to burden Sophia with her feelings for Garret. It wasn't and wouldn't be fair, and she didn't want to burden herself with undue emotion when she didn't have to. She would be far better riding her feelings out by avoiding things and people that reminded her of him.

Yes, the show was not to be avoided, and truly she could not totally avoid Garret if she'd be a "regular" of his, but that was all it needed to be, and soon enough she'd decided to get herself out there and actively date, poor soul whoever it was that was next in line. She was pretty sure she'd do a number on him, but that was her process of healing, and healing was demanded by the logic she forced into her heart.

So she had called Sophia's cell when she knew she wouldn't answer it, and had left her a convincing excuse around a creative impulse, so she knew Sophia would probably leave her alone. Sophia would be fine without their little get together. Sophia was always fine.

Chapter 20

The one thing Carmen did do was call on Fiona that Tuesday as they had discussed to go out dress shopping. She had thought of avoiding it, but realized a trip into the city and a day spent chatting with Fiona might prove interesting, and certainly educational. It's true that learning more about the woman who was Garret's right hand assistant might not qualify as her distancing herself from the man, but curiosity is not so easily quelled. Besides, she needed to do something other than hang around her house painting and moping and mulling, and she'd had so much tea and careful snacks, she couldn't handle any more. She was not one for shopping, so the additional set of eyes, especially those as seasoned as Fiona's, would be welcome wisdom.

They met at a coffee shop mid morning, Fiona looking polished and serene, her hair slicked back as Carmen had always seen it, and dark blue frames surrounding eyes she thought seemed bluer. She was so poised and well attired that she'd be intimidating to Carmen if she wasn't so immediately kind, greeting her with a broad smile, and sincere eyes.

"Hi Carmen. You're looking very well." She said.

Carmen felt at ease right away, not that she thought it'd be otherwise. She herself had dressed more casually, but had made an effort to be more metropolitan than she usually did. She didn't mind dressing up to fit the city chic, and was now getting more used to it since she'd come in to New York quite a bit recently. Even at home, she was starting to be a bit more selective when choosing clothing to wear around town.

"Thanks, Fiona. You too, as always." She sat down, and so did Fiona. They each ordered a simple cup of coffee, and chatted about where they'd be headed to get the job done. Carmen wanted nothing to do with setting their path for the day so sat back and listened while Fiona, who seemed to understand her role perfectly, told her what was what. After they were done, they hopped into a cab and headed straight to 5th Avenue, and Carmen iterated her desire to be properly guided as far as her attire. She would of course buy nothing she didn't like, but she wanted to stun the crowd while also somehow pulling off being demure, which in her mind was roughly equated with mystique—a basic necessity for a successful artist. Fiona listened and did not look surprised at all, and seemed to think it would take no time at all.

"But forget the demure business, Carmen." She said with full disapproval. "You don't usually dress demurely, nor should you. Splash. That's what befits you. And don't be too obsessed--it's not as big a deal as you think, Carmen" She said. "The show's a big deal, but what you wear a bit less so. How you comport yourself, not to add stress to what you've already got going on, is more heavily weighted." She continued since she didn't know what to make of Carmen's silence. "I wouldn't even mention this except I'm worried you're going to try for an air you think is right for the moment. Don't do it. Be who you are, and the night will fly and the guests will be eager to praise and spend."

"I can do that" she said confidently, and she was sure she meant it. She was proud of her work, happy that Mack would be there for some kind of support, even if it was just an arm, and she just had an inkling that it might be a dazzling night. She wouldn't deny there'd be an uncomfortable moment or two, but what was that? It was her night, and no one would be trying to take that from her. In the end, everyone she could think of would be trying to make the evening successful.

"Then let's get some shopping done" Fiona said happily. She couldn't explain it, but she was unusually excited—didn't feel like it was just another art show. She could almost sense the stars aligning, and their quickened pace to the next shop almost felt like a dance.

***

Sunday had taken forever to get there, but was large upon arrival. The morning was cool, but not yet as crisp as a November morning could be, and the fact that not all the birds had chosen to quiet down just yet meant that much of nature still made itself heard and lessened the bluntness of landscape without leaves. As Carmen gazed out her window when first she woke, the fact that an easy mist hung about the place, with blue and sun in the vista, led her to believe the day might be tolerable. She rose and met the morning without even reflecting much on what was ahead, maybe as a subconscious protective measure, and cleaned and puttered around her house, almost in a daze, a smile rarely leaving her face.

She was not so stupefied as to let time elapse without preparing herself, however, and when it was just before noon she switched modes to ready herself for what might prove to be one of the most important days of her life. She was extremely calm as she dressed for her debut. The dress she and Fiona had immediately agreed upon together was nothing short of breath-taking; a brilliant ruby red strapless gown that slung low enough in front, but daringly low in back. It was a tight fitting dress that accentuated her breasts and her waist, and then just below the waist the material flowed into a generous skirt that was no longer tight, and reached grandly to the floor, a shade longer in back than in front, almost as if to match the dips above on either side. It made her think of Spanish dancers, and it made her feel incredible. She chose to wear her hair down, and was bold with her make-up, adding black lines above her eyes to go along with her Spanish fantasy. Despite Fiona's warning not to act any differently, she wanted to at least look the part, but was not entirely sure what that was. Regardless, her reflection made her smile, and after accentuating the dress with earrings, a few rings, and a touch of her favorite perfume, she went to her living-room to wait for Mack, almost giddy when she looked outside and saw Nick already waiting with the car.

She was still off tea, and really would have been happy with just popping open a beer, but decided it might make her want another, and that was one direction she would not take. She didn't want to be the drunken artist, at least not as young as she was. She had just finished tasting a sip of the lemon-water she had decided on when she hear a knock at the door. Butterflies back from the prom fluttered against the walls of her stomach and she giggled self-consciously. Where was that calm from two seconds before? She stopped herself mid-stride and took a deep, soothing breath, and resumed her walk to let Mack in. She passed a mirror en route and took a last passing glance, which renewed her sense of pride and even serenity.

She opened the door to almost a stranger, for how different a tuxedo could make a man look when she was accustomed to him in farm clothes. "Mack". She said, suddenly forgetting her manners. His smile reminded her. "Hi—Come on in." Had he always been this height? She leaned back to let him walk by her. She reached mentally for normality and found it as she closed the door.

"You're right on time." He had turned to her and waited for her next direction, but he was still smiling. "You look very handsome—had to catch my breath, there."

"Thanks, Carmen. You look absolutely gorgeous. " Carmen had not given Mack a chance to gawk since she invited him in right away, but now he was left with few options. It was unfair how much beauty resided in the Carmine family. The two of them, Sophia and Carmen, made him think of fire and night respectively--so basic, so intense, and sometimes even overwhelming. She might not have been as beautiful as Sophia, but she was certainly the more striking, and dressed the way she was lent to the effect. He was pretty sure she'd need no help from him tonight.

Carmen could feel Mack's appraisal, and blushed in his presence. What time was it anyway? She then realized that while they both ogled the other she'd been impolite. "Mack, I'm sorry. Can I get you something to drink?"

"That, Miss Car--Carmen would be exactly what I'd like, but I think we should get going. It's just about one now, and your buddy out there in the limo looked a little anxious."

"Oh". Carmen said, startled, even though she shouldn't have been. "Let's go then."

Together they walked out, Carmen going through her belongings mentally, but she didn't need much. Ninety-five percent of the show was her artwork, and that was hopefully already hanging, and the other 5%, judging from Mack's appreciation, would do just fine.

As they went down her walkway, she noticed Nick was standing facing them, not even leaning against the car like he sometimes did, but standing erect. She grinned when she saw his honest reaction to her, and bashfully dropped her head a bit as she walked towards the limousine.

Nick gave a low whistle. He had come to know, and then like Carmen enough that he felt comfortable doing just that. He knew she would not be offended, that he would not be acting out of his station. He knew, in fact, that she did not believe in stations. "I hope you don't mind my saying it, sir," he said, looking at Mack, "but I should have a glass pumpkin for the likes of Miss Carmine. I don't think I've ever seen anyone so beautiful."

"I don't mind the truth" Mack said, and smiled kindly at Nick.

Carmen was very happy, surrounded as she was by handsome, flattering men. "Oh, Nick. You're making me feel like a school girl. Not that you have to stop or anything. A girl likes complements you know" She said, pretending he didn't.

He took her hand as she approached. "I guess I'm the luckiest chauffeur in town tonight, no small feat."

He helped her into the back. As he did so, she remembered the painting. "Oh, Nick, I'm sorry, but I forgot to bring one more thing—it's my last painting. Would you mind getting it for me? It's just leaning against the wall on the inside porch". She said.

"At your service. Make yourself comfortable." He shut the door gently after Mack got in and went on his errand.

She moved to the far side of the seat so that Mack had plenty of room. They looked at each other a little uncomfortably, but not achingly so. "Haven't been in a long car in quite some time" He said, and Carmen noticed that he did not look entirely at ease. She hoped she wasn't forcing him to do something he was really not looking forward to. She must have given away her thoughts because he added "But they're fun enough, and it'll get us there safer, I hope, than I would. I don't drive in the city much" He explained.

She was grateful for this man, and felt a warmth towards him that simply helped maintain her good vibe. "Me either" She said.

She heard Nick open and then shut the trunk. He got in, glanced back at them and nodded dutifully with a grin. They were off.

***

Garrett paced in his apartment. Where the hell was Sophia? Jean had gotten to her house an hour before departure, and that was an hour before he needed to, all of which was an hour earlier than anything…and he stopped there. No use. Stupidly, he did not have her cell number, merely the number of her home/shop, but he dialed Jean, and Jean answered on the fourth ring.

"Yes, Mr. Darrs" he said.

"Where are you Jean? You were supposed to be here 15 minutes ago."

"Yes, sir, that's true, but things got a little tied up at Miss Carmine's house" he said, and Garrett noticed he was trying to convey more in his voice than by words since Sophia must have been with him. At least that was good.

"I see. Well, when do you think you'll get here?"

"Not more than a half hour, I guess." He said.

Garrett was ready to yell, but gripped the side of his desk instead. Very quietly he said "A half hour?"

He paused, but knew Jean would be mostly speechless right now. "Hear me on this, Jean. I don't care what laws you have to break, just get here quickly, and that does not mean half an hour."

"Yes sir" Jean said unhappily, and in the background Garrett heard Sophia laugh lightly, which did not sit at all with him. He had a fleeting temptation to ask Jean to pass her the phone, but Jean had hung up before he could ask. What would he have said? And why was he so agitated? Even if it took Jean a full half hour, they'd be at the gallery in plenty of time. He reached down and grabbed his well chilled scotch and took a deep draw. It was not an ordinary evening ahead of him, he knew. And it would not be an ordinary evening for Carmen, his protégé, his artist, his…his…his. He had to distract himself from thinking too much

230

about Carmen and opted to glance himself over in the mirror in case he'd missed anything, but the reflection revealed no flaws in his attire, and no obvious chink in stance. He had chosen not to wear a tuxedo, but a well tailored dark blue suit, his jacket buttoned, under which he wore a deep red, thin silk turtleneck. His hair was getting too long, but he had done his best to tame it with some hair product Fiona had given him. He was satisfied with what he saw, and continued his walk around his apartment, and then sat down, uncharacteristically, to watch TV. He was far too accustomed to the late arrival of a woman to let it affect him now.

Sophia sat in the back of the car smiling. She had not been late on purpose, such a conclusion would have been unfair, but really what was the big deal? She wasn't debuting. Her glorious sister was the star and would have to be on time, etcetera. The fact that Garrett had sent the car more than an hour early was laughable, ludicrous, impossible. She had resolved to take her time when she realized she did in fact want to see her sister walk into the gallery. She wanted to see the moment, the always romanticized moment, because Carmen wouldn't disappoint. For that realization she was forced to dress more hurriedly, since admittedly she'd been running behind schedule, and she therefore had less time to really go through her dresses, of which she had many. It was mind-numbing really, but she'd had to opt for her blue silk strapless gown again. She had a wonderful cream colored knit that was almost too exceptional to wear, but she'd found an unexplainable stain on the back. It was unfortunate that Garrett had already seen her in the blue, but that hardly mattered anymore. It was just Garrett.

How right she was when she made such assumptions that it mattered not any more what she wore for the likes of Garrett Darrs. She could have been dressed as Queen Victoria or Cleopatra, and he wouldn't have changed his expression of impatience, albeit that she knew he was trying to hide it. She could do nothing other than smile at him with her infamous "forgive me" eyes, the likes of which he as yet was not privy to.

"Sorry for the delay" She said as he greeted her at the car. "I'd try to explain myself, but I bet you're used to the girl story." She added playfully.

"We've got plenty of time". True enough. "Why don't you come up for a drink before we go?" He suggested, and said to Jean before she could reply "Jean, don't go anywhere, please, and if you could go across the street and pick up a tasteful bouquet, I'd appreciate it."

Sophia was a little miffed he hadn't seemed more pleased to see her, but assuaged herself with the thought she'd get to see his apartment, something that piqued her curiosity both personally and professionally.

When they entered he asked her what she'd like to drink, and went off to go get it. She looked around, and felt immediately at home in such understated luxury. He knew how to put together a room. The neatness meant nothing to her, since he'd not be a man without cleaning help, but the bold furniture, against subdued colors was very elegant, and his walls, though not busy, were well decorated with striking art. Not all of it was to her liking, but the effect of stark masculinity in the furniture, and more romantic scenes on the walls was simply beautiful. And somehow still quite homey.

He came back in the room with her wine, which gleamed promisingly in a magnificent crystal glass, and gave it to her, a satisfied look on his face. The anxiety from outside seemed to have vanished. "Feeling better now, Garrett?" She asked, but didn't wait for an answer. "Your apartment is lovely. Better, even, than I expected.

"Thank you, Sophia. You look lovely as well."

"Thanks. Sorry about the repeat dress though, Garrett, but I couldn't find anything else clean enough. Gotta go shopping". She shrugged.

He smiled at her politely, kindly, and she was made keenly aware that if this was going to be the level of responsiveness she could expect, she'd have to seek another companion when they got there. "Gee, Garrett, don't hurt yourself talking too much."

He snapped out of something, and apologized to her. "I'm sorry, Sophia, it's just that I guess I'm preoccupied with the show. I'll make a conscious effort to be better."

"Why would Garrett Darrs be so concerned about just another art show, not that my sister's art is "just" art, but you know what I mean. You do this all the time."

He knew he couldn't answer the question truthfully—that he wondered how Carmen's ride in was going, whether or not she was nervous, that he wished he could guess what color she was wearing so he could better picture her sitting in the limousine, that he wished he could gently whisper one last encouragement into her ear—so he went with easiness. "We had a bit of an attendance mix-up, and two rather important associates of mine will be there, but I usually invite them to separate occasions since they have a notoriously ugly past and don't get along."

Sophia's spirits perked up right away. "Juicy" She said happily.

They proceeded to sip their respective drinks and talk casually, but it wasn't quite as leisurely as Sophia had hoped. No matter how hard he tried, Garrett wanted to get to the gallery, so after a short while they headed out. Jean muttered something to Garrett about the flowers, who thanked him, and they got in the car.

"What a sister I am. I didn't get Carmen anything" Sophia said with dismay.

"They're not for Carmen. Fiona has been the usual angel all week while I've been similar to the opposite." He smirked at a thought that prompted him to say "Besides, I'm not sure Carmen's date would appreciate it. Especially since he likely didn't get her anything". He was convinced this was true.

Sophia was trying to recover herself. It was heaven sent luck she hadn't been drinking anything. Garrett looked at her skeptically.

"Carmen is bringing someone?" She'd had a couple of seconds for recovery, but still her voice was shrill with surprise.

"Don't the two of you talk at all?" It seemed to him as if nothing were conveyed between them. At least nothing that most women considered quite important.

233

It was a question that sounded like it didn't want an answer, Sophia thought, so she said nothing, and sat in her puzzlement, nodding vaguely when Garrett handed her a glass of wine. Odd, really, that Carmen hadn't said anything. Sophia had made sure to call her that morning and wish her well for today. She'd wanted to at least touch base since they never made it out together Thursday night, but the conversation had not been a long one. Bringing a man to her debut. That was something, alright. The day was getting more delicious by the moment.

***

"Nick?" Carmen said loud enough for him to hear. They were just pulling up beside the gallery, and he was pulling to the side.

"Yes, Miss Carmine."

"Would you mind driving around a bit more? I've got a few things I have to go over with Mack before we go in and I don't want to take up too much curb space." She felt silly, making excuses. Fact of the matter is she should have spoken far sooner, but hadn't the courage, and only now, when she realized she had no choice, had she been forced to do something.

"It's your day, Miss Carmine. You don't have to give me any reasons, not that you would anyway." He smiled warmly at her. "I'll just keep driving, not going too far, and when you think you want to pull back, you let me know."

"Thanks, Nick." She hoped Garrett paid him well enough, but quickly determined it was a foolish wish. Garrett was a smart man. He pulled away from the curb, and Carmen looked over at Mack, who was looking at her patiently. She hadn't thought it'd be necessary to involve Mack much more than his accompaniment of her, but she realized it couldn't be. She smiled at him a bit weakly.

"I'm sorry, Mack. I should have said something earlier, but really, I don't even know how to begin with my idiotic request. Well it'll seem idiotic, anyway."

Mack shook his head, as if to shake off such a notion. "I'm willing to bet quite a bit it won't seem idiotic at all, and I

234

wouldn't question it anyway from a woman such as yourself, Carmen. It's true I don't know, but I know enough of you to have made a positive assessment, and generally speaking my assessments are good ones." He knew that lately that hadn't been true, but saying it didn't hurt since he wanted to make Carmen feel at ease. "Just relax and take your time. Like Nick said, it's your day."

Carmen was aware that it was past three, that the doors had been opened, and the show had begun. She tried not to think about that. One nuisance at a time. She took a deep breath and looked at Mack, who looked very much at ease.

"When I originally asked you to come with me I thought that that's all I would need—you by my side—and largely that's true. But what I did not tell you is that in attendance tonight will be a man for whom I have….." She paused, feeling more ridiculous by the moment. "For whom I care about rather a lot." She was looking at Mack expectantly as she spoke, but his expression hadn't changed. She was also hoping he'd guess what she was after and save her the trouble of saying it, but he didn't accommodate.

She glanced around at the city streets through which they were driving, and was grateful for the noise, muted though it was. She couldn't have raised the separation glass, but in no way wanted her humiliation to extend as far as Nick's ears. She continued. "I…ah…need you to act a bit more like a date." His eyes registered s degree of understanding and she rushed on. "Not anything ridiculous, just subtly I guess. I'm not really trying to make him jealous, but need to authenticate something I might have said about our relationship. I mean, it's just that…" She had stopped looking at him and was staring at her hands playing with a seatbelt. "Perhaps an occasional—"

Mack reached over and put one of his hands on hers. "Carmen, please relax. It's OK. I get what you're trying to say, and I would love to help you." He smiled reassuringly at her. "I promise to adore you—with taste—and not over the top—OK?" He wondered what any of this had to do with Sophia, since Carmen had told him not to say anything to her, but held his curiosity in check.

"Thanks, Mack." It was really all she could say, and she sighed heavily, but was still relieved. She'd wanted to tell him more, but decided it would be wiser not to. After a few quiet moments, Mack looking out at the city scenery and Carmen staring fixedly into nowhere thinking about what lay ahead, she said "Thanks for the tour, Nick. I think we can head back." A quick thought made her stall the course just a bit. "But if you could stop at a fairly reputable lounge on the way, that'd be even better." She glanced at Mack, but he was still looking at the sights.

Nick nodded and saluted her gallantly. "You got it Cinderella".

Chapter 21

The waiting game had begun. Garrett, Sophia, Fiona, William, and Finn were all at the gallery, Fiona walking around making sure everything looked perfectly well aligned, the lights at just the right level and dimness--the stage set, William humming softly and looking over each painting with Sophia, Garrett brooding in the middle of it all, occasionally looking at his watch, and Finn mostly silent and looking amused.

"You look freaking nervous" Finn had told his brother when he saw him in the morning.

"Well, I'm not nervous, Finn." He had said, looking a little annoyed. "Energy. The day is just full of it. Not that it helps you got in so late last night"

"Sorry. Really. There's this girl...." And then Garret had tuned him out, only here and there catching spicy pieces of information on the latest heart-throb. Finn fell in love all the time, but it was never a long flame. Fact is, there was always someone else to fall in love with. Today Garrett noticed it was Fiona, but even there Finn realized this love would remain unrequited, so he tried to flirt as subtly as possible (and besides, William was on to him). Garrett marveled that he was so controlled around Fiona, but of course he had not told Finn that he and Sophia were not an item, which may have put him at bay, if only for now. He had come to feel protective of her, and thought it best neither of them really get to know each other. He was not sure who would be the worse for wear, and he was pretty sure he didn't want to find out.

Before Fiona had turned on some good alternative beat music, the atmosphere had been tight, at best. William and Sophia had a way of making things seem light, but Garrett was elsewhere and wouldn't budge from it. Fiona was recklessly nervous, and wished people would get there quickly so she could be distracted. Garrett had made her promise not to call Carmen for any updates on her whereabouts, not that she knew why, but it was something she agreed with. Much better for Carmen to arrive when all the guests were there and had had a chance to look at what she'd done to get them there. None of that logic was assistance, however, when the minutes dragged by. She turned the music up and fixed herself a virgin sparkling tonic. A certain swagger entered her step when she thought she was drinking, and though she was not psychotic enough to fool herself, the glass, the olive stick, it all helped. And the knowledge she'd make a real one later in the evening did no harm.

Eventually the people began to walk in, and a spark hit the air current. Garrett snapped out of it and did what he did very well—made his guests feel comfortable and well liked. It was a skill Fiona appreciated, because she knew from experience she had the opposite effect, so between them they had learned how to navigate the crowd expertly, and as the guests arrived she smiled broadly and let Garrett do the talking. William was always fond of chiming in with an odd, misplaced comment, which was fun, if a little unnerving to watch, but usually she didn't introduce him as her husband. His games might prove far more embarrassing otherwise.

Fiona watched the crowd's reaction to Carmen's paintings, and it was obvious that her work was going over very well. Garrett was being hounded, as was usual, by questions about the artist, and she thought he was managing the task with aplomb, despite the fact she saw him looking at the entry rather often. She was guilty of the same action, but she had a better reason. She needed to bee-line right to Carmen when she did get there to help her and her guest enter without being attacked.

It was almost 45 minutes into the show when Fiona saw Carmen. A low whistle escaped her lips, because Carmen looked absolutely amazing. A fantasy, really. Fiona had been with her when she bought the red number, had also seen it on her, but Carmen had taken on the personality of the dress now, and the effect was show stopping, for slowly but surely the crowd seemed to hush as they noticed the newcomers. When Fiona's eyes were finally able to free themselves from the lock they had on Carmen, she gazed at the man who was on her arm, a tall, striking man with a serious expression, and, she decided, a protective demeanor. Well, good. She'd have an ally. She knew that those who had seen her would not necessarily know Carmen was the artist of the evening, but they'd be half daft not to think so. With that in mind she roused herself and walked quickly to the pair.

"Hello Carmen" Fiona said, just barely edging in front of a couple that seemed intent on introducing themselves. When she said it she realized now everyone would know it was she, but then that was the idea wasn't it? "How beautiful you look". She looked over at Mack, and introduced herself. "I'm Fiona, here to guide the two of you, or at least Carmen, through this throng that I know will soon begin to overwhelm us."

Mack smiled slightly, and nodded his head politely. "Hello Fiona. My name is Mack, and I for one am happy to have you around. Feel free to be just as bossy as you like."

Fiona laughed, liking this man of Carmen's already. "I won't be too "bossy" I hope, but try to stay with me, especially Carmen, obviously."

Carmen, for her part, was alight with pride, delight and fear, but logically she knew she could hold the pose just fine, knew she was holding it now, but did not know how long she could be quite this breathless. She had known people would look at her since they were supposed to. What she had not realized was that they would not stop looking, even if some tried to disguise it. They had only just begun walking in, and she could not be seen by everyone, but those who could see her did not appear to be looking away, so she smiled politely, alluringly she hoped. She could feel her blood as it coursed through her body quickly, neon-lighted, dizzying and electric. No easy evening would this be.

Her gaze fell on Fiona, and she realized she had not yet spoken a word, wondered how long she'd been just dazing. She swallowed in preparation of speech, and if she could have timed the swallow she knew it would have been many seconds long. Maybe someone had put something in her drink. She blinked her eyes, spoke. "Fiona".

Fiona was prepared for the muteness of her client, and took her arm. "Come on, Carmen, you can do it. This is going to be fun."

Mack walked slightly behind them, thinking that the best position for Carmen's entry. He could perform his boyfriend-like duties once this spell-cast audience had quieted down. He couldn't say he felt at home, and never would in such an environment, but even in the short moments they'd been here he thought it much better than expected. Maybe it had something to do with the fact it was Carmen's art hanging on the walls, and soon he'd go take a serious look when there were fewer gawkers, or that he had an expectant feel in his stomach, but the afternoon was downright alive. He could not help but seek the figure of Sophia. Despite himself he was anxious to see what she was wearing, and had the distinct wish to glimpse her before she noticed he was there. The thought was almost delicious, and he swam in the revelation that it came from himself.

Garrett was tall enough to see what was happening, and the sudden change in the volume of the audience was noticeable. He'd been looking towards the entry when he could between the many diversions that his guests provided, but he missed the precise minute when she arrived. He sought her now with an awareness that could have been fever driven, and she was so easy to spot. She was really the only one there.

Carmen had not seen him yet, and he took those precious moments to watch her, absorb her, and his realm of awareness of any thing else diminished dramatically. He did not hear Sophia muttering something funny about David Beuford, and he did not feel the audacious tugging on his right cuff by an also unseen plump matron. He was unaware that the music had switched to Sibelius, a composer he would not have otherwise agreed to because of its darkness, and he did not see Fiona's signal that his introduction should begin shortly. Red and black together, no surprises--explicable beauty, but the red was brilliant and soft against the curves of a woman he thought he was beginning to understand, and the black was her vexing hair worn down with an old-fashioned glamorous sheen. She had a smile on her face, but he was so mesmerized he couldn't tell it was transfixed, and determined it heart-stopping. She had chosen to accentuate her eyes darkly, and somehow this brought out the scar at her eyebrow, and what a tilted beauty she was.

240

His knowledgeable gut prodded him from his dopamine stare, and he looked and found quickly the man who would be with her, the man just behind her, tall and even formidable.

The timing of glances, exchanged looks and realizations was excruciation, and to say that when the eyes of the two tall men first met there was heard the sound of swords clashing would be dramatic, but something in the air shifted enough so that Sophia looked up at Garrett, since she'd been standing next to him, also eager for her sister to arrive, and she casually followed his gaze.

So there it very much was. Mack had seen Garrett before he'd seen Sophia, for the sheer nature of physical structure, and because of the very nature of the man's stance looked at his face, and saw him looking at Carmen in a way that only a fool would misunderstand. Mack looked quickly back at Garrett, keenly aware that this had to be the man, must be the man that Carmen had spoken of. He looked into the man's eyes, and Garrett's eyes were already there, quickly confirming Mack's guess. He then braced himself for an evening of a different mood, and looked away from Garrett for what he was really after.

When Mack's eyes found Sophia, she was already looking at him, a strange expression on her face, mostly strange because she was in the middle of reacting to an uncomfortable scene—that of the man she loved walking in with the sister she loved. She had been standing next to Garrett and chewing on a silly piece of fish when she'd looked up. The man that was a mountain at the ranch was before her in black and white, defining the word of etched. The lighting of the gallery cast additional shadows on his angular, scarred features, and if it would not have been for the music and bustling, the reminders of sanity, she would have been just a bit afraid. He was a beautiful, frightening man, and she had to look away.

Mack had seen most of Sophia's thoughts in her eyes, because she hadn't been prepared enough to hide them, and he hinted to her a smile. Somewhere in the depth of her eyes he had seen a trace of fear, and it made him feel magnificently primal, his thoughts dangerously careening to their night in the barn. She had looked away from him, and he had taken the moment to appreciate her as much as he could in a hasty stare, but he was not

241

disappointed. The brilliance of the blue silk gown against her vibrant red hair was odd, mismatched, stunning. Her tan had faded enough, and the color of the dress so blazing, that she looked pale and haunting. A damsel, he mused, and widened his smile.

Carmen was possibly the last to be aware of the inevitable, but she had more to think about. Fiona had been gently talking to her as they entered, but Carmen didn't know what she'd said. She'd spent her concentration so much on holding herself erect while trying to appear slinky that she'd been unable to hone in on what she really needed to be prepared for—Garrett in front of her and gorgeous. And with Sophia.

When at last Fiona was able to guide her and Mack to Garrett and Sophia, the crowd dropped back some, understanding the importance of artist greeting owner. Mack stepped closer to Carmen and put his hand on her back, aware and enjoying Sophia's fire observation. Carmen felt the gentle touch on her back, and a swell of gratefulness helped her to clarity, or at least reaction. She'd looked at Garrett, acknowledging him, but not into his eyes, and now she did so. The act itself was so simple, but the reception not as much so, and in the darkness of his eyes she didn't know what she saw. She hoped her smile was brave or nonchalant or anything but what it felt like.

Sophia looked at her sister looking at Garrett, and the blood they shared slapped her with facts that made her draw in her breath and stifle a snort. She mentally cursed their missed discussion, but then realized this might be better. At the same time she understood that Mack's accompaniment was nothing more than a new blessing to her evening, although she'd mostly known it anyway. She was now at odds because of the various twist-ups, and was suddenly very conscious of Garrett's arm in hers, and as subtly as she could, she withdrew it, an action keenly noticed by both men. But it would not be so easy, and Garrett casually put his hand on Sophia's back, somewhat ashamed at himself for why he was doing it.

It had only been tiny moments, but Fiona sensed something she could not yet recognize. "Here she is, Garrett", she said, "The

242

star of the night. Your star of the night", not realizing how intimate that sounded to those concerned.

"Hello Carmen". He said, his voice deep but not laden with anything other than welcome.

"Hello Garrett" she said. "Good to see you" She added, very much meaning it.

He nodded an agreement, but said nothing and looked at Mack. He did not wait for Carmen to introduce, and extended his hand. "Garrett Darrs".

Mack took Garrett's hand and shook it firmly. "Mack Fordham. Good to meet you."

Sophia glanced from one to the other to her sister and marveled at what was happening. She wished to catch someone's eye but didn't know whose. What had been happening?

Fiona only sensed questions in front of her, and tried to glean answers by focusing mostly on the man she knew best next to her husband, but Garrett offered no news. This was silly. "Garrett?" She asked.

He and Mack separated hands and then eyes. "Yes, Fiona?"

"You've got an artist to introduce".

"Yes I do". He said. "Yes, I do." He looked at Carmen and Mack while letting go of Sophia and taking Carmen's hand. "I'll be back".

Carmen walked easily, happily, feeling like an idiot, but a momentarily thrilled idiot. Garrett's hand was warm, and held hers intimately, guiding her to the center of the gallery's showroom. She knew he was unaware of what just that touch was doing, but it was a touch that authenticated her smile for the first time since she'd walked in.

Garrett had not been paying attention to their route as closely as he should have, because Finn appeared suddenly in front of them, almost as if Garrett had intentionally directed her there. He was hoping such a reunion would occur after the introduction. What if this changed her demeanor for the worse?

Carmen gasped in surprise and smiled widely. This was not the expression Garrett expected, nor was it one he was hoping for, but "get on with it" was all he could think of. "Finn! I'm so glad you could make it." There was genuine warmth in her voice, and

243

another sparkle entered her eyes. "I owe quite a thank you, and…."

"Which you've already expressed, so cut it out Carmen." He was smiling large as well, a mote of aw- shucks on his face, and he went over and hugged her.. Garrett was restless, mostly because he could discern nothing but happiness from the two in front of him, but it was a happiness that revealed no history. It told him nothing.

"You look so handsome". She said.

"And you look delicious" He said.

Carmen was visibly blushing under the ravenous eyes of Finn Darrs, and Garrett was starting to redden for entirely different reasons. "The crowd is waiting for us, I would imagine" Garrett said. The both of them looked at him simultaneously, almost as if they hadn't known he was there.

"Of course, Garrett. Sorry. I haven't seen Finn in too long" She smiled at Finn once more before she and Garrett continued their walk. And then she added "You never talk about your family. Finn." She felt his hand stiffen against her back, she thought.

"And neither do you". Was all he said, but it was as perplexing as it was simple to her. She furrowed her eyebrows, but said nothing in return.

As they made their way through, the crowd quieted, slowly all turning in their direction.Garrett waited for complete silence, but did not let go of her hand. How absurd she'd feel such glee from that fact alone. Quiet down they did quickly, and Garrett introduced her.

"Good Evening Everyone. I've told many of you already, but thanks for coming." He looked down at Carmen, who was politely smiling to his guests, quietly dreading the moment her hand would slip from his. "This is Carmen Carmine". It was the first time he'd said it aloud, though a few times he'd mulled it over in his head, thinking of it as ludicrous when first he heard it, fanciful when after they'd met, comfortable after they'd made acquaintance, but now it somehow sounded grand, fitting.

The room broke into appreciative applause, and Carmen looked at Garrett. He asked with his eyes and head movement for her to now speak. Fiona had prepped her, and, with Garret still holding her hand, it was easy to say a few words of thanks and wishes for everyone to enjoy her work and the evening. She bowed slightly, and got another round of clapping.

It was done, the introduction made. Carmen felt physically bereft when Garrett let go of her hand. "Let me take you back to Mack" was all he said, and she heard no resentment in his voice, and bereftment grew.

As they walked back, she said "Thank you Garrett" as she glanced at him sideways.

He smiled back at her, and then put his hand on her back as he said "Oh, it's far from over yet".

She knew that was true, but sensed he meant more and didn't care.

Chapter 22

After Garrett had taken Carmen off to greet the crowd, Sophia had turned to Mack, who was already looking at her.

"Did you read the book I left you?" She asked, actually quite curious.

He thought only for a second and answered. "Yes, Sophia, I did."

Fiona was still standing with them and went in search of William, worried with the fact that she deemed him at that moment a resource of sanity. "Excuse me".

Sophia wasn't sure what the overall vibe was, but she needed to get there. She had made her moves, had made a peace offering, what else?

She put a hand on Mack's arm. "And what did you think?"

Mack disliked himself, but he felt sorry for Sophia, and knew she would hate him for it. He knew she needed him to confirm something positive, but he wasn't going to do it, not here, not now. He could not so lightly put behind him their odd moment in the night, and he was not going to discuss it. He looked down at her, and saw what he always saw, what always made him just a little off-centered.

"I read the book Sophia. And I liked it better, I think, than the first time I read it."

She looked disappointed, and was about to prompt him further, but Garrett and Carmen had returned.

"Thank you, Mack, for lending me the artist" Garrett said, smiling largely and somehow tightly at the same time.

Carmen obediently walked over to Mack, and Mack returned his hand to her back, and said "Thanks for giving her the opportunity". He paused, and then said to her "They obviously love you".

Sophia was looking at Mack and Carmen with an odd expression on her face, but she kept silent. She didn't want to derail anything her sister might have set in motion for whatever bizarre reason.

Carmen was rudely aware of the replacement of hands on her back, but she only smiled at Mack a thank you.

Garrett had also noticed Mack take immediate possession of Carmen, and he looked at Mack fixedly. He then turned to Carmen and said "I know Fiona has told you all about what's going to evolve this afternoon, but as soon as she gets back I'd advise starting the rounds. It'll take a while, especially given their early admiration of you."

"Who needs a drink?" Came a savior's voice, and they all turned to see William with Fiona smiling just behind him, a degree of victory in her stance.

***

After they'd all gone together to the bar, Fiona spoke up.

"OK, Carmen." She said. "It's about that time." She smiled brightly at her.

Carmen took a sip from her wine, and smiled appreciatively at Fiona. "I think I'm ready."

"Follow me" And Carmen began to do so. Mack, realizing suddenly what was happening, ventured a question.

"Fiona?" He said, and the women stopped and turned to look at him. He could not afford to be stuck with Sophia and Garrett. They'd both be looking at him with prying eyes for different reasons, but worse, he knew there'd be questions, and he couldn't possibly know how Carmen would want them all answered. "If it's alright with you I'd like to tag along. It'd be an education, and I promise to be strictly background material."

Fiona thought nothing of it. "Fine with me" She shrugged. "I just figured you'd be bored." She looked at Carmen.

"I thought the same, but I'd love it if you came along". She smiled, and then happened to glace at Garrett, who was looking at her, his expression still. She looked down quickly, but held her hand out to Mack.

Sophia tried very hard to think of something clever to say, but could come up with nothing. She didn't want to sound desperate.

All she could do was touch Garrett's arm in a lame attempt to create a ruse she knew he would not buy.

Garrett seemed not to notice. "Enjoy the show" he said to the three of them, and they went out into the gallery.

"Nice guy, that" William said, seemingly out of nowhere.

Garrett looked over at him. "Really?" This he said in a dubious tone.

"Actually he is" Sophia agreed. "And my parents love him."

Garrett snapped out of his quiet fume. "Your parents?" He paused for time to reapply his sardonic. "I didn't know they were that serious."

Sophia looked at him, confused, but then understood. "No, not that way." She laughed easily and then uncomfortably at the thought. What was Carmen doing with Mack? She continued in order to explain to Garrett and perhaps to confirm to herself. "He runs Twilight Stables, which belongs to them".

Something rang a bell from earlier conversations he'd had with Carmen, and he nodded. "You know him well?" He asked, unable to help himself.

At this point William politely excused himself. He was unfamiliar enough with the topic that he could be of no use, and he wanted to watch Fiona sweetly sachet her artist around the gallery floor. He knew eventually she'd have to come back to him, and that kept a smile on his face.

Sophia didn't hesitate. "Well enough. I like him a lot." She said simply.

Garrett looked at her. "Oh." Was all he said, for indeed what else could he say? Sisterly approval was something he wouldn't question aloud.

But his silence brought on her natural curiosity. "What do you care? Shouldn't really affect your show, I wouldn't think."

"No, Sophia, I guess it shouldn't". He said, and he looked over at them, Fiona gently and politely smiling while Carmen was speaking to someone with freakishly tall hair who seemed riveted by her words. The freakish tall's date said something apparently funny and Carmen tilted her head and laughed heartily. He watched the silk of her dress crease just a bit by the flat of her stomach as she bent just a little, and a twinge hit his groin and his brain simultaneously. There was power in her stance, and as with most success stories that walked out of this building, they picked up a new vibe, a confidence issued from the confirmation that their work was in fact good enough for his walls. He'd wanted that for her all along, even, he thought, from when he'd first viewed her magnificent painting at Luigi's. And there she was, and he could almost see the current she drew and then generously lit out.

Sophia missed none of this. She'd already walked around and looked at her sister's lovely pieces, and comfortably in the midst of no one. She'd been left to converse with the host, and he was beautiful as always, but also ambivalent. She'd had enough to think about, so she had only looked at him when he'd agreeably said "No, Sophia. I guess it shouldn't." And then he had seemed to forget she was there, that maybe they could continue to talk. She looked at him quizzically, amused, about to ask him "Why so odd, Todd?" when she'd followed his gaze. It was Carmen dazzling his customers, Mack slightly behind and to her left, holding what she thought was a patient smile. She looked back at Garrett to ask him who Carmen was talking to, but his face stopped her, made her pause and then think.

There was a hardness to his features as she watched him look at Carmen from behind the rim of her glass. The master of debonair and finesse was in the midst of confliction, and Sophia was fascinated. She might have been jealous or at least envious if she'd thought longer, but it was a bit too entertaining. It was obvious he was very proud of Carmen and her display, and the cynic in her also thought it might be self-congratulatory on his discovery, but he also looked angry. He sported no scowl on his handsome features, but that could have been it. The serenity he presented seemed just shy of dangerous. She'd known Garrett for a few short weeks, but she thought she'd gotten to know him well enough, that they'd formed a bond born out of similarity of character.

"Garrett?" Sophia said, lightly touching his arm.

He did not move his head, but shifted his eyes to look at her, waiting.

"Why don't we go for a bit of a walk?"

He raised his eyebrows. "I'm not sure that's a good idea, Sophia" he said, turning his eyes back to Carmen and company, who had moved on to another set of fans.

Sophia understood his need to stay close to the goings-on. "I don't mean an exit, Garrett, just a walk around, a mingle about for a break from just standing here." And then "Mulling" she said pointedly.

He looked over at her agreeably. "Mulling?" He asked. "What are you mulling about?" But he knew what she meant. He held out his elbow. "Let's go".

She took his arm, and they began to walk through the chattering crew, not ever getting very far because if the guests weren't talking to Carmen, then Garrett was next on the art chain. Sophia obediently stood by his side and conversed when prompted, but she really had just wanted to cruise, and maybe look at her would-be lover from another vantage point. She noticed that Fiona was very good at moving them efficiently from group to group, and Carmen wasn't fading at all, if anything picking up light as she walked. Occasionally Mack would bend his head and say something in her ear, which Sophia found intriguing and disconcerting, but she'd have the whole thing pieced together by the end of this shebang, she was sure, not in the least because she'd part of it figured anyway, and would now concentrate on speeding up the process for those uninformed. She just wasn't very good at ennui.

"Garrett". She stated.

He'd been in the middle of talking to Sam Barston if she recalled his name correctly, and this particular conversation could wait. Garrett glanced over at her and said "Excuse me" to Sam.

Sam had been finding it very hard not to look at Sophia anyway, so the break was welcome. "S'Alright. I'll catch up." He muttered and walked away.

"Sophia. What can I do for you? This is part of that walk you mentioned, you know." He said, but jovially enough.

His eyes were seeking, seeking, and then rested. Sophia didn't follow his gaze because she didn't have to.

"What if I told you something, Mr. Darrs?" She said flirtatiously.

A few hairs went up on Garrett's neck, because questions like that from the likes of Sophia were not easy to answer, and it was a question posed in such a manner to distract him from his vigil.

"What if you did, Sophia?" He asked back slowly, deliberately.

"I may have information that'd better your afternoon, and who knows, maybe your evening" she toyed.

He'd be a fool not to listen, but quite possibly an idiot to fall prey, never-the-less the draw was too strong.

He thought it sage to warn her. "Sophia, God knows I enjoy your company, but if you haven't already guessed, I'm in the middle of an important event, and I'm a little distracted."

In the light of her observations that was a good enough understatement to make her laugh with delight. "That's rich, Garrett." She said, still quietly laughing. "Really."

They were still arm-in-arm, and she drew him purposefully a degree apart from the center of things, just at the base of the stairs that led to the second floor. It almost seemed cozy, intimate, Sophia smiling at Garrett mischievously, and he responding in a vague, happy dread, having no idea what she thought could better this day unless she proposed sabotaging Mack's attire, or maybe his drink. With such glad thoughts he looked at Sophia expectantly.

The beauty of familiar laughter, familial laughter after all, had elicited attention from across the room, where only moments ago Garrett had focused. Carmen heard her silly-go-lucky sister and looked up, a smile on her face. She saw that Sophia and Garrett were off to the side, engaged in close conversation, and witnessing such a picture faltered her smile. Sophia was touching his arm, and Garrett, for his part, had his arm on her back, his head leaning down to hear something private. It shouldn't have shocked her, and she wasn't appalled, but the sight did produce an inward cringe and a jolt out of the sublime party campaign she'd been leading. She had prepared herself for just such moments, and either she stopped expecting it because she'd deluded herself into thinking something was in his eyes when he looked at her, or simply because as yet this afternoon she'd seen no display of affection between them, but she wasn't as prepared as she'd ought to have been. It wasn't of course as awkward as she self-deemed it, but she had been mid-speech, so Fiona took the reigns and spoke for her, no one the wiser.

Neither was Mack entirely fond of seeing Garrett's hand directly on Sophia's soft skin, and his jaw visibly clenched once he noticed. It was just a logical reaction for a man who now considered Sophia his own, despite the fact he'd shared none of this with her. He looked down at Carmen, who had stopped speaking, and understood they'd been drawn to the same pair by the luscious laughter they'd both recognized. He had not known until that evening that he could be a jealous man, but this was all just silliness and it was making him weary. He was fairly sure there were only two confused individuals in the room when it came to Carmen and Garrett, and that would be Carmen and Garrett. Whatever Garrett and Sophia were talking about was not some sexual tryst they'd share or would share later, but something plainly fun—it just happened that no matter what Sophia said she looked sexy doing it. All of this he wished he could explain to Carmen, but he knew it was not the place, and most of these surmises were anyway only instinctual.

"What I think you should know, Garrett, is that my sister might not really have Mack along for anything other than decoration." Sophia gently said, her head close to his ear so no one else could hear.

Stupidly, Garrett's pulse quickened. He felt less a man by stooping, literally, to hear what Sophia had to say, but the words she'd just spoken were hypnotic. He straightened himself, not wanting to appear as though they were huddling, and as he did so he looked over at Carmen who was staring at him. No. At them. Gut reaction prompted a nod of a head acknowledgement to her, but even in that short second, he couldn't help but notice her expression. He turned to Sophia who demanded he give her his attention, and while he attempted to listen to Sophia continue, he was forced to replay that expression in his mind. Was it panic that he'd seen? Would that have made sense? Not at all, but there had been realized dismay, and his stomach felt uneasy.

"I don't think you're listening to me, Garrett" Sophia said, annoyed. He looked at her blankly. "What did I just say?" When

252

he did not respond, she said "Honestly. You're not even bothering to look sheepish." She knew pouting was out of the question with her stupefied friend so she continued.

"You are very obviously attracted to my sister. By that I mean obvious to me." Garrett continued to look at her, waiting. Taking that as confirmation, she went on. "Why don't you do something about it? I know Mack pretty well, and I don't think he's as into her as you think he is." She wasn't sure why she'd taken on the role of matchmaker other than satisfying her own curiosity, but she was also getting bothered by being so ignored.

"I do think your sister is attractive, Sophia" he said, responding, "But she's also the focus of the evening, in case you've forgotten."

"Oh, stop it Garrett, and why would you care if I know?"

"Why, Sophia, would you think Mack is not "that into her" He asked.

She twisted her mouth, displaying puzzlement. She was not in fact sure of how to tell him that piece of the equation enough to respond, and before she could say anything, he said "I thought as much".

He looked up, hoping to still find Carmen in the same spot, but they'd moved on, and Carmen was no longer looking their way. Exasperation was setting in, and he looked back at Sophia. "I suggest we get a drink". He turned and walked in the direction of the bar, and Sophia, momentarily at a loss for words or activity, obediently followed.

Carmen, still doing the rounds, found all her needs brilliantly attended to by William and Fiona, depending on her requirements. Fiona was of course immediately there to guide, introduce and provide additional information when Carmen didn't have it, and William was just a benevolent source of charm, and replenished her drink as needed. She had started with wine, but quickly switched to water, when she realized how thirsty constantly talking made her. Despite her exceptional attendants, Carmen needed a rest, and she wished just to go somewhere and quietly be, even if only for a few minutes. She mentioned this to Fiona, who easily agreed and recommended she go up to the second floor.

"You're welcome to any part of the offices, and it's very spacious." She said. "In fact, Garrett's office overlooks the street, and if you keep the lights off it's a lovely serenity you'll get."

Carmen smiled at her gratefully. "Thanks. I won't be long" and off she went for that promised serenity.

Once she'd reached the top of the stairs, she began poking around a little, and found a front office, which was quite dark, almost so that she couldn't see, but after a few moments she could make out the entry to yet another office, and the only shred of light was coming from in there. She realized that must be Garrett's office, and headed that way. As she walked through the door, a shadow jumped in front of her and stopped her. She might have screamed had her mouth not been immediately covered by a large hand, and she heard a chuckle.

"Just me funny-looking" Finn said, and Carmen immediately relaxed when she heard his voice. He dropped his hand and backed up.

"You scared the shit out of me" Carmen said. "What the hell are you doing in a dark office, you fortified moron?" She asked him, not really mad, but trying only to quiet her racing heart.

"Come on" Finn said, taking her hand. "Let's go by the window and enjoy the silence of twilight."

Carmen smiled to herself. Finn was always Finn, and how she loved him. She'd known him for almost ten years now, and even though they hadn't been together in a while and rarely spoke, they were the type of friends that held fast and true, regardless of distance. They reached the window, and Finn casually put his arm around her, gently holding her next to him. Quietly they stood, each just taking a moment of peace, separation from the excited crowd below.

Garrett was part of that excited crowd, but he had almost visibly separated himself when he had seen Carmen float up the stairs in her red finery. He also clearly remembered his brother going up the stairs not five minutes earlier. His body opposed what his mind was concluding, but still it obeyed by letting him move forward through the crowd. He found himself unable to think as he strode up the stairs, noticing, for example, that the marble needed to be replaced in some places; the gold railing was polished to an unbearable sheen. Despite the noise of the ambiance he was leaving, he strangely heard nothing, just the patter of his shoes on each step. He couldn't tell by listening to them if he was running, but Garrett had cultivated calm, and even in his haze he looked like a confident man just going upstairs.

Chapter 23

Carmen leaned her head against Finn's arm, feeling herself re-balance after getting worked up over too little. She had to cut it out. She had to get back to the woman who knew how to handle men, who didn't really need them. Where was that woman anyway?

Finn startled her by speaking. "What's on your mind tonight?" He asked quietly, gently. "Why are you stepping out on your own party?"

She separated herself from him slightly so she could look up at him. "You think you know me so well, don't you?"

"Nope" He said. "Know I do. Why don't you just tell me instead of bullshitting? You know it won't work, and you don't have time".

Which was true. She did not want to be absent for too long. "You're going to think it's silly, and for that matter, it's not something you can say to any other. Any other."

Finn smiled, but tried to hide it. "You don't have to tell me, but if you haven't told anyone else, it might help to tell me. Plus you know I can be of help."

"I wish that were true" She said. "I wish that were true". Hesitantly she began to tell her short but turbulent tale, with each word feeling more relieved just at being able to reveal it. She'd hinted at it with Mack in the limo, but to Finn she held nothing back, and the physical lightening she felt was sheer heaven.

Finn had listened, no expression changing on his handsome face, just a gentle patience playing at his eyes. When she finished speaking he said "That's it?"

"What do you mean that's it?" She sounded exasperated and slightly hurt.

"You used to be more intuitive than this, I guess" He said, stalling to taunt her.

"And you used to be more helpful" She said, a bit disgusted, turning to go.

256

Finn caught her arm and brought her back next to him. "Sophia is not in love with Garrett. Garrett is not in love with Sophia. Plain and simple. And obvious, I might add." And now he understood why he'd seen various glances in various directions that hadn't seemed at the time to make sense. He then tried to explain, as plainly as he could, what he had seen and why it was obvious—that Garrett had barely paid any attention to Sophia, that he had a weird anger vibe around Mack, that Mack could not keep his eyes off Sophia and she returned the stare (whereupon he noticed a quizzical look on Carmen's face, but didn't pause for what he deemed irrelevant), "I don't know if he feels for you as you do him" Finn concluded. "But I've had the time all afternoon and evening to observe—a rarity for me since I'm usually part of the action." He added as if to himself "I think I'd like to do more of it. How entertaining everyone can be."

Carmen wasn't sure if Finn knew what he was talking about, but he sounded like it—all except for the part about Mack and Sophia. Dare she believe any of this? Dare she begin to think that her love for Garrett was not one-sided? She felt a smile tickling, tingling her brain. Surely she shouldn't let the thoughts of her rogue roommate make her stand straighter and happier only to have the rug pulled from under her later.

Garrett had reached the top of the stairs, and calmly straightened his tie. Absently he looked below, but it remained a boisterous hum, and only a few admiring eyes were looking his way, to whom he nodded an acknowledgement. He was not in the mood to go hunting or even to admit what he was doing, but he was not the trespasser after all. He did not hurry his gait or veer in any other direction than his own office. He was hypnotized by the scent of her perfume which ever so smugly teased the air through which he walked. He had not thought about what he would find, since it was quite clear. There was really not much else up here that was not also downstairs, other than quiet and solitude—the opportunity for stolen moments. He smiled a polite smile as he rounded a bend of the hallway.

"You know" Finn began again. "It's time to go back to the party, and wrap this thing up. Maybe we can go out after it's over and you can humor me some more with your odd ways." He gave her a light punch on her arm.

Carmen nodded, and smiled up at him. "OK. Maybe. Although I've got to see if it's alright with Mack." She added.

Gently Finn put his hand on her cheek. He felt a tenderness for Carmen now, and always had. He did not know why he had never attempted more, though perhaps he had and it was beyond the realm of his memory, but it didn't matter. Ever since they'd lived together in college they had enjoyed a sincere friendship. She forgave him his many foibles, and she entertained him with hers.

"Buck up, beautiful". He said. "This is all going to be just swell."

Garrett noticed, as he walked round the last bend to his offices, that no light was cast through the open main door. His body registered nothing other than searing conviction, though he slowed and quieted his pace. The air was suddenly a little thick, and he was pristinely aware of humming white noise seemingly drowning out the now distant music and voices from downstairs. He felt his face tightening, and now his heart did actually forget composure and beat harder as he drove himself through the moment. He had reached the entrance and strode a few steps in quietly, waiting for his eyes to adjust to the darkness. And it was quite dark, but slowly, his own office with the large street-side windows shed enough light so that he very soon witnessed the fine silhouettes of Finn and Carmen right in front of those windows. Carmen was looking up at Finn, and he down at her. No expression from this distance or in this light could be discerned, but Garrett quickly noted Finn's hand on her cheek. Something not unlike hatred shot through his rigid frame, and he touched his head to fend off the headache on its way. He stood motionless, waiting. He heard them talking, but it reached him as mere faint sounds. Tender sounds. He knew it wasn't possible, but the air seemed soupier, and he was sure he felt pulses of heat coming from an unseen vent.

What a silhouette they made, he thought. Finn, so tall, looking down at her, and Carmen looking fragile and demure next to him. He had to admit it was a handsome picture, and unbeknownst to Garrett, his expression grew somber. Such melancholy may have persisted had the moment not changed.

Carmen looked at Finn dubiously, and she could not help but be cheered by his light-hearted enthusiasm.

"You'll see" He said, and leaned down to kiss her gently on her forehead, his hand still on her cheek. While his head was still lowered he said "Just wait".

And because Finn had said this in the ear that faced Garrett, and because hearing gets better and desired perception can meet its mark, those two words made their way to Garret Darrs as he stood watching, wondering what to make of anything. The words were seconds after the soft kiss on her forehead, but to Garrett's eyes, it was a far more intimate, deliberate affection than either Finn or Carmen could have guessed.

Carmen felt a draft and rubbed her shoulders. "Did you hear something?" She asked Finn, inkling a frown. She turned to look about the office, and thought she caught movement in the outer office, but chided herself for such foolishness.

"Just your guests. Come on; let's get you back to it. Garrett'll be freaking out if you're gone too long." And with that sentiment, they walked through the darkened rooms out into the hallway to make their re-entry.

Garrett stood in the shadows, watching their exit, noting that Finn had his hand on Carmen's back as they walked by him, and, in fact, until they reached a point in the hallway beyond his vision, after which he knew the hand would drop. He had felt a distinct pleasure knowing that if either one of them would have turned around while leaving, they would have seen him. Now, after their departure, he felt a little dizzy with displeasure, and behind his eyes, if anyone were looking, they would see something like rage poured neatly over ice.

***

Carmen walked down the stairs with Finn, feeling much better than when she had risen them, not so much because she held conviction in what he'd said to assuage her, but because most of it was logical and coincided with what she felt somewhere deep inside herself, and that maybe she'd been misreading things about him and Sophia. That Mack and Sophia were seeing each other was a little unexpected, if he were right, but she would make sure to ask questions. For now she smiled at Finn's side as they reached the bottom of the stairs, and lightly gave him her thanks.

"No need to thank me, Carmen" He said. "All I did was tell you what I see. And I bet I'm as close to right as anyone".

But Carmen was losing her interest in this conversation and this companion, much as she cared for him. She beheld the gallery's guests, and now with a lighter heart, just smiled at Finn and said "I've got to run for a little while—maybe we can get that drink", but neither of them really thought they would, and Finn watched as she departed with an expression not unlike that of a proud brother, even if a little rueful.

As Carmen waded through the slowly thinning crowd, she had a small, but legitimate smile on her face. She'd made it through the rigorous beginning, witnessing Garrett in all his splendor, being introduced to the throng, and meeting many people that were not part of her world, the likes of whom she would continue to meet if she was successful. She wondered what on earth the next day could possibly offer in wake of such a large event, and hoped it would not be so anti-climactic as to prove stagnating. She had not yet begun anything of real substance, but a tiny part of her brain she kept shushing worried about a creativity block, logical or not. What if it now became forced? And as she continued her organized meander in search of Fiona, she realized her painting may not suffer—that it might change in light of her experiences, but in fact that is the nature of all art—the reflection of life. The thought of painting sent sunlight in a part of her brain that mightn't have wanted it. Her painting, the one they'd grabbed last minute and put in Nick's car--she had left that to Nick. Terror then seized her, motivated her. She hoped Nick was inefficient, that he hadn't found William or anyone to help him with it, but as she changed her destination, she knew such hopes to be ludicrous. If it had been hung, it would be difficult to unhang. She thought with a panic about what she had painted, and a rueful but crazed smile escaped her.

"Shit" she said, and quickened her pace.

*　*　*

After Garrett had taken a few silent moments to calm his body down, he went downstairs to reacquaint himself with black celebration. In what amounted to a few minutes he had become a changed man, and this time it was visible. Whereas one couldn't deny the debonair, the sophisticated, the handsomeness, a new edge had appeared that dimmed the previous qualities while heightening others more properly kept private. Before descending the staircase he gave a look about the room below, putting his position in perspective to all others he now deemed relevant.   He felt very much in control of the evening, even while it was apparently shattering before his very eyes. A grim smile affixed itself to his features as he came downstairs, and his eyes didn't focus on anything in particular, but then rested on the bar and a few familiar faces in front of it. It didn't trouble him that Mack was standing with Sophia, or that, despite the fact that Sophia was theoretically his date, Mack was looking like a man before a feast. He might have felt sorry for him had he been in a better mood. What was the world coming to when sincerity became so unimportant? He did not want to think too deeply, or pretend he was a man of incredible moral standing because he knew he wasn't, but people in his immediate spectrum had approached the ridiculous. No one was who they seemed to be, and with that thought he glanced around the room seeking Carmen, though he loathed himself the weakness. He finally saw her fiery presence on the far side of the gallery going at a speed that suggested determination, but he looked away abruptly. He knew he was off balance enough already that he should not tempt real madness.

Mack looked up to catch Garrett looking at him as he approached, and only nodded.

Didn't have the decency to look guilty, Garrett thought. What kind of conceited thug had Carmen invited? But then, he corrected himself, what kind of conceited thug was she? And for the first of what would be too many, the picture of Finn's hand on Carmen's face in the darkness cast itself before him.

"Sophia". Garrett said.   "Mack" he acknowledged.

261

"Hello, Garrett. After you deserted me so suddenly I went off to find this strapping man to keep me company." She said, eying Mack with a wide smile.

"Sorry, I had to attend to some immediate business". Garrett said, truthfully.

Mack's gaze was penetrating, for he knew who had been upstairs. He knew who, but had not known exactly what to make of it, and had also shifted his attention because he knew Carmen could take care of herself, and that it wasn't any of his business. Looking now at Garrett, however, he was not so sure. "Yes, I saw you head upstairs" was all he said, looking directly into Garrett's eyes. He did not like a new presence he saw there, and decided he should go find Carmen now that she'd returned to the party. "Excuse me" he said to Garrett. He turned his head and looked at Sophia. "I'll talk with you later." Garrett was no idiot, and he watched Mack walk away, knowing Mack's departure was something of a reaction to his presence. He had not seen a reflection of himself, but there was no way that what he felt inside was not somehow cracking his outer veneer. He realized Sophia was still next to him, and looking at him strangely. He spoke before she could say what he knew she was thinking about. "Seems to finally be thinning out". For this fact he was glad. It was time for him to get out of here before an eruption took place.

Sophia agreed. "What a show! I'm so happy for Carmen, and I haven't even had a chance to tell her."

"I saw her on the far side of the room if you want to tell her" He said stonily.

"What happened to you?" She asked as lightly as possible, understanding enough already by the darkness he emanated.

Garrett sighed with patience. "Sophia, I like you too much to go into my mood, because yes, it has gone sour." He paused. "Let me also add that I don't think you know your sister very well." Silence again for a moment. "And neither do I."

She was about to voice her protest, now grasping that he must somehow be upset about Carmen, but he cut her off with a quick peck on the side of her head. "Jean will be waiting for you when it's time to go. I have to disappear for a moment." And just like that he was gone.

Chapter 24

Carmen had painted something she was very proud of, and had badly wanted to include in today's debut. It bore her soul, how she'd been feeling, but until the actual debut it had not been obvious. Certainly, any onlooker would have seen passion, maybe sadness or sympathy, but there could not have been made a personal link to the artist. Yes, every piece of work was a personal link, but "The Mirror" was a little too true.

When she had painted it, just over a week before, she could not have foreseen how events were to unfold. She had depicted the scene of an extremely beautiful woman, sitting in her parlor chair looking at her mirror, but instead of looking at her reflection, she was looking in the reflection into the eyes of a handsome man looking at her. It was obvious they were in love, caught up, in fact, with being in love. There was also a bedroom window, made to appear at the far side of the bedroom, and the face of another pretty woman was looking in, no mistaking the envy in her eyes. The anguish. Such a display would not have been so damning had she not inadvertently put the seated woman in a blue silk gown. The woman was not a red-head, but it didn't matter. If Garrett saw that painting, her secret would be out, and she couldn't afford the humiliation. Why had Sophia worn that dress? She wore the stupid thing all the time. Wasn't her opening worth a new gown?

As she reached the bottom of the middle of the gallery, she didn't care what any remaining guests were thinking as she walked determinedly through them, wishing William would light a beacon so she could find him all the more quickly. She cursed herself for not having realized it sooner. When had she first seen Sophia?

"Carmen" She heard the accused say.

She turned to the direction of Sophia's voice, and forced calmness. "Hello, Sophia." But she kept walking.

"Carmen" Sophia said in a manner to stop her sister.

Fiona also arrived on the scene. "Carmen?" She asked. "Are you alright? Why the look of dread?"

Sophia looked at her sister closely, for she hadn't noticed.

"I'm fine. Where's William?"

"William?" Fiona repeated. "I think he went to find Garrett and Mack." She looked up and around. "He was hoping to find them at the bar."

"I just wanted to know..." She started.

"Know what? I doubt William knows more about something involving you than I do." She said plainly.

Sophia would have interrupted since she wanted to take Carmen aside and talk to her, complement her, whatever she had time for, but Carmen did look fixated, so she held quiet.

"Of course, Fiona." Carmen said, and sighed deeply. "There was a late painting, and..."

"Yes, Nick brought it in."

Carmen's heart sank, and regret welled inside her, but she said only "Oh." And then "Where did you put it?"

Fiona looked shamefully at the ground. "I'm sorry, Carmen. We couldn't put it up..."

Before she could finish, she saw that Carmen was now elated.

"Where is it now?" She asked.

"I Saw Nick take it to put back in the trunk to go back with you, although we've sold so many you might as well leave it and we'll hang it this week."

"No, no. That's alright. Perfect, really. Thank you, Fiona." She smiled, and then looked at Sophia, forgiving her the blue. "Sorry, Sophie. You want to get something to drink with me? It's been a long afternoon." She felt suddenly tranquil, even happy with the knowledge of this accidental prevention.

"Sure, but can we just talk for a few moments first? We haven't been able to, and I think you ought to know a couple of things."

They walked arm-in-arm to another suite that was darkened, boasting work by other artists. When they'd found a bench, they sat down together, both sighing peacefully, simultaneously.

264

"So what've you got?" Carmen asked, assuming it was some kind of gossip.

"The other day when we talked on the phone, do you remember how you assumed it was Garrett I was talking about?"

The question brought Carmen to full, pristine attention. "Assumed?" She said, the startle not hidden from her voice. "Who l else could you have been referring to?" Though now her conversation with Finn came back to her full blast.

Sophia smiled, and shook her head. "Mack."

"Mack." She said, quietly confirming. "Why didn't you tell me?"

Sophia put her hand on Carmen's arm. "I tried to. We really should have gone out to dinner as planned, and I'll tell you all about it, but that's not the most important piece of it, really."

Carmen doubted that. To her the most important piece was that she did not have to now feel as guilty for feeling the way she had been for Garrett.

"Does Garrett know how you feel?" she asked, calmly.

"He doesn't know about Mack and me, though I think he might have guessed by now. But nothing ever happened between Garrett and me, and it's you he..."

"Nothing ever happened?" She guffawed at the prospect. "But that doesn't make sense. He…." She dropped off as she recalled that day in the street when he'd kissed her, and when she assumed he was being a sister-hopping idiot.

Carmen remained in a mummified silence as Sophia prattled on. She explained how it had been obvious to her immediately how Carmen felt about Garrett, that just looking at the two of them was something, and that she quite frankly had had to do something about it. Here and there Carmen nodded dumbly, possibly at the right points, as Sophia further explained how she had tried to do a bit of match making by, forgive her, expressing her thoughts to Garrett. "Or at least I tried to tell him." Sophia said. "But all I got out was that you and Mack aren't hot and heavy. Actually, I'm not sure he even believed me. He's been kind of weird."

"Oh." Was all Carmen could think of to say immediately, but something calmly happy was stealthily making its way into her

265

bones, her muscles, even the end of her nose. She smiled like a kitten might. Perhaps the gentle touches from the beginning of the afternoon, and some of his glances had not been misinterpreted by her. Maybe her secret joy at such trivial physicality might not have been one-sided, a tantalizing thought. At some point she would find him tonight and thank him for all he had done, and just maybe that would lead to other sincere words. From both of them. Just maybe any queasiness at facing one another could end.

"Thanks for letting me know, Sophia" Carmen said. "I'm going to go find Mack, and maybe Garrett, because I think this thing is…."

Mack had appeared almost out of thin air. He nodded a hello, but looked quizzically at Sophia. "How did you beat me to her?" He said, referring to Carmen. "You were next to Garrett when I left."

"Your intuition is not always dead on, I guess. You went in the entirely opposite direction. I had no idea where you were going." She teased him, and smiled. "Besides, Garrett left me two seconds after you did, so I was effectively stranded." Annoyance crossed her eyebrows.

Mack let some tension out of his frame as Sophia's presence amused him, and when he let himself really look at her, other tension replaced that which had set him looking for Carmen. Even when she was not posturing at all she looked sly; suggestive. The late afternoon and bustle of the event had not affected her beauty, but the invariable hint of dishevelment was present and dangerous.

Carmen, now educated, found it hard to believe what she now beheld. It had been just seconds since his arrival, but Mack's attraction to Sophia was quite obvious. How had this not been visible? But she supposed she'd been so preoccupied with her own emotional sensations that she'd noticed nothing else.

She smiled now, thinking that pieces were slowly coming into place—the world was not spinning as inaccurately as she'd thought.

"I think I'll go find Fiona and Garrett, Mack, if that's OK" She said, still smiling.

Mack's expression changed focus from Sophia to her, but otherwise seemed not to reveal anything else. "I think Garrett had to go take care of something—um, anyway I don't think he'll be easy to find." He said while remembering Garrett's formidable stance. And then because he did not want Carmen to still go looking for him, added "I don't think he really wants to be found."

This was an odd comment that Carmen found surprising, but she wouldn't go seeking Garrett out, even if she couldn't bear not seeing him now that true belief of existing love was in her heart. "Oh. I'll go find Fiona, then. I'll be back before we have to go." And Carmen walked away from the handsome, if enigmatic pair. How had that happened, she wondered, no less glee in her demeanor.

***

Garrett Darrs sat behind his desk facing the hallway, the street light behind him. His desk was positioned so that one couldn't exactly see very far into Fiona's space without the lights on. Which was just fine. He had done what he should not have done and poured himself a generous portion of scotch from his private stock. Customarily at these functions he nursed one or two such drinks at most, but today he was on his sixth. He was in darkness so that no one could see what his thoughts had done to him. Though he did not look clumsily inebriated, he did not look entirely sane. Frankly, he did not feel entirely sane.

It was fine to demand of himself logical explanations, for there could be plenty, but the part of his brain that whispered rationale had been driven back, drowned by liquor until he heard it no more. When that tiny voice had still been audible to him, he had supposed it was possible that Mack was only an associate or friend of Carmen's, and it was possible that Finn had merely been too demonstrative of feelings they'd shared in the past, but eventually the fact that such things were only possible was far outweighed by what was likely. Despite his gut feelings about Carmen Carmine and her virtuous nature

Virtuous nature, indeed. He made a snort in the dark, and then laughed at the ridiculous sound. He had not been sitting for ages, maybe ten minutes, but it had given him more time to think—the last thing he should have allowed himself other than scotch. He was unsure why he was not angrier with his brother. Truly he held contempt mostly for Carmen, barely a trace for Mack or Finn, but he did not realize, or chose not to, that he was more angry at his misinterpretation of Carmen. She had waltzed in casually with Mack, and they had by no means been a physically distant pair, and then she had shared secret, sexy moments with Finn. Possibly a lover from the past, but now possibly not. He could have argued for her had she not so easily accepted his touch, his gentle whispers. She had not stepped back, offended. She had not stepped back and laughed off the attention. She had not done anything but drink it in, he recalled. He hated twists. He hated scandal, and he hated that she was not the woman he'd fallen in love with.

A fresh pulse of anger stirred him from his rigid seat, and he stood to his feet, only a little off-balance. Why should he be hiding in the dark, sulking? He had done nothing wrong, and it was his gallery, and bottom line, it was his show. He had not actually bumped into her since the beginning of the show, and now a crooked grin crossed his already strangely accentuated features. Would she be able to pull it off? Would she feel guilty at all--yet be able to hide it? Or would guilt not show simply because she felt none? A bit of devil-may-care added a lighter side to his ominous aura, but it did not make for a less threatening appearance. He knew he was far too sophisticated and truthfully not as violent, but he fancied himself just then as the big bad wolf, the lady in red in his sights. Silly, he thought, scotch addling his humor, since she wasn't a lady at all.

Chapter 25

Carmen had found Fiona and told her she wished to depart so that she was not the last one to leave. "But before I go I was just going to walk around and take a look at my work. I know I've seen it all, but I haven't actually gotten a chance to see it in this beautiful gallery. Not really see it, if you know what I mean". She'd been walking through it all afternoon and evening, but hobnobbing allows no appreciation.

"There's no reason for you to stay, and you're right. Late entry, early exit." Fiona smiled. "You did marvelously. Really. I hope we can do this again." Fiona was tired, but she meant it all. Carmen had a way about her that was easy, sincere and entertaining.

This made Carmen pause, because she realized she had not properly thanked Fiona, who had been sheer brilliance throughout, and she did not now wish to sound insincere. She smiled to her, and the result was truthful and demure. "So do I, Fiona, so do I. Thank you for all your help." They hugged briefly, as time would allow, and then William popped up to add his own slant.

"Well you guys look all happy-smoky." He said, a laugh always in his smile.

"Happy-smoky?" Fiona said, shaking her head. "Go ahead, Carmen. I'll talk to you soon."

Carmen meandered slowly to the main suite, and on the way noticed most everyone had gone. She looked around at her paintings, since she had not gotten such an unpeopled view, and was filled with pride at what she saw.

Carmen breathed in what she hoped would be an uplifting breath, and set out to give herself a tour of her own work. Garrett had explained to Carmen how the lay-out would be, and how many rooms would be adorned with her work, but she was not prepared for the overwhelming feeling she got when she looked around. All she saw was painting after painting of hers, works that she cherished, in one way or another, and here they all were. Not only that, but the way they were displayed, each with its own under-light in an otherwise relatively dimly lit space, made them more vivid and alluring than she thought they were. She was mesmerized, and walked slowly about the rooms, looking at each piece, amazed at the clarity, amazed at the brilliance. It really was art! What a thing to think, but it had always been—just here it became majestically so. She then noticed many of them had a red sticker by the title! Which could only mean one thing. She quietly said an appreciative "Ooh."

"Yes, you've done well, Carmen."

When she heard his voice from behind her she froze, but at the same time felt desire in the pit of her abdomen. "Thank you" She managed. "We've done very well, I hope". She hadn't seen Garret since the beginning of the show even though she'd thought of him often, and now hearing him behind her reminded her of his absence. She did not know why, but thought herself brave, and turned to face him. It was suffocating to see him so close and stunning in his dark blue suit, his hair now tousled, and him better looking because of it. But that had been her first reaction. After a few seconds, reality showed her a picture of someone perhaps tired. Was that what she saw? Because if she hadn't known Garret, it seemed he looked….calculating. And how could that be? Her face betrayed an expression of doubt. "Hello, Garrett…."she had been in the middle of saying. She noticed a smile on his face, normally a sign to put anyone at ease, but she didn't recognize this particular smile, and mentally she reached for a shawl. "Um…" she said, now unsure of herself, "I was just taking a look at my work on the walls since I haven't really gotten the chance."

Garrett said nothing to her explanation even while she seemed she wanted one. "Carmen, if you always paint like this, you will be world famous one day." He said sincerely. "I know the whole parade today was exhausting, and you might not have gotten to enjoy it as much as those of us that relaxed, but I hope you took something away from it." Because you took something from me.

"You look tired, Garrett" Because she knew she couldn't use any other adjective without sounding strange, and she didn't think she yet had the right to be intimate.

"I think maybe I am." He said distantly.

Carmen realized again that something was off, and it could not have been insignificant.

"I just learned a lot tonight" He added, "that really I had no inclination or time for. But I guess that's part of the business."

"I never thought you the cynic" She said, now feeling slightly alarmed at his words and his demeanor. She would find Mack and leave, safest for all. "Anyway," she said, hoping to shake off unwanted vibes,

"It was a lot of fun, and I thank you for that, Garrett. Really." She smiled at him, tired but sincere. "Now I must find my date and go home, I guess." She said and turned to go.

But Garrett had only just begun his evening, and he grabbed her wrist gently and stopped her, causing her to turn back to him, though now he had pulled her a good degree closer.

"You looked stunning, tonight, red" He said, his voice now deeper, and he took a sip of his drink. "You make an amazing silhouette", He added, knowing it would be heard without understanding, but didn't care at all.

Carmen was rendered unsteady, glad for the leverage his hand provided her, though she hoped he hadn't noticed. There was something in his eyes she couldn't explain, and didn't think she liked. And she positively did not like being referred to as "red". She watched him closely as he gazed at her, and she saw that he was drunk, or nearly so. She knew she needed to exit before he said more than she wanted to learn.

"Thanks, Garrett". She said quietly with a small, shy smile. She pulled her hand firmly free of his and walked away.

But she heard him say "Until later then, Red." She heard him rattling the ice in his drink, she and the scotch getting colder.

***

Sophia knew Carmen would be leaving soon, but all she cared about was that it meant Mack's departure. He was talking to William and Fiona who had appeared shortly ago, and as her eyes left the general gallery view to look at him she realized he actually looked comfortable, possibly happy. It was a pleasant sight, she thought, but somehow the half smile on her face would not go full mast.

What she mightn't have understood yet was that she was not comfortable when Mack was out of the usual element, Twilight Stables. At an event such as this, her Mack was supposed to be at odds with his surroundings, more obviously disgruntled. She was the one who was cultured, sought after, a socialite damn-it! He saw her looking at him and bowed his head a bit, but then returned to his apparently engaging conversation. The Sophia known and loved by most felt as though she were losing ground, that by mere virtue of the fact Mack was at ease in her typical surroundings, he would not need her. The idea that she was labeling herself that transparent did not occur to her, and the fact was that perhaps a trace of such nature was indeed within her, but she was now letting such musings hamper her confidence and shine, the very things that Mack found most alluring. Was this how awful true love was? Was becoming unhinged a reasonable side effect? Someone stirred her out of her unwelcome reverie by saying her name.

But she was thankful for it, and it turned out to be Mack inviting her to their conversation.

"What's on your mind? Did you enjoy the debut?" He asked her, sincerity seemingly apparent. William and Fiona looked with a degree of interest to her, but she suspected that was it. Fiona might have liked Carmen, but Sophia knew she hadn't proven her credentials to her yet.

"How could I not? Carmen, my very talented sister, presenting as she did and looking as she did? And besides…" But she dropped off mid sentence because she'd noticed her sister approaching, looking a bit off center.

"Hi". Carmen said, almost nervously. "Look that bad, do I?" She smiled weakly.

Sophia said "Well, you don't look pleased. And a few minutes ago you were beaming." She had a question mark on her face. Mack said nothing, but looked around for some unknown explanation.

"I know, weird, right?" Carmen said. "Strangest thing, but my stomach started feeling odd. Maybe delayed stage fright."

Sophia looked doubtful. "Well, it's the end of the night and you were going to leave anyway. You've said your good-byes to the people that matter, right? And now I'm saying good-night. Go find Nick and get out of here."

"That's a great idea, Sophia" Mack said. "I think I'm starting to fade as well".

"Thanks, I appreciate it."

She and Mack turned together and said good-bye to Sophia, who smiled a brilliant but disquieting smile. Mack stopped for a moment.

"Good-night Sophia" He said. Wishing deeply that he'd had more time to spend with her that evening, that maybe he could have walked with her to view her sister's artwork, but it had not been the right occasion.

A glaze came off Sophia's eyes and she looked at him, now focused. "Well good-night, Mack. I think you must have had a wonderful afternoon" she said, not quite meaning to sound condescending, but not quite regretting that she did.

Mack's features hardened and also registered disappointment, and Sophia immediately felt the pangs of ruing. Always, always, always her voice betrayed her, but silent she held lest the more worrisome possibility—apology—surface.

"I know I enjoyed myself, Sophia. Carmen is excellent company. I hope your ride home provides you with a fitting end to the day" He said in his cryptic fashion.

What a clever man, she thought. He knows now damn well I'm to ride home alone.

Carmen looked from one to the other and realized she was not the only one experiencing turmoil. All of us to greater or lesser degrees, and she cast a hasty glance about them to make sure they could leave the gallery without any other run-ins. But Garrett was nowhere to be seen, not that Carmen was put at ease, because there was a charge in the air she could almost see, madly

273

dashing against the walls, flying through the air, millions of tiny static. Out, out, out, she had to get out.

Fiona looked concerned, and could not fathom the change in Carmen. "You sure you'll be OK?" She asked,

"Yes, sorry, really I am." She looked at Mack with a plea.

The four of them made their way through the front entrance into the cool night air, welcome refreshment to all of them.

"I can't seem to find Garrett, Carmen, but I'm sure one of the straggling guests has his ear. I'll have him call you tomorrow." Fiona added, hiding her disapproval of Garrett's not being available.

"There'll be no need for that" Garrett boomed, his voice coming from the street. They all looked in that direction to see that in fact Garrett was present, that he had to have been around the front corner of the cement building wall. "I can tell her right now how splendidly the show went."

The crew of four stared at Garrett, possibly baffled. Garrett's voice was louder than necessary, and though his words were a compliment, they were delivered more as a taunt. While they watched him, he drew closer, casually. His look had grown darker, messier, more chaotic.

And embarrassing, as far as Fiona could tell. "Garrett go inside, and we'll go over the show's receipts in your office. Now." She was stern, and he looked at her as though for the first time realizing her presence. William put a hand on her arm, hoping she would not set something off, but Garrett merely smiled ruefully with a shaking of his head.

"The office, Fiona?" He said more quietly. "The office?" He was not slurring his words, but stressing words in an eerie enough fashion that it was obvious to his observers he'd been drinking. The smile had not left his face, but affixed itself more firmly, and the effect was not gentle.

The group of them facing the street barely even registered Nick pulling up in the limousine, because Garret's stance had entranced them into a disquieting stupor. Mack saw that Nick was there, that he should guide Carmen to the car and get out before something odder happened, but Garrett hadn't actually done anything truly wrong, though Mack knew this type of reserved menacing to know an explosion was not far off.

Carmen couldn't believe that anything was real, and she realized the electricity she'd been feeling was the energy Garrett was sending out, and she was frozen to the spot, wishing just then that Mack would pick her up and carry her to the car. It was only just steps away, after all. Garrett's actions were inexplicable and were making her doubt her understanding of him.

"The office?" Garrett said once more, but turned his gaze to Carmen, and walked close enough so that he could see the expression in her eyes. The expression was fear, but he read it as fear of publicized sins. "I was in the office earlier tonight, Fiona". He said, keeping his eyes locked with Carmen's, who could not look away.

The fear and angst she'd been feeling began a steady progression to dread. Head-stabbingly slowly a haze was lifting, and letting her envision what she thought Garrett believed he had seen. This could not be what he was referring to. There had been no one upstairs. She remembered seeing Garrett below as she had gone up the stairs. Her heart was beating too fast, and now her stomach did feel awful. Too much.

"Garrett, please let's…" Fiona attempted.

"Except, of course," Garrett continued, "the lights weren't on at the time. You and I, we'll need them for the paperwork, I suppose." His voice had risen again in volume, and now everyone except he and Carmen were baffled by his strange words.

Carmen was weak enough so that she leaned back against Mack, who put his arm around her protectively. "Garrett, that's enough. Sleep this off. We're leaving." And he began to lead Carmen to the car, ignoring everyone else, but Carmen couldn't stop staring at Garrett, and wished she could speak, but there was too much to say as explanation and it would sound feeble.

"I see" Garrett said more softly. "You chose Mack for the night, Carmen."

Carmen wished Mack were faster, wished she were faster, wished Garrett would make some sense.

"Because I was sure, judging by your bohemian actions, that it's my brother you wanted to fu…" But he never finished his

275

sentence because Mack had stopped, turned, and very quickly smashed one of his fists into Garrett's right eye. As Garrett reeled backward and fell, Mack shook his hand out, for he hadn't used it for this type of thing in a while.

"You're an idiot, Garrett. And you've made a ridiculous fool of yourself." Mack said. He went back to Carmen, who could no longer speak, but who had tears falling from her eyes, and picked her up.

Nick had not heard most of the goings-on because he'd had his own plans to focus on, but the time was getting to be when Ms. Carmine should be coming out, and he occasionally peeked out for her, as he would not want to miss much of her walking in that red dress. So he happened to catch Mack's well-placed punch, and leaped out of the car to defend his boss, but when he heard Mack's words, and saw how upset everyone else was, he realized he should tend to his passengers, and opened the door for Mack.

***

Fiona could not let Garrett just sit there on the pavement, bleeding and suffering silently. Mad as she was at him, she would not desert him, especially when he so obviously needed help. She had asked William to go in and get a wet cloth, which he did grudgingly, and then she walked over to Garrett.

"I'm not going to talk to you tonight about this or any invoices, so don't start talking to me. I'm going to help you with your face, and when I come in tomorrow we'll talk about whatever you'd like. Right after you make atonements to Carmen, which I don't know how you'll do." Fiona said, all the while examining his face.

The punch in the head had not been of value to his state of inebriation, so he chose not to respond to Fiona. What would the point have been, anyway? She hadn't seen anything, knew nothing because he told her as close to nothing as possible. She did not know that his favorite artist in the world was a two-timing, shallow Bohemian, and that he was not even half of the two-timing equation. He sat with his head in his hands until William, accompanied by Finn, came out with a cloth.

"Please take him out of here, for a walk, whatever. I don't want any of the left-over guests to see him like this." Fiona said, and William and Finn led him around the building towards a separate entrance.

"William, I've got it from here" Finn said. And William, astute and eager to find his wife, smiled a thank you and left.

They were in a side alley, and Finn paused, his arms still around Garrett.

"What the fuck is the matter with you?" He said, exasperated, desperate. "Do you know what the fuck you just did? Do you know what you've jeopardized?"

Garrett backed off his brother unsteadily as he laughed. "Your tryst with an artist?" But he was tired now, and along with the scotch, this now made his words less distinct.

Finn looked perplexed and even crazed with it. "What?"

But Finn didn't know that Garrett had witnessed and then misinterpreted his affectionate discussion with Carmen. "You are really drunk. And stupid." He said disgustedly, but not unkindly. "Carmen's got it bad for you."

Garrett laughed harder, and then winced at the pain it caused his face. "I guess that makes three of us", and his laughter became almost maniacal.

Finn, still perplexed and impatient to get back to his waiting conquest at the gallery, said "OK, let's get you inside. You can sleep upstairs." He led Garrett, who had grown subdued, up the back entrance stairs to an office that accommodated late night work and moments such as this.

Finn watched as Garrett silently loosened his tie, and took his shoes off, beginning the process that would put him safely in bed, and hopefully not bothering anyone else.

"I'll lock up with Fiona. Just go to bed." He turned off the light as he left, fairly confident his date would be waiting for him.

Chapter 26

The coolness of the air let in through the car's window and the smell of sadness were hard for Mack to bear, but bear it he did. He had gotten Carmen inside the car safely, and laid her down on the longest seat, and told Nick to make haste to her house. Perhaps Carmen's unhappiness even soothed him, because he was an angry man, appalled at what Garrett could say to someone so obviously good. He did not know her well, he knew, but there are some things one just knows. He leaned back against the leather as they pulled away from the curb, and stared out the window, just in time to see Finn and William take Garrett away. He looked at Carmen because she'd raised herself.

"Carmen, lie down. Don't worry—you're tired and you need rest." He said, believing it, but also not knowing what else to say.

She smiled weakly at him, and he noticed that only tear tracks remained, that she'd only shed a few for that horrible boob. "You're right, Mack, I am. And foolish, I guess." And she almost did cry again, thinking about the brash words uttered by a madman a few moments ago. If all Garrett had seen was she and Finn close together, how could he have doubted her? Was his perception of her that fragile that he let slip such awful accusations? In front of everyone. She shivered, reliving it.

"I don't know enough to make any passing judgement, but you're no fool. The only idiot present tonight was Garrett." Mack said. Gut feeling made him add "And maybe you should steer clear of him, business or otherwise. He was drunk, but that's no excuse".

Carmen had begun to set her brain on comatose, finding it better to stare out the window, but not actually see, her eyes glazed over. "I wish you were wrong, Mack, but you're not". She said, distractedly.

"I wish you were wrong."

Mack wished she'd just lie down, but he knew he'd said enough and that Carmen had either a lot to think about, or a lot to put out of her mind for this particular ride. He wanted to make it as easy a difficulty as possible, and opted to quietly pour himself a drink.

Nick was experiencing his own turmoil as he occasionally glanced in his rear-view, even though Mack had raised the glass immediately. He felt as though he had somehow betrayed Garrett, but it was obvious Garrett had somehow upset Carmen, and that would not do. He had tried calling him several times, but got no answer on either of his lines. All he could do was get Mack and Carmen back home, though after that he was not sure. "What have you gone and done, Mr. Darrs?" He occasionally muttered as he drove, trying very hard not to drive too fast.

An hour into the trip, Carmen had leaned her head against the seat and dozed for the last few minutes of the ride, though Mack had sat simply, remaining vigilant. When they reached her home, Mack walked Carmen to her door.

Before he could say anything, Carmen said "Mack, I'm so sorry for the way the evening ended, but I want to thank you from…"

"Please, Carmen, don't thank me, or wait 'til tomorrow. You need rest." He paused, but looked as though he had something else to say. After a moment he continued. "Would you like me to stay? On the couch in your living-room, just until the sun comes up? I…"

But Carmen had been shaking her head and smiling as he asked this part. "Thanks, Mack, but really that's not necessary. He may be awful, but he's not violent." And then realized she wasn't entirely sure.

Mack seemed to accept this, and said only "You have my number." He watched as she closed the door, and stayed until he heard her lock it.

When he got back in the waiting car, Mack lowered the glass.

"How ya doin', Nick?" He asked, sincerely curious. He imagined Nick might have his own problems with the situation.

As Nick pulled out of the drive, he glanced furtively at Mack in his mirror. He made an expression of "wish I knew", and said

"Not sure yet, Mack, not sure." He paused and kept driving, now making it a point to keep his eyes on the road. "Is there anything I need to know?"

"I don't think so. Just that Garrett drank too much and was out of line." Mack was only being kind to keep Carmen's privacy. He also had to satisfy his own curiosity on her behalf. "You know him better probably than most. Does he get out of hand like this a lot?" Mack stared at the mirror, knowing that Nick would have to look, and the returned eyes were immediate. "Never. I've only known him for two years, but he's solid. A good man. And even when he drinks too much, which isn't much, he's still a good guy." He shrugged his shoulders. "You hit him pretty good". He added, and this evened his mood enough to make him laugh a little.

"Guess I did". And even Mack smiled, and then went on to direct him the last mile to the farm.

* * *

Carmen closed the maw that was her front door, knowing no solace lay on the side that was once a comforting home. Her Bohemian home. Not even usually an insulting description, but the way he had said it was so unkind, aimed at being demeaning. She shed her shawl, throwing it haphazardly across a chair, and headed for light. After she found that much, she walked into the kitchen where she poured herself a glass of wine. She'd deprived herself of alcohol for wise reasons, but now it would be unreasonable not to have a taste. She was tired, but there were too many thoughts in her head for outright sobriety. One dark moment in a solitary office had cost her more dearly than she could have guessed. She walked to and about her living-room, touching things, putting things in order that were already so. She looked in one of her full-length mirrors, and still saw a remarkable beauty looking back at her, but it was not the same woman. She walked closer to study herself, with each step riveted and somewhat horrified at her haunted appearance. She saw no other wrinkles, but she was older. She shook her head, knowing it was silliness, that one night could not age one too much even if it had ended with the scare of a lifetime. She slipped her shoes off and sat down, willing calmness, or at least acceptance, for the night. How would she ever sleep? She took a sip of wine as if this would be of some assistance, and took up her habit of staring at a blank TV screen. The whole thing was ridiculous, insane and improbable, but it had happened. The ultimate of misunderstandings had occurred while she hadn't been paying attention. She had in fact over-accomplished her wish of making Garrett jealous, and was in fact now deemed a whore. That he could think such things of her with such meager evidence astounded her, and hurt her more profoundly than she could say. The night had been about to end so well, she remembered, after she had spoken with Finn and she had learned about Mack and Sophia. She recalled going back down the stairs in what felt at the time like a beautifully spun cloud of plain old happy.

He had been so cold, unrelenting and disgusted. And he had been drunk. She would not allow that to excuse him, because truth had to be underlying for spirits to elicit such scathing words. She was angry, but nothing could outdo the hurt and the regret. Regret for having fallen for a man who did not exist, regret for not having been able to defend herself, and regret that she thought she was still in love with him, beast or not. And that was the worst regret of all, that she was so weak she still yearned for his angry presence if only to tame it, beat it out of him somehow. She rose, in her pathetic state, and traipsed to her room where she quietly disrobed, and moped through teeth-brushing and face-washing. She turned off the lights and fell into bed, deflated enough perhaps to fall asleep.

***

Sophia could not have said she'd had the best night of her life, but she knew the night had not been about her, and she might have been consoled if she thought Carmen had done tremendously, but she didn't think so. True, the sales seemed to be exceptional, but Carmen had not left happily. To top it off she had not been able to find Garrett, and a tight-lipped Fiona had said he was occupied with important business, but she had spoken in a

281

manner that suggested it was anything but business. She was Mack-less and felt now totally out of any loop, so she chose to pout on the ride home, that much more because she'd failed to raise the separation glass early enough, and now didn't want to seem rude. Not that that couldn't be taken care of.

"Jean, I'm going to nap the rest of the way, so will say good-bye for now" she said as the glass rose.

"OK, Ms. Carmine, that seems like a good idea, especially seeing that you...." And voila, the seal was made.

If she were in her bed she'd have been tossing and turning. She could not rightly land on any given conclusion, only that there had been no resolution, only banal conversation, and avoided steady gazes. She wished she could have ridden with Carmen and Mack, but could not and would not have asked, was not slighted when the offer was not made. There had been some revealing exchanges of words between a few of them, but she didn't know how complete the knowledge was, and the need for the expected ride home still existed. She didn't resent it, but considered it a waste of a beautiful fall night, and a long sexy car.

One thing was sure. She had made her peace, apologized in her own way—not directly, but through gestures—magnanimous for her, and that should be enough. Who was Mack to think he should get more than that, especially since all she did could only be considered heavy teasing? She thought disgustedly about her mildish-mannered attempts at snippets of tripe-ly talk, and said an "ugh" out loud. It must have been the tuxedo. The thought of which brought her immediately back to what she felt the moment she'd first seen him--aghast, bewildered, transfixed. She had tried not to watch him too often, a difficult task at best, but once she had mentally confirmed he was Carmen's escort only, she came to appreciate the nature of his companionship to her, not that she totally avoided the pinches of jealousy when she saw his hands touch her. She wondered about him, what his past was like. She hoped for another day at the beach, intentionally planned this time, when they could share intimate stories, and she could learn what made him so hard. Visions of the beach and shared moments were not typical of Sophia's ideals, but now she yearned for it, wished more fervently for that than she did a completion of their passion. Mack Fordham, a virtual enigma to her, was turning her into a similar creature.

When Jean dropped her off she thanked him, and went inside. It was only a bit after nine, and normally she would have poured herself a glass of wine and turned on the television. Tonight she instead went to her bookshelf and chose something to read, dressed in soft clothing and climbed into bed. She lay against her pillow and was comfortable in a quiet little spell until midnight, when sleep beckoned her to turn off the light.

***

Twilight, however, provided no serenity for Mack. After he got home his mind wouldn't let him alone. He had poured himself a usual dash of whiskey and turned on the TV, sat back in his welcome and welcoming couch, but the TV may as well not have been on.

He'd had an exceptional day, as Sophia had so oddly, snidely—unlike her—noted. He had been in the company of a real artist, a beautiful woman at that, and had led her around a roomful of what seemed mostly like well-meaning people, a stunner of a fact to him. He was not an idiot. He knew he was far too cynical, and probably unfair, but he'd had fun. Even though he had spent a good deal of time at Carmen's side, he'd had a few opportunities to have interesting exchanges, amusing conversations, and the whole atmosphere had just fizzed and popped.

But then it had popped so much it was an explosion. He wasn't sure what the hell Garrett was talking about, just that he had ruined a perfect event for Carmen, though thankfully it had not been witnessed by any other than a few close-knits. And despite the rather sad ride home, Garrett's misbehavior had not fouled his night, making him feel a shade guilty, but only just that. Whereas he didn't totally trust Garrett, he suspected Garrett was acting out of real jealousy. Whether or not it was well-founded he didn't know, but he had enough of his own to think about without letting two other confused souls screw up his equilibrium.

283

Beautiful, cruel-to-be-kind, fascinating Sophia. That woman was something else, and all afternoon and then evening he always felt her, and struggled not to turn and just look at her, and he knew she was mindful of him. She thought he held a grudge from the other night, but she was wrong. He hadn't even been as mad as she thought that very night—he had just wanted to let her know he wouldn't tolerate some of her antics all the time.

And of course he was brought back to that night, her missing clothing and near utter disarray. He felt desire begin its course, and closed his eyes and clenched his teeth. He would not be able to wait much longer, and he glimpsed a vision of her house, where he thought he could reasonably demand she open the door, and where he thought she would only pretend she didn't want to, and then he could do what he wanted and recklessly. But he was not that man, and his body's patience could return with a cool shower. As the TV droned on, and the laugh-track amused another audience, he let his mind dwell instead on what she might be doing while he was just sitting. He found this more comforting, and with such ideas ended up shutting off the television and finding his way to bed, a satisfied look on his now weary features.

Chapter 27

Garrett woke precisely at 5:02 in the morning to pitch black and a piercing head. He was not immediately familiar with his surroundings, but after almost a minute realized he was in the gallery's spare room.

And then awareness of a very different kind poked at him, intensified his head-ache. He sat up abruptly and reached for his eye, wincing the moment he touched the area. The pain was quite bad, between his head and the eye, but something awful in the pit of his stomach was more acute. He fumbled for the lamp, for despite the occurrence of dawn, the thick curtains on the large window were drawn shut.

Pulling the bulb string produced just the ugly effect Garrett was expecting, and he turned his head to look around the room. No crime scene this, and he laughed miserably at the evidence of his guilt. Well maybe not here, but he remembered well enough to know that there was indeed a crime scene of sorts, and it had involved his artist, his beauty, his faithless Carmen, and he put his head in his hands for the first time that day.

But today there was no scotch, no falsity-inducing liquids, and he thought he might have been wrong to have so accused her. He was certainly wrong and cruel for having spoken as he had in front of others, possibly defaming her in an unforgivable fashion for what might not even be accurate. Rudely the picture of Finn and Carmen assaulted him, but he had sought the picture, wanting to affirm his right to anger and his right to distaste. He rose out of bed, subconsciously willing a return of the torch that had driven him to the brink the night before. In truth, he wanted so badly to have mislabeled her, but the weight of his guilt was pushing for the other side of the coin.

He walked to the bathroom to wake up, for he had no ability to go back to bed, and when he saw his reflection he stopped short. Mack's handiwork shown brazenly in the fluorescence of the room, and his hair was oddly matted. He smiled to see what it looked like and was satisfied when he saw it offered no improvement. It was a bruise he deserved and he would wear it accordingly.

After getting himself some aspirin he sat down again, not sure what to do at this hour, and he was not as steady as he wished. It was possible he was still a bit tipsy, and this fact made him disgusted with himself. He started to fixate on the events of the afternoon and evening, and seeing new slants to a day already transpired, and it was driving him mad. He raked a hand through his wrecked hair and opened the door quietly, not sure why he thought anyone else would be around at this hour.

He felt in his pocket for his phone and discovered he had quiet a few (predictable) missed calls, and switched it off because he would not want to talk to anyone for a while. Too many people were expecting something like an explanation and he did not have one. As he strode down the stairs to the main part of the gallery, Garrett Darrs was not sure who he was anymore. He had behaved in a manner last night that was nothing like him, and he could blame it on the scotch and jealousy, but there was more to it and it was tearing him apart.

When he reached the bottom of the stairs, he was newly overwhelmed, but this time not by his own thoughts, but by the beauty his silent gallery presented. The large front windows let in the beginning of light, and all paintings had their mandatory lighting shining on them. His pace slowed as he looked around and, regardless of the chaos he would return to, for a moment he felt serenity at its most divine. That most of the art was Carmen's only added to the peace, and a touch of sadness joined serenity. It was in that moment that he recalled Carmen's face while he'd been speaking, and the fear he had seen, but now he sensed it had been misinterpreted, and the sinking in his stomach from earlier returned with a stronger tide. His head was not better yet and the light that looked so peaceful and angelic just moments ago was making him dizzy. He walked alongside the walls, and now reached to steady himself; fairly certain he would be sick. With the idea that fresh air would help him, he headed for the main entrance, but paused there again, not sure he should venture out so instead sat down in one of the foyer's two exquisite leather chairs.

He breathed deeply, trying very hard not to think at all so that he could make his body concentrate on getting better. As he began to relax he noticed something against the pillar by the door. It was a package, or a t least something wrapped in brown. Quite possibly it was a painting, which made Garrett curious, and he could use the distraction, so up he got, ignoring the protests his body gave him. Upon closer review he realized it was actually a painting, so he lifted it carefully and gingerly pulled away the wrapping. Vaguely he noticed deep colors, and he carried it so as to prop it up on a table against the side wall, and glanced first at the lower right to determine the artist, not terribly surprised to see Carmen's interesting double C, and also not surprised to feel a tug of something odd in his gut, knowing it was not his gut at all.

And what Garrett would behold was the one painting Carmen had wanted to and believed to have escaped the gallery by way of Nick to the trunk. She had later forgotten it because how could she not, but it had stood against the wall, unnoticed by everyone, almost especially by the few that were to have taken it out of harm's way.

Garrett backed away from the painting to help appreciate it, and almost right away he understood that it should have been on his walls. In some ways the colors seemed wrong, and the angles strange, but the raw emotion was simple and stunning. He looked at the face of the beauty looking in the window enviously at the couple in love, and he felt for her, wished her entry into such a passion but he sensed it might not be.

He then looked back at the brilliantly blue-clad star of the painting and it jarred something in his mind. It could have been the haze of physical illness that slowed his reaction, but finally there was a snap. He changed his expression from a gaze of admiration to a focused stare.

It was lovely Sophia sitting in that blue dress—the very dress she had worn yesterday to the show, and it was he, Garrett, that was looking back at her lovingly. True, the woman's hair was not red, but it didn't matter a wit. This is what Carmen had painted, and he looked now at Carmen's depiction of herself, and perhaps that is when the real torture of his day began. He looked in her eyes, willing her to look away from the couple and to look at him standing in the gallery, but it was a painting after all.

At once he was re-assaulted with all the images and harshness of the prior day, and he covered his eyes to block the onslaught, backing up and sitting down hard in the chair as he did so. He pounded his fists against the armrests and let out a groan of despair. As soon as he did so he became aware of time and its passing. He looked at his watch, but it was only just getting to 6 in the morning. He felt miserable, but now his anguish and regret had taken over, and he hoped he could come up with something, anything to simply undo.

Nick answered on the first ring, having not slept well at all, worried as he was about Garrett.

"Yes sir" He said.

"Need your help, Nick. How soon can you be at the gallery?"

"15."

"Thanks, Nick. I'll be waiting" And then he hung up, glad he would be moving, but still a man with an obvious sheen of panic on his face.

"Oh, Carmen" He said quietly. "Carmen, I'm so sorry".

***

The weight of emotion had kindly granted Carmen a sound sleep, and she rose at her usual early hour. But of course sleep had erased reality for a while and upon waking she felt the first pangs of "oh, that really did happen". She walked through her house haphazardly in a self-induced fog, her subconscious deciding she'd have to think about breakfast, and then she'd have to think about cleaning the bathroom, and then she'd have to think about painting, and then…one mundane step after the next, but it was enough to help fake herself out.

She went through elaborate preparations. This would be no eggs and toast Monday, since surely it was a special week? She had sold many paintings, and that should mean her next set, whenever she might finish it, should sell just as handily. Assuming she painted as well. Assuming she had a gallery to go to. She twisted her mouth as she mixed the batter for French toast, for she had not thought of business yet—of how that might be affected. Logic told her Fiona would make sure that side of things would work out alright, and that her future with Gallery Darrs might not actually be jeopardized if Fiona was her sole contact. But it would be weakness to help Garrett profit after what he'd said to her. The supposed cutting of ties must be absolute to give her any validity as a principled artist. A principled human.

She looked up from what she was doing and stared outside, noticing the goings on outside for the first time. It was not a pretty morning in the conventional sense, but it matched recent events and moods to a tee. Though it wasn't raining, the promise was darkly there, and the wind was gusting. She fancied it bizarre she'd only just perceived such weather, and thought she'd better take a long time eating breakfast because such lack of perception was not a good sign for brilliant painting. She laughed lightly at herself, returning to less perilous thoughts, and finished most of her cooking while listening to the wind and occasionally glancing at the inky sky.

"This one's going to be a doozy." She said, and then hummed her way to the front door to grab the paper. She opened it just a bit, knowing the wind might blast it back, but it was between gusts and she let it stand open as she ran down the drive to get the paper, clad only in a long, white gauze shirt that only just covered her hot-pink underwear, and did not hide its color by virtue of its relative transparency. She was not normally so lightly clad when retrieving items in somewhat public sight, but Carmen had not yet arrived at who she was. So doing would require a deeper acknowledgement of pain, and then a morning swept up in tears for things lost. As such, she looked younger and more care-free than she was as she ran back up the drive, paper in hand. She found herself thinking that she forgot to take out the butter to soften, and that she was possibly out of jam.

***

In fifteen minutes Garrett had managed to run back upstairs, take a quick shower and don clean clothes. Just jeans and a white linen shirt, but it was all he needed. He kept a half full closet at the gallery not so much for nights he'd sleep there (which were rare since they usually meant late work nights), but sometimes it was more convenient to change at work than run home. He looked in the mirror as he quickly combed his wet hair, and he did not like what he saw. The punch had been hard enough that in addition to the swelling and purple-blue, it had achieved a small cut on his cheekbone next to his eye. Honestly, if he had a pirate's patch, he would have put it on.

Nick winced largely when he saw him come out of the building. "Ouch. That's some shiner, Mr. Darrs." Then he thought about it. "Sorry. I guess it might not be my place to…"

"It's your place. Say what you want. I deserved it." He shooed Nick back towards the car. "Let's get out of here, I'll get my door".

"Yes, sir" Nick said, jogging to the vehicle and getting in.

When the doors were closed, Nick looked back at Garrett, still not able to facially hide his thoughts on Mack's work. "Where to?" He said, dreading the answer.

Garrett was silent for a moment, and this did nothing to allay Nick's worries.

"The apartment, sir?" He attempted.

"No." Garrett sighed heavily, and Nick shook his head imperceptibly. "We need to go to her house, Nick."

"Mr. Darrs, if…"

"This is not something I'm going to discuss, Nick. Go." Garrett said sternly. After a minute or two, and after Nick had eased out onto the street to begin the journey, he said "I'm not saying it's a smart move, and believe me I appreciate your thoughts on things, but this is something I have to do. I do not have the ability not to go."

"OK, Mr. Darrs. I'll get us there quickly". And once the inevitability of the journey was established, Nick felt somehow better. Not without qualms, but better.

Garrett sat back in the seat, hoping for comfort. He felt only slightly better physically, but his insides were chewed up with guilt. He tried countless times to imagine Carmen's ride home. Had she ridden with Mack? Had he witnessed her unhappiness or had she been able to hide it until she'd gotten home? And how much of what she felt for him had been demolished by his bitter sentences? He wished he could curl up like a little boy and lie down, even if he did not deserve to.

He did not know what he was going to do, of course. At least he did not know what he would do beyond what would only come across as a feeble apology. He understood she might not even open the door. He understood she would look at him with pity and with loathing, and that the hints of what he now was sure was once love, would be absent. He understood it could be a very sour, very bad morning, but he also knew he could not go back to his apartment without having seen her, without having tried to convey his remorse. He could not go home.

As they crossed into Connecticut the skies grew heavier, and the trees danced more vigorously at the whim of the impending storm's breezes. Garrett smiled ruefully at such obvious significance, and Nick just bit his fingernails.

Chapter 28

Sophia went to Twilight Stables, with the full intention of not giving a flying rat's ass whether or not Mr. Mack Fordham was there or not. She was aware she'd recently been approaching the barn with those thoughts in mind, but she was almost convinced she meant it this time. She'd slept extremely well, was proud of her night reading studiously and falling asleep, and she'd woken early and made herself breakfast, something she'd not done in some time.

She knew it might not be an ideal day for riding, that in fact thunderstorms were predicted for later in the day, but so what? She didn't have to ride forever, and she'd missed riding the day before for the sake of Carmen's show. Problem was, she knew damn well she'd get an earful if Mack was around. She was pretty sure he would not be able to hold back from telling her she shouldn't go out. It was just who he was, and how well he thought he could take care of her. She realized some of it might stem from the part he actually cared for her, but today she decided to treat it as an annoyance.

When she arrived and got out of her car, the wind addressed her skirt sharply, and she was taken back by it some, and she looked at the sky, disconcerted, because it did look more threatening than she liked. Never-the-less, she walked to the barn, determined to fit a short ride in before heading home, even though she had enough time to dawdle since she'd asked her friend Lucy to watch the shop. She'd been leaving closed signs on the door more and more recently, and decided it didn't make good business sense, or sense at all for that matter.

No one was in the barn, and even Envy did not seem like she wanted to see her, let alone go out for a ride.

"Boy, girl, this is not what I was hoping for. Where's your sense of adventure?" She asked, lightly scolding.

"It's what they call animal sense" Mack said as he strode in the barn from the direction of the drive.

Despite herself she was glad to hear his voice, and turned to say hello, but without any gladness too evident. "Hhmph" she said. "There's no rain yet. Can't hurt to go out, and Envy is quite an adventurous sort." She added, not really sure she agreed with what she was saying. He was dressed in jeans and a thick, black sweater, matching the overcast sky, and looking not much less scary, but she was trying to get used to his overall demeanor, so she wouldn't let it ruffle her.

He stood there, looking at her, trying to gage where she was today, and decided he saw something feisty—attractive but tedious--the usual. "You're right, Sophia, no rain yet". The sarcasm did not go unnoticed. "And you're dressed just as appropriately as ever" he added, looking at her long, wide skirt, and thin sweater. He noticed she wasn't wearing a bra, and let his gaze linger longer than might have been polite, and certainly longer than he would have a week ago, but he thought her his to stare at now.

She watched him look her over, and damned herself as she felt her skin grow hot, and quickly turned her head as if Envy were her sole concern. "I have a jacket in the car I intend to put on." More lies.

Sincerely he said, "Sophia, please be careful. Even if you haven't heard the forecast, it's obvious something violent is brewing." He could not actually stop her from going out, even though the ranch, and anything that happened on it was his responsibility, because she would fight him harder if he did. The best thing to do was air his concern as he had done, and let her go. Hopefully she'd recognize the folly soon and turn round without enough resentment to prevent wisdom.

She heard the sincerity in his voice, and appreciated it. "I promise" she said, and looked over at him. "Do you have a lot of work today?"

He had turned to walk out, but said "Not if the forecast's right", and walked towards his house.

She watched him walk away, the strength in his stride, the lean, but muscular shape of his butt and thighs, and other thoughts more imperative and beautiful than countryside came to mind.

"Let's do this thing" she said to her horse, and she led Envy out slowly, once again looking above at the sky. Maybe it was a shade lighter? But she really didn't think so.

She opened the gate, and after letting herself and Envy in, closed it behind them and mounted her. She couldn't help it, and glanced back at Mack's house, but it was dark, no evidence of anyone inside or watching her depart. She clicked her heels against Envy's side, and told her to go.

But Mack had not gone home, because he would have to follow Sophia, a task he thought he'd probably have to do again and again, based on her stubbornness alone. He guided one of his favorite mares, Sorceress, out to the same gate Sophia had only just gone through and began the pursuit. He would stay far enough back so that she would not see him, and keep an eye on the weather and make sure he was close enough. As long as her pace was not as fickle as her personality, he had a good chance of staying close.

He did not have to wait long for things to turn ugly, and therefore prompt Sophia to action. They had been riding for only ten minutes or so, though at a fairly good clip, when the first crack of lightning split the increasingly black sky, and not long after a low rumble of thunder. Sophia might have risked a longer ride, but horses don't like storms, and Envy bucked, letting Sophia know they'd have to turn back fast. Mack knew he had to find some brush to hide behind, but his camouflage attempt turned out to be less difficult than he anticipated because when the rain came, it was only light for a minute and then turned torrential. His first concern was for being this ridiculously drenched, but then he realized just how poor visibility was, and got atop his horse to make sure Sophia could see. No longer did he care if she spotted her chaperone.

Not ten blinks after he mounted Sorceress he heard Sophia ripping by, but he didn't see her. Judging from the direction he heard her going, she was moving correctly, and he followed, but now returned to a more distant pursuit since he knew she was alright and headed to the barn. Another streak of lightning sparked the left sky, and this time the thunder was louder. He was not afraid of storms, but he was afraid of what a horse might do in a storm, particularly Sophia's horse. She could handle herself well, he knew, but she was tempting nature and nature was getting closer and louder.

Sophia was drenched, and she could barely see. She led Envy as quickly and accurately as she could in the horrible weather, but she'd be lying if she claimed she wasn't afraid. She hoped Mack had gotten on a horse to find her once the rain had started. She wouldn't blame him! She promised! But she rode on, knowing she was going the right way, just more slowly than she would have liked, and sick with worry that they were in such openness, and the storm seemed to be almost on top of them.

At last she caught sight of the barn in the distance, and bee-lined for it even if Envy didn't really need direction. "I'm sorry, Envy" she said when they were under the protection of the barn. She took Envy to her stall and immediately began drying her off, hoping the horse wouldn't get sick. She got her horse blanket and draped it over her tenderly, thankful that they had not been out too long. Sophia was not happy with herself for going out. She was smarter than that. And now she was thoroughly soaked, her clothes heavy and sticking to her. She'd have to ask Mack for something dry, if only to drive herself home in, or at least that was what she made herself believe.

After she tucked Envy in, and felt sure about the horse's happiness, she braced herself for the dash she'd have to make to Mack's house. It was only a few hundred yards, but the rain was still coming down hard. When she got to his doorstep she knocked as hard as she could to make sure he heard her the first time, and grew annoyed when he didn't answer. She was starting to get cold, and another clap of thunder reminded her of what else she wanted to avoid, so she banged again as hard as she could.

All this Mack watched patiently from the haven of the barn, which he'd quietly led Sorceress into once Sophia and Envy were in the stall. He knew the sound of the rain on the roof would drown out any incidental noises he'd make. Until he saw her banging on his door he was still trying not to let her know he'd been tailing her, but now he was just curious at what she'd do next, even if part of him felt guilty at her wet rat state.

Sophia was puzzled. She could not imagine he wouldn't answer the door in this weather, so she determined he must be possibly taking a shower or doing something (sleeping?) that didn't let him hear her knocking, so she decided to make one last ditch effort of finding him and walked around his house to go window-snooping. It was a well manicured garden, in the English garden sense, and despite the rain she admired the lay-out of the small plot, which was not so evident from the usual angle of the barn. When she found a back window, she went over to it and peered in, leaning in close enough to touch her nose to the pane. There were a few trees next to this side of the house, and she was not getting quite so battered by the rain, and she patiently peered at what must be his bedroom—stark, but not un-homy.

When Mack saw Sophia begin to go nosing around his house, he decided he'd have to watch her. He was already as wet as the rain could make him, and seeing what she was up to would add a bit of sunlight to the day. When he saw her at his window-side, he was able to observe unnoticed, and he took in her disheveled appearance, this time possibly no fault of her own. The rain had muted the fire of her hair, and created thick, matted strands haphazardly falling down her back. He knew well enough she was looking for him, but it wouldn't hurt to pretend otherwise. He walked closer and came behind her, and she was peering into his house so closely that she never saw his reflection. He grabbed the wrist that was acting as a visor over her eyes, and twisted it gently behind her, while covering her mouth with his other hand. His action was so swift he hadn't had a chance to determine his own motive until he was in the middle of it.

Sophia, as he expected, let out a small cry, but she had not been as scared by a man accosting her in such a manner as he would have thought. Perhaps the rainstorm was a bigger threat to her at the moment.

"You're trespassing on my property" he said, and with those words took his hand from her mouth, because she wouldn't scream again (presumably) if she knew it was him, but he did not let go of her wrist.

Sophia's body had tensed, but she was too smart to say "let me go". Instead she said "Where have you been?", and now that she was inches from the glass of the window, she saw him, looked him in the eyes by reflection. "I've been trying to come in, and you didn't answer, so I went around to see if you'd hear me from another spot". She looked at what little of him she saw, how rugged he looked—more so in the rain. She noticed he was just as wet as she was, that he had not just come out into the rain. She concentrated on the way he felt, and even though she might have been too damp herself to tell, he did not feel dry against her. She smiled to herself, because that could only mean one thing.

Quietly he said "I hear you now, Sophia". And then he realized he couldn't just let her go. He was falling under her wicked spell, and demonizing himself. The hand that had left her mouth had dropped to her shoulder, but now he moved it down to her breast as he stared at her reflection, looking into her eyes.

Sophia hadn't been prepared for such an affront, even if she'd had an inkling things would get dicey. She couldn't help but draw in a breath of excitement, which she knew he must have felt. "Move your hand" she said in as much of an order as she could muster.

"Gladly" he said and squeezed her breast roughly, watching her cry out, feeling her fight against him, knowing it wasn't really a true fight. He was captivated by the feel of her breast beneath the wet material, so close to being fully in his hands, but stopped by some cotton flimsiness. He eased his hold on her wrist and turned her around. Enough rain was coming through to add an altogether different pique to his interest, and he looked as her thin clothing clung to her, outlining what he'd only briefly seen before. He was getting hungry, brought his eyes back to hers, curious to see if she understood what he now had to do.

"We've got unfinished business, you and I" he said thickly, putting his hands on her shoulders, then using one to grab the back of her head and bring her face to him. He grabbed her mouth with his and kissed her hard, locking his tongue with hers, but he did not kiss her long, because he just couldn't. He felt her breathing heavily, and was spurred to action by what he would only read as approval.

Sophia was on the brink of climax even if nothing had really happened yet. She was helpless, and would give him what he wanted, mostly because she no longer had power to deny it, but also because part of her knew that this time he would not stop even if she so bade him. She felt him biting and licking her neck and the steady slaps of rain on her face. His bites were not gentle, but all she heard from herself was out-of-breath moans. She thought she might fall against him, but wasn't sure he'd notice. When she felt herself get stronger with peaking desire she grabbed the back of his neck, hoping he'd kiss her again, because it had ignited her like no other kiss.

And her wishful hands sent the message he wasn't going to wait for, but was glad to receive. He moved his hands and reached beneath her sodden sweater, feeling at last the softness therein, but the neckline was unjust--holding him back, and he stood back, breathing unevenly.

"Take your top off" He said. "Please" he added, when he thought he saw hesitation.

When she did so, he watched the rain pitter patter on her perfectly proud nipples and skin, and his head swam, and he fell on his knees as if about to pray, but instead grabbed her slippery breasts and massaged them. After his hands were satisfied, he took a breast in his mouth, now sucking gently, a deep groan coming from him. Sophia had let her head fall back against the window, enjoying the change of pace, and the sensual motion of his tongue on her nipple. And as she closed her eyes, Mack slid his hands on her waist, and she was dizzy with want.

"Please" she heard herself say in an unrecognizable voice. "Please" again.

And that was that. Mack snapped out of his own sucking of skin reverie, and slid his hand between her legs over the material of the wet skirt, turning gentle rubbing into a harder, rubbing pressure. Sophia began breathing heavier, but it wouldn't be enough for her, and Mack knew it was not enough for him. He stood up and used both his hands to lift the back of her buttocks onto the sill, and Sophia supported herself with her hands against the side sills. He spread her legs firmly, and expertly reached under her skirt to remove her underwear, which made Sophia shiver, and then he stood between her legs, one arm helping support her where she was, and the other hand went back up her skirt, and he slipped his finger inside her, wanting to tempt himself just a few moments more. Sophia moaned in part delight, and part agony. She wanted him, she wanted him, she wanted him. Mack felt the silkiness of her, and knew he could not endure longer without true penetration.

Sophia stared at him hungrily, now looking every much the beast that Mack was, entranced with the vision of him unbelting, and letting his pants and underwear down his legs only far enough to do what he needed to do. He looked at her deeply, leaned in for a last tender kiss and then thrust himself into her as hard as he could. Sophia did scream then, but Mack had expected it, and had covered her mouth, and he did not ease up, but continued to penetrate her in long, hard strokes. His hand had left her mouth because Sophia no longer screamed, but widened her reception, telling him he could do what he wanted, and except for his hands and the fierceness of his penetration, she was caught up only in reaction. And when he had spent them both, she fell against him, aching, bruised, but serene. He stood against her, supporting her, both of them quiet and listening to the continuing rain, which actually seemed to be picking up again. When several minutes had passed, Mack spoke gently into her ears.

"Let's go in and put something dry on." He lifted his head to look into her eyes. "But not before I do you justice".

She leaned over and kissed him on the cheek. "Help me down, please".

He did so, and got her sweater which she'd strewn to the side, now a sodden grassy clod. Sophia was not bashful, and they'd not a long way to his door, so she merely propped it in front of her chest as Mack guided her, his arm around her protectively.

When they got inside the door, Mack did not let her go very far, and reached to grab her. His body, now partly sated, wished to experience her otherwise, wished to find the softer side of her, and let her find the gentler side of him, something she had not yet witnessed. He kissed her slowly, letting the moment flow over time, and then before he let it go back to madness he sent her to take a warm shower to get the cold out of her skin.

"But…." she objected, wanting to experience more of that splendid kiss.

"My house, Sophia" He said. "My rules. Besides, I'll meet you in there and give you the soaping you deserve" and he smiled a handsome smile.

So it went, the cleansing. In the middle of steam and scents of grapefruit and pine, they washed each other tenderly, administering to the task of washing and bubbling. These were moments almost the opposite of passion, but moments not without equal intensity. Sincere emotion was shared by just such gentleness, and mutual need. Hundreds of thoughts and feelings were likely exchanged in the misty warmth, and they did not speak often. Not so much intentionally, but out of subconscious, shared reverence.

When at last they exited the bathroom, they went to Mack's bed quietly, and lay there adjusting to the more bracing air of the rest of his home, and faded into a nap. But that was the end of their quietude for that day, because upon waking, new desires surfaced, and Mack wanted to do as he promised—tend to his mistress in the manner that more befitted her and his talent. All of that Monday they spent together, undoing any washing that had occurred earlier, seeking the outreaches of passion and doing things neither of them might have dreamed of. Theirs was not an ordinary lust, borne as it was out of more turbulent waters, and their first encounter by the barn and then later by Mack's house was what their physical love was fashioned after. No less needy or brutal, but there was also no less authenticity to the feelings behind the actions. Mingled with the sweating and moans, there was in the air a hint of desperation that came from both of them, but it was at least now desperation not so keenly honed. Both Mack and Sophia were lonely souls in different ways, but they had found each other, tentatively, denying, maybe clashing on the way there, but they had persevered to find their own forever.

Chapter 29

By the time Nick pulled reluctantly into Carmen's drive, Garrett was nervous and still without any idea of how he should approach her. As the car pulled up by the house, though, he quickly decided this was no time for dallying.

"Nick, pull out of here and drop me at the end of the drive."

Nick shot a bewildered look back at Garrett, but said only "OK".

The sky was less friendly and looked about to break, but Garret noticed the weather no longer. Once outside the view of the house Garrett said "Stop the car and pop the trunk." For he had put Carmen's re-wrapped painting within as he knew it might help him apologize. "Stay close." And he got out of the car, grabbed the painting gingerly, and shut the trunk.

What on earth he was doing he didn't know, but a degree of exhilaration had entered his blood, and for the first time that day he felt a brighter side of courage. As he walked up the drive he wondered which window was her bedroom's, but he thought he could probably guess that right, not that he knew why the hell he should be thinking about nosing at windows, and a glimmer of that courage wavered. Thunder had been distant and not distracting, but now a clap arrived with a respectful enough force that Garrett jogged the rest of the way to the door just as the rain began. Soon it would be pouring, and he looked at the package in his hands, which had to stay safe. He raised his hand to knock on the door, but couldn't do it. Off to the right of the door a few yards away was a small porch and he put the painting there against the wall of the house where he decided it would be fine. At the same time he looked at the cozy seats this small haven provided, and opted to relax for the moment and think about what he would do as the rain now began to come down in sheets.

The canvas covered settee creaked lightly as he sat, and he smiled at the homey feel of it, found himself thinking if Carmen spent much time out here, and if she did how she spent it. Thunder continued, but the sound of the rain was outright powerful, yet soothing enough in its rhythmic way that he closed his eyes, enjoying his slightly illegal moment in her beautiful garden. He could have sat like that for easily ten minutes, and would have, but he heard the front door opening just yards away. The sound was horrific in its own right, because it meant he'd have to face facts sooner than he'd expected, but he also breathed a sigh of relief for the same reason. He watched as Carmen came running out with a flowy kind of see-through shirt, and he caught his breath. He had waited for her to look at him and perhaps start screaming, but she didn't see him, never thought to look his way, just to hurry in the rain. Where the hell was she going? She had not headed for her garage, but was running down the drive-way, and he found himself hoping Nick had driven somewhere. He looked absently back at the door and saw that she had not closed it behind her, which meant she would be coming back and soon. The mail. He looked back at the door and mentally slapped himself for taking so long to do the obvious. He grabbed the painting and made a mad dash for the door. Once inside he took off his shoes quickly and put them under a chair in the living room. He did not have much time, and did the only thing he thought made sense at the time. He ran into the kitchen and unwrapped the painting quickly, leaving it standing against the counter where she would see it, noticing g as he left that she was about to eat, and his own stomach reacted to the beautiful setting she had put out on her table. He went quickly back through the living room to the hallway that led to the rest of the house, where he waited. He heard the door shut just as he got there and began to regret his break-in. But he had at least given her a warning, and now, since he knew she would be heading to the kitchen to eat, he came out from the hallway and stood in the living room to wait for her.

***

Carmen was soaked, and when she looked down at herself she marveled she'd gone out. The gauze was sticking to her and

302

her nipples might as well have been bare. She shook herself a little and wished for a towel, but first things first. She had to avoid fire and turn the toaster off.

Garrett was transfixed. He was standing still, and observing Carmen, drenched, shivering and beautiful. He longed to go over and give her his coat, but now he could not. He had assumed she'd do the same straight-ahead walk to the kitchen as she had when he'd been on her porch, but he'd not thought about the effects of rain on such flimsiness. He watched her move, contemplate what she was doing, and felt thankful when she headed for the kitchen, even though it was just a delay of what he knew her reaction would be upon realizing his presence.

She trod into the kitchen, her bare feet slapping against the tile shaking her head, now amused at her silly flight to get the paper. The aroma of what she had cooked greeted her warmly and she debated the necessity of getting a towel at all since she was so hungry. As she rounded the island to get to the toaster, something out of kilter sent her eyes looking downwards. She had caught the presence of something that had not existed moments ago. Upon changing the direction of her gaze, she was faced with "The Mirror" very suddenly, perhaps feeling so sudden because she knew very well she did not put it there. She stood still, the mid-stride halt jarring her body and her mind to full attention. She stared at it, a growing dread grabbing her and staking claim to her stomach. She had not put it there. Knowing she had not put it in that spot made her recall that she did not remember getting it out of Nick's trunk at all, that she had not even asked about it since she'd spoken to Fiona about it at the gallery. Unbeknownst to herself, her head was shaking, as if trying to deny what might be happening. She looked around at the rest of the floor, the room, hoping to get clues or additional evidence she knew she didn't need.

Garrett stood, waiting, as she made her way into the kitchen. It was one of those obvious moments when she noticed the painting, because he felt everything stop. He closed his eyes, preparing for some kind of blood-curdling scream, groan, utterance of horror, but there was nothing. He tried to imagine her thoughts, but abandoned such attempts and focused instead on

303

preparing himself for her inevitable walk into the living room. He thought about the way he looked then. About his darkened eye, the cut, the blood-shot eyes and hair gone awry from the rain and ran his hand through it, and then decided it was time to speak. The waiting was enough and the suspense was not something he felt like tolerating.

"Carmen" He said quietly, but loud enough to carry to her. "I'm in the living room."

When she heard his voice Carmen moved her eyes immediately to straight ahead, away from the painting she'd been staring at. She had tried to imagine what the significance was and why he had placed it in her kitchen, why he had brought it over at all. She thought maybe it was a ploy, but of what? What could he hope to accomplish with it? Last night assaulted her afresh, and she let out a soft moan, for living through the pain she had felt in that moment when she realized he thought so little of her was an agony she had been delaying. Her mind had been keeping her in a sort of stupor, but now she was beginning to feel and become an aware person once again. Garrett's presence was forcing the matter.

She felt herself moving, and he heard her steps. He was looking forward to seeing her look at him even though it would not be easy moments. He wanted her beautiful eyes looking into his so he could say everything he needed in the hopes of ridding himself of the wrenching guilt. Surely she would forgive him, because she was in fact the woman he had always thought her to be. She came through the door, and as she did so he apologized.

"I'm sorry, Carmen" He said evenly. He did not want to sound weak or pathetic even though he knew that perhaps he was. "I'm very sorry that I hurt you." She had stopped at the far side of the room and was staring at him, no marked expression to her features. "I may not be forgivable, but I'm asking for it anyway. I…" He found it hard to continue without her saying something, anything, even if it was "Get out".

It was hard to look at him without feeling sympathy, because it was barely him, but she did not let her face betray such feelings The punch Mack had sent flying had made its mark with violent color, and the rest of his face seemed damaged in ways she could not define. He too had been dampened by the rain, and she realized absently how he had entered her home. What would he have done had she not gone out for the paper? He looked awful, but she was so glad to see him, and hated herself for it. He did not look the wreck of a man who had confronted them last night, but a man filled with sin and reeking of wildness and guilt.

"You found my painting" She stated simply, and decided it was foolish. What did she hope to begin? She was glad for his remorse, and believed him, but other than that she saw nothing. She couldn't understand why he'd brought it over other than to show her that he knew what she felt for him, but he was not gloating. He was not acting like a man who had powerful knowledge, and he was not wielding anything other than apology. So maybe that was it. She saw nothing other than apology. Maybe he just used it as a clue to her that he was in her house.

Garrett was not ready to discuss her painting, and she looked slightly deranged with her lack of facial expression. "I'm sorrier than I can possibly say about what I said last night, Carmen." The pain he felt at what he'd done renewed itself, and he shook his head slightly as he spoke, as if to ease the burden with such a movement. "I completely understand if you want to sever any ties with me, if you never want to talk to me again. I had no right to say what I did to someone like you in front of others--or at all." He stopped, because his heart was hurting, and he felt like sitting. This was worse than he had expected. He felt like he was saying the words all over again, but sober this time, and miserably aware of every possible reaction. He tried to see as much as he could when he looked into her eyes, but still saw nothing. Better than hatred, he supposed.

"I forgive you, Garrett" She said, meaning it, but now tired and wishing to get on with it. "I know you were not yourself" And then said "I have to change." She walked by him and he caught the scent of rain and last night's perfume, and it was alluring even in such treacherous minutes. He had not looked at her body when he had spoken to her, but now he watched her retreat, the material clinging to many skinful points, and he stared fixedly, not able to quite quell desire, much as he should. What he had not liked was her tired tone. She had forgiven him, she

305

said, but she was distant and anger lurked somewhere therein. At least she showed something. Prior to that he had seen nothing other than catatonic oblivion. He stood there for a moment, a sense of dissatisfaction about him. He should be happy he hadn't been thrown out, and thrilled that his apology had been accepted, but of course now that he had that he needed a bit more. Before he thought about what he was doing, he headed for her bedroom to figure it out.

When he opened her door she was at the far side of it, looking for something in her bureau drawer. Possibly clothing, since she wore none. She had changed from her outrageous hot pink underwear to a yellow and black lacy number, and her brazier matched. He was glad he had not caught her naked because she might have been more upset, but this was actually better anyway. The underclothing was scanty and he stared at her body openly, now caring less if she objected. He had gotten his forgiveness after all, so it was on to the next affront.

"Garrett, what are you doing in here?" Carmen had not expected Garrett to barge in, and she was supposed to be upset, she knew, but his look had changed. He was not remorse-stricken any longer, apparently, and looked in fact like he'd forgotten all about what had occurred the night before. He was actually walking over to her. Quickly.

Something had come over him when he walked in her door, or maybe it had been when he smelled the rain in her hair when she walked by, but he was now reckless, hungry, and desire-driven. Her wet hair clinging to her skin, the sweet cadence of her cleavage, the quizzical look on her face, were zinging his blood, and making him all too aware. He watched her face as he closed in, going from merely curious to breath-taking alarm, and the fact that he'd maybe made her a little afraid served as additional ignition that took him by welcome surprise.

"Garr...." But he had grabbed her by then, pulled her head to his, and placed his mouth firmly on hers where his name was swallowed back. He put his other arm around her waist to bring her up against him so that he could feel as much of her as possible. From that moment Carmen did not object, but let herself be thusly taken. She kissed him fully back, enjoying the succulent feel of their tongues colliding in a fiercely exotic kiss. Garrett was thrilled that she was kissing him back, and changed direction with his arm so that he could feel her breasts. He let his palm move over her skin from her back, down her waist, over her stomach—where she began to tremble—to finally lay claim to one of her breasts. He squeezed it gently at first, enjoying its supple firmness, but then couldn't handle such patience and squeezed harder.

Carmen let out a groan of pleasure. She wasn't sure what was happening entirely, just that she had no control anymore. Garrett had stridden in as if he owned her, and confirmed it when she fought back not a whit. He kissed her like no other man she'd known, and his hands were nothing other than magic. She felt tingles all over her body, was drunk with need, and felt as though she'd soon be begging for more. She had both her arms around him and was feeling the tautness of his back through his clothing, the beauty of his form, and she clutched him hard whenever he made her do so. It was getting painful to stand.

But Garrett was also going silently mad, feeling just out of reach of satisfaction. Invisible reins were keeping him from getting where he needed to go since he wanted to maintain a modicum of discretion. His want to please let him move one of his hands gently down her belly, and over the top of her underwear. He pulled his lips off of hers and began to kiss her neck while his hand then slid underneath her underwear. If it was not the groan Carmen made when he touched her there, it was the way he saw her eyes roll that caused him to abandon decorum. He had stopped brushing her neck with his tongue so that he could watch her face while he rubbed his hand against her clitoris, but it was too much for him. He swept her up and carried her the short distance to her unmade bed and dropped her gently, looking down at skin and lace and sensual rarity. He was breathing heavily, wiped the back of his hand against his forehead.

"Tell me to stop and I will" He said deeply, fairly sure that what he said was not true.

She only looked back at him, and made a motion with her hands as if to grab him down to her when she couldn't reach.

He was enjoying himself now, assured in his role at her telling. As quickly as he could he took off his shirt and unzipped his pants while she looked at him, breathing in what she found to be virility made out of skin. There were fine beads of sweat on his chest, and even his battered face was catering to her need for a bit of vulgar. She had not imagined this moment would come to pass at all, and was overwhelmed with it being now and quite so magnificent. When he took off his underwear she couldn't stop herself from just a small gasp at the hardness she knew was not far from reaching inside her.

Garrett stared into her eyes as he leaned down, naked, and pulled off her yellow and black. He was thrill-sent while hearing her breathe so hard, enraptured she was merely waiting to have him. He wished fervently to finally look upon her breasts while he made love to her, and almost tenderly unclasped her bra's front hook. He pushed it to the side and groaned at curves and cream and the welcome her breasts gave him, and then he grabbed them, knelt down to put his mouth greedily on her nipples, knowing he was still teasing his groin. Carmen threw back her arms against the bed, feeling a helpless woman. This is not how she had intended moments to pass if she had intended anything at all, but the man on top of her was not someone she would stop. He was getting slightly crueler, and she felt his hand once more find her, and this time he did not stop toying, and very suddenly she felt his finger inside her, seeking, flirting, thrusting. She let out a long moan and pushed him away, because just that had to be replaced.

Garrett was out of breath and confused. Passion had broken him to the point he was thankful for her refusal. He resolutely kissed her gently and deeply while he then entered her, and he felt her stop kissing him for a long moment as he sucked in her scream of delight. The bewilderment, teasing and expectation was over, because so was any hesitance. He went into her again and again, getting less conscious of her, and really only feeling his pleasure increase by the beauty of the slide. They both groaned, moaned, succumbed. It might have been arduous, sweaty and thick, but somewhere in its midst, Garrett ceased the solo ecstatics and held on to Carmen's face with one of his hands, prompting her eyes to search for his.

"I love you Carmen Carmine." He said, barely able to because of his tired lungs. "I love you".

Carmen had been on the brink of climax, and no, the words did not finalize the physical reaction, but as her body bore the exquisite tide, her thoughts were able to match it. Mere seconds after he heard and felt Carmen peak, Garrett came with such force he cried out in what could have been interpreted as pain. Their bodies held to each other, Garrett being careful not to crush her, as they slowly caught their breath, and gently he rolled to her side, and turned his head so that he could look at her openly, honestly for what really was the first time.

Carmen looked over at Garrett, who was staring at her fondly, and she knew she saw love in his eyes, and wondered why she'd never seen it before.

"That was fun" she said, and he laughed.

"It was at least that". He said.

Their laughter subsided, and Carmen grew more serious as she thought about how they had wound up in her bed. She understood it was jealousy that had driven him to his absurd rudeness, and it made the forgiving absolute.

She looked into his eyes. "You know I love you" She said, a statement.

Garrett propped his head up on one hand and used the other to touch her cheek softly. "I know you love me." He smiled, and shook his head a little. "Wish I would have known it a touch sooner."

And from that point on the conversation was easy; they exchanged thoughts and laughs about the evolution of her show, and the various misunderstandings that had taken place. It was an enjoyable discourse, spent gently in each other's arms, and when at last they tired of talk, they fell into a quiet nap, both of them truly happy.

When they woke later that morning, they woke to more thunder and pouring rain. Garrett was the first to stir, and waking in Carmen's room prompted a review of the area, and the woman that lay by his side. He turned to look at her, and stroked the top of her hair, which slowly brought her out of her own dreamland, and when she opened her eyes to see him, she smiled warmly, and he leaned over and kissed her. Still with the slight fog of sleep and the crashes of hard rain, they made love slowly, easily, but not less hungrily. There were whispers, light caresses and almost ghostly moans, a scene altogether different, but touched by something divine.

Chapter 30

Finn stared out the window of the train, easing back into his seat as he watched some late passengers make their way on board. He now thought himself almost brilliant to have booked the speedy Acela instead of driving down. He had enjoyed his stay with his brother, and felt like he saw some essential part of evolution, even if it was an admittedly small realm. It was hard to believe his older brother had finally fallen smitten but good, and it had been odd to see him weakened by jealousy and inebriation being that Garrett was all about control, but he supposed Carmen was an understandable source of such havoc, and he smiled—happy for the two of them and happy for the world into which she had entered.

A bunch of them had gone out for drinks just the night before to clink glasses, and maybe to somehow say without saying that for the moment life was shimmering with good. The interaction between Mack and Garrett was free and easy, as if Mack hadn't smashed Garrett's face only two days prior. They made jokes and laughed in a manner that suggested a longer relationship, and Finn just stared. He saw Carmen absorbing it all, happy, transfixed, positively dreaming up some kind of artwork he was sure. She was radiant, occasionally catching the eyes of Garrett's, which rarely looked away from her, and despite all they'd shared still smiled at him demurely. Sophia, back in her confident but not too defiant element and just as radiant, kept Mack busy, who Finn had quite quickly come to like. Honest, fierce-some, protective—not just of Sophia, but his newly-knit group, looking sometimes as though he might be waiting for someone to walk up and disrupt the balance he was happy finally to have reached.

And clink they had, their glasses, but the headier potion was not in their cups, but in the thoughts that danced in all their heads that night--so obvious an elixir Finn had marveled, and marveled enough to think a bit longer and about things he usually didn't. He'd acquainted himself too well with envy as he watched them, remaining at the fringe of the conversation most of the time, but therefore heard more keenly and absorbed magical material he subconsciously tried to fend off.

He felt the train begin to ease out of Penn Station, departing gently with a comforting sound of whining steel and expected wind. He was looking forward to going back to Boston and thought perhaps he'd even go in and see how the restaurant had fared without him. He trusted most of his staff implicitly and knew there was no real need to go in until the next day, but he might have needed the company. He wanted to find his own surroundings, something of which he was a part--not just the watcher, he. He wanted the exotic aromas to envelop him, coax him sweetly and easily into the Finn who had left Boston less than a week ago.

Maybe Josh would make him his exceptional tomato sandwich, and he smiled at the thought as the train pulled out into the light to head home. He shrugged New York off at the prospect of Boston, at the prospect of what he knew would return him to his old happy self. He would eat that delicious sandwich, wash it down with a beer, and definitely make time with Fallon, a favorite waitress of his. He'd talk to a few of the regulars, get into the cool vibe of the swing they'd be playing that night, and the world would once again be his.

"Maniacs" He said, not loudly. "I know what I need."

Convincing was Finn Darrs with his words of solace, bravado and see-if-I-care mirages. Convincing.

Just not convinced.

ABOUT THE AUTHOR

Narcissa Lyons lives in Massachusetts with her husband and two boys, and Artless is her first novel. Narcissa was born as a first generation American to her Hungarian mother and British father, along with her five siblings. Hers was a rich, European childhood experienced in the deep country of Connecticut and in somewhat dicier towns when times were a little tough. She started writing very young, honed her craft in high school and college, and contributed as a free lance journalist to a local paper in Massachusetts. Only recently, however, has she begun sharing her unique style through her blog, "if not for Passion", and now her first novel, "Artless". She is currently working on the sequel to that, as well as finishing a sci-fi/fantasy she began in the mountains of Vermont.

.

Connect with the Author

You can read and see more of Narcissa Lyons' work at ifnotforpassion.com and sign up for email notifications of her articles and stories. If you wish to send her a note, please use her email ifnotforpassion@gmail.com.

 Narcissa_Lyons

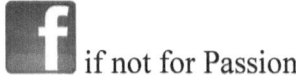 if not for Passion

www.ingramcontent.com/pod-product-compliance
Lightning Source LLC
Chambersburg PA
CBHW052017240626
47153CB00006B/1842